A True
Cowboy
Christmas

A True Cowboy Christmas

CAITLIN CREWS

St. Martin's Paperbacks

This is a work of fiction. All of the characters, organizations, and events
portrayed in this novel are either products of the author's imagination or
are used fictitiously.

A TRUE COWBOY CHRISTMAS

Copyright © 2018 by Caitlin Crews.

For information address St. Martin's Press, 175 Fifth Avenue, New York,
NY 10010.

ISBN: 978-1-250-29523-1

Our books may be purchased in bulk for promotional, educational, or
business use. Please contact your local bookseller or the Macmillan Corporate and Premium Sales Department at 1-800-221-7945, ext. 5442, or by
e-mail at MacmillanSpecialMarkets@macmillan.com.

Printed in the United States of America

St. Martin's Paperbacks edition / November 2018

St. Martin's Paperbacks are published by St. Martin's Press, 175 Fifth
Avenue, New York, NY 10010.

10 9 8 7 6 5 4 3 2 1

To all the cowboys out there.

And in our hearts.

Acknowledgments

Thanks to Monique Patterson and everyone at St. Martin's—especially the art department for this delicious cover!

Thanks to Holly Root for making my dreams come true, every time.

And thanks, as always, to Jackie, Nicole, and Maisey for talking me off ledges and into complicated stories. Thanks to Jane for introducing me to cowboys in the first place. And to Rusty for her unwavering support and all the rest of my wonderful friends for encouragement, breath, laughter, book recommendations, "research" trips, love, and more laughter. What would I do without you?

And to Jeff, always and for everything.

1

Everetts had been going to their eternal rest in the same remote plot of land with its breathtaking view of the same range of gorgeously unforgiving Colorado mountains for at least three generations. And counting.

Gray Everett had always understood that sooner or later, he'd follow suit.

Today was one of those bright and blue November days that seduced a man into pretending he couldn't feel winter kicking there in the snap of the air against his face, sweeping down from the snowy heights to tug at his bones and make him feel every one of his thirty-eight years. It was the kind of sky that made Gray imagine he might be immortal. Colorado sunshine was nothing if not deceptive, even in an autumn that had already dusted the jagged peaks around the remote Longhorn Valley with a couple of teaser snowfalls, just to get the blood pumping and the snow tires ready.

And today it was Gray's famously ornery father who was carrying on the inevitable Everett tradition. He was being interred into Everett land in the simple pine box he'd requested in the will he'd drawn up years ago, and had thereafter theatrically amended with a red pen at the dinner table any time he felt irritable or slighted.

And Amos Everett had pretty much felt nothing but ir-ritable *and* slighted, every day of his miserable life.

Gray was the one who'd had to keep the ranch running, no matter Amos's many feuds and grievances. He was the only one of his brothers who'd bothered to stick around and take care of what was theirs, so he'd long since stopped paying attention to his father's dark mutterings and peri-odic pronouncements of who was in and who was out. He'd had actual fences to mend, calves to brand, colts to halter-break, bulls to move from one pasture to another. Amos's dark obsessions had been a distraction, nothing more.

The pine box was about the only thing the old man hadn't changed in all these years of will amendments.

And there were worse things than an eternity spent in this pretty family plot, miles away from anything, draped in wind and quiet, snowstorms and summer breezes. Shaded by cottonwood trees overlooking the icy blue river that tumbled down from the higher elevations and had given the four hundred acres Gray's ancestors had claimed its name. Cold River Ranch. The seat of the Everett family as long as there had been Everetts in Colorado.

His trouble, Gray thought as his reluctant family and the few neighbors who didn't outright hate Amos gathered around the grave Gray had dug into the chilly, resistant earth the previous morning, was that it turned out he might want more from his life than the Everett family tradition being interred in front of him.

He'd come from this land and like it or not, he'd be re-turned to this land, sooner or later. Staring at his father's grave brought that home to him with a kind of wallop.

Gray had spent his life deep in the harsh realities of running cattle, committed to handling Amos's nonsense as best he could, and dedicated to the raising of his daughter the way he'd been doing since Becca's mother had taken Gray's truck and crashed it on the mountain on her way to see one of her lovers ten years back.

He stared at his father's casket sunk deep in the ground and figured it wasn't the worst idea in the world to see if he could enjoy his life before he found himself stretched out beneath an adjacent patch of grass. And maybe make Becca's life easier than his had been while he was at it.

Everetts historically lived mean and more than a little feral, out here where the land had a mind of its own, cattle and weather wreaked havoc at will, and the pretty town of Cold River was an iffy mountain pass away. Everetts tended to nurse the bottle or wield their piety like a weapon, spending their days alone and angry until they keeled over in a barn one day. Gray's grandfather had been found one morning slumped over his tractor. Amos, who Gray really should have been taking this opportunity to mourn in the way a good son surely would have, had staggered off to the barn to saddle up his horse on Halloween morning and hadn't come out.

Gray's grandfather Silas had been a tough man, but a good one. When he had died, the whole valley had turned out to pay their respects. To this day Gray couldn't make a trip into town without some old-timer gruffly reminding him he had the look of his grandpa about him. He was fairly certain it was a compliment.

Amos, on the other hand, had been as bitter as he'd been spiteful and had taken it out on anyone who'd happened near. He'd run off a pair of wives, a series of girlfriends, not to mention two of his three grown sons. He'd also gone out of his way to alienate just about every resident of this cold, protected valley a world away from Colorado's fancy, glittering ski slopes and a solid few hours of hair-raising driving from the city lights of Denver.

Gray wasn't given to dramatics, but he could see his

future as well as anyone if he didn't change. He didn't have to like it or the way it was mapped out right there in front of him to accept it.

Today's grumpy hermit is tomorrow's bitter, old man, he told himself.

He didn't love thinking about himself that way, and he wasn't thrilled at how much he sounded like Amos inside his own head, so he frowned around the small graveside service instead. His two younger brothers stood to one side of him, looking solid and grounded as if they hadn't gotten the hell out of Cold River at the first opportunity and left Gray to handle everything all these years. Across the way, loyal neighbors like old Martha Douglas and her capable, dependable granddaughter, Abby, stood with the sprawling Kittredge family who had land farther out in the valley. The longtime hands had lowered Amos's casket into the autumn earth and now stood there, taking part in the moment of silence.

Gray didn't know what anyone else was feeling, except for his daughter, whose muffled sniffles seemed to indicate she was actually mourning the bitter, old man in question's passing. But then, Becca was fifteen and had tried her best to dote on her grandpa as if the mean, old geezer was some kind of substitute for the mother she'd lost way too young. The mother Gray maybe should have tried to replace.

Gray couldn't say he or his brothers had tried all that hard with Amos. They'd learned better a long time ago.

When the simple service was finally over, everyone headed back toward the ranch house despite the fact there was supposed to be no gathering, "celebration of life," or any of that nonsense, per Amos's pissy wishes etched out in thick, red pen on that damn sheaf of papers he'd called his will. Becca gave him a hug before jumping in a truck with one of the Kittredges, but Gray decided to hike the mile back from the river with his brothers as if they were close.

They weren't. Even way back when they'd been kids, it had been every man for himself in Amos's version of family.

"Congratulations," Brady said as the three of them settled into the walk at Gray's brisk pace. "Dad's dead, Gray. That means you're free."

Gray adjusted his collar against the biting wind that rushed down from the snow-topped mountains and tended to remind a man exactly how small he was. A feeling Gray had always liked because it put things into perspective. He knew Brady hated it, because Brady had complained about it pretty much constantly throughout his teen years. He eyed his baby brother, all polished and fancy like the city slicker he'd made himself in his years down in Denver. Gray didn't want to imagine what the fool had spent on those boots of his.

"No man with four hundred acres is free. Or maybe you forgot what ranch life is like."

"I didn't forget. That's my point. This ranch is a cross no one asked you to carry. And one you can put down anytime now, in case you wondered."

Gray didn't want to have this conversation. Ever. And certainly not with Brady, who'd never made any secret of the fact he hated not just Cold River Ranch, but the town of Cold River and the entire Longhorn Valley too. Brady, who had never sacrificed a thing, was filled with all kinds of opinions. And yet had done nothing but run away.

Which was fine by Gray. But it wasn't him.

"I'm not selling," he said gruffly, to end the discussion.

Brady glared at him. "Not sure that's up to you, big brother."

On his other side, their middle brother Ty threw back his head and laughed, hard enough that the wind couldn't snatch it away and long enough that Gray and Brady stopped glowering at each other and turned it on him instead.

"Let's really get into it," Ty suggested when he fully had their attention. "Throw a few punches, leave a few bruises, and roll into the house with enough blood to horrify the neighbors and make sure we're the talk of the valley. Isn't that exactly what Dad would have wanted us to do to mark his passing?"

Gray's mouth curved despite himself. "The old man did like to cause a commotion."

Brady shook his head. "He could pick a fight with a tree. And win."

"He was banned from every bar from here to Vail, repeatedly." Gray almost sounded . . . nostalgic. "Lately, though, he liked to hole up at home with a bottle of whiskey and list his enemies."

"Did ungrateful sons count as enemies?" Ty asked lazily. He sounded as cool and unbothered as the hotshot bull rider he was, and was exhibiting only the vaguest hint of a limp to remind anyone looking at him that the last bull he'd tried to ride had stomped him good on the way down.

Amos had pretended not to be aware that Ty rode bulls on television, because he'd always refused to acknowledge anyone who'd wronged him by leaving, from the ex-wives he'd bullied to the sons he'd chased away. But when others mentioned the famous Ty Everett, he'd certainly always seemed to know everything there was to know about his superstar middle child's career.

"We were disappointments, not enemies," Gray assured his brothers.

Brady scoffed. "How are you a disappointment? You're

just like him. You might as well be a Cold River wet dream."

Ty snorted. "I definitely don't want to hear about your wet dreams, baby brother."

Gray didn't want to hear from either of them. He tuned out their bickering as they hit the crest of the hill, because there was his life's work laid out before him. In every direction, as far as he could see, there was nothing but Everett land. Sweet Angus beef, Colorado mountains, and the sweat and tears and stubborn dreams of all the family who'd come before him.

He took a deep breath, then let it go, his gaze fixed on the ranch house where he'd lived most of his life. He remembered his brothers grousing about it way back when. They'd each called the place claustrophobic, in their own ways, and each of them had made tracks out of the mountains as soon as they'd turned eighteen. Ty to the rodeo, Brady to school.

Only Gray had stayed. Only Gray had endured.

Because what Gray saw when he looked around wasn't the ball and chain Brady imagined or the chokehold Ty had never wanted.

He saw his home.

The place he'd raised his daughter. The place he planned to stay until it was Becca walking down this hill from the family plot, leaving him behind.

"This is the loneliest place I've ever seen," Brady muttered from behind him.

"Lonely is as lonely does," Ty replied, all drawl and the sound of his famous smile. "Which in my case is usually a whole lot of whiskey until I fancy myself a pool hustler."

Gray didn't turn around.

"I'm not selling," he said again, more seriously this time. "It's not happening."

He could feel his youngest brother's impatience. And he was sure he could *feel* the two of them exchanging glances back there, behind his back.

"Then tell me your plan," Brady said, using the rational, corporate voice he probably got a lot of mileage from down in the city. It made Gray want to swing on him. Which he didn't do, of course, because he was a grown man who was supposed to have a cool head on his shoulders.

"Same plan as always," he said instead. "Run cattle. Sell beef. Nothing changes here, Brady. Isn't that the reason you never come home?"

"What kind of life is that?" Brady demanded.

Gray cut his gaze to the side to find Ty there, a lot less belligerent than usual. A lot less swagger and a lot less of his typical showy crap too, now that he considered it. Maybe that last bull had actually stomped some sense into him.

"It's my life," Gray told Brady quietly.

"You could live an entirely different life if you wanted to."

"I don't want to."

"You could sell this land and never have to work another day in your life."

Gray shook his head. "What kind of man doesn't want to work?"

"There are developers from here to Grand Junction and back who would kill for this kind of view."

"And I'd kill them all with my own hands before I'd let them turn our family legacy into a sea of tacky condos. Forget it, Brady. Dad didn't want to sell and neither do I."

"He left the ranch to all three of us."

"He did." Gray would turn the supreme unjustness of that over in his own head, in his own time, likely while continuing to be the only one of the three who actually put any work into the land that now belonged to all of them. That had been a kick in the gut. But Gray wasn't accustomed to showing the ways he hurt. "But it requires a unanimous vote to sell."

Brady looked frustrated for a moment, but then he blinked and his expression turned canny again. Like the slick finance guy he'd turned himself into. "What about Becca?"

"What *about* Becca?" Gray growled. "You have a sudden interest in my kid's well-being? I'm real happy to hear it, but you better break it to her gently. You're nothing but a face in a photograph to her."

That wasn't entirely fair, but Gray was okay with that. He was a lot less okay with that edgy, uncomfortable feeling in his own chest, making him restless and far meaner than he wanted to admit.

Maybe you're not as different from Amos as you like to think, that spiteful voice in his head chimed.

And maybe he needed to pay more attention to his daughter's well-being himself, and figure out ways he could make her life on the ranch better, though he didn't plan to admit that to Brady.

"You might have bought the legend of the Everetts hook, line, and sinker, but that doesn't mean she has," Brady replied, uncowed. "What if she wants to go to school and learn a few things, instead of spending her life neck-deep in cattle and dust and endless drudgery?"

"Whatever *my daughter* decides to do," Gray said, very distinctly, not touching the "drudgery" remark because if he did, he really would give his kid brother a bloody nose like he was thirteen again, "it has nothing to do with you."

"But—"

"Just like the ranch has nothing to do with you, Brady.

That was what you wanted. That was what you got. Don't think you can come back here because the old man is gone and start acting like you care what happens to the land, or Becca, or me."

Gray started down the hill toward the house, his stride longer than before, not just annoyed that he'd taken the bait in the first place—but that he'd imagined he could actually have a conversation with his brothers without wanting to smack them upside the head.

Apparently he wasn't going to grow up any time soon. Even if his brothers were adult strangers now instead of the snot-nosed brats Gray had always had to corral while their parents were busy fighting.

"Brady's just trying to point out that there are options," Ty said, reasonably enough, matching Gray's pace a touch too easily for a man who'd sustained injuries bad enough that he'd had to drop out of the bull-riding circuit in the spring.

But Gray didn't feel reasonable. About any of this. He was a thirty-eight-year-old man who'd poured his heart and soul and entire adult life into this land. He'd lost his wife to it. Oh, sure, he knew Cristina had cheated on him, just like he knew that some people weren't suited to marriage in the first place—especially not with a rancher who could never take those extended vacations she'd longed for or ever leave the land long enough to buy her the pretty things she'd been so sure would make her happy.

But he also knew that if he hadn't been more married to his land than he'd ever been to his woman, he might have prevented her from taking his truck that night and skidding over the side of the pass on her way into town.

If he had to live with that, he'd rather do it out here where there was nothing but the wind and the evergreens bristling on the sides of the mountains, his cattle in the distance, and his land beneath his feet.

He didn't expect Brady, who'd never stuck with anything or thought much beyond himself, to understand that.

Sometimes he wasn't sure he understood it himself.

But he knew one thing. If he didn't want to end up as bitter and twisted as Amos, and he didn't, Gray was going to have to figure out a way to live this life without drowning in his own darkness out here like so many of his ancestors had. And he had to believe the way to do that was to make sure Becca didn't succumb to it either. That the legendary Everett tendency toward wholescale self-destruction ended with Amos.

The brothers walked in what Gray held to be blessed silence the rest of the way down to the house. Despite Amos's clear instructions—delivered to get out ahead of the decided lack of interest in celebrating his miserable carcass, in Gray's opinion—there were trucks and a few SUVs parked in the yard. He recognized almost all of them, and the ones he couldn't identify he figured were his brothers'. Otherwise it was a showing of Kittredges, Douglases, and Everetts, the way it had been almost a hundred and fifty years ago when the three families had come to settle these mountains from different points back east.

There was something about that he liked. It settled in him like a long pull of the whiskey he enjoyed as much as every other man in his family, but preferred to limit so he never behaved like any of them. A good, warm weight of the history here, bound up in all of those who stayed.

"Listen," Brady said when they made it to the yard, a kind of warning in his voice that put Gray's back up.

"Not real interested in listening to you lecture me on ranch life, Denver," Gray drawled.

"Hilarious." Brady squared his shoulders when he faced Gray, reminding both of them that he wasn't a kid anymore. He was built more like a quarterback, and not all of it came from the weird gym he was obsessed with, where they flung tires and carried bags of sand around in the middle of a city as if that was more worthwhile than an honest day of backbreaking ranch work. "It's going to be just you out here, Gray. Becca's going to leave you sooner or later."

"She's fifteen."

"So you have what? Three years? Then she's off. And there's going to be nothing here but the Everett legacy, too many freaking cows, and you."

"And the quiet, Brady. Don't forget the quiet. That's sounding pretty fantastic right about now."

Ty laughed at that. Brady didn't.

"It drove Grandpa crazy, in the end," he said with a certainty that made something Gray refused to call dread or foreboding knot in his gut. "He got weird and you know it. And God knows this place never did anything good for Dad. It poisoned him. It scared Mom so badly she ran off to California and never came back."

"I'm pretty sure Dad made that happen all by himself."

"And what about Cristina?"

"Jesus Christ, Brady," Ty interjected then, sounding slightly less lazy than usual. "You're relentless."

"What you are is out of line," Gray said, cold and sure. "There have been Everetts on this land for more than a century. That's not going to change on my watch. But rest easy, little brother. It doesn't have to be you saving the ranch. No one's expecting it to be you, least of all me."

"Great," Brady replied hotly. "Die of loneliness, bitter and mean and crazy, like all the rest of them."

And they'd put their father in the ground less than an hour ago, which was the only reason Gray kept his fist out of Brady's face. The only reason he bit his tongue and stood there while Brady shouldered his way into the house. Amos might not have been much of a father to any of them, but that hardly mattered. They'd had to bury him all the same. The world was going to feel wrong without the old man in it, whether they'd liked Amos all that much or not. And Gray pummeling his uppity younger brother until he shut his mouth wouldn't help anything.

Not today, anyway.

The back door slammed behind Brady, leaving Ty and Gray standing there in all that brightness with the cold right there beneath it.

"He's only trying to help," Ty said after a minute or two.

"And maybe sell our birthright to fatten up his bank account," Gray agreed. "Sure."

"I think he actually just hates the ranch."

Gray turned his scowl on Ty then. "Do you?"

He expected one of Ty's usual careless replies, tossed out for a laugh or adoration. But instead, his brother looked back at him with an odd expression on his face. Gray couldn't quite place it. He was used to that faint scar at Ty's temple and the loose way he carried himself, all cowboy swagger and bravado, which he guessed a man needed if he was going to fling himself on the back of a pissed-off bull. Repeatedly. For sport. What he wasn't used to was Ty, of all people, looking . . . thoughtful.

"I don't know," Ty said after a moment. His smile seemed longer in coming than usual. "What's home supposed to feel like?"

"According to Brady, a kick in the gut."

"I don't think I'm that emotional." Ty nodded toward the ever-watchful mountains that rose all around them, catching the light and casting shadows and making Gray's chest feel tight. "Besides, I like the view."

Gray nodded at that, and didn't say anything when Ty walked into the house too.

That left him alone, which was how he preferred it. He had a hundred chores to do, dead father or not. He always did. There was a part of him that liked it that way. He didn't feel tied down here—he never had. He felt needed.

The land didn't take care of itself. Neither did the cattle. That was Gray's job. And Brady was right—Becca would leave, sooner or later, whether she went to school or married one of those punks down at the high school in town. The very idea gave Gray indigestion, but that was reality. Kids left and many of them stayed gone. Look at his brothers.

Gray breathed in the only home he'd ever wanted. The change of seasons in the wind, smelling like fresh snow from the higher elevations. The rich scent of the livestock mixed with the sharp slap of the pines. Cold and clear, sunshine and cedar.

Home.

He'd tried marriage once, but for all the wrong reasons. He'd been young and hot for Cristina, and had made the cardinal sin of confusing his hormones for something more. He was still paying for that mistake, but two good things had come out of his reckless, doomed early marriage. Becca was the first and most important thing, of course, hands down.

But the second was the fact he would never, ever be that stupid again.

Gray didn't mind being on his own. But that didn't mean he'd ever intended to live his life lonely. Much less keep Becca from the kind of family she'd clearly always wanted, or she wouldn't have tried so hard to make Amos the cuddly, sweet old grandfather he wasn't.

That was the piece he was missing. And unlike Amos, he didn't plan to endlessly repeat his mistakes until he keeled over of his own sheer orneriness one day.

He'd always intended to fill this house with a family and hope that he made at least one child who got bit by the ranching bug the way he had and grew to find he or she didn't want to leave. It had worked for Amos, despite what a misery the old man had been to live with, so why not Gray too?

What he needed was a practical woman. A solid, dependable woman who understood reality and could commit as much to the legacy of this land as the man who worked it, instead of making demands and dreaming of far-off cities Gray would rather die than live in. Or even visit. A woman who knew who she was and didn't set off to find herself in every smile a cowboy threw her way. A woman who wanted the things he did, would work beside him to get after them, and help keep his obnoxious brother from pretending to be concerned about him when what Brady really wanted was his third of the profit from any sale of this land.

Better still, a woman who could be the kind of mother to Becca that Cristina hadn't been. And Gray hadn't either, these past ten years.

The back door opened again, and when Gray turned, Abby Douglas was standing there in the wedge of space between the screen and the doorjamb.

"I'm heating up some chili," she told him, sounding perfectly comfortable in his kitchen. "Do you want some?"

He'd never really paid much attention to Abby Douglas because she'd always been there, as familiar to him as the long drive from the ranch house to the county road, or the mountain pass that wound its way into town.

Abby Douglas, whose roots stretched back as far into this valley as Gray's did. Abby, who was a year or so younger than Brady and lived with her grandmother on the old Douglas homestead out there on the road into town, making her Gray's closest neighbor.

Plain, sweet, easygoing, and helpful Abby, who had stuck close to home despite having a flighty mother folks still whispered about. Solid, practical Abby, who'd worked in the coffee shop in town through three or four owner and name changes, so long people had started to call it *Abby's* instead.

Abby Douglas, who was nothing if not steadfast and pragmatic.

She blinked at him, and Gray didn't know why he'd never noticed her eyes were that shade of hazel before, nearly gold in the light. It had to be all that bright November sunshine, dancing over both of them and presenting him with the perfect solution to a problem he'd only just realized he needed to solve.

As soon as possible.

"If you don't want chili, that's fine," she said. "I threw together a few sandwiches too."

And this time when Gray's mouth curved, it felt a lot closer to a real smile than anything he'd plastered on his face since he'd found Amos in the barn on Halloween.

It felt real.

And it held the promise of a much, much better life than the one he'd just buried.

2

Abby Douglas had spent most of her life fantasizing about Gray Everett, which as far as she could tell was a favorite pastime of most of the women in the Longhorn Valley. If not all of Colorado. She couldn't blame them. Gray was six feet and three inches of straight-up cowboy fantasy, and what red-blooded Colorado woman could deny that siren call to her cowgirl roots?

Abby had fallen head over heels with Gray, literally, when she'd been barely five. She'd fallen down at a church picnic, he'd picked her up and set her right, and she'd never quite been the same after. She'd spent long hours in high school daydreaming about touching Gray Everett. Kissing Gray Everett. It hadn't ended when she'd graduated either. As she'd grown and settled into her quiet, simple life in Cold River, she'd indulged in a great many detailed fantasies about her gorgeous, remote, gruff, and fascinating neighbor. Her imagination had always done much, much more than simply let her live there on adjoining land, as her family had done with his as long as there had been settlers in this part of the Colorado mountains. And as Abby had been doing her whole life.

Her imagination was never satisfied with merely *yearning* at him.

Not that he'd ever noticed what she did or didn't do.

All the ladies in Cold River might smile a bit more brightly when Gray Everett walked by, it was true, but Abby had always longed for the man that much *more*. And had accordingly resigned herself ages ago to the bracing truth that she was destined to spend her life mooning over a man who paid about as much attention to her as he did to the scenery. Less, if she was honest, because she'd actually observed Gray stopping to take in the pretty view that surrounded them upon occasion.

And yet despite the fact he had never appeared to see her as any different than her own grandmother, and had exhibited roughly the same amount of romantic interest in the both of them—which was to say, none at all—Abby had spent whole years imagining infinite variations on Gray proposing to her.

Some sweet, some angsty. Some wild and hot, in a rumpled bed somewhere. On one knee, over a romantic dinner, or even on the back of a galloping horse. She'd covered every possibility.

Except this one.

She was having some trouble believing it was real.

Because in all the many versions of this moment that she'd imagined over the years, she'd never imagined it happening in the comfortable sitting room of the Douglas family farmhouse. The cozy, happy place where her grandma had taught her how to mend her own clothes, how to convey acres of emotion and reaction with a single arched brow, how to enjoy the pleasure of her own company, and best of all, how to hide really good books behind unremarkable works of seeming piety so Abby could better amuse herself during boring family discussions.

But unlike every one of her fantasies and all of her favorite racy books, now that the proposal she'd always wanted was happening somewhere other than inside her head, Abby didn't want to fling herself into Gray's lean, hard arms, she . . . kind of wanted to kill him.

"Let me make sure I'm understanding you," she managed to say into the awkward silence, threading her fingers together on her lap as if she were sitting in church.

Not that Gray looked awkward. Abby couldn't imagine a man like Gray ever really looked or felt awkward about anything. He was too . . . *elemental*.

So elemental, in fact—so commanding and *big* with those dark green eyes that never failed to make her belly flip over and a body too solid and smoothly muscled to really fit in that armchair he'd chosen to sit in—that there had almost been too much noise in her head to fully comprehend what he was saying to her.

Almost.

Gray's mouth curved, that fascinating quirk of his firm lips Abby had spent quite a lot of her time contemplating. She'd been doing exactly that when he'd appeared at the front door of the old farmhouse that only company ever used, which was why it had taken her longer than it should have to realize he hadn't come by today to share what passed for the usual neighborly news and information out this way. Cows busting through the fences or horses leaping out of their paddocks or rumors of coyotes. The usual.

She'd told him her grandmother was in town, and he'd aimed that half smile at her, which Abby assumed had no other purpose than to make her knees weak. Then he'd told her that was just as well because he was there to see her.

Abby had been rendered speechless by that declaration and had no idea how she'd managed to move from the front door to the sitting room. It was lost forever in the tumult inside of her.

Though that had subsided a bit, she had to admit.

And normally the rare sight of Gray Everett this close to her, much less his version of a smile, would have left her feeling giddy. Today, she had the urge to smack it. Him.

He was sitting there in the chair that had once been her late grandfather's, except he was much taller than Grandpa had ever been, a fact that was impossible to ignore with his long legs stretched out in front of him. He was dressed in his usual uniform of boots, jeans, and a T-shirt—a long-sleeved T-shirt today, beneath something flannel and that barn coat of his. He was holding his cowboy hat in his hands, though he wasn't fiddling with it, because of course Gray Everett was the only man alive who could ask a woman he wasn't dating or even really connected to in any way to marry him and never feel the slightest urge to fidget.

Correction, Abby eyed him. *He didn't exactly* ask.

"You want to marry me," Abby said, and it was interesting in a kind of clinical way to hear herself say that. Out loud. *To* him.

Some part of her expected him to belt out a laugh. To tell her she'd misheard him and had completely gotten that wrong. To then wonder why she'd ever imagine he would say something like that to her. She was half blushing already, ready for that kick of humiliation—

But Gray nodded. Decisively. "I do."

Abby felt too hot. Her head was spinning. She went to sit down and then remembered she already was, there on the old sofa with the cheerful printed cabbages she'd always loved. The sofa where she'd read a thousand books before the fire, fitfully slept off her colds and flus beneath throws her grandma had knitted over the years, and had watched her grandparents grow old as they'd raised her when her mother couldn't be bothered.

This was reality. Gray's bizarre proposal wasn't. It couldn't be.

"Your father's funeral was last week," Abby said as gently as she could, because Amos's death had obviously hit him harder than anyone had imagined. "It's possible you're having a reaction to that."

That curve in the corner of his mouth deepened, and even though this was all crazy, it still seemed to sizzle straight through her. "You think I'm breaking out in spontaneous marriage proposals? Is that a thing?"

She reminded herself that he was insane with grief. Clearly. "You've never glanced at me, Gray. Not once. In your entire life."

"I've glanced at you."

Abby couldn't argue with him on that, since it would involve explaining that she would have known if he had or hadn't glanced her way because she was always, *always*, paying entirely too much attention to what, where, and who he was looking at.

She smiled politely instead. "You don't know a single thing about me."

"I've known you since the day you were born."

"I've known most of the people in this town since the day I was born. That doesn't mean I *know them*. It means I know whether or not to pretend I see them in the supermarket on any given day."

"I already covered this," Gray said patiently. Too patiently, as if Abby were the one being crazy here.

"Right. Something about shared goals and roots, and did you call me *uncomplicated*?"

Gray regarded her for a moment. "That's a compliment."

"I think you'll find that no matter how you phrase it, there are very few women who like being called *uncomplicated*."

"Because you'd rather be an impenetrable mystery?"

Abby frowned at him. It felt weird—likely because it

was the first time in her entire life she hadn't *beamed* at this man, hoping against hope that he might finally return her smile. Or better yet, her feelings. He never had.

"Not impenetrable, necessarily. But consider the other things you find uncomplicated. A tractor, I'm guessing. A cow. Your barn. Most of your appliances."

"I like things I can depend on."

Abby wanted nothing more than to be one of those things, even if that meant he lumped her in with his washing machine or his John Deere, but . . . not like this. Not this . . . offhanded chat as if they were discussing livestock.

It occurred to her that they were. Or he was, anyway. That unless she'd had an aneurysm when she'd answered the door and was even now in a coma, hovering close to death and making things up again, Gray Everett had come over to inquire after her as if she were some kind of . . . broodmare.

"You don't know if you can depend on me or not," she pointed out.

Politely. So politely. As if this were as normal as the way they'd all sat around in Gray's house last week, pretending to eat something because that was what people did around death to prove they were alive. The way everyone had made awkward conversation that steered clear of potentially thorny topics like why none of Amos's exes had turned up to pay their respects, what was going to become of the ranch everyone knew Amos had left to all three of his sons instead of just Gray, and the simple fact that didn't require discussing that most folks in the valley weren't expecting to miss Amos and his drunken nonsense much.

"Everybody in Cold River knows they can depend on you," Gray was saying, in the same calm, unbothered way he'd talked about the annual snow pack and the proposed new residential developments out on the county line in his own living room. "You live with your grandmother when you could have moved out on your own. And you're the only reason anyone knows the current name of that coffee shop in town."

He said that as if the very notion of a coffee shop was newfangled and odd. As if he was in his seventies instead of his thirties. But then again, she'd always considered that a part of his charm. Before now.

"It's called Cold River Coffee, again, the way it was fifteen years ago when they first put a coffee shop in the old feed store building," she supplied, as if he cared. Or that was the point of this conversations. "It was Human Beans for a while there, but apparently there was a copyright issue."

"You're a local girl. More than that, you're a Douglas. A lot of folks head out of here as soon as they graduate from high school, but you stayed. You know your own roots."

"My grandparents raised me," she replied, feeling unduly stung by his list of facts about her life, all of which she suspected he knew, the way people just knew things about each other here. It was all part of the scenery, really. Meaning Gray certainly hadn't had to pay any particular attention to her to learn any of those things. "After Grandpa died, I didn't see leaving my grandmother all alone."

"Like I said. Dependable."

"I could have a secret life as a phone sex operator for all you know," Abby blurted out.

Where did that even come from? And had she really just mentioned *phone sex* to Gray Everett?

His green gaze was steady on hers. Her cheeks burned. "Do you?"

"No."

"Then I think we'll muddle through."

"Muddle through . . . a *marriage*?"

There was something besides patience in that green gaze of his. And Abby didn't understand why her throat was dry, or worse, why there was a kind of tight grip around her chest.

"You're asking a lot of questions," Gray pointed out, all drawl and that unwavering gaze. "But you haven't said no."

"Haven't I? I feel certain that I have."

"You haven't."

"Oh. Well. That's really just an oversight."

He leaned forward. He rested his elbows on his knees, and Abby couldn't seem to tear her gaze away from his hands. They were a rancher's hands, that was for sure. Big, tough. A couple of nicks here and there, which only made her imagine what those callused fingers might feel like against her skin.

She jerked her gaze back to his and sat there, mortified. Because for some reason, she was sure he knew exactly what she'd been imagining.

He didn't smile. But there was something in his gaze that made her feel as if he had.

"Here's what I think, Abby. I suspect you're as practical as you seem. Salt of the earth, through and through."

"Does anyone actually want to be called salt of the earth? Isn't that a lot like saying, 'you're deeply boring and easily ignored, but you're always there, so I'll use the word *salt* because it sounds less offensive'?"

"I need a wife. Becca needs a mother. I'd like it to be you." Gray held her gaze. "I'm not a man given to compliments, but that doesn't mean I don't appreciate a good thing when I see it."

Abby felt like the pig in that kid's movie. Two gruff

words from a farmer, and she was contemplating flinging herself on the floor and pressing her face against his boot.

Not really, she assured herself.

Or anyway, she didn't think she would actually do something like that.

But the worrying thing was what she wasn't doing. She wasn't kicking him out. She wasn't gathering her tattered dignity around her like a cloak and sweeping out of the room, refusing to entertain the madness that he was throwing at her. She wasn't laughing in his face.

He might imagine that was because she was *the salt of the earth*, since he apparently imagined it was every girl's dream to be compared to condiments and dirt, but she knew better.

She knew the real dirty secret was how tempted she was to say yes, no thought required. As if it were still the 1880s and she was a pioneer woman preparing to head out to the frontier in the company of any old stranger she tripped over in Boston Harbor. Which she was pretty sure was the actual true story of how her Douglas ancestors had made it out to Colorado.

"You sound very serious about this," she said after a moment.

"I don't spend a lot of time talking about things I'm not serious about."

"Really? How funny. I'm pretty sure that's one of those things people learn during a normal dating process. You know. Likes, dislikes. What to be serious about and what's pure silliness. That's Online Profile 101."

"I hardly trust a computer to do my banking. I'm not about to trust one to find me a wife."

"Do I need to tell you what year it is?"

Another curve in the corner of his hard mouth. "Are you looking for a date, Abby?"

Once again, that stung when it probably shouldn't have. Gray wasn't the type to get a dig in like that. But she was a bit touchy on the subject. It had never been her intention to become one of the vestal virgins of the Longhorn Valley. It had certainly never occurred to her back in high school that she would be one of those women whose lack of a dating life was discussed right in front of her with a side helping of pity and every now and again, the teensiest hint of scorn.

"For all you know, I date all the time," she told him, and ordered herself to unclench her jaw. "Maybe I juggle men like a circus sideshow and enjoy it so much I've never had the slightest inclination to settle down."

"I feel like I would've heard."

"Because you're really tuned in to Cold River gossip? Why do I doubt that?"

"I have a fifteen-year-old daughter. You'd be surprised the things she wants to talk to me about on those long drives to and from school."

"I wouldn't describe myself as looking for dates, exactly," Abby replied, rather than touching the topic of Becca. Lithe, lovely Becca, who looked like the ghost of her beautiful late mother and was exactly the sort of girl Abby had longed to be while in high school. And had not been. In any way, shape, or form. And who Gray now claimed he wanted Abby to parent in some way. "But if you don't do online dating, how do you date?"

"I don't date."

"You prefer to just show up on doorsteps and issue marriage proposals. Got it."

"Abby. You're making this complicated. It's a yes-or-no question."

Her throat went dry again, and her hands ached like the arthritis her grandma complained about on cold mornings.

She frowned down into her lap and saw that she was still clenching her fingers together. Hard. She let go, then spread her hands out on the tops of her thighs in the hope that could make them stop throbbing.

Or make Gray make sense.

She hadn't dressed for a marriage proposal today, that was for sure. She was wearing her favorite pair of leggings and a slouchy sort of sweatshirt that felt a bit like a wearable cave. It was the perfect outfit for a November day in this drafty old farmhouse that Grandma refused to heat much because she'd prefer to use the stove or build a fire. Abby's hair was in its usual serviceable ponytail, and she never wore much makeup anyway, though when imagining marriage proposals, she'd always assumed that mascara would be involved. To top it all off, she was wearing an extra thick pair of bright orange socks emblazoned with foxes as a stand-in for curse words she didn't utter in front of her grandmother.

Actually, if she thought about how embarrassing it was to be sitting here with Gray Everett dressed in what her grandmother called her *day pajamas*, she might die.

"It's not a simple question," she found herself saying. "You're talking about marriage, not a ride into town."

"Okay. But it's pretty easy to say no, Abby." The way he was looking at her seemed to change then. It was as if he moved closer, though she could see he didn't. But there was no air in the room. And even less in her chest. "It seems like what's complicated here is that you don't want to."

"What would you do if I did say no? Work your way down a handy list of appliance-like females in Cold River who you feel are equally dependable? How many others can there be?"

And as soon as she said it, she realized she really did

want to know the answer. Was she unique in her *salt of the earthness*? Or was that a quality Gray found everywhere he looked?

You are pathetic, she lectured herself, but that was old news.

"More questions. Still no answer, though."

He shifted in his chair then, and Abby still kind of wanted to kill him. She still didn't understand why any of this was happening. She wasn't sure she liked any of the things he'd said to her about why he would choose her for what sounded like an old-fashioned sort of frontier marriage that shouldn't have appealed to her at all. She was sure she should have been significantly more outraged than she was.

But she was suddenly terrified that he was going to get up and leave, and that struck her as much worse than all the rest.

"Let's assume I accepted this ridiculous proposal," she said, frowning at him. "What would that look like?"

"What do you think marriage is supposed to look like?"

She stared back at him and very carefully did not mention what his first marriage had looked like, to every last soul in Longhorn Valley. Before and after its sad end.

But something must have shown on her face, because his lips flattened. "Not looking to be cheated on again, if that's what you mean."

Abby felt her face flame. Again. But almost as soon as that wave of embarrassment—or shame, really, that she'd brought up something so sensitive and upset him—passed, something else followed in its wake.

Something a lot more like temper.

Because if she'd actually been dating this man, these were the kinds of things she could and would ask about, surely. She might not have gone on a whole lot of dates herself, or any, but she'd read enough to know better.

"I'm sorry," she said stiffly. "Is your first marriage off-limits?"

"What do you want to know?"

His green gaze was cool. Steady.

And the thing was, Abby wanted to know everything. She'd been fifteen when he'd married Cristina. Fifteen and absolutely, utterly lovesick over twenty-three-year-old Gray. She had spent hours upon hours worrying over every last aspect of his marriage—or what she knew about it, anyway. She'd cried at his wedding. And then she'd viewed the next five years as an opportunity to keep a stern vigil over Gray's happiness. She couldn't have him, of course. She was just a kid. But Cristina did have him, and Cristina ought to have loved him the way he deserved.

She still remembered exactly what she was doing the first time she'd heard the rumors that Gray Everett's tempestuous wife, the one he'd met when he'd gone over to Colorado Springs to watch his brother ride some bulls and had brought back to tiny Cold River like some kind of prize, was stepping out on him. That was what gossipy old Charlie Dunn had said to one of the Winthrop girls, right there in the coffee shop where Abby had worked after school. Back when it had been called Grounds & Grace.

She had to lock herself in the back room while she'd sobbed for Gray's broken heart.

But she didn't share any of that with him. How could she?

"You've had one marriage that didn't work out," she said. Carefully. "What makes you believe that this one would?"

A crease appeared between his brows as if he hadn't

thought about that. Or hadn't expected her to think about it. "You and I have a lot more in common."

"So far the only thing we appear to have in common is that we live here."

"That counts for a lot."

"And you still haven't told me how you imagine a marriage between us would work. Practically speaking. For example, do you want more children?"

She didn't say anything about sex. Because the phone sex operator thing was still living inside her like its own kind of horror movie, thank you. She supposed she didn't really have to say the word for it to shimmer there between them. Because as far as she was aware, there was only one direct way to have children.

There was a gleam in his gaze that hadn't been there before. "I'm open to the idea."

"Okay. Well, I do. Want more children. Or I just want them, I mean, because I don't . . ." *He knows you don't have any children.* She pushed forward. "And you're asking me to step into the role of stepmother, as well. That's not something you should do on a whim."

"Becca needs a solid family, but she's fine."

"What does that mean?"

"It means, she's fine. It'll be good for her to have you around, but you don't have to worry about her."

Abby's mouth was open. She shut it and shifted against the sofa, suddenly unable to get comfortable. "So in your conception of this marriage based on nothing except proximity, I wouldn't actually be a stepmother to your only child? Or are you imagining a marriage where I'll stay here with Grandma, and we'll just say we're married for tax purposes or something?"

"What the hell kind of marriage is that?"

"I don't know. But then, I also don't know any fifteen-year-old motherless girl who's *fine*."

Abby had always loved where she lived. Cold River was beautiful, it was home, and the fact that so few people lived here seemed as much a bonus as a burden some days. But it was right here, sitting in the front room of the Douglas farmhouse with Gray Everett, that the true beauty of living in a place like this became clear to her as it never had before.

Because she didn't have to tell him why she was the expert on motherless fifteen-year-old girls in this room when he had one and she didn't. He already knew. As many stories as Abby had heard about Gray and Cristina and their doomed marriage, she knew he couldn't possibly have avoided hearing a similar number of stories about Lily.

Lily, who had never liked *Lillian*, the name she'd been born with. Lily, who had always made it clear to Grandma and Grandpa and every last citizen of Cold River that she deserved better—and that she, by God, would get it. Delicate, manipulative Lily, who had left home after high school and had taken herself off to whatever bright lights and big cities she could find, only to return a few years later, pregnant and seemingly abashed.

It hadn't lasted. Abby had been a baby the first time Lily took off and claimed she'd be back at the end of a long weekend, or so the story went, only to turn up weeks later. She'd been nearly ten by the time everyone involved stopped pretending. Lily wasn't ever going to come home for long, and she was never, ever going to be any kind of parent to Abby.

But sure. Abby had been *fine*. Still was.

"Sounds like you and Becca can do a lot of bonding, then," Gray said after a moment, as if this conversation was going exactly the way he'd planned it. "Something else in favor of you marrying me."

"I don't . . ." Of course there were a million reasons people didn't go around marrying their neighbors for the hell of it, but Abby couldn't come up with any of them there and then. "You don't really think something this sudden would work."

"Abby. Listen."

He didn't move any closer. He didn't take her hands in his or shift so he was gazing deep into her eyes. He stayed where he was, the wide brim of his hat in his hands and his elbows resting on his knees as if he could sit there all day. As if she was one more fractious animal he could soothe with the power of his voice and the force of his steady attention.

She hated that he wasn't wrong about that either.

"I've always liked you," he told her.

And somehow—*somehow*—Abby didn't let out the bitter laugh that crowded her throat then and made her wonder if she might choke.

"You have?" she asked instead. Not bitterly. Not exactly. "Are you sure? Because I'm pretty sure you don't know the difference between me and any piece of furniture in your house."

"I like all the furniture in my house."

Gray waited as if he expected her to respond to that, but it was as if something heavy were parked on her chest. And there were too many harsh words in her mouth that she didn't want to say. Not because he couldn't take it. But because it would be much too revealing.

"I can see why you want to stick your fingers in my first marriage and tear it apart, or dig into this proposal and make it something it's not. But I'm not hiding anything. I'm not crazy, I'm not grief-stricken, and I'm nothing if not practical myself. This is simple." His gaze was direct and uncompromising, as if he could convince her simply by looking at her. And her heart pounded against her ribs because it felt as if he really could. "Just marry me. We'll keep on doing what we already do, we'll just do it together. It's a perfect solution."

It was that word that got to her. *Solution.*

"Oh." The word came out like a sigh, and she didn't know if it was relief or despair. "Is this one of those will situations where you have to marry someone to save the ranch or something?"

"No." Gray's head canted slightly to one side. "This isn't a soap opera, Abby."

His tone was reproving, and Abby didn't like the way it made her feel so . . . bright hot and melty, all at once.

Or maybe she liked it too much.

"It must be the out-of-the-blue marriage proposal from a man who's never spoken more than a handful of complete sentences to me in his entire life." She waved a hand. "I'm seeing soap operas everywhere."

Gray sat back at that. And then he . . . lounged, as if his entire body became his own low drawl. "You keep saying things like that. But what I can't help noticing is that you're still sitting here. Talking about the details of a marriage you can't seem to decide if you want or don't."

"Details you haven't shared with me."

"What details do you want? Be precise. And stop talking about furniture and appliances."

Abby didn't see any reason to hold herself back further in the face of such insanity. "Will it be a marriage in name only?"

"Name only?" he echoed.

Her courage waned the hotter her face got, it turned out.

But she pushed on. "Are you looking to pretend or do you want it to be real?"

That seemed to hum in the air between them, hanging over the hooked oval rug in the center of the floor where Abby had played board games when she was a child. Or maybe it was just that she couldn't seem to breathe when she saw the arrested, amused expression on his face.

"You're talking about sex," Gray said after what seemed like a thousand years, his voice a low rumble. And Abby's wild pulse took over her whole body. His eyes were particularly green, then, and the longer he looked at her, the more intense his gaze got. "Yes, Abby. I want there to be sex in my marriage."

3

Gray didn't know what he'd been expecting.

The whole thing had gone a lot smoother in his head. He'd figured that he'd come over, state his case, and that would be that. Practical, dependable Abby would see the wisdom in it and give her agreement, and everything would fall into place.

Except now they were talking about sex.

And Abby Douglas was staring back at him, her face flushed in a way that made it impossible not to notice how intriguingly red her cheeks could get. Which got him wondering all kinds of things that made him . . . restless. Her eyes, which he couldn't recall ever noticing before the other day, were even more gold than before, and more, he couldn't seem to *stop* noticing them.

That was disconcerting enough.

In fact, everything about Abby Douglas was disconcerting. The way she looked, the way she looked *at* him, the things she said—it should have been all the reason he needed to call this off and get the hell out of the Douglas farmhouse.

But he didn't make a move for the door. It was almost as if he couldn't tear himself away, though that didn't make any sense.

There was something about the way she fired questions at him. As if she was interviewing him for the position of husband. And he was amazed how interested he was in getting that job when he'd been so sure she'd act grateful and pleased that he'd proposed to her in the first place.

But it was more than that. Gray felt very nearly agitated, and he didn't like that at all.

He focused on her instead, not her eyes or all that rosy color on her cheeks. "You keep saying I don't know you, Abby, but I do. I watched you grow up. You're nice to my kid the same way you're nice to your grandmother's friends. No one in this town has a bad word to say about you, and you know as well as I do that there's more than a few who have nothing but bad words to say about everyone and everything. You were even nice to my father, no matter how raucous he got, and there's not a lot of folks who could say the same. Including me."

"And because I'm so nice, we should marry each other for very, very practical reasons. And also have sex. Will that also be for practical reasons?"

Gray hadn't given a lot of thought to the fact that Abby was likely to have a whole host of her own opinions. About appliances, apparently. About what marriage ought to be. About his previous marriage. And, it seemed, about his method in proposing to her.

There was an itch deep inside him that he knew he couldn't reach. That he had to sit with. That was how it felt to sit here and talk to Abby about something he'd expected to go sweet and easy, no complications at all. He wasn't sure how he felt about it.

He hadn't really expected to *feel*.

"The great thing about sex is that it's fun whether it's practical or just practice," he heard himself say, in the kind of voice he would have said wasn't him at all. It was better suited to one of his brothers, low and loaded, like he was flirting.

Of course he wasn't flirting.

"Oh." Abby breathed more than said that, and Gray found himself looking at her mouth, of all things. And there was something wrong about that, he knew there was, because this was *Abby Douglas*, for God's sake. But her mouth was another part of her that, once noticed, couldn't be unseen. It was as full as it was soft, and Gray wondered how he had gone every year of his life so far without noticing it.

And yeah. Maybe he was flirting.

It made him feel lightheaded, all these years after he'd figured *flirting* was something he'd buried with his ex.

"Oh?" he echoed. Because apparently he was picking it right up after a decade. "Are you opposed to sex? Or fun? Or are you not the marrying kind?"

It occurred to him then that the peculiar feeling inside him was *enjoyment*, and that was the funniest thing yet in this strange afternoon. Because despite the numerous comments he'd suffered from his brothers over the past few days, Gray did, in fact, know how to enjoy himself. Or he had. It was just that his enjoyment usually came in the form of pride in his daughter or his land or in his sheer survival year after year without going under.

People tended to mistake a man who kept his own counsel as some kind of grim reaper. But Gray wasn't grim. He considered himself a pragmatist who preferred the company of his horses and the enduring quiet of the mountains, that was all.

Abby was much more entertaining than he'd anticipated. And that had to be a good thing. It opened up all kinds of possibilities.

"I support sex *and* marriage, generally speaking," Abby

said, carefully, as if she had to give the matter some thought.

Gray tapped the wide brim of his hat against his leg as he sat there, watching her. Everything had shifted when he'd looked up in his own backyard and seen her there in the doorway. He'd decided he ought to marry her there and then. And just like that, he'd started seeing her for the first time. That mouth, for one thing. Those pretty eyes.

When he'd always considered Abby nice enough, like he'd told her, but he'd never looked twice.

He was having trouble remembering why that was.

"You support sex and marriage generally. How about specifically?" His fingers were too tight on his hat. "As in, specifically you and me. Because yes, I'm going to want to make babies the old-fashioned way. And likely do a lot of that practicing while we're at it."

Sex had been the only decent thing about his first marriage. Gray had imagined that he'd sleep with this woman he was proposing to, sure. But somehow it hadn't occurred to him until right now how much better than decent things could be.

She swallowed. He could see her throat move, and that was another thing about Abby he'd failed to notice before. It turned out he liked the line of her neck. He liked the droopy collar of the sweatshirt she wore that slid down one rounded shoulder in a manner he could only call inviting.

Had she always been inviting? Gray had dropped by today with no warning, so he knew he'd caught her off guard. It meant she was just . . . like this. And he didn't know what it said about him that he'd never noticed either way.

Nothing good.

Maybe it was true, as Brady had suggested more than

once since the funeral, that Gray had spent too much time brooding around the ranch these past ten years. Brady was sure it was because Gray had been mourning his marriage, or at least Cristina's death. Gray figured everyone thought that, and he hadn't exactly gone out of his way to disabuse anyone of that notion.

Are you mourning? Ty had asked the other night, his gaze too shrewd. *Or do you just really like the taste of martyrdom with your ranching?*

Gray didn't want Abby to think he was in mourning. And he refused to consider himself any kind of martyr.

"We really have to talk about the fact that you should probably be having this discussion with a therapist," Abby said after a moment, sitting straighter in her seat.

"I have to say, I didn't see that one coming. A therapist?"

"A therapist, yes. You need one. Badly."

"The only therapist in town is Bobby Garcia, and I'm pretty sure his focus is on traumatized children. And anyway, I don't want to marry Bobby. He's much too old for me."

Abby let out a small, frustrated noise that Gray was surprised he found . . . cute.

It was a slippery slope. He was noticing her mouth. He was fixating on where the collar of her sweatshirt moved down her upper arm and the soft skin beneath. He was thinking of her as cute, everywhere.

Not that it was a bad thing to decide he lusted after Abby Douglas. Especially when he wanted to marry her. He was thrown by how fast it all had happened. Was happening. Because he could feel a whole lot of interest in the situation, suddenly, heavy and hot enough to make him shift where he sat.

"We're sitting here talking about sex," she said, turning

a brighter shade of that red as she said it. But she lifted her chin and kept going. "That's crazy. You and I don't sit around. Or have discussions. And certainly not about sex. *People* don't sit around discussing sexual exploits with people they hardly know."

He studied her for a moment that turned into two, and that flush rolled down her neck toward the dropped shoulder. "Some people don't talk about it all. They just do it. Other people hold out for a few dates before the topic comes up. I'm offering marriage from the get-go."

Abby looked flustered, but she still frowned at him. "You can't expect me to believe you think it's normal to wander next door one afternoon and proposition the first person you see. Marriage, sex, children. What kind of person wants to jump into all of that blind? You have no idea if we would get along with each other. On any level. I would say there's a ninety-nine point nine percent chance that we won't. At all. Are you prepared to discuss the divorce right now too?"

"I'm not a big believer in divorce. When I make promises, I intend to keep them."

She didn't say Cristina's name. But it still seemed to hang there between them, because that was the curse of a small, remote valley like this one. Everybody knew everybody's business. Whether people wanted them to know it or not.

Abby looked away, as if she was filing the information somewhere in that fascinating head of hers while she gazed out the window toward the old apple orchard that had been her grandfather's pride and joy.

"I'm not crazy," Gray found himself saying gruffly, though he had never believed in explaining himself. He had always wanted to be known for his actions, not the words he strung together to clarify them. "I want what everyone with acreage out here wants. I want my land to stay in my family, and I want that family to work it the way Everetts always have. I don't want to sell it off into tidy, manicured condos so rich city people like my brother Brady can come up here on the weekends. There's only two ways to do that. A whole lot of legal nonsense or a big family. Seemed like it was a good time to start working on the latter."

"You want a wife." She kept her eyes trained on the gnarled apple trees, stark and bare this time of year despite the November sun that made them gleam. "Any wife at all. It's a role you need filled. It isn't personal. Is that what you're telling me?"

"It's not . . . *not* personal." Gray felt a different kind of agitation settle in against his sternum, and he didn't like that at all. This whole thing was supposed to be a path toward getting rid of his agitation, not making it worse. "I didn't pick a name out of a hat, Abby. I picked you, specifically. I watched you grow up a lot kinder and sweeter than you had to. Everyone knows how your mother went off the rails, but you didn't use that as an excuse to follow her example the way a lot of folks might have. You're a pillar of the community, and you're barely thirty."

"A pillar of salt? What a compliment. Or am I getting my romantic metaphors confused in all these . . . condiments?"

"I don't have a list of other women I'm going to propose to if you say no."

He hadn't exactly meant to say that. But something changed once he did. Abby turned back to him and regarded him solemnly, the red gone from her cheeks and those golden eyes of hers unreadable.

Gray decided to take that as a good sign.

"When I decided I wanted to get married," Gray said, more gruffly than necessary, "the only one I considered was you."

Her lips parted, her cheeks lit up again, and there was something glassy in her gaze that suggested there was a lot going on beneath her surface. Gray found himself surprisingly focused on her, as if the moment he looked away, he would break the spell, and she'd laugh in his face.

Something it hadn't occurred to him she might very well do until he'd been knocking on the door.

He watched her closely, and he couldn't decide if she looked stricken or intrigued. Both, maybe.

But then she was the one who broke the spell—not that Gray believed in things like spells anyway—by surging to her feet so she was standing there before him.

He was still stuck on sex. Marital sex. Long and lazy. Unhurried. No need to cram it all into a night or pretend it was anything other than what it was. No need to do anything but slow down, take his time, and learn every last thing about her.

He had only vague memories of Abby's mother over the years. She'd always been much too glamorous—which was an insult, to Gray's way of thinking. Lily had taken after her father. Richard Douglas had been tall and thin, no matter how many pies his wife baked from his apples or how he liked his steak and eggs in the morning. Gray had distinct memories of Richard putting away more pancakes than the high school boys at those firehouse breakfasts, but the man had always been as gnarled and skinny as the trees in his orchard.

But Abby was built like her grandmother. Martha Douglas was no-nonsense from the top of her head to the soles of her feet. Solid. Not skinny, not fat. Broad farmer's shoulders as befit a woman who'd lived on a farm every day of her life. Martha's people were still dairy farmers a few valleys over, which meant Abby was rooted deep into Colorado soil on both sides.

"You're forgetting that I knew your first wife," Abby was saying, crossing her arms in front of her as if she was warding him off. While Gray was imagining all the ways he could enjoy a woman who wasn't likely to break in half if he touched her. He had to shift in his chair, again, to pay attention. "And at least three of your previous girlfriends. I'm not your type."

"I don't have a type."

"Of course you have a type. Everybody has a type."

"What's your type?" he asked, genuinely curious.

She scowled at him, and he had no idea why it made him want to laugh. "The girls you like are all hip bones and gleaming, glossy dark hair. They're usually three to five inches shorter than me, and looked like delicate little dolls next to all your—"

She cut herself off.

Gray raised a brow. "My what?"

Abby sighed. "Your . . . whole thing."

He didn't know what that meant. "I know what you look like, Abby. I'm sitting here, looking at you."

"I've never been married before, so I'm clutching at straws here, but surely you have to be more than neighbors. You have to have more in common than an address on the same dirt road. It's easy to sit around in my grandmother's living room and talk about sex and children, I guess, no matter how bizarre it might be. But relationships are year after year after year. Children don't make them any easier. And I don't see how you jump into that if you don't have a few really important secret weapons already." She started ticking them off on her fingers. "Attraction. Some kind of shared sense of humor, I hope. And an actual relationship, with real tests and history. Without those things, I don't see how you could possibly last."

Gray wasn't losing his patience, exactly. But she wasn't even slightly excited by the idea. Or even faintly intrigued. He could work with *intrigued*.

"I think you're attractive," he told her, shortly. The strange thing was that he'd never thought about her attractiveness one way or the other before, but now it seemed so laughably obvious to him that he couldn't understand how he hadn't noticed. "You're entertaining, though I don't know that I need a stand-up routine, if that's what you mean by a shared sense of humor. And our families have been tangled together since the eighteen hundreds. What more could you want?"

"Oh, I don't know. Chemistry, maybe?"

There was temper in her voice and splashed all over her face, and that should have been a red flag. He'd had enough rocky weather to last him a lifetime. He'd vowed that he'd never tolerate that crap again. That he'd find the sweetest, quietest, most biddable and even-keeled female who'd ever existed if he ever went down this road again—but maybe Gray really didn't like them all that biddable.

His own mother had been quiet until she'd packed up and left. Cristina had started off sweet and *whatever you think* and *you decide, honey*, hadn't she? And look how that had ended up. Sweet and biddable were good qualities in cattle, but not so great in a rancher's wife. A good rancher's wife needed to be independent, stubborn, strong-willed, and capable, or she wouldn't last a single winter out here.

Much less a few rounds with Gray.

He told himself that was why he found himself grinning as he rose to his feet to stand in front of her.

"People put a lot of faith in chemistry," he said. "But

there'd be a lot fewer people wandering around this planet if we all sat around waiting for chemistry to hit us."

Her scowl deepened, which shouldn't have been possible. "Is that supposed to be a positive? Are you going to tell me that a good marriage requires I lie back and think of England?"

"Why would you think about England?"

"Why would you try to tell me that chemistry doesn't matter? Of course it does."

"I'm not saying it doesn't matter. But sheer stubbornness matters more." He heard the intensity in his voice, but did nothing to temper it. "If people want to stay married, they do. If they want that marriage to be a good one, they work on it and make it that way. It's not rocket science. It doesn't require your online profiles. You don't need to get matched on your smart phone. You make a commitment to someone, then you keep it. It's as simple and as hard as that."

He watched in fascination as her hands curled into fists at her sides.

"I appreciate that you have experience being married, and that gives you a platform to make sweeping statements," she said, her voice low, as if she was fighting back her own intensity. "That's great. But you're missing that I'm not interested in the state of marriage in a general sense. I'm telling you I am not going to marry someone I have no chemistry with. That has nothing to do with me being stubborn, not stubborn, or insufficiently committed. It's actually all about the fact that I'm not staggering around in a grief-induced daze, proposing marriage to people I've never looked at twice before in my whole life."

That should have annoyed him, because he wasn't dazed. Amos had been a mean, unhealthy old man. His death hadn't been a real surprise. Gray wasn't sure he was grieving him so much as the father Amos had never been, and he knew he wasn't crazy with it. But he couldn't seem to lose his grin, especially when he moved closer to her.

Because when he did, she lost that scowl. Her eyes went wide, that cute flush brightened up her face again, and she had to tip her head back to look at him. Not as much as some of the other girls he'd dated had, as she'd pointed out. Gray liked that too. He didn't have to hunker over her.

She was . . . right there.

He had an urge and went with it. He reached over and curled his fingers around her ponytail, then pulled them gently along the length of it.

And figured the chemistry question was answered by the way her breath went shuddery.

But he didn't end it there.

"If I'm following all this," he said, his drawl low. Thick. "You don't actually have any objections. You think we maybe ought to date first. You're worried we don't have chemistry. But at the end of the day, you're not opposed to the idea."

"It's crazy. And I'm worried that *you're* crazy, in a clinical sense."

"If you agree to marry me, I'll take you on a date or two. If that's what you want." His hand was still tangled in her hair, and he was close enough now that he could catch her scent. Gray breathed deep. She smelled like rosemary. And something that reminded him of the pies she and her grandmother had brought over the day after the funeral, warm and good. *Right.* "But we can settle the other question right here."

"What do you mean . . . ?"

Gray didn't wait. He didn't answer her question, half stammered out with her hazel eyes so wide they looked like summer gold.

He used his free hand to cup her cheek, flushed and smooth beneath his palm. Then he bent—only a little, which struck him as unexpectedly hot—to take her mouth with his.

He felt her tremble. And there was something about the way she melted into him as their lips touched, then brushed, as if she was being pulled by some kind of magnetic force he was half certain he could feel himself.

Gray had only meant to kiss her to make a point. The way a gentleman might, not that he'd ever met too many gentlemen out here where the mountains and the land were the only things that mattered.

But Abby's lips were soft and velvety beneath his. And she made a tiny sound in the back of her throat that he could feel like a flickering flame.

Before he knew it, Gray was angling his head to one side and licking his way into her mouth.

As if he couldn't help himself.

And everything got hot. Bright. Impossible.

This was Abby Douglas. *Abby Douglas*. There was something deliciously wrong about it being Abby that made it hotter, wilder.

It rolled in him and made a joke of him imagining he was in control of any of this. Of her.

Of this sudden storm of sensation that would have taken him off his feet, if that didn't mean he would have had to let go of her.

When the door slapped open, both of his hands were sunk deep into her hair, and Abby was up on her toes, pressed against him, her arms wrapped around his back.

It turned out Gray wasn't going to have to worry about easing his way into some or other form of eventual chemistry with the woman he already knew would make him a good rancher's wife. He was going to have to worry about what the hell to do with all this chemistry—so much it was like a lightning storm and he kept getting hit—with a woman he'd never paid the slightest attention to until his father's funeral.

The fact that the front door had opened penetrated the heat and fog that was swirling around him.

Finally.

"My goodness," came Martha Douglas's familiar, scratchy voice, laced through with a ripe sort of amusement Gray couldn't identify entirely, but had no doubt was aimed right at him. "That will teach me to go into town for the bingo. Look at the show right here in my living room."

"Mrs. Douglas," Gray gritted out as a greeting, stepping back from Abby and not sure he liked how difficult that was. Especially when she looked as if separating from him . . . hurt her. "I don't mean any disrespect. This isn't what it looks like."

"I'll thank you not to treat me like I tripped and fell into your daddy's grave along with him, Gray," Martha retorted, her gaze level on his. "I haven't forgotten what a kiss looks like, especially when it's happening to my granddaughter right here in the room where I taught her how to walk."

4

Martha Douglas was many things—and in her later years, had gotten a bit looser with the edge of her tongue—but she was no gossip.

That simple truth had frustrated Abby when she was younger and had longed to dig into their friends and neighbors the way everyone all around the valley seemed to do with such relish. Martha had always steadfastly refused. It wasn't that she didn't have opinions, but she wouldn't share them until she judged it the right time. Until then, she wasn't one for unnecessary or idle chatter—especially when it was none of her business.

But tonight, her grandmother's solemn refusal to ask a single question about what had transpired earlier might actually eat Abby alive.

Gray had left shortly after Grandma had come home.

After that first moment, no one had mentioned the fact that Gray and Abby had been kissing. *Kissing*, for God's sake. There had been about three minutes of awkward conversation about the calves Gray had shipped this season and those he'd kept back to wean in his corrals, the usual exchange about the weather forecast and the cold front moving in, and then he'd been on his way with only a single dark look Abby's way.

After the sound of his truck had disappeared entirely from the dirt road outside, Abby waited for Grandma to ask her what had been going on and what on earth she'd been doing, kissing their neighbor in the front room when anyone with eyes could see the man needed grief counseling.

But Grandma didn't say a word.

It had been like any other weekend afternoon in the farmhouse. There were the usual housekeeping chores to do, laundry and the weekly clean of the rugs and floors to set up for the week ahead. Tasks Abby usually found oddly meditative, but today couldn't seem to concentrate on. Because she kept flashing back to that kiss and *marriage proposal* and all the other impossible things that had happened to her on this otherwise perfectly ordinary day.

She couldn't really grasp it. And she'd lived through it.

Or she'd had an extended hallucination. It was maybe telling that there was a part of her that hoped it really had been all in her head. Because a complete break from reality and sanity seemed liked it might be easier than . . . whatever this was.

Abby couldn't think about it. She couldn't think about anything else either, but she definitely couldn't think about it. Not about Gray. Not directly. Every time she started to remember his mouth against hers, she skittered away from the memory, her heart pounding and her skin flushed and clammy, as if it were some kind of flu that threatened to take her to her knees.

After full dark fell hard out the windows, coming down like a curtain the way it always seemed to this time of year, Grandma started to pull together their dinner. Abby helped without being asked, the way she always did. They were long past the days when her grandmother took care of everything and Abby was the dependent child who had to be asked to contribute. They were more like roommates now, bustling around in the kitchen together and then sitting down to eat at the kitchen table, because Grandma didn't believe that good food and decent companionship should be frittered away in front of the television.

"He wants me to marry him," Abby blurted out when she couldn't take it any longer, staring ferociously at her pork chop.

Grandma made a noncommittal sound.

For a while there was nothing but the usual noises of the farmhouse. The creaking from the old porch swing outside. The summery song of the wind chimes dancing out there in the dark that Abby needed to remember to take down before winter hit in earnest. The wind itself, moaning a bit as it rushed past the windows, sneaking inside in the form of the drafts they'd spend all of the cold months battling.

"That's why he was here," Abby continued, because now she'd started, she couldn't stop. Because she was either having a serious mental health episode or, far more frightening, it had all really happened. "Apparently, Gray Everett woke up this morning over there in his big ranch house, decided he was in need of a wife, and looked no farther than the farm next door."

"I've always appreciated practicality in a man," Grandma said, after a moment. And even smiled as she said it.

Abby stop pretending to eat. "I could be anyone, Grandma. He has an opening he wants to fill, that's all. And I guess when he looked around, he felt there was a shortage of capable, dependable, *salt of the earth* single women in Cold River, so he landed on me. By default."

Her grandmother dabbed at her mouth with her napkin. Cloth, of course, because Martha Douglas didn't like the waste or expense of paper.

"You've been silly about that Everett boy as long as I can remember," she said, matter-of-factly, which didn't exactly take away the sting of it. Given this was something they'd never discussed. Ever. Abby felt her face burn, and the steady way Grandma eyed her from the other side of the table didn't help. "Did he ruin it when he kissed you?"

Abby blinked. "Ruin it?"

"Nothing is worse than kissing a man after a long buildup only to discover that he's terrible at it. Sloppy. Or worse, too much—"

"Grandma. I beg you not to finish that sentence."

Her grandmother raised her famous brow, capable of silencing small children and stopping grown men in their tracks. "I hate to offend your delicate sensibilities, Abigail, but I have in fact kissed and been kissed a time or two in my day."

Abby sighed. "I fully support any and all kissing you've ever done. I just don't want to hear about it."

"I'm not certain I wanted to wander into my own front room to find my granddaughter locking lips with the neighbor boy, now that you mention it, but I've rallied."

"But that's the problem. We don't have any relationship. He's never looked at me twice. Or even once."

"Maybe he's finally come to his senses. Sometimes men get there on their own."

"He didn't have any senses to come to," Abby retorted, the heat in her cheeks in her voice too, and constricting her throat. "It's not like he's been nobly resisting me for all these years. As far as Gray Everett is concerned, I might as well be one of the fence posts he's forever putting up all over his property. And now he wants me to actually be on his property too. As his wife. Because he seems to think it's perfectly reasonable to get married when you don't know the other person at all."

Grandma sat back in her chair and regarded Abby for a moment.

It was times like this that Abby normally took comfort in the fact they were so alike. She even looked like her grandmother, so much so that staring at Martha's creased cheeks and gnarled hands was a lot like staring her future in the face—something Abby would have said she found comforting. Usually. They had the same wide, capable shoulders, a hand-me-down from the generations of Grandma's relatives who'd been slopping milk pails around on dairy farms since the dawn of time. Grandma had been strong and sturdy all her life. She'd turned eighty-three in September and was less of both than she had been while Abby was growing up, but wasn't slowing down. Grandpa's death seven years ago had left her more frail for a while there, but she hadn't let it take her under. She was a proud, fierce woman who knew precisely who she was and was grateful for it daily.

She was exactly who Abby had always intended to become one day, when she finally grew up.

And tonight, she was looking at Abby as if she was a remarkably silly girl who wasn't likely to get there anytime soon. If at all.

"Your generation thinks all the knowing each other has to happen before you get married. It used to be you liked a person, married them, and then whiled away the years getting to know each other as you went. You might call that inside out, but I promise you, it worked fine for hundreds of years."

Abby wanted to ask her grandmother questions about her marriage to Grandpa, but didn't. Because she wasn't sure she wanted to know the answers. Her grandparents had married late, there in the supposed calm after the second World War. They'd had Abby's mother when

Grandma was thirty, which must have seemed ancient in a place where teenagers marrying right out of high school was still common.

Had they spent their childless years before Lily's arrival getting to know each other and turning into the solid unit Abby had always considered them? And if they had, did she really want to know the details?

"You can't possibly think that I should consider Gray's offer," Abby said instead, rubbing her hand on her chest because it felt as if she had her own draft, chilling her from the inside out. "Not seriously. He's obviously insane with grief over his father."

Grandma sniffed. "It's hard to imagine anybody grieving a bully like Amos Everett much at all, much less to the point of insanity. Especially not his own son, who knew him better than most and had to live with him day in and day out. The poor boy."

"But . . ." Abby felt drafty inside and uneven outside, as if the sturdy old floor in the farmhouse kitchen was pitching and rolling beneath her feet. "This is all ridiculous. People don't run around marrying people they have no actual relationship with. That's a recipe for divorce."

"Here's some free marriage advice, Abby. If you want to stay married, don't get divorced. The end."

It was a lot like what Gray had said. Abby didn't know if that made it better or worse.

Abby rubbed her hands over her face. "Is this . . . Are you . . . You're *supporting* this? I was positive you'd laugh."

Her grandmother studied her for a long moment. "There are worse things than a marriage proposal from a man you're already sweet on."

"Most grandmothers would be appalled at the very idea of their granddaughter marrying some guy who turned up at the door one day. Out of the blue. And approached the whole thing like he was negotiating for a few more acres of adjoining land. Aren't you the one who spent my whole life telling me I should know my own worth?"

"I also told you that a bird in the hand was worth two in the bush."

"I still don't know what that means. Why would I have a bird in my hands? Why are there so many birds that it's turned into some kind of shrubbery situation? Why does everything end up a Hitchcock movie?"

"Abigail. There's no need to get wound up. You know Gray Everett as well as I do."

"Meaning . . . enough to bring a hot dish to a family funeral, the way you would for every person in this valley."

The look her grandmother aimed her way then was familiar. It was the same one she used whenever Lily rolled into town, and the same one she'd used more sparingly during Abby's own, far more infrequent, teenage episodes.

And Abby, predictably, felt instantly chastened.

"You've watched him work that land. You've watched him run cattle. You've watched him raise that girl of his. You watched him marry that Cristina, and better still, watched him take the high road when it all went bad. Every man has his own private life, I grant you, that's not necessarily on display outside the walls of his house. But he's not a mystery to you. He's not some stranger who showed up on the porch this morning."

Abby wasn't sure she'd ever felt so . . . helpless. As if she'd been shoved off the edge of a cliff, and like it or not, she kept on falling. Her heart was kicking at her. Her palms felt as damp as her mouth felt dry.

"Are you telling me I should marry him?"

"It's not up to me to tell you who you should or shouldn't marry. But I do believe that a marriage proposal deserves celebration. Whether you accept him or don't, it doesn't matter. You're the same girl who used to lie on your bed and cry your heart out, telling me that no one would ever want to marry you."

"I was thirteen. No thirteen-year-old thinks anyone is ever going to want to marry them. That's the joy of puberty."

"Well, I told you you were wrong then, didn't I? And I do like to be right."

Abby didn't know whether to cry, the way she had when she'd been thirteen and distraught about everything and nothing. Or whether she should find a way to laugh all this away before it got any more real, which should have been impossible, because this was all impossible.

While she was dithering, her grandmother rose from her seat, moved over to the counter, and uncovered a freshly baked pie Abby had been so distracted she hadn't even noticed sitting there. Something that should have terrified her, given her deep and abiding love of all baked goods.

But she didn't seem to have any more room for terror tonight.

"That's the thing," she said quietly while Grandma pulled out plates and clean forks. "When I imagined somebody wanting to marry me, I imagined that they would want to marry *me*. Not any old woman who fit their idea of what a wife should be. I might as well be a mail-order bride."

"Your great-grandmother was a mail-order bride," Grandma replied serenely.

Of all the things Abby imagined her grandmother might say, it wasn't that. It had the immediate effect of clearing Abby's Gray-muddled head.

"You've been telling me stories about your grandparents as long as I can remember, and you never mentioned that one of them was a mail-order bride," she argued, feeling . . . breathless.

She'd imagined her ancestors as pioneers in covered wagons, but never something so *specifically* western. And somehow thrilling.

"My mother's mother was raised in a big family back east in Pennsylvania," Grandma said calmly. That part Abby knew. "They didn't have much, so when she came of age, she answered an ad from an enterprising young man with a few acres out here in Colorado, and the rest is history."

Abby felt more shaken than she should have. More than she would have been the day before. Too invested, maybe. She'd seen pictures of her great-grandparents, stiff and faded in their old sepia ovals like the world might end if they gave away any hint of their actual personalities while they stared at the camera.

"Were they happy?" she heard herself ask, as wistfully as her thirteen-year-old self might have.

Grandma came back over to the table, holding two plates heaped with pie and freshly whipped cream, the way they both liked it. She took her seat across from Abby and fixed her with one of her looks.

"Happy isn't something you stumble over on the street like a penny, Abigail. You can't pick it up, put it in your pocket, and consider it done. Happy is something you choose. And keep choosing."

"Grandma." Abby hated that her voice cracked on that, but she couldn't seem to help it. "Even if I believed that Gray meant it, I couldn't possibly say yes. Because that would be taking advantage of somebody who's clearly taken leave of his senses."

"He seemed perfectly normal to me."

"You don't live your whole life next door to somebody,

never pay them any attention, and then wake up one morning determined to marry them. That's not how it works."

"Oh? How does it work?" Grandma asked, much too placidly, in Abby's opinion.

"I don't know. If he was really interested in me, me as a person rather than some tab he can shove into the appropriate slot, he would . . . ask for my number. The way people do."

"What people? He knows your number. You've had the same number your whole life. Which is also my number, by the way."

"I have a cell phone, Grandma. And you know that's not what I mean. He could ask me out. To dinner. Or coffee, if dinner is too much pressure."

"The man runs a cattle ranch. He also has a teenage daughter. Until recently he also had the primary care of an ornery old man who'd made an enemy of every last person in the Longhorn Valley. I can't imagine when you imagine he's supposed to be painting the town red and going on coffee dates."

"You can't possibly think it's perfectly normal for him to show up one morning, knock on the door, and tell me that he wants to marry me." There was something like panic clawing at her insides. "Whatever else you want to call it, it's not *normal behavior*."

Grandma took a big bite of her pie and chewed thoughtfully for a moment or two. She took a swig from the milk she still drank at all three meals because she had dairy farms in her bones. Literally. Only then did she meet Abby's gaze again.

"I wouldn't say I think it's normal, necessarily, though it's true that burying a parent can be clarifying in all sorts of ways. But I'm surprised that you're focusing on the possibility something's wrong with him and ignoring the more important part."

"How can there be something more important than the fact he's acting completely out of character?"

"You've never so much as looked at another man," Grandma said quietly. With far too much uncomfortable knowledge in her gaze. "Maybe now you don't have to. Seems to me you should stop worrying that he's lost his mind and start considering the possibility that if he hasn't, you might just get everything you ever wanted."

Obviously Abby had no intention of considering anything that . . . impossible.

She'd rather worry about Gray's sanity than accept that he might have meant it. Because if he meant it . . . if he'd really meant every word he'd said and didn't actually require a therapist . . .

Well. That forced her to face all kinds of possibilities she'd ruled out a long time ago.

She refused to consider any of them as she tossed and turned in her little bed tucked up under the eaves in the farmhouse that night. She rejected them all over again when she woke hours before dawn, shivered through her shower because the old pipes were temperamental at best, and stomped out to her car to head into town for her early shift at the coffeehouse.

Abby usually liked the days she had to open the shop. She liked being up so early that it felt as if the world was only hers, especially out in these fields where she couldn't see any lights but the ones she'd left on back in the farmhouse kitchen for Grandma when she woke up.

She waited until her serviceable old car warmed up, then pulled out onto the dirt drive that cut through the fields and led to the county road she'd driven nearly every day of her life. It was a kind of reflex to turn right and ease into the familiar route she knew as much by feel as sight, at this point.

Her grandparents had sold off the bulk of their farmland to the Everetts not long after Abby was born. Grandpa had been ten years older than Grandma, and arthritis had already been sitting on him, hard. Selling to the Everetts wasn't the same as passing the farm on to his own children, Grandpa had always said, but no one expected Lily to come back and care for the land that had been in her family for so long—and it was a sight better than handing it over to one of those corporate farm operations that Grandpa had always hated.

Abby had grown up with it like this. A scant seven acres that were still Douglas land tucked in with all those miles and miles the Everetts owned and worked. Room enough for the farmhouse, Grandpa's garden and orchard, and space to breathe besides.

This morning, it was frigid and cold and unquestionably November. The dark seemed thicker than usual, inside and out, as if it were sticky, somehow. Her car was old and cranky, or maybe that was her, and she couldn't seem to get warm as she sped along the lane toward the mountain pass that led into town. It was too dark to see the mountain itself before the road started to climb, but she could feel it there. She could sense it, looming over her in what was left of the night, waiting. Abby tucked her chin into the scarf she'd wrapped around her neck a few times, and she tried not to think too much about what Gray had offered her.

Or that kiss.

That kiss that made her feel chills for a completely different reason.

She forced herself to consider the land instead. Because she was supposed to be so practical, wasn't she? Wasn't that why she was the whole of Gray's shortlist for a wife? And she couldn't think of anything more practical than marrying an Everett so that Douglas land belonged to a Douglas again.

She knew perfectly well that people in these parts had married for a whole lot less in their time. Land was land. And family legacies meant something out here, where people threw around the names of the Cold River founding families as if they were all still ambling up and down the streets of the quaintly preserved town in period attire.

It's definitely not about kissing Gray at last, a voice inside her said, deeply sardonic. *You tossed and turned all night long because you're worried about* the land. *Not the taste of him. His hands in your hair. Or the way he slanted his mouth—*

"Stop," she ordered herself. Out loud.

Her voice sounded strange in the dark. Her rickety old heater was starting to spit out the tiniest bit of warmth, better late than never. She wrapped her gloved hands around her steering wheel and frowned fiercely at the road ahead of her as it started its incline. The mountain between the farmhouse and the town of Cold River wasn't much of one by general Rocky Mountains standards. Only a few thousand feet. But it didn't pay to take it for granted. Gray's first wife wasn't the only fatality on a road that was always slicker and more perilous than any on the valley floor.

Luckily, Abby was safe and dependable and a pillar of salt, or whatever, even when no one was watching. Because she drove the speed limit, cautiously making her way over the hill and down into Cold River at last.

Town always seemed like a miracle to her, no matter how many times she saw it spread out before her on her way in. Cold River still sported Old West buildings lined up along Main Street, pretty brick structures that hearkened back to the early days of the Colorado Territory. She liked the long drive down from the mountain, the climb over the river that had given the town its name, then down on into the historic town itself. This time of year, there were pretty holiday lights on the outsides of all the buildings, making everything gleam against the night like a real, live Christmas card.

For a blessed moment, Abby wasn't thinking about kissing Gray after approximately twenty years of imagining what that might be like. She wasn't thinking about her grandmother's surprising support—it seemed like support, anyway, because Grandma certainly hadn't sounded at all opposed—to the idea of marrying him. She wasn't even thinking about taking up the mantle of mail-order brides that was, apparently, family tradition.

Because there was nothing quite like soaking in the quietness in her pretty hometown. It had soothed her all her life. It made her feel . . . right and rooted.

The things Gray had said to her yesterday swirled around inside her. That she'd never left home, the way so many others did. That she had chosen instead to stay right here in Cold River, where nothing ever really changed. Where there was the pushy Longhorn Valley Historical Society forever at war with the Chamber of Commerce to make certain nothing changed too much, ever, no matter the march of progress or the clamoring from the tourists for fast food and Starbucks.

Abby had been waiting to feel badly about staying her whole life. Her own mother took it upon herself, every time Abby saw her, to point out how provincial Abby was. How small town and therefore *less than*.

Just another dumb country girl, Lily had said once, with that half smile of hers.

Because that was the kind of charming thing a woman like Lily said to the daughter she hardly knew and had, in fact, abandoned.

And here in the quiet of her car as she drove down a deserted Main Street in Cold River, hours before most people were anywhere close to waking up, Abby could admit that half the reason she'd always claimed she had no interest in going anywhere was in direct response to Lily's inability to stay put.

But it was more than that. Spite could only take a girl so far. There had to be love too, or she'd be as bitter as her mother was—a fate worse than death, as far as Abby was concerned.

Abby wasn't bitter. She hadn't made her choices out of fear. Or not entirely, anyway. She'd also believed her grandparents had needed her, and she'd wanted to be needed. Didn't everyone?

She parked her car around the back of the coffeehouse the way she always did, and then pushed her way out into the cold again. She stood there for a moment in the crisp, clear dark with only the faintest suggestion of a bluer dawn to the east. She breathed it all deep into her lungs, filling herself with the clean, sweet mountain air. It smelled like winter. That aching little lilt, like tears in the wind. Like foreboding.

But she'd always chosen to call it hope.

Gray Everett had kissed her.

She laughed wildly into the solitary night because one of the dearest dreams of her childhood had come true when she'd least expected it. And she wanted to cry in the next breath—because one of the dearest dreams of her childhood had come true, and she didn't know what she was supposed to do now it had.

She heard the sound she made then, a kind of shuddery thing, here where no one could hear her. There was nothing around but a coffee shop she had yet to open, pretty lights on all the brick buildings, and looming high all around her, the watching mountain sentinels that made her feel exalted and humble all at once.

The same way Gray Everett always had.

He'd kissed her. He wanted to marry her.

There was no going back from that.

Whatever happened next, whatever happened between them or didn't, Abby understood out there in the dark that nothing about this safe, sweet, comfortable life she'd loved so much was ever, ever going to be the same.

5

Abby was wiping down the tables in the cozy back part of Cold River Coffee, outfitted with several couches around a decorative fireplace, a bookcase filled with much-loved romances and thrillers that operated as a community honor-system library, and battered brick walls that made her unreasonably happy every time she looked at them. She was listening to Noah Connelly, the latest owner of the coffeehouse and its resident chef, bang his pans around the way he liked to do to announce his typical bad mood to all and sundry. The music playing from the speakers was brooding with a side of acoustic guitars. There was the usual scattering of locals and tourists at the long, family style, shared tables toward the front, some with laptops open and others bouncing infants on their laps.

She cleared off the table in front of her, adjusted the festive holiday centerpiece she'd set there, and let the coffeehouse's particular magic work on her. Abby had started working here part-time when she'd still been in high school and had moved to full-time after graduation. And instead of putting in the usual six months to a year that most baristas did before bailing, she'd stayed. She'd been promoted to manager two owners back and Noah had asked her to stay in the job when the business changed hands because she knew it backwards and forwards. She did the books and most of the orders.

Abby hadn't necessarily meant to end up running a coffeehouse, but here she was. She knew some whispered that she was stuck here. *That poor Douglas girl with no prospects,* she'd heard gossipy Theresa Galace whisper overloudly to one of her friends a while back as Abby had been making her drink. That had stung, but she didn't want "prospects," she thought darkly as she moved from one table to the next.

She'd never had any desire to move on to something else. She loved the coffeehouse. She loved working in a place most people in town treated as a part of their extended living room. It felt like home.

And Abby loved her home. She wasn't like some other people she knew, who were forever worrying about what was over the horizon and what they might be missing. She liked Cold River. She liked her life as it was, happy and sweet and hers.

She was complimenting herself on her choices when the front doors slapped open, letting in the bite of the November afternoon. It was a reflex to look up from wiping the last table in the section—but when she did, she froze.

Because Gray was shouldering his way inside.

It was Gray, except that was impossible, because Gray Everett didn't drink fancy coffee.

Abby blinked, but the vision didn't go away. It was still Gray. He was dressed for ranch work the way he always was, which made his presence in this place of polished wood and brick . . . confusing. When Abby pictured him, she realized, she pictured him outside. He wore a different flannel and different long-sleeved T-shirt beneath that barn coat of his, but for some reason all she could concentrate on was the way his jeans outlined every single muscle in his thighs.

Who knew there were so many?

She watched him as he frowned up at the big, chalkboard menu that hung behind the cash register and pastry cases, as if the very concept of a coffee shop was a scam and he was bracing himself for the inevitable con. He looked as if he'd never darkened the door of such a questionable establishment before.

Because, of course, he hadn't. Gray was old school in every possible way and that included getting his coffee for $1.25 in Mary Jo's Diner down at the other end of Main Street, where working men in the Longhorn Valley had been devouring huge plates of food with cheap, strong coffee as long as anyone could remember.

Abby wasn't one to make mountains out of molehills, especially if the molehill in question was her. But she couldn't come up with a single reason Gray would break from his decades-long tradition. Today. After that conversation in the farmhouse. And the kiss that had gone with it.

Except one.

She almost knocked over the cheerful holiday decoration she'd put in the center of each and every table in the coffeehouse the day after Halloween. It was a vague sort of Christmas tree made out of sparkly balls that Abby had assembled herself with help from sleek crafting blogs that did them much better. She cursed under her breath and fumbled to keep the centerpiece from tipping over.

When she looked up again, Gray was buying his coffee from sweet little Amanda Kittredge—who Abby supposed really wasn't all that little anymore, since she was in her twenties—and it was all too much for Abby to process.

What was next? Would Gray wander down to the Sensitive Spoon, an organic restaurant that prided itself on its local produce and hipster-farm aesthetic? She didn't have to ask Gray his opinion on the place, since all the locals liked to complain about the expensive restaurant and the owners who'd relocated to Cold River after a ski vacation in Aspen. Abby knew, deep in her soul, that Gray Everett ate neither massaged kale nor hand-selected vegan cheeses, and would choose the greasy sirloin down at Mary Jo's every time.

She would have bet everything she had that he held similar opinions about espresso drinks and the establishments that served them.

But here he was. Standing in the middle of Cold River Coffee.

And Abby knew the precise moment he saw her, because she had about as much chill as the average Tasmanian devil, and she was staring right at him.

He didn't smile. His hard mouth—*that she had now tasted*—didn't curve in the slightest. But his dark eyes gleamed.

Gray accepted his coffee from Amanda, held it between his hands as if he expected it to explode like a grenade if he wasn't careful, and took his time crossing the floor to Abby.

Almost as if he knew that every local in the place was gaping at the sight of him here, the same as Abby, and wanted to give them a show.

She realized she'd wiped down the same table approximately twenty-seven times already and forced herself to stop. To stand still. Some hair had escaped her ponytail, but she only blew it out of her way as he came to stand before her.

That dark gleam in his gaze was a lot more potent up close.

"Abby."

"Gray."

He let his mouth curve. "I'm sure glad we settled that."

Gray being sardonic made her blood feel too hot in her own veins. Too hot in her veins and too slippery everywhere else. Abby cleared her throat, stood straighter, then forced herself to smile. The way she would if she saw anyone else she knew, whether they were frequent customers or not.

"I'm in shock," she told him. "I didn't peg you as a fan of artisanal coffee."

Gray slanted a look down at the sixteen-ounce cardboard cup in his hand. "This is art? Are you sure?"

"That probably depends on what you ordered."

"I have no idea. I told the Kittredge girl to give me her favorite drink." When Abby couldn't manage to muffle her laugh at that, his dark green gaze slammed into her again. More reproachful this time. "That's funny?"

"I don't know if it's funny. But it's probably sweet. Very, very, *very* sweet. And I'm going to go out on a limb here, but I feel pretty confident that you're the sort of person who likes his coffee as black as he likes it strong and unfussy."

"I'm not ninety-five years old, Abby. I do try new things on occasion."

"Do you?" Her tone made it clear she doubted him. "Like what?"

She wasn't prepared for the teasing light in his eyes. Or the indisputably male look that made his face . . . change as he gazed at her. She wasn't prepared for how tight it made her own chest feel. Or how, lower down, something sharp and soft at once began to hum as if her body was trying to sing, just for him.

"Like you," Gray drawled. "Just to pull something out at random."

Abby was so flustered—and something else she couldn't put her finger on, that made her feel like she was quivering, deep inside—that she lost track of the conversation. And the world.

It wasn't until that curve in his mouth deepened into a full-on grin that she realized she was standing there.

Staring at him.

"Uh . . . do you want to sit down?" she asked, feeling so awkward and exposed she worried she might actually combust. Or maybe she only wished she would.

She sank into the seat closest to her, right there at the table that was now the cleanest surface in the valley, fairly certain that if she'd let it drag out for another second, her knees might have given out from under her. Gray was still grinning as he slid into the seat across from her, and she couldn't really process anything that was happening. Or the fact it was happening right here in full view of far too many people who knew both of them.

It was much, much worse than yesterday.

She couldn't tell if that constriction in her throat was tears or anxiety or embarrassment for her inevitable humiliation, but whatever it was, she had to swallow a few times to keep from succumbing to it.

Gray. Her. A small two-person table tucked away in the back of the coffeehouse, that tempted her to forget they were out in public.

Public. The word was too bright inside of her, and she flushed again, aware that just because she couldn't see past

Gray's wide shoulders didn't mean everyone else couldn't see *her*.

"You doing all right over there?" Gray asked mildly. "You look like you might keel over."

"I've never fainted in my life." Though if anything called for a strategic swoon, it was this madness. Abby made herself smile. Politely. "I'm wondering how many people will call my grandmother in the next five minutes to report that I'm sitting at a table with you."

Gray's shrug was unconcerned. "You can't worry about what people think. They're going to go ahead and think it no matter what you do, so you're better off doing what you want in the first place."

Abby eyed the cowboy sitting there across from her as if it was the most natural thing in the world for him to be here and for the two of them to be sitting around *chitchatting*. She ignored the fact that her heart refused to settle down, that it kept tapping out a wild rhythm in her chest, only making it worse. Because he couldn't see that part.

"That's a great philosophy. In my experience, however, it's only a very specific sort of person who can live that way."

"A person who knows who they are," Gray said, as if they were agreeing. "And doesn't spend a lot of time worrying about anyone else."

"I would have said, a person who happens to be a man. And who therefore doesn't have to think about anyone else."

She felt her ears singe as she said that, and her stomach sank. Because that was exactly the sort of comment that she was sure had helped her stay resolutely single at the age of thirty.

That and the fact she'd always been in love with her unrequited crush.

But mostly, she'd discovered that men her age weren't exactly enamored of a woman who didn't work very hard to guard her tongue around them.

Gray didn't say anything. He also didn't storm away. He picked up his coffee, took a long pull, and then winced. "Sweet Lord."

Abby nodded. "Literally."

"What *is* that?"

"I couldn't say exactly." Abby waved a hand. "Amanda cycles through a few different versions of her sugar bombs. Is it chocolaty or vanilla-y?"

"I don't know. I might be having a heart attack. My teeth hurt."

"The good news is, when they stop hurting, you'll feel like you have rocket thrusters attached to your feet."

"That's a good thing?"

Abby figured that was a rhetorical question. Or maybe she simply became too entranced watching the way Gray lifted his coffee cup and put it to his mouth again. It was his hands. Or maybe it was his mouth. Or maybe it was that she didn't know how to handle the fact that the mouth he was putting on that coffee cup, right there a foot away from her, was the same mouth he'd put on her the day before.

She definitely didn't know what to do with the wash of heat that swamped her at the memory, so she focused on him instead. Hard.

"Not that I don't think the whole town shouldn't enjoy the coffeehouse whenever they want, but you never do. So why are you here?"

Gray grimaced at his cup and set it down. Then he settled that stern green gaze of his on her as if he expected this might take some time. He didn't lean back, lounging in his chair the way men did sometimes, taking up as much

space as they could. He sat forward, his hands loose around the cup in front of him and his shoulders blocking out everything else.

"I thought this was what you wanted," he said, in that gravelly voice she couldn't help but feel everywhere.

"The song is 'I'd like to buy the world a Coke,' not a cup of coffee, though I guess I can see how that's confusing. They both have caffeine."

She was babbling. That was what his voice did to her.

"Isn't sitting around having coffee in a place like this supposed to be a date?" Gray asked, apparently unfazed by the babbling.

Abby didn't say that she wouldn't know, having never been on a date in her life. She didn't say that she'd spent some fifteen years working in this very same coffeehouse and had therefore witnessed any number of dates play out before her. She also didn't ask him what kind of awful dates he'd been on in his past, that he couldn't seem to figure out if this was one or not.

She concentrated on the practicalities. "Everyone will think it is, the longer you sit here with me. As you never sit anywhere with anyone. Are you prepared for that?"

Again, that quirk in the corner of his mouth that really wasn't fair.

"I asked you to marry me, Abby. I'm not the one who's unprepared."

For a moment she couldn't breathe at all. Because there was a part of her that was sure she'd imagined it all. What he'd asked her. The fact he kissed her. All of it.

Because she actually had imagined all of these things a thousand times before.

"But no," she heard herself say, as if she'd been possessed by a creature far more talkative and relaxed than she felt. "This isn't a date."

"You, me. Coffee." Gray shrugged. "Feels like a date to me."

"I'm actually working. You didn't ask me if I wanted to have coffee with you, you showed up at my place of business, ordered yourself coffee, and are now sitting here. That's not a date. Just like it wouldn't be a date if I drove out to one of the fences you were mending without telling you I was coming. And then was . . . just there."

"I don't know about that." Gray's drawl was low. And heated her up in ways that should probably be illegal in a public place. "I suppose it would depend what you did once you got there."

Abby wondered why Noah was making so much noise clattering his pots and pans together all of a sudden. It took her a dizzy little minute to realize Noah wasn't making any noise at all in the kitchen. It was happening in her head. It was the ringing in her ears.

It was the fact that Gray Everett was *flirting* with her, and it made her want to cry, because she was so woefully unequipped to handle such a thing.

"I don't know how to do this," she whispered.

It was all too much. So much that she couldn't even be embarrassed she sounded like that. Broken. Confused. Deep in over her head.

"Hey." Gray reached across the table and hooked his fingers around her wrist, and just like that, the world stopped. There was no coffeehouse, no acoustic music from above. No people other than the two of them. Abby looked up from the hard wonder of his hand on her to find him studying her, concern and something darker and more intent on his face. "I'm not playing games with you, Abby. I wouldn't do that. I meant what I said yesterday."

"I meant what I said too," she said in a fierce whisper.

"You can't run around marrying people on a whim. Look at your parents. You could look at mine, but I don't even know who my father is. Why would I want to repeat any of that?"

"We won't repeat it."

"You don't know that." Her voice was still low, that odd whisper she was sure revealed entirely too much, but in the heat of this particular moment she couldn't bring herself to care. "How could you possibly know that?"

His hand was still wrapped around her wrist, and that didn't help. She could feel the warmth of him. The fascinating calluses that made his fingers rough. That easy strength he carried so carelessly. She could feel everything, and it was killing her.

This might actually kill her.

"I sure hope I'm not my father," Gray said matter-of-factly. "I don't think you're much like your mother. Why would the two of us together be anything like either of them?"

"The truly funny thing about my mother is that every single terrible thing she does make perfect sense to her." She knew she should pull away from him. She ordered herself to do it. And didn't. "People can rationalize anything away. And do, given the opportunity."

"Abby." His gaze was so steady it was almost as if it propped her up where she sat. As if he were his own brick wall, and he was inviting her to lean against him if she needed. His voice changed, impatience laced through that rich drawl she heard in her dreams, but the steadiness never wavered. "I wanted you before I came over yesterday. By the time I left, I was absolutely certain that you're the right wife for me. All you have to do is say yes."

"I . . ."

"Give me your phone."

That wasn't what she was expecting. "What?"

"Your phone."

He let go of her wrist, which felt like the sort of thing she ought to spend a year or so grieving beneath a black shroud. Then he curled two fingers at her, demanding she obey him.

Abby didn't really know what it said about her that she didn't argue. Or stall. Or question his lofty hand gesture. She reached right down into the pocket of the apron she wore and pulled out her phone, then set it down on the table in front of him.

"You should lock this," he told her as he picked it up and swiped at the screen.

"Why should I lock it? I have nothing to hide."

"It's about security, not secrets."

"Please. I was raised by a woman who hasn't locked her doors in eighty-three years. Grandma doesn't believe in locks. She thinks they're for sad, crowded city folks who don't know any better."

Gray lifted his gaze to hers, then returned it to the typing he was doing.

Abby had mooned after this man her whole life, and she'd never known that he could hold entire conversations without speaking. She might have found that fascinating—and likely would, when she had time consider it in the privacy of her bedroom in the farmhouse where she could also scream into her pillow if she wanted to make a quiet, personal scene—if she hadn't been in the middle of it.

And if that gaze hadn't seared her straight through.

"Here you go." He handed the phone back to her, and she took it. Because of course she took it. She really ought to mount a resistance, yet she couldn't seem to do anything except stare at him in what she wanted to call affront—but was a lot more like wonder. Sheer wonder. "I programmed in my number and called it."

"Um. Thanks?"

"You can call me tonight. Tell me what you decide."

That didn't sound like a request, really. He'd said *you can* but it was clear he meant *you will*, and Abby should have mustered up some outrage about that.

Instead, she swallowed. Hard. "I don't know that I'm going to have a decision tonight."

He treated her to that half smile of his again, and the look in his dark gaze made her fairly certain she would never be able to stand or walk or *breathe in oxygen* again.

"Then you can just call."

"Because you're the kind of person who really likes to settle in on the phone and have a nice, long chat about nothing."

"Tonight, Abby." Gray pushed his almost entirely untouched coffee across the table toward her with a gentleness that she very badly wanted to *mean things*. "Just call me tonight."

He reached over, touched one of his fingers to her lips because he apparently wanted to ruin her completely, and then he left her there.

With his number, her heart thundering to the point she was afraid she might need medical attention, and the remains of his coffee.

Abby watched the doors swing shut behind him. And the way every head in the place swung back around toward her, faces bright with the kind of speculation she'd never caused in all her life.

She didn't know whether to laugh it off, scowl, or cry. So she did the next best thing and chugged the rest of his coffee.

Because if Abby couldn't figure out what she should do—and she really, really couldn't, the same way she couldn't actually breathe well at the moment—a sugar high seemed like an excellent back-up plan.

6

"I thought we were friends," Hope Mortimer said theatrically when Abby pushed through the doors of Capricorn Books later that day, after her shift at Cold River Coffee was up, and she'd finally stopped sitting in the back office staring at Gray's number in her phone.

Like an overwrought teenage girl. Like the very overwrought teenage girl she'd been herself, if she remembered those years correctly.

As with everything else involving Gray and the past twenty-four hours, Abby didn't know whether to laugh or cry. Or both. It had taken a ridiculous amount of effort to shove her phone in her pocket and leave the coffeehouse. It was taking even more effort not to pull the phone out again—right here, right now—and make sure Gray's number was still in there.

Because it was the only thing that proved any of this was really happening.

"Of course, we're friends," Abby replied, shutting the door with its happily tinkling bell behind her and inhaling the musty, comfortable smell of books that never failed to make her feel at home. Even if one of her best friends was still glaring at her.

Hope sniffed over the piles of books on the messy

counter that she and her sisters never neatened up entirely because they all preferred a wall between them and the customers. It was a kind of cave in this bookstore that Hope and her two sisters had been running ever since their mother and *her* sister had decided that all things considered, they'd had enough of Cold River and the state of Colorado. Stella and Helen intended to find themselves in the hills of Santa Fe, they'd told anyone who'd asked and many who hadn't, and then they'd left the store and the house out back to the next generation.

And apparently their true selves were truly good and missing because it had been three years so far and counting.

"Friends do not let friends find out incredibly important personal information in a series of dramatic texts from Rae Trujillo," Hope said, all accusation and outrage.

Only about 30 percent feigned, if Abby had to guess.

"You're also friends with Rae Trujillo," she pointed out mildly. "I'll remind you that in fifth grade, you decided you and Rae were best friends and I was only your second best friend."

"Not that you're holding on to that or anything." Hope rolled her eyes. "And I demoted her."

"Not until seventh grade. Your devotion has been suspect ever since."

"My devotion is the foundation of your entire life, and you know it," Hope shot back. She shook her head. "And now you've been standing in my shop for more than five seconds without *immediately confessing* there's a Gray Everett situation happening to you. At last."

Capricorn Books was one of Abby's favorite places in the world. As a little girl she'd spent hours here, crawling around the nooks and crannies of a bookstore that was filled with stacks of used books in the back and new ones up front in no particular order, because the Mortimers believed that books found you, not the other way around. It had always been treasure and magic to Abby. That she, Hope, and Rae had grown up hanging around the store together on all those school day afternoons, absolute best friends even through the fifth grade debacle, just made it better.

It also meant Abby didn't wait to be asked to come in and make herself comfortable. She moved around behind the counter and took her usual spot in the overstuffed armchair there after dislodging Orion, the ancient, ever-affronted tabby cat. And then she poured out the incredible, unbelievable story of the past day to her friend.

She even offered her phone with Gray's contact page open as evidence.

Hope stared at the entry and the number, then handed the phone back, her eyes wide.

"I still don't understand why I'm hearing about this now, instead of three seconds after it happened. Yesterday."

Abby blew out a breath. "Because I didn't believe it was true. I still don't."

"Oh, it's definitely true." Hope settled herself on the wide arm of the chair next to Abby, and for a moment, they could have been any age. Seven. Twelve. Seventeen. Always in this same configuration, and often with Rae on the other arm. "Rae said that three separate people came into the Flower Pot and told her that her good friend Abby Douglas was on a coffee date with Gray Everett." She grinned. "So even if it wasn't true before, it is now."

"That's what I told him."

A customer came in then, bringing in a rush of cold

with the jangling bells. Abby stayed where she was while
Hope swiftly found the book the man was looking for,
acting as she always did, as if there was a Capricorn
Books shelving system that made sense. And Abby found
herself grinning down at Orion, who was cleaning himself
with obvious, murderous umbrage at her feet, as Hope
talked the man into two more books besides. Because that
was Hope. There was something about her smile that
made her impossible to resist—a power she used for both
good and evil.

"What are you going to do?" Hope asked once the
customer—one of the tourists Cold River got more and
more of these days as overflow from the resort traffic along
the I-70 corridor meandered off that well-beaten path into
more of the Colorado wilderness—finished thanking her
profusely and headed back out onto the street. She settled
on the arm of the chair again and angled herself so she
could look Abby full in the face.

"What do you mean, what am I going to do? I can't . . ."
Abby sighed as her friend stared back at her. "Oh, come
on. I can't marry him."

"The first time you told me you were going to marry
Gray Everett was in the second grade."

"I also wanted to be a princess in the second grade. And
an astronaut. Simultaneously, if possible."

"*Second grade*, Abby. And it's not as if your feelings
on him have wavered since."

But Abby didn't think her feelings were the issue. "I
don't know why he wants to get married again, and I
really don't understand why he would pick me. Except the
fact I live next door. And am convenient."

Conveniently close. Conveniently single. Conveniently
so boring that there would certainly be no more scandal
attached to the Everett name if she took it.

And conveniently without anything better to do, which should have offended her the most.

Hope frowned. "You don't marry someone because they happen to be located on the same road."

"That's what I keep saying."

"Apart from all the reasons that's true in emotional terms, the man has access to any number of vehicles, including a big old truck. He knows how to drive it. I've seen him driving it. It's not like he's imprisoned in his house and wants you because you're the only female he's laid eyes on in years."

"It just doesn't make any sense."

"It makes sense to me." Hope's voice was as steady as her gaze. "You're loyal and steadfast. You're completely trustworthy. And when you love, it's forever. I don't know the inner workings of Gray Everett's head, but given how his last marriage ended, I'd bet all of those are high on his list of preferences."

That scraped at Abby, making her feel like she should jump in and defend Gray when Hope wasn't exactly attacking him. *Down girl,* she ordered herself. She stared at the cat fiercely, as if she could figure all this out if she watched Orion angrily lick his fluffy haunch long enough.

"First of all, even if all that were true, Gray doesn't know any of that about me because he doesn't know anything about me, period. And second, you just described a dim-witted Labrador retriever."

"Abby."

"It's *ridiculous,*" Abby burst out, and she could hear the emotion heavy in her voice. She could feel it, threatening the backs of her eyes. "He's *Gray Everett.* And I'm . . . me. How's that going to look? No one's going to believe he actually . . ." She broke off because her throat was so tight, and her face so hot, it actually hurt. She made herself swallow, then push on. "It's embarrassing."

Hope's expression was flinty. "I have no idea what you're talking about."

But Hope pretending she didn't understand didn't make what Abby was saying any less true.

"Gray Everett belongs with someone like Cristina, not me."

"You mean the same Cristina who cheated on him and left him to raise their daughter alone because she couldn't bear to stay home that night? Or any night?"

Abby's cheeks blazed, and she was surprised they weren't shooting off sparks, igniting all the books and papers around them. "I'm not talking about how she acted. I'm talking about the whole package. He needs someone like her. Or you. Somebody . . ."

"Somebody . . . ?"

Hope's raised brows were relentless, and some ugly thing inside Abby was almost grateful. Saying it out loud was better. Because no one else would pretend. They would come right out and say it when she wasn't in the room. *That poor girl,* they would tut. *Just so* plain, *bless her.* Surely it was better for Abby to say it herself. Surely that would take away the power of the whispers that would follow her otherwise.

"Somebody beautiful," Abby said, because in the end it was that simple, and it didn't matter if there was too much heat behind her eyes. "People are supposed to marry people like them. They're supposed to match. Otherwise it looks like . . . pity. Like I'm trying to be something I'm not."

"The only person who doesn't think you're beautiful is you," Hope retorted, her voice as fierce as the light of battle in her gaze.

That hard, choked knot inside of Abby eased, but only because this was familiar ground. Hope and Rae had been giving her some version of the same pep talk since they'd all decided they liked boys, way back when they didn't know what *liking boys* even meant.

But even then, Abby had understood that Rae was delicate and Hope was magnetic while Abby herself was too tall, too awkward. She couldn't laugh like Rae and she couldn't smile like Hope, who both drew people to them effortlessly. She'd decided she was an acquired taste.

That no one had yet showed the slightest interest in acquiring.

"I love you for saying that, but you know it's not true," Abby said quietly. "For example, somehow, despite this great beauty that you claim everyone sees but me, every single man alive has managed to resist me for the past thirty years."

"Men are notorious idiots." Hope nudged Abby's leg with hers. "But you wouldn't know either way because you've always been completely unaware that any other men exist."

Abby sucked in a breath, horrified at how uneven it still sounded. How unsteady she felt, even here in this sprawling armchair where she'd never been anything but comfortable.

"We can argue about how secretly beautiful I am some other time," she managed to say unevenly. "Right now I need you rational. Because I know there's no way you can sit here and tell me *rationally* that I should marry a man who's never really spoken to me before. No matter how long I've had a crush on him."

Hope shifted on the broad, flat arm of the chair. "You're the one who keeps telling me there's no such thing as the Mortimer family curse."

"Because there's no such thing as curses."

"And yet here we are. Another generation of eternally lonely Mortimer sisters holed up in this town and running this bookstore. Just like Mama and Aunt Helen before us."

"You're not cursed, Hope." It was Abby's turn to nudge her friend for emphasis. "You wish you were, because that would make it a narrative instead of . . . life."

Hope's eyes narrowed at that, and Abby watched her decide not to argue the point.

Possibly because it was true.

"If I'm not cursed, then you're not the ugly beast you seem to imagine you are," Hope argued instead. "If I have to accept it, so do you."

Abby made a face. "I'm not an ugly beast. I'm . . . *fine.*"

That was the trouble. She was fine. Okay. *Plain,* she'd always told herself, with an upgrade to *decent* when she made an effort. The sort of woman who should have been born generations earlier, when capability was more prized out here in these unforgiving hills than an insubstantial prettiness that would fade at the first sign of winter.

But she wasn't a pioneer woman. This was the twenty-first century, and no one was ever going to write her a love poem or make grand, romantic gestures to win her favor. There would be no besotted lovers fighting for her hand or even her phone number. She'd given up on that long ago. Until this moment, she would have said she'd accepted it.

"If you were fine in any real sense of the word, you would have let Tate Bishop ask you out in high school," Hope said after a moment.

Abby made no attempt to hide her sigh. "Not Tate Bishop again. How many times can we talk about Tate Bishop in one lifetime? I would argue we've already exceeded the maximum by about eight million."

"He liked you, Abby. He really liked you."

"The only person who thinks about Tate Bishop is you, Hope. I didn't think about him then. I'm not thinking about him now. I'm not sure Tate Bishop thinks about *himself* this much."

"Tate Bishop is a representative of the whole Abby Douglas story."

"There is no Abby Douglas story."

Hope looked at her pityingly. "I know. That's my point."

"You have high school Tate in your head. You missed post-high school Tate, the grim march of his bad decisions, and that whole arson situation."

"That was never proven."

"Hope. If Tate had a single, golden moment, you were the only one who saw it. Then you went off to college. You weren't around to witness his downward spiral, but I was."

"If you'd let him ask you to even one dance in high school, who knows, you could have averted all that spiraling," Hope argued, as she had before.

Many, many times.

"I'm not prepared to take responsibility for Tate Bishop's life choices," Abby said with a roll of her eyes. "But it's becoming apparent that your obsession with him might actually point to a deeper illness."

"All I'm saying is, you've always been a lot more desirable than you think you are," Hope said, the laughter that had infused their half-faked squabble fading as she settled back against the chair and kept her gaze steady on Abby. "For some reason—and we both know what that reason is—you decided to be invisible a long time ago. And that's what you've done, ever since."

Abby didn't want to talk about her mother. Much less her friend's theories about her mother. She'd wasted too many hours of her life that she would never get back talking about Lily, and this wasn't the time.

Besides, she already knew what Hope would say. Because she'd said it a thousand times before. That was the comfort and exasperation of very old friends.

"Maybe that's true," she said now, though she didn't believe it for a second. She just didn't want to argue about it. "But, Hope, Gray wants me to call him. He wants me to give him an answer. How can I give him an answer when the question is ridiculous?"

Hope didn't answer immediately. The phone rang, and she got up to take the call, told the caller the store's hours, and then replaced the receiver. She took her time leaning back against the counter to face Abby, gazing at her as if she'd never really looked at her before. And Abby did the same in return.

She couldn't expect Hope to understand. Hope was beautiful, like her sisters. Tall, effortlessly slim, and always that little bit more polished and put together than everyone else in Cold River. And yet Hope didn't have the sort of easy, unmistakable beauty that made Abby feel like a lumbering oaf in comparison. The way she had around, say, women like Gray's Cristina. Hope's was the sort of beauty that made everyone around her feel beautiful too.

Damn her.

"Do you want to marry him?" Hope asked.

"What kind of marriage can you have with someone who doesn't know you from a can of paint?"

"That's not what I asked you."

"There's a difference between fantasy and reality. They're not the same thing. I'm not sure that's bad either. People want things in fantasy that they would never want in real life."

"That's an interesting theory. But still not what I asked you."

"I think about marrying him and what that would look like, realistically," Abby said carefully. She let out a sigh. "What people would say. *Oh, Gray Everett took pity on that homely Douglas girl.* Or, *did you hear that Abby Douglas took advantage of poor, grieving Gray Everett?* Those are the two possibilities I keep circling around."

Hope actually laughed. "I don't even know where to begin with that."

"Because you know I'm right. That's how it would happen."

"Number one, you're not homely. Two, I've never heard of anybody taking advantage of any Everett, but especially not Gray. Speaking of things that are completely unimaginable. And most important, I don't know who you think wanders around this town talking about you that way."

"Everybody in this town talks about everybody else in this town, and you know it."

"I personally exult in it. But nobody talks about *you*, Abby. Not like that. You're not some horror that will be inflicted on the person who marries you."

"That doesn't mean they won't—"

"And I can't help noticing you still haven't answered the actual question I asked you."

Because she couldn't.

Because there was only one word that she could say, and she was afraid to say it out loud. Abby was afraid it was written all over her. That it was stamped on her forehead like the tattoo she'd never gotten and right there on her tongue, so close to spilling out every time she opened her mouth that the effort of keeping it in make her feel slightly ill.

"And I'm not talking about any tediously adult, depressingly realistic discussion about what an egalitarian partnership looks like these days out on a working ranch." Hope leaned forward, her tone as intense as the look on her face. "I'm asking if you, Abby, in your heart, still want to marry that man the way you did when you were seven."

"When I was seven, I thought dreams came true," Abby replied quietly, before she knew she meant to speak at all. "I thought my mother would come home to stay. I thought my father would hunt me down so he could meet me. I thought both of my grandparents would live forever."

Hope reached down and took both of Abby's hands in hers, startling them both, because they'd never been big touchers. They generally kept it to an odd hug here and there, like when Hope had come back on visits from college, or finally moved home for good.

But today, Hope took her hands and even squeezed them for emphasis. "We both know it's a trick question. Because we both know the answer. It's always been the same answer."

"It was never a real question!" Abby protested.

"And now it is," Hope retorted. "So I have to ask. What are you going to do with this opportunity to get everything you've always said you wanted? Are you going to step aside and let someone else marry him for the wrong reasons because you don't think he wants *you* for the right ones?"

Abby sat with that all the way home, on that long, usually peaceful drive around the side of the cold mountain and out into the winter fields that seemed to spread out before her like a warning tonight.

She turned it over in her head as she and Grandma

moved around the kitchen in their usual easy dance, the lights bright and happy against the wall of brooding night outside, but not quite bright enough to calm the turmoil inside of her.

It rolled around inside her while Grandma went off to take her evening bath, leaving Abby to settle down with her book, there on the sofa where she could trace the familiar cabbages with her fingertips as she lost herself in the pages.

But tonight, she didn't open her book. She stared at her phone instead, as if it might leap to life before her eyes. As if it might sprout horns or perform gymnastics on the sofa cushion beside her.

She thought about what Hope had said. About Tate Bishop, of all people, who Hope and Rae had stoutly maintained throughout the years was a perfect representative of all the boys Abby didn't see or even notice had interest in her.

Her friends were being kind, but it didn't matter. Because even if they were absolutely correct and Abby had been careening through her life with blinders on, it wouldn't have made any difference. Then or now.

Because there had only ever been room in her heart for one.

She'd always believed she'd been made defective, but maybe she'd been made for this.

And the whole town might whisper about her. They might cluck their tongues and call her names behind her back. Sad, for example. Pathetic. Poor, plain Abby Douglas and a man who wanted a woman in his house—so any old woman would do.

But she couldn't control what people said about her. She knew it was more than likely they said all of those things already.

And if Gray was going to go ahead with this plan of his to locate a wife based on her ability to fit seamlessly into his life with a minimum of fuss or unruly emotions or any of that mess—and she hadn't seen anything to suggest he was kidding—Abby couldn't really see why she should step aside and let him fill that slot with someone else.

If he was going to go ahead and marry *just anyone*, why shouldn't she be that anyone?

Because she already knew what it was like to yearn at him from afar. She'd already experienced what it was like to watch him marry another woman. She was familiar with that ache and the way it sat on her, until she felt pale with all the frustrated longing and the self-hatred that went along with having feelings for another woman's husband. She'd already lived through it once.

If she was being as reasonable and rational as she liked to imagine she was, she knew that if she turned Gray down, it would very likely turn out that he did, in fact, have a list. And that he would move right along to the next name on it.

He wasn't in love with her. But then, she'd loved him for so long and with such single-mindedness that she had to believe it was possible she could love enough for both of them.

And while she was busy loving Gray from close by, for a change, she could try to be the mother figure for Becca that she'd always wished someone had been for her. She could try to help.

Maybe it wasn't ideal. But what was?

And Abby would rather be needed and useful in some way, like an appliance after all, than ignored.

She picked up her phone and scrolled to the name he'd

programmed in himself, then told herself it was silly to have butterflies in her stomach. True, she hadn't practiced this like everyone else she knew had in middle school, horrifying her grandmother by calling up boys. She told herself the only reason she was so nervous was because it was new. And because all of this was so crazy.

If there was craziness going around, she might as well try being crazy with Gray for a change rather than the solitary crazy she knew too well.

She hit the button to dial his number and held her breath as the phone rang. And rang.

"Hello, Abby," came Gray's unmistakable drawl, sending a ribbon of textured heat winding through her. "I was beginning to think you weren't going to call me at all."

She was sweating. She was afraid she might drop her phone. She had no idea what she was doing. "I'm sorry if I woke you."

"It's eight o'clock at night." There was that dark current in his voice again, the way there had been in the coffeehouse earlier. *Laughter,* Abby thought, dazed. "You really do think I'm a geriatric, don't you?"

"I don't think you're a geriatric." Not with that body. She paused for a moment, unable to tell if she'd said that out loud or not, God help her. When he didn't respond, she made herself keep going. "I do think you're a rancher, who probably gets up at the crack of dawn to tend to all your land and livestock. Don't you?"

"I don't go to bed at eight."

There was something so intimate about his voice in her ear like that.

Abby had never given a lot of thought to the intimacy of telephone calls before. But then, she'd never had a phone call with Gray. She'd never found herself sitting in a quiet room, able to do nothing at all but press herself back against the couch and imagine what he might be doing on the other side of the fields that separated them.

She'd never considered how . . . dangerous it could be to tell herself stories about what he was doing. Was he sitting at his kitchen table? Helping Becca with her homework? Crashed out on his own sofa, which she knew was made of faded leather, wide and masculine and perfectly him?

Was he . . . fully dressed?

Abby had never felt more like a vestal virgin than she did then, when the very idea of Gray Everett in a state of undress threatened to give her the vapors.

"The fact I don't have a geriatric bedtime seems to have thrown you for a loop," Gray said after a moment. "Not sure I know how to take that."

"I was considering how bizarre phones are. If you really think about it."

"I'd be surprised if anyone thinks about it. This century."

Abby squeezed her eyes shut, but her mouth had a mind of its own. "Isn't it strange that you hold this thing in your hand that can let you sit somewhere and have conversations with people as if they're sitting next to you, when they're not?"

He made a low sound, a kind of dark laughter that echoed inside of her like fire. "Maybe I'm not the one who's secretly geriatric."

"I'm not saying I'm preoccupied with telephones. Or a technophobe or anything. It's one of those things that hits you every now and again when you—"

"Abby."

And God, the way he said her name.

Maybe she could be forgiven for changing her whole

life to hear him keep saying it. Just like that. Amused and faintly frustrated, low and deep.

"Yes," she whispered, sealing her fate.

Because it was better than the alternative.

Because it was better. Because anything that was with him had to be better, she was sure of it. "Yes, Gray. I'll marry you."

7

"What do you mean, you're getting married?"

It was too early in the morning for this. Gray cupped his hands around the mug of coffee he'd just filled and congratulated himself on keeping them to himself. Instead of planting them in his little brother's face.

Because Brady was annoying. And the most annoying thing about him currently was that he was *here*.

Cluttering up Gray's kitchen and more than that, his life. Brady had claimed he wasn't moving home—that he had no intention of ever living on the backside of beyond again—and yet here he was, up from his fabulous, fantastic life in Denver that he professed to love so much. Again. He'd come in late last night, uninvited as usual. Gray had already been in bed, but the headlights crossing over his ceiling had kept him wide awake and glowering at the walls.

He should have known better than to answer honestly when his brother had asked him how he was doing. Especially at 4:45 in the morning, according to the old clock on the wall, when a man wanted silence and caffeine to get his head on right.

"Not sure why the concept needs explaining, Brady," he drawled, his gaze out the kitchen window toward the barn and the outbuildings he couldn't see at this hour. His mind was on all the things he had to get done that day, before and after he ran Becca to school—a job he'd decided long ago he'd take on himself unless there was a legitimate emergency, because he refused to raise his kid the way his father had raised him. Meaning, with total indifference punctuated by occasional bouts of violent, drunken rage. "Pretty sure it explains itself. Or maybe they do things different down in Denver these days."

Brady was pushed back in one of the old wooden chairs at the solid kitchen table made from a slab of wood that had once been part of a barn door and still had marks from all Amos's red-pen will rewriting. His fancy laptop that he carted around like it was made of solid gold was cracked open before him. He was wearing a faded Colorado sweatshirt with the CU insignia on it, reminding Gray of Brady's college years the same way his presence here did. It was another thing that made Gray want to clip him one. It wasn't bad enough that his little brother had taken it upon himself to treat the ranch house like his own personal hotel. He had to loom around in the kitchen every morning, as if it was his goal in life to disrupt Gray's peace of mind and beloved schedule.

If memory served, he'd done the same thing when he'd been home from college. Underfoot and mouthy, then and now.

"Since when did you start seriously dating? Or dating at all?" Brady demanded, that scoffing note in his voice rubbing Gray the wrong way. "As far as I know, you've been doing the same monk impression since Cristina died."

Gray didn't know what was worse. That Brady felt comfortable talking about Cristina's death like that, as if it weren't a touchy subject that was better tiptoed around and treated carefully. Or that . . . it wasn't a touchy subject any longer. Gray felt nothing when her name came up, or her death was mentioned, except the same old sadness that he and the woman he'd married had done nothing but hurt each other. If it weren't for Becca, he doubted he'd think about Cristina at all these days—and he had the sneaking suspicion that said some pretty dire things about him.

But he wasn't about to share that with his obnoxious brother.

"I didn't realize I was expected to clear my dating schedule with you."

"You have a dating *schedule*?"

"Had I known you were so interested in how to date a woman, I would have invited you along. You should have told me you needed help."

"And this isn't even dating you're talking about," Brady continued in the same scandalized voice, ignoring the swipe Gray had taken at him. Though Gray could see his eyes glittering in the window's reflection and knew it had hit him all the same. *Good.* "Marriage? Really?"

In a tone that suggested marriage was crazy in general but *particularly* insane for Gray.

It was possible he was projecting that last part. It was also possible Brady was enough of a jackass to believe he could go there.

Either way it wasn't yet 5:00 in the morning and this conversation was like slamming his head into the nearest wall, except less fun.

"Brady." Gray turned. He fixed his gaze on his brother directly and didn't much care that the longer he looked at him, the more Brady scowled. "You're confused. I wasn't asking your permission. You asked me what was up with me and I told you."

"Have you told Ty?"

"Not real interested in his opinion either," Gray replied,

fighting back his temper. "But if the rodeo princess wakes up before noon one of these days, sure, I'll tell him. Assuming you don't race out there and tell him first, because apparently what you do now is run your mouth like it's your job."

Brady raked his hands through his dark hair as if he was also having trouble keeping them to himself.

Try it, Gray urged him silently. Almost gleefully. *See what happens.*

But as Gray watched, braced for a fistfight he'd dearly love to have and lessons he was dying to teach, a canny sort of look took over Brady's face. As if he were sitting there running one of his money games, except this time it wasn't some investment he couldn't properly explain, it was Gray's life he was planning to gamble away.

"How did Becca take it?" Brady asked after a moment.

Like Gray couldn't read the deliberately even tone he used.

"That's not your business, little brother. My daughter is my responsibility, not yours."

Brady rolled his eyes. "Is there anything on this ranch or in the whole world that *isn't* your sole responsibility? Am I allowed to be a member of the family, Gray? Or do you get to decide that too?"

"Mom asked me my opinion on that when she was pregnant, and I said no, Ty was more than enough." Gray shrugged, enjoying the fact that a memory he was more than half convinced he'd made up could still agitate his little brother. "No one listened to me then. Why should anything change now?"

Brady's gaze was darker and his expression a whole lot less canny. "You must practice this whole hard-bitten cowboy thing you have going on. In the mirror, I'm guessing, so you can make sure you *look* laconic."

"The sun hasn't come up yet, and to be honest, this is way too much drama for me to take in with so many chores waiting for me." Gray wanted more coffee, but he didn't want this conversation. He put the mug down and grabbed his battered Stetson off the counter. "Feel free to jump in and help me with the chores, since you're here all the time these days. Or is this like when you used to come home from college and acted as if you were doing us a favor by pretending you couldn't remember how a ranch was run?"

Brady responded to that with his middle finger.

Gray nodded as if that was the response he'd expected and headed for the back door, because if he didn't get outside and get a lungful of cold air, he might actually lose his cool. He couldn't remember the last time he'd let his temper get the best of him, but it had always seemed like his baby brother had been put on this earth to test him.

As far as he could tell, it was the one thing Brady was really good at.

He walked out into the yard and stood there a minute, taking a deep breath. Then another. It was a sharp, sweet sort of shattering intake of air that instantly grounded him. It reminded him who he was. Why he was here, on this earth with his feet on this land. It told him, every morning, what the point of all this was.

His upcoming marriage included.

His upcoming marriage most of all, if he was honest. He was ready for the change. He was ready for the next phase.

Hell, he was ready to get laid again.

That Brady had called him a monk burned in his gut, but he forced himself to ignore it. What Brady didn't know about Gray's life could stretch across the whole of the Rocky Mountain range and back again, twice. Brady had never been married. He hadn't had a baby. And he certainly hadn't had to navigate life in Cold River with a daughter to raise and a ranch to run while Amos drank himself meaner than dirt, and the gossips in town tracked their every move.

Of course Brady thought Gray was a monk. And more, that he'd chosen it. As if he'd woken up one day and decided what he'd really enjoy was all work, no sex, and a decade of knowing that even if he could wrangle a few days away somewhere, that would mean . . . what? Picking up random women in a bar and sneaking in and out of motel rooms while someone else watched his little girl? That had never been Gray's style. Cristina had been the single spontaneous decision he'd ever made—and look how that had turned out.

He tried to breathe all the old ugliness out in a great puff against the cold, dark air.

There was a vague hint of the coming day high up over the mountains on the eastern side of the valley. The horses knew he was awake—they probably knew the minute his feet hit the floor beside of his bed, smart and attentive creatures that they were—and were already making their usual morning noises in the barn. There were clouds tossed here and there across the vast sky, slightly darker against the gradual creep of light like some kind of warning. Gray loved every part of ranch life, *his* life, but it might have been these quiet, still mornings that made him the most grateful that he got to be here. That he got to be him. That he got this life he'd always wanted, and he got to decide what made it better too. And do whatever he had to do to make it that way.

Even live like a damned monk for ten years.

But Brady wasn't done. Gray heard the back door slam again behind him, and gritted his teeth. "Are you ever going to quit?" he asked without turning back around.

Brady didn't respond immediately. Gray heard his feet on the steps, then shuffling across the yard until he was standing there at Gray's shoulder as if he'd been invited to come along.

"Not everything is an attack on you," Brady said in a low voice, with all kinds of his own temper in his tone.

Gray slanted a look his way, but didn't comment on the fact his brother wasn't wearing a coat against the sharp morning air. Not his business. And it might even teach his citified baby brother a few pertinent lessons about the life up in these mountains he'd worked so hard to forget.

"I can't quite see the difference between you making conversation and you gearing up for another run at me," he said instead. "I know it's a big surprise to you that a man might take offense the idea that his brother wants to sell his land out from under him, but here we are."

"Hey. It's my land too."

"So you and that damned will tell me." Gray shook his head. "I guess I'll continue to do all the work while you sit around comparing real estate prices and coming up with new and exciting ways to take everything I've worked for my whole life and turn it into what? Condos for pampered people who think a little dirt on their designer shoes makes them a cowboy?"

"Jesus Christ, Gray," Brady muttered beneath his breath, but Gray heard him. And didn't jump on it, which made him feel purely virtuous from his head to his boots.

He could barely make out the outbuildings in this light, but he looked in the direction of the one Ty had taken since the funeral. His own private bunkhouse, which at least Gray could say he'd earned. Ty had donated money he'd won bull riding more than once, if the ranch's ledgers their father had kept so ineptly were to be believed. It was more than he could say for Brady, who could have used his college education to give back to the ranch that had paid for all those classes that made him think he was better than everyone else. But hadn't.

Gray doubted it had even occurred to him.

"Can we just have a conversation for a change?" Brady asked, his voice fierce. With something else beneath it Gray didn't want to acknowledge. "Or do you get something out of constantly being in a fight with everybody?"

Gray wasn't in a fight with anybody, because there was no point fighting when he already knew who'd win, but he didn't tell his brother that. He made himself take a breath. Two.

"I like conversation as much as the next man," he said when he was sure he could sound completely unbothered. Because he was enough of a jackass himself to enjoy the prospect of getting right up there beneath his little brother's skin whenever possible. "But every time you open your mouth, it's to comment on my business. My life. My choices. And yes, Brady, *my* land."

"Excuse me for being interested in your life and giving a crap what happens to you." Brady's voice was clipped and hard. "Particularly when you make sweeping, random announcements out of nowhere that you're marrying a woman who, as far as I know, you're not dating."

"You don't have to come to the wedding if you don't want to," Gray replied mildly. More to rub some salt on the wound, he could admit. To himself. "It won't hurt my feelings, though I can't vouch for Abby's. You were in high school together, weren't you?"

Brady had his arms crossed and his hands tucked beneath his armpits against the cold, but that didn't prevent him from pivoting, slowly, to glare at the side of Gray's face.

"Abby Douglas is a sweet girl," he said in a voice that broadcast how pissed he was without him having to yell.

"She was a couple of years behind me in high school, as a matter of fact, and she's not your type."

Gray hadn't much cared for it when Abby had said the same thing to him. He really, *really* disliked hearing his snot-nosed brother echo it.

"You an expert on her too?" Gray didn't know where that came from, his voice like steel and bad weather. "How many times do you figure you've spoken to her in your entire life? Three, total, including at Dad's funeral?"

Brady made a rude, anatomically impossible suggestion.

"I would," Gray threw at him, "but I'm Cold River's resident monk. Isn't that what you just said? None of that for me."

Brady sighed as if he were in actual, physical pain. "Maybe sweet Abby Douglas deserves more than this life you say you love so much, that's all. Stuck out here with nothing but mountains and cows for company. I'd ask you what kind of life that really is, but I don't think you know, because you seem to like it no matter how many women it drives crazy. Mom. Crist—"

"Brady." Gray didn't know how he managed to keep from shouting. Or letting his hands do the shouting for him. "My daughter isn't your business and neither is her mother. And *sweet Abby Douglas* isn't a problem you need to worry about solving. All you need to know is that she and I are getting married. You can do with that information what you want, but I'd advise you to be real careful how you talk about it around me."

He didn't wait for whatever smartass remark his brother might make because he wasn't sure he'd be able to handle it. Not in a way that wouldn't leave one or both of them bloody in the dirt, which wasn't how he'd wanted to start the day, thank you.

He headed for his truck, swinging himself into the cab

and ignoring the fact the Brady was still standing there in the dark. Watching him go, as if Gray was the one being unreasonable.

Gray found himself stewing on that all along the winding dirt roads that led out to the pastureland he used for the herd during the winter. He didn't know what Brady wanted. Other than the money selling the land would put in his pocket, and Gray knew he wasn't very reasonable where that was concerned. But why should he pretend to be reasonable about something like that? He didn't want to sell. He didn't want to give up his life's work. His home.

The Everett family legacy.

And he wanted to beat the crap out of his own brother every time he mentioned it.

That's why you're getting married, he reminded himself.

It was one of the reasons, anyway. Because he had to believe Brady would find it more difficult to get excited about kicking Gray off the ranch if there was a real family to consider displacing when he did it. He had to believe his brother couldn't see the ranch as a home because, in fairness, it had never been much of one for any of them. Amos had been a tyrant when he hadn't been passed out somewhere, and once she'd left, their mother had made it clear she was perfectly happy to have a distant relationship with her own sons if that meant no more dealing with Amos.

Brady didn't understand there was a pull here that had nothing to do with one mean old man.

But that pull was all Gray had.

And he wanted to pass it on to Becca.

He could drive up to the pasture blindfolded, though he was never reckless enough to test that theory. He knew every hump and hollow beneath the truck's tires as he went. And the more he contemplated marrying again and making the ranch a family operation—this time in a way that didn't involve Amos's various reigns of terror—the less he concentrated on the bumpy dirt roads he knew so well. And the more his thoughts turned to *sweet Abby Douglas* and the fact she'd agreed to be his wife.

She'd actually agreed.

The sense of satisfaction that gave him didn't make a whole lot of sense, given he'd only come up with the idea at his father's funeral, but there it was. It sat in him, solid and warm, like a slab of rock baking out in the summer sun.

I don't want a big production, she'd told him during one of their evening phone calls that had become a habit over the past week. *I don't need all that commotion.*

Because after making such a terrible choice the last time, Gray had managed to stumble into perfect when all he'd been looking for was practical.

And better yet, she was right next door. Sure, "next door" was about six miles out here on these back roads that crisscrossed the fields and looped up into the hills, but that was part of what made Abby the right choice. She wasn't his mother or his late wife, both outsiders who'd imagined their lives out here would be like a lazy summer's afternoon beneath that endless blue Colorado sky. Abby wouldn't have to figure out a way to adjust to the brutal winters or the aching quiet of the land that Gray knew some felt like loneliness instead of hope. She knew how far it was into town and the fact the road over the hill shut down at least three or four times each winter. She'd grown up in these fields, with nothing some days but the howl of the wind and the kind of inbred country stubbornness that allowed a person to call that "invigorating."

She was the perfect choice. The only choice. Gray couldn't believe he hadn't realized that sooner and saved himself and Becca all these years alone.

He'd been all for getting it done as soon as possible, since they suited so well and Becca had been all for it when he'd told her the news.

This is a fantastic idea, Dad, she had said. *Really. Abby is great.*

Gray was all for heading down to the courthouse and calling it a done deal.

Or we could try getting to know each other, Abby had countered, her voice scratchy and hushed over the phone, as if she was cradling it between her cheek and shoulder. An image that stuck with Gray, for some reason, and made him wonder about all kinds of things. The scent of her skin. Its softness. What she might do if he tasted her there in the crook of her neck. *I'm not suggesting we date or anything so outlandish, but we could try talking to each other before we jump headfirst into an entire marriage.*

Gray didn't really want to wait. Or talk. But he did.

Because really, was she asking that much?

They'd settled on Thanksgiving weekend as their wedding date, which was slightly more than three weeks since Amos had departed the mortal coil with a lot less fanfare than he'd required while alive. Family and friends would already be gathering for the holiday, so they could throw a party or something after their trip to the courthouse, which Abby had assured him *she* didn't care about. But it turned out Martha Douglas had insisted.

And Gray wasn't about to start off his second round of married life by getting on the wrong side of Martha Douglas.

It wasn't too long of a wait, he told himself now as the

truck jolted its way up the side of a hill. It was next weekend, which only felt like forever because he was finally at the end of all his years of forced solitude.

And then it would be done. Abby would move in, they would get to know each other better, and they would figure out how to build a decent life on this ranch whether Brady approved or not. Gray might not have seen it done, not in his lifetime anyway, but he persisted in imagining it was possible.

Everetts had been here forever. Some of them had to have been happy. Somewhere down there in the tangled roots of his family tree, or there wouldn't have been so many of them through the generations.

Gray didn't see why he and Abby couldn't be happy too. He was convinced it had to be better to dive into a marriage with no unrealistic expectations. With everything laid out on the table up front. That had to take the edge off—and Lord knew, Cristina had left him pretty much allergic to any kind of edginess. He wanted a different kind of sweet this time. Simple and real. Not a woman who pretended one thing to his face and was something else entirely behind his back.

He wanted Abby, who had somehow managed to get him talking on the phone. Just talking. Something he couldn't say he'd ever done. Not deliberately. And certainly not every night for a week.

Gray had learned a lot of interesting things in that week.

He learned the different tones in her voice. The way she laughed, or even giggled occasionally. He discovered she wasn't any kind of pushover. She was happy to argue with him if it mattered to her, which he respected. He learned how she sounded when she was teasing him, and the somber note she used when she was being more serious than she wanted to admit.

Gray had never spent much time on the telephone. He considered his cell phone a necessary evil, because he was a doer, not a talker. But he was the one who had started them down the road of phone calls, and he couldn't say he minded ending his evenings by talking to Abby.

It boded well for the evenings they'd have together in the ranch house. Soon.

The sun was starting to peek up over the eastern range in earnest when Gray finally bumped his way up the last bit of hill to the pasture. There were already trucks there, his foreman and hands drinking coffee from their thermoses while they waited for him, and he knew he needed to stop brooding about his personal life.

Because this was just another day at the ranch. Brady might not understand that. Maybe it wasn't fair that Gray expected him to, because if he was capable of grasping what the ranch meant, he wouldn't have left skid marks getting away from it when he was eighteen. He would have stayed. He would have put his sweat and blood into the land the way Everetts had been doing for nearly a century and a half.

The sun pushed itself over the ridge then, bathing the cold fields with thick, golden light. And Gray knew that really, he didn't need his little brother to understand.

He just hoped like hell that Abby would.

8

"I don't know how to tell you this without coming right out and saying it," Grandma said in a too-steady, too-intent way that instantly put Abby on her guard.

Grandma was peeling potatoes at the kitchen table in the farmhouse, her expression placid while her gnarled hands moved deftly. It was the Tuesday before Thanksgiving. Abby was getting married—*married*—on Saturday. To Gray Everett. *Gray Everett*.

It was all her dreams come true, and none of them, all at once.

So of course there was bad news.

"That always bodes well," she said, trying to remain upbeat. Or at least sound it.

Grandma didn't react to that. She kept peeling her potatoes as if she could keep doing it forever. More importantly, she didn't look up.

A heavy, all-too-familiar weight thickened inside of Abby, three parts dread and one part sick experience. It was always there, lying in wait and ready to roll out and smother her at a moment's notice.

Because there was only one reason for her grandmother to worry about telling her something instead of coming right out and saying it the way she did everything else. And it was always and ever the same reason.

Lily.

"Your mother has decided that this is one of her *on* years," Grandma said evenly. Because that was the charming shorthand they'd developed to discuss the times Lily actually condescended to appear in the general vicinity of a major holiday. "You know I always invite her to Thanksgiving dinner."

"That doesn't mean she has to come." Abby found herself scowling ferociously at her own pile of peelings. Bright orange curls of carrots because she and Grandma loved their carrot cake in addition to the carrots they'd use to make more traditional side dishes. "It's been five years, at least. I was under the impression she was never coming home for the holidays again."

"No one is more surprised than me."

Snick. Snick. Snick. That was the only sound in the kitchen for what felt like an eternity as they peeled, the heaviness of all the things they weren't talking about seeming to expand with every second, blacker and darker than the late autumn night outside the kitchen windows.

"We're not having our usual Thanksgiving," Abby said fiercely, fighting to keep the thickness out of her voice. "Does she know that?"

Thanksgiving usually involved treks deeper into the mountains to the dairy farms where Grandma had grown up, where Abby had swathes of second cousins and huge, loud family dinners to choose from. Lily had declared herself allergic to what she called "the milk run" ages ago. But this was an odd year in every respect, because Gray had suggested Abby and her grandmother come over to his house—the house that would be hers too in a matter of days.

Seems like a good opportunity to spend some time to-
gether as a family, he'd said in that raspy, lazy voice of his
that was the last thing Abby heard before she went to bed
at night and the only thing she thought about all day.

She got overheated thinking about it.

"She knows." Grandma sounded resigned. "And you
know your mother. It's more than likely she won't turn up.
But I wanted to give you a warning."

Abby suddenly felt a searing sort of pain at her temples
and wrestled her shoulders down from around her ears.
She cleared her throat. "Grandma. Please tell me you didn't
tell her . . ."

"That her only child was getting married? Of course
I did."

"Grandma."

Grandma put down her potato and her paring knife, and
met Abby's gaze. "I didn't tell her to hurt you, Abby. But
she is your mother. And my daughter. Not telling her felt
like a lie."

And Martha Douglas was no liar. She didn't stretch the
truth. She didn't pretend this or that to save someone's feelings. She shot from the hip, and that was one of the things
Abby had always loved most about her.

But it also meant . . . situations like this.

If it had been up to Abby, she would have written her
mother off years ago. Instead, she was always waiting for
the other shoe to drop where Lily was concerned. She
could turn up at any time and had, because she knew she
was always welcome in her parents' house. The fact that
her only child wanted nothing to do with her didn't appear
to concern her in the least.

On the contrary, she seemed to delight in it.

Abby had spent her life blinking back angry tears, torn
between feelings of betrayal on the one hand—Why

couldn't Grandma and Grandpa stand up for her? Why couldn't they dismiss Lily the way she'd dismissed them a thousand times?—and a sad sort of compassion for two parents who couldn't really understand the child they'd brought into the world or the damage she did.

All while she nursed this scraped-raw feeling, so big and bright in her chest that she sometimes wondered if she would collapse into it. When she thought about *family* with Gray, she had no idea what that would look like, but she wanted . . . more than these terrible, vicious moments that made her feel small.

She wanted more than the ache inside her like a tide, pitiless and mean.

Abby frowned at her carrots so hard it made more than her temples hurt. "What did she say when you told her I was getting married?"

"You know your mother," Grandma replied, sounding as if she was forcing that calm tone. "It's hard to say what she feels about anything."

And that was the end of the conversation, because further comment would slide too close to gossip, to Grandma's way of thinking.

Because whether or not Abby stewed over the conversations they didn't have and the things she couldn't say was neither here nor there and never had been.

She didn't mention it to Gray in their phone call that night.

"You okay?" he asked a few minutes into their usual back and forth, these little discussions about nothing in particular that Abby kept telling herself mattered. They were a foundation. They were a start, anyway.

"I'm fine," she assured him. She was curled up in a knot on the bed she'd slept in all her life, staring around the bedroom that had been the center of her world all that time.

It was hard to imagine that this time next week, she'd live
six miles down the road.

With him.

She had to take an extra couple of breaths.

"You usually talk more," Gray said quietly. "Second
thoughts?"

Abby hardly knew what to say. He knew the story of
her mother, the way everybody did in Cold River. That
didn't mean she wanted to discuss it. Not with this man
who she still couldn't quite believe she would be calling
her husband in a matter of days. This man who she desperately wanted to like her. To think highly of her.

To want her.

The idea that he'd imagine she'd back out of this now
made those same frustrated tears prick at the back of
her eyes. Because like hell would she let Lily ruin this
too. Like hell would she let her mother strangle all the
possibility out of this fragile, magical dream Abby hardly
believed in herself.

"Oh no," she said, with maybe too much fervor. But she
didn't rein it in. "I'm not having any second thoughts. Are
you?"

"None."

He sounded certain. Absolute.

And Abby dared to imagine she wasn't the only one
who sat there a minute after they hung up, smiling into her
empty room.

Still, she slept badly and woke up cranky, and it wasn't
because she had Gray on the brain. Because she always had
Gray on the brain. She sleepwalked her way through her
usual morning routine, almost burst into tears when her car
choked as she tried to start it in the frigid predawn, and
failed to see the usual magic as she drove in to town.

One more thing to blame on her mother. One more reason to wish that one of these days, Lily really would just disappear for good. She didn't only ruin lives, she cast a black cloud over otherwise perfectly happy days too, and she didn't have to be in the vicinity to do it.

Abby hated that she had such ugliness in her head, no matter if it was warranted. Whether she liked it or not, Lily was her mother, and surely she should find a way to have some kind of feeling for the woman inside of her. Or maybe that was the problem. She had *too much* feeling inside her. Too much feeling, too much experience with Lily's broken promises, and entirely too many memories of Lily's casual cruelty.

"It doesn't really seem fair that I have to put up with Lily in the middle of all this," she blurted out to Rae in the coffeehouse's back office some hours later.

It was getting on lunchtime, and her friend was in town before her own shift at her family's florist shop down the street. The Flowerpot sourced all its flowers from the Trujillo family plant and flower farms north of town, with a number of largescale greenhouses and deep, deep roots in the valley. Rae was all about roots—though no one was allowed to talk about the kind of roots she'd married into and then cut off, so abruptly that she was still barely on speaking terms with the whole, sprawling, historic Kittredge family who roamed all over the valley. And in the case of Amanda Kittredge, the youngest of the big family, who worked right here in Cold River Coffee.

Today was not the day to test the water on Rae's current feelings about her brief marriage to Riley Kittredge and all the ill will it had caused ever since. Especially when Abby could see that Rae hadn't ordered herself a coffee drink, which meant she was quietly avoiding having to interact with Amanda.

Still.

"Nothing about your mother is fair," Rae said. She folded her arms over her chest, which made the bright red shirt she had to wear at the florist's stretch over the figure Abby had envied since the day in seventh grade Rae had woken up with it. Rae raised a dramatic dark brow. "There's a lot of unfairness going around, now that you mention it."

"I'm talking about my pain, Rae. Why are you interrupting me to give me a hard time?"

Rae waved a hand. "Pain comes and goes, Abby. But the agony of not being asked to be a bridesmaid in your best friend's wedding? That lasts forever. In the wedding pictures, particularly."

"It's not that kind of wedding."

"Every wedding is that kind of wedding. Maybe you've forgotten mine. It was like a parade."

Abby hadn't forgotten. That awful iridescent dress lived in her memory like a virus and was right there in her closet should the awful details get fuzzy. But Rae's short, unhappy marriage was so sensitive a subject that neither she nor Hope had dared bring it up directly in years. If Rae couldn't manage a civil exchange with Amanda here in the coffeehouse, the mention of Riley Kittredge himself might send Rae right over the edge.

Rae tipped her head to one side, and Abby tried to stop thinking the name of her ex, in case Rae could somehow sense it in the air between them. "Are you *forbidden* to have a wedding party? Is that part of the deal with this whole whirlwind thing—he gets to make all the rules?"

Abby threw a ball point pen across her desk, and Rae laughed as she batted it aside.

"Don't make this into something it's not. Gray doesn't *forbid* me to do anything. This isn't a romantic thing, that's all." She lifted her chin. "I don't see why it has to be."

"He might not think it's romantic because he's a man and he's *him* and sometimes it looks like a smile might kill him, much less a romance. But that doesn't mean you can't find it romantic, right?"

"No. I don't know." Abby rubbed at her overly dry eyes, wishing she'd slept for more than fifteen minutes here and there. "He isn't the one who's had a crush on me all these years. And I don't . . ."

She didn't want to finish that sentence.

"You don't want to tell him because you're afraid he'd change his mind about marrying you if he knew."

Abby realized she should have expected Rae to deliver a punch like that, straight to her heart. Because that was Rae in a nutshell. A delicate creature, all anime eyes and Pied Piper laughter, and yet so direct sometimes it left scars.

"It is what it is," Abby heard herself say, in as measured a tone as she could manage.

Rae made a small noise. "I've never understood that expression. *Why* is it what it is? Can you change it? Why can't it be something else if that's what you want? *It is what it is* always sounds like defeat."

"In this case, you know exactly what it is and so do I. He might as well have advertised for a position in the *Longhorn Valley Tribune*. It happens to be a position I want to fill, that's all."

"And one you can quit if you want." Rae's voice was dark then, which Abby suspected was another reference to the marriage she ordinarily pretended hadn't happened.

"I'm not going to quit," Abby said, and it felt like a vow. Because everything felt like a vow this week. Maybe she was getting prepared. "Some people go through their whole lives looking for their place in the world, but not me. It's mapped out for me, and I think that's a good thing."

"I think he's an idiot."

"He's not an idiot. You know he's not an idiot."

"You deserve to be loved, Abby," Rae said with a sudden rush of ferocity. "You deserve everything. You don't have to prove yourself—"

"What I deserve doesn't matter," Abby said fiercely in return. "Because this is what I have. And it's what I want."

"Are you sure?" Rae sighed when Abby glared at her. "I'm not trying to give you a hard time. But I have to wonder if having part of him is worse than having nothing at all."

Thanks for that, Abby thought and would have said if her throat didn't feel sealed up. *Thanks for articulating my absolute worst fear.*

She had surrounded herself with direct, take-no-prisoners people in this life. Usually this was something she treasured. Because it had never occurred to her before these past few weeks that there were very good reasons most people preferred some gauze and self-deception wrapped around their lives.

"I guess I'll find out," she said. Maybe too grimly.

Rae's eyes widened. "I didn't mean—"

"I really do know what I'm doing, okay?" That was a lie, but she was doing it anyway. And she would keep doing it, because this was the path she was on now. There was no going back. She didn't *want* any going back. "We're not having any kind of bridal party. Grandma has insisted on a party after the courthouse, though. That's going to have to do."

"I love you, Abby," Rae said, her dark eyes filled with distress. "I don't want to hurt you. That's the last thing I want."

"I know." Abby pushed back from the desk and stood. Then she made herself smile because she didn't want to

hurt Rae either. Not when all her friend wanted was to protect her. "I really do know."

But what she knew wasn't the same as what she felt,
Abby reflected as she took a shift at the cash register up
front. This close to the holiday, Cold River Coffee was
packed full of familiar local faces, college students back
home for the rest of the week, and old friends who only
turned up at this time of year.

Abby lost herself in the familiar hustle of a busy day
slinging coffee drinks. The sun came up late and set early
this time of year, and contending with that required a
whole lot of caffeine and sugar. One of the things she liked
about working here was being out front during rushes
like the one today. Making drinks, making change, so it
was impossible to do anything but concentrate on the task
at hand.

She liked to lose herself in the rhythm of it, especially
when there were so very many things she didn't want to
think about.

Abby was so busy focusing on getting a round of drinks
out to a pack of chattering tourists who'd day-tripped over
from Aspen that it took her a moment to understand the
girl standing there at the bar, trying to catch her eye, wasn't
waiting for a drink.

It was Becca.

Gray's daughter, Becca.

"Hi," Becca said when Abby's gaze collided with hers,
with more self-possession than most thirty-year-olds. Or
this thirty-year-old, anyway. Abby had to remind herself
the girl was fifteen. "I had the idea we should get to know
each other better before tomorrow."

"Tomorrow?" Abby echoed through the sudden panic
that gripped her.

"Thanksgiving." Becca's mouth curved into a smile a

lot like her father's. "My dad said you were coming over for Thanksgiving dinner. Did he get that wrong?"

It hit Abby then that she was messing up her first interaction with Gray's daughter now they both knew Abby was set to become her stepmother.

Stepmother. The word had never seemed quite so heavy as it did then.

"Yes," she said, trying to sound as if she'd never heard of anything heavy in her life. "Tomorrow. He didn't get that wrong. I'm out of it today."

Abby wiped her hands on her apron, then indicated with the tilt of her head and a grateful smile that the barista next to her should take over. She walked out from behind the bar, smiled at Becca like the kind of mature and easy-tempered stepmother she hoped she would be, and led the teenager over to a table.

Not far from where Abby had sat with her father.

Except this time she might be even more nervous.

"I hope this is okay," Becca said as they both sat down, with a bright, wide smile that wasn't like Gray at all. "We got out of school early, and I thought it would be fun to swing by. I know we've met before, but, you know. This is different."

"I hope you're okay with this," Abby said. And then wished she hadn't, because what if she'd opened a door she wouldn't know how to close?

"I love Thanksgiving. The more, the merrier." Becca wrinkled her nose to show she was kidding. "And yes, I'm more than okay with it."

Something about that scraped at Abby, no matter how much she wanted to take it at face value. She tried to shove it aside. They'd all have ample time to get to know each other after Saturday, wouldn't they?

"I've never been anybody's stepmother before," she said

after a moment. "Between you and me, I don't want to mess it up."

Becca smiled at her again, and she suddenly looked so much like her mother it made Abby's breath catch. All that glossy dark hair cascading down her back. The flashing dark eyes, the graceful, easy smile. Abby had never seen pictures of Cristina as a teenager, but she would bet money she'd looked exactly like this.

She couldn't help but wonder if Gray saw a ghost when he looked his daughter.

Then hated herself for the thought. Gray saw his own daughter when he looked at Becca, she was sure. It was Abby who saw Cristina everywhere.

"It's going to be great," Becca told her in the same tone. It took Abby a moment to realize she sounded *determined*. "I've wanted my dad to get married again for a long time. And I'm so glad it's you, because I already know you. It would probably be weirder if it was a stranger."

Weirder, but not insurmountable. Noted. Becca clearly wanted him married. To anyone.

"Why do you want your dad to get married?" Abby heard herself ask, which was a prime example of bad stepmothering because she was so obviously fishing. But she couldn't seem to help herself.

"Because he's so lonely. Don't you think?"

"I think he's solitary," Abby said carefully. "But that's not the same thing."

Becca smiled again, and there was something about it that tugged at Abby. It was too practiced, maybe. Too studied. There was no fifteen-year-old girl on the planet who was *quite* so self-possessed with the random adults in her orbit. Especially when said adults were marrying into the family.

Not without reason, anyway. She couldn't think of very many good reasons.

"I know that sometimes stepparent things are, like, intense," Becca said. "I want you to know we're not going to have any friction. Not on my end."

"We're not? I mean, that's great."

"I want my dad to be happy, and if you make him happy, then I'm happy."

"That's a lot of happy," Abby said, taken aback. Though she couldn't put her finger on why.

"Great!" Becca sat back in her chair and almost looked . . . relieved. "Then I'll see you tomorrow at Thanksgiving. You're coming with your grandmother, right?"

"Yes." Abby tried out her own self-possessed smile and felt silly. "And maybe my mother too. If she shows up."

The smooth, happy smile that Becca was aiming across the table slipped. "Your mother?"

"I don't know if you've ever met my mother, because she certainly isn't one for visiting the neighbors. I can't remember."

"But isn't your mother . . ." Becca's voice cracked on that last word and her cheeks got red. "Well, I mean, I heard she was . . ."

"She's never had the best maternal instincts," Abby said judiciously. Because Becca was a fifteen-year-old. With her own mother issues. She didn't need Abby's on top of that. "But people change. In fairness, she could be waiting at home for me right now, filled with regret and desperate for my forgiveness. It's possible, right?"

"No." Becca's voice was flat, and there was no trace of a smile then, studied or otherwise. "It's not possible. People don't really change. Not that much."

"Hey." Abby wanted to reach over and grab the teenager's hand. She, who never wanted to grab anybody's hand for any reason. But she didn't know Becca that well and didn't want to start off this new relationship of theirs too oddly, so she settled for sliding her palm across the surface of the table and stopping halfway, to indicate that she would have reached farther. If she could. If they were different people. "Fifteen is young to write people off for good, isn't it?"

"Not really." Gone was the happy, outgoing, self-possessed creature who'd appeared at the coffee bar and asked for a meet-and-greet with her new almost-stepmother. And in her place was a child with a storm in her gaze and what Abby would have called too many bad experiences twisting her mouth. "Some people don't deserve forgiveness."

"Becca . . ." Abby began.

But it was as if a switch flipped. There was Christmas music playing and someone was crooning about snow and mistletoe. And Becca looked as if she took the caroling personally. Because she smiled again, even brighter than before, but Abby didn't buy it this time. Then she pushed back her chair and stood.

She was pretty like her mother, but that self-possession was all her father. Abby wondered if Gray's was as much an act as she suspected Becca's was. She filed that away as Becca zipped up the down parka that made her look waifish—instead of the marshmallow roll Abby resembled when she wore a parka—and tugged on a bright hat with a pom-pom on the top.

"I don't want to keep you," Becca said. "I know you're working. I only wanted to officially welcome you to the family and make sure you knew that was coming from me, not because my dad, like, forces me to do it tomorrow."

She offered an awkward, yet adorable little wave. Then

Abby watched Becca turn and head for the door, where a group of friends waited for her. The girl would be her stepdaughter come Saturday. They would be living together. And hopefully, Abby would find a way to be some kind of decent parental influence, whatever that looked like.

For the first time, the enormity of what she was preparing to do crushed Abby where she sat. The coffeehouse was hopping all around her, conversations rising and falling, the whir of the espresso machines and the squeals of small children. Abby was aware of all of it, yet somehow miles away at the same time.

What the hell was she doing?

Rae was absolutely right. She was crazy, at the very least, to consider signing herself up for the kind of torment it was going to be to be close to Gray, and yet as far away as ever. She couldn't pretend she wasn't afraid of exactly that.

Just as she couldn't pretend that she was only risking herself. There was Becca to consider.

Abby forced herself up and onto her feet, then worked the rest of her shift in a daze, not sure if she was grateful any longer that it didn't give her time to think.

She did the last of the Thanksgiving grocery shopping before she left town, and then drove out over the mountain. The fields opened up before her with only a few lights here and there, and she knew who'd lit every one of them.

It felt as good as peace.

She reminded herself she was choosing this. That there were people who married on a whole lot less than the number of things she and Gray shared, plus that one kiss.

That one, life-altering, utterly devastating kiss.

A few generations ago, there might have been even less than that. And somehow, the world had kept on turning, through mail-ordered brides and all manner of strangers getting together and making the best of things. There were human beings scattered all over the earth, and surely some huge percentage of them had to come from marriages a lot worse than the one Abby planned to have.

After all, she didn't have to be Becca's mother. She didn't have to fill the shoes of a dead woman it seemed Becca had no intention of forgiving for her sins. Abby could relate.

She could more than relate, especially when she made the turn off the county road and drove down the dirt lane to the farmhouse.

Abby blew out a harsh breath and stared at the strange car parked in the yard. It didn't matter that she'd never seen it before. That it was different from all the other cars she'd ever known her mother to drive, because the woman changed cars the way other people changed hairstyles.

She turned off the ignition and sat there a minute, trying to ignore the way her heartbeat hit so hard and so fast her ribs felt tight. She could remember all the other times she'd come home to find a strange vehicle in the same spot out back, and had been forced to face the fact that Lily was here again.

She remembered how excited she'd gotten when she was younger. How desperately she'd clung to the hope that her mother was back home to actually be a mother, for a change. As she'd gotten older, she got angrier—and more afraid that one of these times Lily might make Abby go away with her. She could remember, much too vividly, the time Lily had turned up for Christmas morning when Abby was just about Becca's age. Abby hadn't been able to control all the competing emotions that had buffeted her and her reward had been her own mother laughing and calling her a dumb country girl.

Abby had never showed Lily any emotion again.

"Not today, Satan," Abby muttered out loud in the car's interior.

She told herself she was made entirely of steel, like Gray, and climbed out of the car. She took her time getting the grocery bags together, and then she started toward the back door. The trouble was, she never knew what to expect. Lily didn't actually have to do anything to be the bogeyman. She just had to turn up.

Abby shoved her way in the back door and was surprised to find the kitchen empty. She slung all the shopping bags up onto the counter, shrugged out of her coat, and hung it on a peg by the door, then told herself there was no point hiding back here. It would only put off the inevitable.

She walked from the kitchen toward the front room, like she was headed toward her own execution. Which didn't even feel melodramatic.

When she got to the arched opening that separated the front room from the dining room, she stopped there. Grandma was sitting in her favorite chair, the way she always did. And Lily was perched where Gray had sat, there in Grandpa's old armchair, which was just . . . wrong.

But this was Lily. Wrong was probably the point.

No one bothered saying hello or making any small talk. Lily gazed at the daughter she'd never wanted, and Abby stared right back. She didn't dare look at her grandmother because she was afraid she would do something terrible if she did. Like burst into tears, when she'd vowed that she would never give her mother that kind of power over her again.

"Your grandmother tells me you're getting married," Lily said as if that was something Abby had been deliberately keeping from her. As if they chatted every day on the phone and Abby had neglected to pass on that information. "To one of those Everetts, apparently."

Abby didn't like the way she said that. *One of those Everetts*. As if Abby was a chip off the old block and scoured the earth for men to leech off of the way Lily did.

"Yes," she said. Because what else could she say?

"You grew up with the Everetts yourself, Lillian," Grandma said, in that particularly serene voice she used when she felt anything but.

That almost made Abby lose it. She hated the fact that Lily got under Grandma's skin so much it made her feel lightheaded.

"*Lily,* Mom. I've asked you to call me Lily for years now."

"You can call yourself anything you like," Grandma said in that same way. "But I'll call you the name I gave you the day you were born, thank you."

Lily's eyes were glittering with a fury she wasn't trying that hard to repress when she looked back. "You're very smart."

"Thank you." Abby knew perfectly well it wasn't a compliment. "That feels like an upgrade. Some people think of me more as a dumb country girl."

"My God." Lily let out a tinkling little laugh and settled back in Grandpa's chair as if she owned it. "Everything is so dire in this house. I don't know how you can live here. Of course it's smart to marry into that family with all the land they have. This is Colorado. Land is money."

"I'm pretty sure land is money everywhere," Abby said stiffly. "That's basically the entire history of the world in a nutshell."

"I knew you had to have a bit of me in there." Lily delivered another one of those laughs. "I'm glad to see I was right."

Abby didn't vomit right there on the carpet. She didn't even scowl. Instead, she looked at her mother like the stranger she was.

"I don't have a single shred of you in me."

And because Grandma was right there, she didn't add a hearty "hallelujah."

"If you say so," Lily said idly, but Abby was sure there was malice in her eyes. "How convenient you found the only single man around with thousands of acres of prime Angus beef to his name."

"I'm marrying somebody who lives here in Cold River," Abby retorted, something too thick and deep to be simple fury bubbling through her. "Someone who I've known for my entire life, because I also live here, and all that Everett land has been the view out my bedroom window since I graduated from a crib. I haven't run off anywhere. I'm not imagining I'm going to find a better life somewhere, like a pot of gold at the end of a rainbow. We're not similar at all, actually."

Lily smiled, and that was worse. "The difference between you and me, Abby, is that I know what I am. I'm not sneaky and deceitful. If it looks like you're a gold digger, you might as well admit it, because you better believe that's the only word anyone else is going to use."

"Lillian. That's enough."

"I call it like I see it, Mom." But Lily's gaze was on Abby. Waiting for something Abby refused to give her. She flatly refused.

"This is already a delight, as usual," Abby said with fake brightness to the room, while the phrase "gold digger" ricocheted around inside her like a terrible bullet, punching holes wherever it touched. Or maybe she was talking to the little girl tucked away inside of her who still had it in her to be surprised that her own mother was always, always . . . this. "Happy Thanksgiving to us."

9

Before it even started, Thanksgiving was not exactly the happy, carefree, and tensionless family gathering Gray had been imagining.

He had been sure that things would be fine, mostly because he wanted them to be. But also because this was the first year they'd get to experience the holiday without taking part in the Amos Everett show the way they usually did, like it or not. Thanks to Amos's usual behavior, Gray was fairly certain he and his brothers suffered from a kind of holiday-onset PTSD that started in late November and held on until well into the new year. Every year.

Not that their aversion to holidays with their father had prevented them from gathering together anyway, year after grim year, so Gray and Brady could stare at each other across the table while Amos and Ty got drunk. And then drunker still while all four of them played an extended game of chicken to see who would be the first to admit that these expected, unmissable family gatherings were . . . terrible.

All while Becca broke Gray's heart more and more each year by trying her hardest to make it all come together anyway like one of those Hallmark movies she sometimes insisted he watch with her. For the past few years she'd cooked the customary Thanksgiving dinner for the hands, then another dinner for family, and had focused on the whole production as if she expected to get graded on it.

"This will be great!" she told him that morning as she and Gray did a last clean of the house before company turned up. "And this year we don't need to worry about Grandad breaking anything!"

If Gray had any regrets, it was the fact he'd subjected his daughter to Amos in the first place—but he hadn't known how to avoid that.

"No one better break anything," he replied, and was startled when Becca came and put her hand on his arm.

"It's going to be *perfect*," she told him with a ferocity that made him blink while he was wiping down the table in the dining room they used twice a year for meals and all the rest of the time as Becca's desk for homework and her various projects. "Absolutely *perfect*."

He didn't ask her why she was so invested. He nodded and thought, not for the first time, that raising a daughter wasn't for the faint of heart. It was one more reason he was changing his life. He didn't want Becca's only family experiences to be his jackhole brothers and her drunk grandfather. He wanted to build a decent family life with someone as committed to that particular dream as he was. Someone who would, among other things, help him make sure a reign of terror like Amos's couldn't happen again.

Someone like Abby, he thought with satisfaction when he saw Martha's old red truck heading up his drive around three in the afternoon. He'd been out in the barn with the horses, but walked out and waited for the truck as it pulled up next to the house.

"You remember my daughter, Lillian," Martha said as she climbed to ground, as spry as if she were still in her fifties.

"Lily," corrected the woman who followed her—without offering her mother a helping hand, Gray noted. She was shorter than her mother and daughter, her eyes were already narrowed, and she was hollow-cheeked in that way they always were in places like Vail, where people's goals included looking well-manicured in fur-trimmed jackets with ski pants on while porters tended to their boots before they hit the slopes. She made Gray want to roll around in the dirt. And when she smiled at him, it was only her lips that moved. Faintly. "And I remember you, of course."

There was something about the way she said *of course* that Gray didn't like, but this was Thanksgiving and he had his own family issues, even without Amos's dark presence. He didn't need to involve himself in any Douglas family tensions.

He tipped his hat to Lily without comment. But his eyes were on Abby as she came around the side of the truck, a huge platter in her arms with tinfoil stretched across the top of a sizeable turkey. She walked to him and stopped, almost as if it was a habit to come straight to him when he knew it wasn't.

Not yet, he told himself. *But soon. Very soon.*

Gray took the platter from her without a word, and something warm moved inside him when she blinked at that, then smiled at him as if he'd given her something pretty instead of taken something heavy.

All those practical reasons he'd chosen her faded away, because her face opened up when she smiled. Or it did when she smiled at him. And for a moment Gray forgot everything. His brothers. His cattle. The stack of paperwork on his desk he needed to get through before morning if he wanted to stay on top of it, and the endless fallout from Amos's bad choices and debts that he was still uncovering.

All of that just . . . went away.

For a moment, Abby was a part of the great stillness he loved so much. The majestic sweep of quiet peaks to soft fields that were as much a part of Gray as his own bones.

Like she was home.

Gray was suddenly, uncomfortably aware of his own arousal—especially when his kid was standing in the doorway only a few yards behind him, exclaiming over Martha Douglas's contributions to the meal and greeting the infamous Lily in a slightly more subdued tone.

"You sure you're up for this?" he asked Abby in a low voice, out there by the truck where it was only the two of them.

"The question isn't if I'm up for it," Abby said, in that way he recognized from all those phone calls they'd been having. As if, left to her own devices, she would tip over into laughter in a moment but was holding it back to be polite. There was a dent in her cheek he hadn't noticed before and now couldn't look away from. "The question is whether you're ready for the Lily Douglas holiday tornado. Highlights usually include people storming from rooms, vows never to repeat the experience, and her nastiest quotes ringing in your ears for the next five years like a hangover."

By the time she finished, she didn't look as if she was on the verge of laughter any longer. And that clawed at Gray like it was something inside him, trying to get out. But he didn't know what to say. And his hands were full or he'd—

"Get a room, lovebirds," Ty drawled at them as he ambled across the yard toward the back door, a whiskey bottle hanging from his fingers and that careless smile of his across his face.

Abby's cheeks flooded with color, and Gray wanted to hit something. Ty, preferably.

But if he hit anyone as much as he thought about hitting his brothers, they'd all be pulverized by now. That was his father in him. That dark shadow deep in there he knew better than to let out, no matter how he sometimes daydreamed about giving into his violent impulses. He ignored it again now, following Abby into the kitchen and setting the platter on the counter next to the oven Becca had already fired up to Martha's specifications, aware that she didn't make eye contact with him again.

This Thanksgiving he'd wanted was happening, like it or not.

Gray watched Martha Douglas bustle around, taking over his kitchen with her usual brusque efficiency. He watched Lily look around his house with an expression that suggested she smelled something vaguely unpleasant, then settle herself next to Ty and his personal whiskey bottle out in the living room.

Ty was already drunk, of course. The kind of drunk that made Gray wonder exactly how many days in a row he'd been drinking without coming up for air. And if this was the kind of problem Gray should jump in and try to solve.

The fact that Ty was neither sloppy nor mean when drunk, like their father had been, didn't make him feel better. Especially not when Ty and Lily started sharing that bottle. Gray found himself sitting in his own living room wondering why he kept imagining that if he could only arrange the right set of people around him, this family thing would work out the way he wanted it to. No drama. No whiskey raging down the length of the house. No whispering in corners over a bottle in a way that could only cause trouble.

Abby and Becca walked into the living room from the far side some time later, suggesting that they'd been deeper in the house.

"I gave Abby the grand tour," Becca announced. She was talking too fast, too bright, the way she did when she was nervous, but Gray figured that was fair enough on a high pressure Thanksgiving with a brand new stepmother on the way. "I can't believe you didn't, Dad. Were you going to wait until she moved in?"

Any tour Gray gave Abby would end in an extremely non-family-friendly manner, and it took a lot to keep from saying that.

"I figured she could sleep outside for a while, until she got the hang of the routine here," he said. "It's not *too* cold in the barn."

Becca rolled her eyes at Abby. "I *think* he's kidding. He always claims any dog we have will be an outside pet, and then they always end up inside living like kings. And usually sleep in his bed."

She didn't wait for a response. She charged into the kitchen, leaving Abby standing there before Gray, her cheeks warm and those eyes of hers dancing as they both imagined sleeping in Gray's bed. Or he hoped that's what she was imagining because he sure was.

"Here's hoping I get treated as well as the average dog," she said, her voice filled with the suppressed laughter that made Gray want to . . . do things.

He didn't do them. One more reason to rethink this whole Thanksgiving deal.

"This was my dad's house," he told her instead, feeling

nothing but awkward as he spoke. "He was responsible for how it looks. But you can do whatever you want to it."

Abby gazed around as if she hadn't seen the living room before, with its comfortable old leather couches and the fireplace at one end. She looked as if she was about to say something, but then her attention landed on Ty and Lily. Ty was kicked back in his seat, his legs stretched out onto the ottoman, the picture of lazy ease. It was Lily who'd gone and perched on the leather footstool, her hip a scant inch from one of Ty's legs. It was Lily who was leaning in much too close to a man who could be her son.

And it was Abby who looked like someone had reached out and slapped her.

"I can break that up," Gray promised her in a low voice. "Right now, if you want."

Abby took a moment to focus on him, and when she did, the smile she aimed at him made something in him ache. "If there's one thing I've learned from the holidays over the years with my mother, it's that not every train wreck is mine to prevent."

She left Gray with that, following Becca into the kitchen.

All he could see then were train wrecks. Whatever the hell was going on with Ty that left him deep in a bottle and impossible to pin down on any subject at all. Abby's mother, who clearly had her own agenda. Then there was Brady, who was pissed about everything and happy to let everyone around him know it however he could. From his unsolicited critiques of the Broncos' performance this football season to comments about the weather over in all those famous ski resorts no one in Cold River cared about, Brady was prepared to dig in and argue *everything* to the death.

Gray's death, apparently.

But then, Gray had expected Brady and all his nonsense. If he didn't feel the need to throw in a comment about what a drag ranch life was every three minutes, Gray might have even found it . . . nostalgic, almost.

"Why are you staring at me like that?" Brady demanded at the end of another rant about . . . something.

So, yeah. Gray wasn't feeling nostalgic after all.

"Sometimes I think you complain about every damn thing because you're afraid if you don't, you might actually like it here," Gray said, without thinking it through. "And then what will you do with yourself?"

Well, what the hell, he thought, maybe too defensively, as Brady's jaw clenched tight. *Why not?*

"I don't hate it here," Brady gritted out. Gray got the impression he was trying not to snap back the way he normally would. The magic of Thanksgiving at work, clearly. "But there are better ways to spend your days than working on land that's never going to give you anything back. Or care if you live or die."

"Do big, bad cities like Denver care if you live or die? It must be my rural, uneducated ignorance talking here that I didn't know that."

"It's land, Gray." Brady held his gaze. "It's not a life."

Gray might have gone after that, but it was a freaking family holiday and he didn't want to scare Abby off. He stood instead, moving over toward the makeshift bar Ty and Brady had set up on the side table because neither one of them wanted to walk a few more feet into the kitchen if they needed a drink.

Gray wasn't much of a drinker, but it wouldn't be the worst thing in the world to blur his edges before he lost his cool when there wasn't any food on the table yet. Amos had always waited for the actual food to come to flip his lid, and sometimes the table with it, the better to ruin everyone's appetite as well as the holiday. And Gray was nothing if not a stickler for tradition.

He smelled perfume, floral and cloying, and in the next second, Lily Douglas was right there beside him. A little too close beside him.

"Gray Everett," she purred at him, filling up a glass with white wine Gray was certain she didn't need. "   grown up handsome?"

A lot like one of those women Gray had gone out of his way not to meet in a sleazy bar somewhere. As if her daughter, the woman he was marrying in two days, wasn't in the next room cooking for them.

Gray fixed her with the kind of blank look he usually saved for unscrupulous bankers, which was to say all bankers, and then excused himself.

But he watched her. She had too much to drink with Ty, then even more all by herself when Ty roused himself to help Becca set the table, and Gray figured she'd decided that gave her license to let loose when they finally all sat down. A snide comment here, a sly sort of smile there, just to liven up the festivities.

Mashed potatoes couldn't make it down the table without a comment about "stick-to-your-ribs farm dinners." The stuffing, which made Gray want to weep with joy though he would never actually do that kind of thing, made Lily muse about fitting into her high school jeans. Loudly.

Gray would have ignored her entirely because she appeared to be talking to herself, but Abby stopped eating. She bowed her head and stared at her plate instead. Gray watched color stain her ears and had to talk himself out of throwing a few choice words Lily's way. Lily was her mother, he reminded himself.

He didn't get mouthy with people's mothers *no* matter how drunk they were at his table.

And no matter how wide his own daughter's eyes were as she looked back and forth between Abby and Lily.

"I can't tell you how grateful we are," Lily cooed when everyone except Abby had stuffed themselves silly on Martha's good cooking and were sitting around the table, trying to breathe.

"Grateful?" Abby asked, her voice tight and her gaze still on her plate. "You? Are you sure that's the right word?"

Lily ignored her daughter. She leaned forward, her smile like a razor and aimed straight at Gray. "Here between family, I know it's all right to say that no one expected our Abby to catch any man's notice."

Lily let out a peal of laughter to go along with the scorn in her voice and didn't seem to know—or care—that no one was laughing with her.

"Lillian Douglas." Martha sounded tired and, for once, as old as her years. "You know full well this isn't the time or place."

"What?" Lily asked, smirking as she sat back in her chair, a triumphant look on her face that Gray couldn't read. But he knew he didn't like it. "You might not be grateful, but I am. It kept me up nights, wondering what would become of her."

"*Stop*," Becca whispered harshly from beside Gray. It was a sound he'd never heard her make.

But before he could react to it, there was a scraping sound. It took him a second to realize that it was Abby, pushing back her chair and getting to her feet.

She looked pale. But strong. She stared down at her mother for a moment, then shifted her gaze to Gray.

"It's only going to go downhill from here," she said quietly. Steadily. "And here's a spoiler alert. It always goes downhill."

She didn't wait for him to answer or for Lily to laugh at her some more. She walked stiffly from the room.

Becca was gaping at Gray like she expected him to fix everything. Brady was glaring across the table as if Lily was his next rant. Even Ty was frowning, suggesting something had finally penetrated his whiskey haze. But Gray didn't need any help getting his temper up—he needed to make sure he didn't lose it and make everything Amos-level worse.

He stared at Lily. Lillian. Whatever the hell she called herself.

"You're a guest in my house," he said quietly, and for once Brady didn't break in to argue whose house it was. "A house that's going to be Abby's before Sunday. And I don't care who you are. If you talk to her like that again beneath this roof, you're going to have to leave and you won't be welcome back."

He found himself up and on his feet, looking in the kitchen for Abby. But she wasn't there. He wondered if she'd headed upstairs or into the living room, but then he saw flash of movement at the corner of his eye, through the kitchen windows, and realized she'd headed out into the yard.

Without a coat when the temperature had been dropping all day.

He grabbed his off the peg, and an extra fleece. He walked outside and breathed in the wind that rushed straight down from the snowcapped mountaintops, filling his lungs and clearing his head. He shrugged into his jacket as he moved, keeping his gaze on Abby. She'd stopped at the fence next to the barn and was already shivering, her arms wrapped around her, trying to warm herself up when she was only wearing the thin layer of the pretty shirt she had on.

Gray stopped next to her and settled the fleece on her shoulders. Hesitantly, like she was one of the jumpy, nervous animals he spent so much of his life trying to soothe. But she didn't try to bite or kick at him. She threaded her arms through the fleece's sleeves and zipped it all the way up to her chin.

They stood there together out in the wind and quiet, staring out at the winter fields through the falling dark.

"Well," Abby said after a while, with a kind of pointed brightness that seemed to wedge its way between Gray's ribs and stick there, "that was humiliating."

"She always like that?"

Abby made a noise that could have been a sigh. Or a sob. Or anything in between. "No. Sometimes she's much worse. Believe it or not, she was on her best behavior for you today."

Gray was no good at talking. He was no good at digging around in emotions and finding the right words. But he hated feeling helpless, especially when he could tell that Abby wasn't only upset—she was trying her best to hide it.

He didn't know why that about killed him.

"Hey." He reached over and took her shoulders in his hands, turning her to face him. And then he didn't let go the way he should have. "The only thing that matters is you and me. Not what anyone else says or thinks or does."

Her mouth trembled, and he would have liked a punch to the face a lot more. He wouldn't have felt it shatter its way around inside of him. He wouldn't have *felt* it like this.

"I don't . . ." She swallowed, and Gray was lost somewhere between her too-bright eyes and that mouth. She was looking at him like he could either pick up the planet and carry it around with him, or break her in two. And like she had no idea which way he was going to go. "I never wanted you, of all people, to hear the things she says about me."

"I don't care what other people say, Abby. I care what I think."

"She wears people down. It's her gift. You have no idea what she can—"

"All she is to me is the woman who had you and left you with your grandmother a long time ago," Gray interrupted gruffly. "What can she do? And why would I listen to a word she says?"

"I don't know." She looked small then. Or miserable, maybe. Her gaze got brighter, and that pointed, wedged thing in Gray's ribs started to ache. Especially when her voice broke. "Maybe you should. Maybe she's right."

Gray was aware of the wind and the crisply sweet scent of impending snow. He could smell the earth beneath him, the horses and the barn, but better than all of that was Abby and the way she looked there, zipped up in a fleece that had once belonged to Ty or Brady. It was much too big, and she was everything he'd wanted and nothing he'd expected, and he didn't recognize the urge that made him hold her shoulders tighter.

On the other hand, he had no trouble recognizing the need that rolled through him, pooling heavily in his sex. More than that, he understood that if he didn't taste her again, right now, he was going to lose it in a way that had nothing to do with the temper he was determined to keep locked down tight.

Gray pulled her closer and liked the way her expression changed. Her gaze heated and that flush warmed her cheeks again.

And when he lowered his mouth to hers, she met him. She was hot and yielding, sweet and *right*. She surged up on her toes, and he felt her hands on his stomach where he hadn't closed his coat.

He remembered that kiss in her grandmother's house like it had been in black and white, but this was all color, bright and wild.

And he wanted more.

He wanted everything.

Gray angled his head, and everything was hotter. Fire and need, and a longing so pure and so intense he might explode with it.

He wrapped her in his arms and bent her back, unable to get close enough. He wanted her naked. He wanted her beneath him, above him.

God, the ways he wanted her, shooting through him like wildfire and clouding his head.

He backed her into the fence and fit himself between her legs, leaning a bit so he could get himself where he wanted to be, cradled between her thighs.

Abby moaned against his mouth, and Gray shoved aside that last tiny part of him that tried to whisper that there was something bizarre about the fact it was *Abby Douglas* who was lighting him up like this.

She was everything he wanted. She was so much more than he'd imagined.

He laughed when she gasped as his hand found its way beneath her fleece and shirt.

"Too cold?" he asked.

"Uh. Not cold at all." Her face reddened, her lips were full from his, and Gray had no idea how he wasn't inside her. "Just . . . new."

He kissed her again, deeper and harder, and traced a lazy little pattern right there above the waistband of her jeans. This way, then that. Just his rough fingertips against the impossible satin of her belly.

And he could taste the way she shook. He could feel it.

He pulled his mouth from hers while all the need and chaos clamoring inside him was still this side of manageable.

"We're outside. In full view of the house where my daughter and your grandmother are." He gritted the words out. And had to bite back a groan when Abby opened her eyes, and he could see they were a dazed dark gold that made him feel like a god. A god who was so hungry for her that he seriously debated carrying her off to the barn right here and now.

"Not to mention your brothers," she said, as if she was coming back to him from far, far away.

"I try not to think about my brothers. And it would be okay with me if you never did, especially at a moment like this."

Her smile was so big and so wide then, he thought it might dwarf the mountains all around them. He didn't realize he was smiling too until she reached up and touched his jaw as if she'd never seen anything like it. He knew the feeling.

Gray pulled his hand away from her soft belly and wrapped it around hers.

"Come on," he said, his voice too rough and that powerful need making his knees want to bend. "We need to go back inside before we . . . don't."

Abby didn't move. "Would it be a bad thing if we . . . didn't?"

Gray was tormented with scorching hot visions of what he could do in that barn. All the ways he could feast on this woman, making Thanksgiving look like a light snack in comparison—

"No," he said. As much to himself as to her. "I don't want our first time to have anything to do with your mother.

want it to have everything to do with you. With me. With us. We're getting married in two days. We can wait and do it properly."

Abby frowned at him, her face still flushed and her mouth still soft, and it might have been the cutest thing Gray had ever seen.

"What if I don't want to wait?" she demanded in a voice he could only call sulky.

He shouldn't have liked that. Yet he wanted nothing more than to pull her close and eat her alive. And this time, he could feel his own smile as he looked at her.

"Abby Douglas," he drawled in mock outrage. "I'll thank you to respect my virtue."

"I don't see why you holding onto your virtue trumps my wanting to get rid of mine," she retorted. "Right now."

He wasn't sure he saw either. But he reminded himself he had a houseful of people, including an impressionable teenager and at least two drunk family members. They'd be married soon enough.

Even if two days currently felt like centuries.

"Because I'm bigger than you, and I say so."

Her frown deepened, but it only made Gray laugh. He pulled her close again and kissed her, hard. She sighed at that, there against his mouth, but when he pulled back her face had softened.

"You'll make it," he told her, and he was buzzing with all that need and desire, mixed in with a kind of hope he was afraid to look at too closely. Could things really be this good? Was this truly going to work out the way he'd been half-afraid to imagine it could? "And I'll make up for this, I promise."

All that heat was in her eyes when she slowly smiled back at him, that flush he was quickly becoming obsessed with making her cheeks glow.

"I'm going to hold you to that," she said, quiet and deliciously needy.

Making him wonder how the hell he was going to make it through the rest of the day, much less to Saturday.

10

It seemed to take whole years, long and torturous ones, but Saturday finally came.

Abby had spent late Thursday night and all of Friday packing up her things. She'd never moved anywhere before, and she found the process of going through everything she'd collected over the course of her thirty years as daunting as it was fascinating. Why had she kept every note she'd passed to Hope and Rae in class? Why had she carefully assembled boxes full of her old stuffed animals? And did she need to carry them with her into her new life?

"You don't have to decide whether to take it or trash it today," Grandma had said on Friday morning when Abby had come down into the kitchen for more garbage bags. "This house isn't going anywhere. You can leave things here if you like."

"We're only supposed to keep things that bring us joy. Not store them away in the attic because we don't know why we have them."

Grandma had gazed at Abby for a moment over the coupons she liked to clip and save, yet always forgot to use. "If *things* are what bring you joy, Abigail, you can expect precious little of it."

That stuck with Abby as she finally unburdened herself of the clothes she was never going to fit in or like enough to wear more than once a year. And she'd put a name to that fizzy, almost-uncomfortable feeling in her gut. It was hopeful. It was . . . longing, maybe. It was as close to joy as she knew how to get.

Because, yes, she was marrying a man she'd known all her life and yet didn't really know at all. But there was the kissing to consider.

Different from the way he'd kissed her here in the farm-house. Different but better. Hotter.

Abby wasn't entirely certain how she'd survived it. The whole thing seemed like a dream—the kind of dream she'd had a lot, actually. Lily's usual behavior over the Thanks-giving table, Abby's decision to walk away rather than en-gage, but instead of the usual, unsatisfying conclusion to interactions with her mother, Gray had been there to sweep it away. To make it better, simply because he was . . . him.

Solid. Sure.

That would have been enough. If all Gray had done was make sure she was warm and stand there with her a while, out by the fence with that sweeping view across the Ever-ett fields, it would have been more than enough. Abby would have held that, warm and sweet, inside her. Maybe forever.

But he hadn't stopped there.

With every box or bag she'd taken downstairs since those deliriously hot moments out in the cold with him, she'd run the gauntlet of her mother's snide comments. Lily had set herself up in the front room, likely because it allowed her to watch the comings and goings of everyone in the house, and had taken the opportunity to work her usual magic.

"I want to come back in my next life as a husky, giant

farm girl," she said once, not glancing up from the phone she kept in her hand at all times.

Because she loved nothing more than to comment on Abby's weight and build—though she never used those words, of course. Or said anything directly.

Lily lived for plausible deniability.

But Abby had Gray now, impossible as it still was to believe. She'd felt the way his hard hands had curved around her shoulders. The way he'd looked at her, stern on the surface and that other, warmer thing beneath.

I don't care what other people say, he'd told her. *I care what I think.*

And then he'd kissed her silly.

The more boxes Abby piled on the sun porch to move over to Gray's house that weekend, the more Lily felt the need to muse loudly about things like the way everything smelled like manure out here in the boonies, especially the people. Or how she could never tolerate the lack of sophistication out in these fields, but she knew some simple women enjoyed being stashed away in a barn while their men found more invigorating company in town.

But the more Abby bit her tongue and thought about Gray—being near Gray, looking at Gray, touching Gray, *kissing Gray*—the less those comments seemed to sting.

Then it was Saturday at last. And she was standing in the childhood bedroom that no longer looked like hers after she'd emptied it of all her things. She climbed into the simple gown she planned to wear to the courthouse to become a wife—*Gray's wife*—and her mouth still didn't feel like hers.

She could see her hands in the mirror and knew she wasn't shaking, so she didn't know why it felt like she was anyway. Like there was a trembling thing lodged deep inside of her that made it hard to pull in a breath. Because even that shook.

Still, she wasn't scared at all. The way maybe she should have been.

She was . . . excited. Probably more hopeful than was wise. She concentrated on that fizzy, buoyant feeling and told herself it was as real as she made it.

Because she was ready.

She was ready to marry Gray. She was ready to be a wife and maybe someday a mother. She was ready to change her life in every conceivable way with this one, possibly lunatic act.

She wasn't sure she cared how crazy it was. She knew every nook and cranny of her life as it was now and she didn't hate it, but she also knew that it would be exactly the same ten years from now if she didn't do something to change it.

Abby wanted to change. She wanted to see if she *could* change.

And she really, really wanted to kiss Gray some more.

When she was dressed, she made her way down the stairs from her bedroom for the last time as a single woman, wishing she didn't have to go through this part. She could already hear her mother's voice in her head, and she felt herself stiffening with every step—

"Surprise!"

Hope's voice there at the bottom of the stairs didn't make sense. Abby blinked as she took the last few steps, but the vision didn't go away. Hope and Rae were standing there in the arched opening to the front room, grinning wildly at her. And more than that, dressed in matching navy dresses.

Abby blinked again, but this time, to keep herself from tearing up.

"You said you didn't want bridesmaids," Rae said through her smile. "And we absolutely listened to you."

"Of course, we listened to you," Hope agreed staunchly. "That's why we're here as your chauffeurs, nothing more." She waved a hand over her dress, then Rae's matching one. "As you can see, we're wearing the appropriate uniforms to perform this necessary duty on this, your special day."

Abby's eyes filled again, and blinking didn't do a thing to stop it. She didn't know whether she was smiling or crying, or maybe both.

But it didn't matter, because they were all hugging each other, tight and familiar. If this wasn't the kind of occasion that called for the sort of group hug they would normally avoid like the plague, nothing was.

When they pulled away, Abby saw that her friends' eyes were suspiciously bright too.

"I'm so glad you're here," she whispered fiercely.

"Of course we're here," Rae replied instantly, in the same tone.

"Especially with the gorgon in town," Hope added.

And, being Hope, didn't bother keeping her voice down.

Abby opted not to look past them to see whether her mother—coiled in Grandpa's chair the way she always was, because she loved nothing more than making her petty little statements from the very place Grandpa had always dispensed his measured, calm wisdom—had heard.

Her heart was flipping over and over in her chest in a way that she would have worried was unhealthy on any other day. Today, she suspected it was merely that same fizzy joy.

Excitement. Anticipation. Worry mixed together with hope.

All of the above.

Grandma took a few pictures of the three of them and waved them off as they'd piled into Rae's rattley old truck the way they'd done hundreds upon hundreds of times before.

It could have been any Saturday from back in high school. The three of them on a bright morning, sharing that long drive into town. Abby sat in the back and gazed out the windows as Rae drove too fast down the county road. She stared out at the fields she knew so well, in all seasons.

She was leaving these fields for the last time as Abby Douglas, resident vestal virgin of Cold River and the surrounding valley. She would return to them as Gray Everett's wife, and there was something in her that didn't know whether to mourn the loss or celebrate the change.

Both, she was sure. *It could be both.*

She could already feel homesick for the easy, comfortable routines of her grandmother's house even as she was excitedly looking forward to a new life in that ranch house Becca had showed her, room by painstaking room.

Including the one she'd be sharing with Gray.

The feeling that moved through her *glowed*, then rode that same internal shiver down to lodge between her legs.

Hope and Rae were bickering good-naturedly over the music the way they'd been doing since they were all ten years old. Abby tried to school her expression into something that didn't scream *Gray's bedroom, Gray's bed, Gray's body* when Hope turned around in her seat to stare at Abby in the back.

Over and over again.

"You're making me self-conscious," Abby complained after approximately the fifty-fifth time.

"I can't help it. You're beautiful."

Abby knew that wasn't true. But today, in a car with her

closest friends on her way to marry the man she'd loved forever, she let it slide.

More than that, she allowed herself to imagine that maybe, just today, it could be a little bit true.

It seemed to take no time at all before they were winding their way down into Cold River. It was one of Colorado's bright blue days that looked as if it might shatter if the wind picked up. And the sunshine made it look a whole lot warmer than it really was.

Abby was usually cold, especially as the winter weather moved in, but today she couldn't seem to be anything but boiling hot.

As if she were already someone else.

"Are you ready to marry Gray Everett?" Rae asked as she sped toward the river. "Are you ready to become Mrs. Gray Everett, at last?"

"Abby is a modern woman, Rae," Hope chided her. "You don't know what name she's going to choose. Or use."

"She used to doodle *Mrs. Gray Everett* all over her notebooks in eighth grade," Rae retorted. "I feel like she made this choice a long time ago."

"Family names are very important, loaded choices in a woman's life," Hope said loftily, as if she'd dedicated her life to studying the issue of surnames despite only ever having the one herself. "I don't want you to pressure her."

Rae's response to that was typically profane, if more muted than usual because she was pulling up in front of the courthouse.

As her friends continued to argue—with their typical laughter and obvious enjoyment of each other, but it was still an argument—over what Abby might or might not call herself in a few hours, Abby looked out the front window of the truck.

Her heart kicked at her. Hard.

Because Gray was there.

Waiting.

And when relief flooded her at the sight of him standing tall and strong and utterly still at the top of the stairs, Abby understood that despite all those boxes she'd packed and carried down the stairs, and despite the way he kissed her on Thanksgiving that had kept her going for the past two days, some part of her had expected him to change his mind. To come to his senses.

But there he was.

He looked better than any dream she could have conjured up. He wore a dark jacket over a button-down shirt that clung to the chest she'd felt pressed against her, too briefly, out there in his yard. His belt buckle looked polished, and he was wearing his darkest jeans. And his boots and his Stetson, in case she'd forgotten that every inch of him was a cowboy.

Her cowboy.

Because before noon, she was going to be his wife. Abby's heart might actually burst wide open. It was possible it already had.

"You guys are the best chauffeurs ever," she said, cutting off Hope arguing about medieval property rights, of all things, "but you're missing the most important part of this ride."

"If you mean Hope's inability to admit other people might have a point of view just as valid as hers," Rae said hotly, "even if she doesn't agree with them, I'm with you."

But Hope followed Abby's gaze through the front window and up the steps to the courthouse doors.

"She doesn't mean that at all," Hope said, her smile widening.

Rae swiveled forward to look, and for moment, all three

of them sat there in the truck, gazing out the window at Gray.

Abby felt that slipping, nostalgic sensation again, as if this were one of the thousands of times in their past the three of them had sat somewhere and done exactly this. Because they had. All over Cold River and the surrounding valleys, including those shameful years when they'd conducted embarrassing drive-bys out in the fields to see if they could spot Gray working on one of his fences.

Preferably without a shirt.

"Well," Rae said after a moment, her voice thick, "who doesn't love a happy ending?"

Abby leaned over the seat and stuck her head between her two friends. She looked back and forth between them and did her best not to be the one who let her tears spill over. Again.

But it was close.

"I know you guys think this is a bad idea," she said softly. "I'm not sure I disagree with you, to be honest. But the fact that you're willing to come with me and act like it's nothing but happy endings and dreams come true means more to me than I could ever say."

"If you make me ruin my eyeliner, I will kill you," Rae whispered fiercely, blinking furiously.

"That's our job, Abby," Hope said. "One we will always do, no matter what. Believe it."

Abby took a deep breath. And somehow she kept herself from tipping over into the great sob that was expanding in her chest, tempting her to lose it completely.

But she was getting married because she was practical, not emotional. She doubted Gray would be impressed if she fell out of the truck in a sea of tears. So she pulled herself together and pushed open the door, then stepped down out of Rae's truck with as much grace as she could muster. Only then did she head for the man who waited there for her.

For *her*.

And Abby knew she wasn't beautiful. She'd been plain every day of her life and in case she'd been tempted to forget it, Lily had made her disappointment in her only child's looks clear over the past couple of days.

The word "plodding" had been used. Repeatedly.

She knew she wasn't beautiful, and she told herself that didn't matter to her, because it shouldn't. It had nothing to do with her life. It had nothing to do with this wedding.

Still, there was something about the way Gray's gaze locked on her when she started toward him. The way his dark green eyes lit when he saw her, then held.

Abby knew perfectly well she would never, ever be beautiful, but today she was wearing a long white dress. She had her hair down around her shoulders, and Grandma had helped her curl it, with a whole lot more patience than Abby had ever lavished on herself or her looks.

She might never be beautiful, not really, but she thought *this is what it feels like*.

Especially when Gray met her halfway down the steps, took her hand in his, and stood there for a moment.

As if it wasn't twenty-nine degrees. As if they had all the time in the world, out here on a breathlessly cold November morning with the sun dancing over the river and shaking the bare tree branches.

"Are you ready?" he asked.

Abby wanted to wrap herself up in Gray's voice. Rough and low, all drawl. All cowboy.

"I'm ready," she said.

She didn't tell him she'd been ready for years.

"I see you brought some witnesses," he continued, and

Abby felt her face go red, the way it seemed to do every thirty seconds around this man.

"I'm sorry. I know we agreed to keep it small, but—"

"I brought one myself," Gray said, in that soothing way of his that made Abby want to do something horrifying, like purr. "Becca read me the riot act. She's turning into a little general."

But he grinned while he said it.

That was how, even though Abby had agreed to a wedding ceremony that was purely municipal, because this marriage was supposed to be only practical, they ended up with a small crowd.

Abby couldn't say she minded. It felt right that she had her friends and Gray had his daughter as they did this thing. Colorado allowed couples to marry themselves, but neither one of them had wanted that. Or, it turned out, to do the courthouse thing alone.

"I asked your grandmother," Becca whispered to Abby in the courthouse hallway as they waited their turn. She was wearing a dress too and had obviously taken time with the braids she'd put into her hair and made into a kind of crown. "She said she had her hands full already, and that she trusted me to take pictures. So don't worry. I will."

Abby didn't know whether her grandmother had meant her hands were full with Lily, or with the reception Martha had decided she was throwing whether Abby liked it or not. Who argued with Martha Douglas when she was on a tear?

Way back when, Grandma had babysat for Douglas Fowler, the patriarch of the Fowler family who had owned and operated the Grand Hotel that had been standing on the corner of Main Street and River Road since there'd been nothing to the town besides a feed store and a few big dreamers. She'd informed Abby that it took her a single phone call to secure a big enough room so Martha could invite the whole town to her only grandchild's wedding reception.

There had been no real response Abby could give but a thank you.

"I trust you to be an excellent photographer," Abby assured Becca and watched the girl bloom a bit as if Abby had showered her with praise. It made her want to keep doing it.

But they were being called in. Gray was taking her hand again, warm and sure. Her friends were behind her, and Becca was looking at her with almost too much delight to bear.

Now that it was finally happening, Abby would have given anything to slow down again. She wanted to lose herself in each moment. The things she had to sign. The way they stood in the fussy room with its Colorado flag, drenched in the sharp sunlight from outside. She wanted to linger over every vow Gray repeated in his uncompromising way, as if he was making it law. She wanted to stretch out in the words she said in return. Love. Honor. She wanted to stop time, standing there in front of a judge with so many smiles at her back she was sure she could feel them holding her up.

But it went so fast.

Her heart was beating wildly in her chest as Gray took her hand in his and slid a gold band into place on her left ring finger.

Abby said, "I do."

And just like that, she was Gray's wife.

She stared at the ring on her hand, trying to make sense of it, but couldn't. Then Gray's hand was on her jaw, tipping her chin up to angle her face toward his. And he settled his mouth on hers once more.

This part felt real. That hard, hot punch of heat. The way the touch of his lips rolled all throughout her body, making her ache. Making her long for more.

Making her forget where she was.

Her ears were ringing, but then she realized that it was their witnesses. Hope, Rae, and Becca, cheering for them.

Hope and Rae started talking about getting over to the Grand Hotel, but Abby couldn't seem to catch a full breath. And she couldn't tear her eyes away from Gray.

She loved the way his eyes crinkled in the corners. She loved the way his hard mouth curved—and if she wasn't mistaken, even more than it had a few weeks ago, when he'd made his outrageous proposal in Grandma's living room.

He'd dropped his hand from her face, but he kept hold of her hand.

She could touch him now, she marveled. Whenever she liked. His hand was wrapped around hers, and no one would glance at it twice, not anymore.

They were married. It was done.

Which meant the only thing left of this quick wedding of theirs—before they started their actual marriage and got into all those big life changes Abby was almost fully certain she was ready for, as practical and levelheaded as she was meant to be—was the wedding night.

The one thing she didn't feel practical or levelheaded about at all, no matter what she might have said on Thanksgiving.

11

After the ride over from the courthouse in Gray's truck with Becca talking excitedly from the back and leaning forward to show Abby photos every few seconds, Abby and her new family—a word that seemed to sit like a smooth, sweet stone in her gut as she considered it—walked into Cold River's Grand Hotel together.

The Old West landmark still maintained its nineteenth-century splendor. There were bright chandeliers, glorious moldings, and embossed ceilings. Abby knew the back bar had been imported from the east by wagon and that robber barons and copper kings had spent their nights here when the hills of Cold River had been rumored to hold more gold than Breckenridge. The fanciest parties in town had been thrown here then, and they still were.

But the kinds of parties that happened here these days would have made Abby feel like an alien, if she'd ever been invited. The hotel had made a name for itself as a destination wedding jewel, bringing in trade from Denver brides who wanted a touch of Colorado's Old West history in a charming, accessible mountain setting.

"This isn't really my style," she said nervously as Gray led her through the lobby, under paintings of famous outlaws and former local heroes alike, toward the grand ballroom Abby had only been in once before. For a charity auction. She'd put down what she'd felt was a generous fifty dollars on a local painting that had been auctioned off for thousands.

"It could be *my* style," Becca said from beside her.

Abby was a coward because she focused on smiling at Becca and not whatever Gray might feel about this place as a location for the reception he hadn't wanted. She was terrified he would judge her as the kind of person who thought she belonged in the Grand Hotel—

He married you all of fifteen minutes ago, she told herself, the voice in her head sounding as brusque and matter-of-fact as her grandmother's. *Even if he thinks you're a princess, he's not going to divorce you tonight.*

Gray pushed through the doors to the ballroom. Abby held her breath.

But she should have trusted Grandma, who wasn't any kind of princess herself.

The room was beautiful, just as Abby remembered it, and just as she'd seen it photographed on the town's tourist-friendly website. But this was no black tie event today. It looked like a church picnic that happened to be inside. It made her smile.

"Your grandmother told everyone it was a potluck," Becca said at Abby's side. "She even told people to bring blankets to sit on."

The town had delivered. There were old high school classmates camped out on thick blankets with their kids running around together. There were tables heaped with the sort of casseroles and chafing dishes that made up the backbone of small town communities. Abby knew at a glance that Genna Dawson had made her taco cups and Whitney Morrow had pulled through with the shepherd's pie she brought to wakes and showers alike. Abby didn't know if they'd all come in support or because they wanted to see the spectacle, but she found that for that first moment when everyone cheered the happy couple, she didn't care.

Gray was swept off into a lot of manly slaps on the back that turned quickly into the endless debate about what was the best and most cost-effective calving season. Abby waded through her own set of well-wishers, spanning every year of her life, until she found herself with Rae on one arm and Hope on the other.

"You seem like you have a mission," she said, looking from one to the other and back again. "Which we all know never ends well."

She could see Hope's sisters across the room and was tempted to remind her friends of the last time they'd decided to scheme over tarot cards and candles and had nearly burned down the bookstore's back storeroom. Abby wasn't sure Faith, the oldest of the Mortimer sisters, had ever really forgiven them.

"You're well and truly married now," Hope said, as if such near-tragedies had never happened. "I saw it with my own eyes. And you know what this means."

"It means I'm married."

But Abby knew full well that wasn't what Hope meant. And they'd all been friends since the dawn of time, so they all knew she knew. Hope and Rae exchanged a speaking sort of look.

"We meant to do this on the drive over," Rae murmured. "But it didn't seem like the right moment."

"Because who knows? Anything could have happened at the courthouse. Not that I thought it would," Hope added when Rae frowned at her.

Abby sighed. "I can guarantee there's no way I'm interested in having this conversation right here, in a room filled with my grandmother, every pastor in town, and my second grade teacher."

Rae shrugged. "I'm going to go out on a limb and guess that Grandma Douglas, as salty as she likes to be on occasion, didn't cover this subject adequately, if at all. And I know Lily certainly didn't step up to the plate at any time during her not-infrequent-enough visits over the past fifteen years."

"I got *the talk* right next to you in sixth grade," Abby reminded them, already flushing from embarrassment at the prospect of this discussion she didn't want to have. "Miss Ellison lecturing us about *a woman's special place* and how best to care for it will haunt me forever. I don't know why you would bring it up today unless you want to hurt me."

"This isn't health class," Rae chided her. "This is real talk."

"Because the two of you are made of sexual experience all of a sudden?"

Hope liked to talk about sex, but had always been remarkably cagey about her own experiences—or even if she'd had very many of them out there in the big, bad world. Rae, on the other hand, hadn't dated anyone to Abby's knowledge since her marriage to Riley had ended.

"Neither one of us is a virgin, Abby," Hope said with exaggerated patience. "Let me break this down for you as simply as I can. When a man and a woman love each other very, very much, or are drunk in a bar somewhere—"

"Speak for yourself," Rae interrupted, making a face. "I would no more run off with some guy in a bar than I would prance naked down Main Street in full view of my parents."

"Both hideous images, so thanks for that," Abby muttered, flushing brighter because she could see Rae's parents a few tables away, talking to their neighbors. "Why are those the choices?"

"I'm simply offering options," Hope retorted. "*I'm* not judging anyone."

"Have you forgotten that we're all charter members—and, in fact, the only members—of the Too Dirty to Admit It Book Club?" Abby protested. "I've read everything there is to read about the things a man and woman can get up to in bed."

"I know you have," Rae said, the laughter draining from her face as they made it to the drinks table, and Hope busied herself pouring them all glasses of wine. "But books aren't real life. Real life is . . . different. It's not words on a page and your imagination, all fluffy and sweet. It's bodies. It's intense. Do you have any questions?"

"What makes you think Gray and I haven't already . . . ?" Abby began, blushing furiously. "As a test run before we jumped into this whole marriage deal?"

"The red face, for one thing," Hope said dryly, dispensing the wine she'd poured. Abby took hers and clenched the stem of the glass. Too tightly. "But also because if you had, in fact, relieved yourself of your vestal virgin status and didn't tell me?" She shook her head, as if the consequences were too dire for her to voice them.

"Does it really hurt?" Abby asked, and she was sure she hadn't meant her voice to go so soft and uncertain, there. But even though that was humiliating, she pushed on. "The entire internet seems to be divided in half, and yes, I googled it. Some say it's terrible, but then they usually go on to tell upsetting stories of how they lost their virginity in the first place. And then other people claim that it's all some weird, made-up thing, and it doesn't hurt at all because it's like a . . . high five, or something."

Rae and Hope met eyes again over their glasses.

"I would not call it a high five," Hope said after a moment. "Because the last time I checked, nobody high fives inside their body."

Rae nodded. "Realistically, it might hurt. But how much really depends on him. And I've seen Gray Everett with his foals and his calves and his own daughter. He doesn't strike me as a kind of man who won't slow down and take his time when necessary."

Abby felt as if she were being smothered where she stood, but didn't want to call attention to herself by gasping for breath. "That's a good thing? Slow?"

"Slow is fun," Hope assured her, her eyes sparkling. "You want to feel so much good stuff that by the time it's actually happening, if you do hurt a bit, it'll all sort of disappear into everything else you're feeling."

"And if he isn't . . . careful?"

"Then you tell me," Rae threw out at once. "And I will personally smack him upside the head with a shovel—"

"Who are you smacking upside the head?" came Gray's voice, low and amused.

All three of them jumped, then turned to see Gray standing there next to the knot they'd made. Abby didn't know why she kept feeling like a teenager again, today of all days. She was the bride. *His* bride, in fact. She was a grown woman.

Yes, she happened to also be the same scared little virgin she'd been at seventeen, but that wasn't exactly common knowledge.

At least, she hoped it wasn't.

It might be a rumor, sure, but no one aside from Hope and Rae *knew*. Including Gray.

Especially Gray.

"Hi," she said, doing a great impression of her shy and awkward seventeen-year-old self, and felt her cheeks singe.

She knew it was only the fact that they loved her with all of their hearts that kept Hope and Rae from laughing at her.

But Gray made no particular attempt to hide the way his lips curved.

"Hi." He let that hang there for a moment, then relented. "I'm not much of a dancer, but this is a wedding."

He held out his hand.

Abby felt as if she was under a spell. She was vaguely aware of Hope taking her wineglass from her, but all she could focus on was Gray. She slid her hand into his, because she couldn't imagine doing anything else when he was holding his hand out like that. She didn't *want* to do anything else. She didn't even fully understand what he'd said, but she wasn't sure she cared when she was touching him again, and it became clear soon enough anyway. He drew her through the crowd of Cold River townspeople until they were in the center of the room, and then he pulled her into his arms.

Abby still couldn't believe any of this was real.

Especially not when music started playing nearby, from a few of the local musicians who hung around Cold River Coffee on the weekends. Nothing fancy, but Abby hadn't realized how powerful *simple* could be until now, when all Gray did was hold her in his arms, there in front of people who'd known them both all their lives.

Then they danced.

It was more of a swaying, really. Back and forth, an easy movement along with the music, but all of Gray's considerable attention was focused on her. And Abby could feel the entire town staring at her too.

She might have died of embarrassment if Gray hadn't been there to hold her up.

"You looked like you were enjoying yourself a minute

ago," he said after a moment of nothing but too much attention, his hand on her back and the other tucked against his chest like a real couple. "Now you don't."

"This became a whole lot more public than I was anticipating, that's all," she managed to say, lifting her chin so she could look him in the eye and try to ignore the riot going on in her pulse.

"I wasn't planning to keep the fact I married you a secret."

"That's not what I mean. It's just . . . everyone's staring."

"Everybody loves a bride."

"Maybe. I'm not sure they like *me* as a bride, though. It might be the spectacle."

He didn't exactly frown, though she could tell that she'd displeased him somehow. And she didn't like that at all.

It was amazing how much she didn't like that.

"You keep acting like you deserve it if people look at you funny," he said after a moment. "When maybe they're just looking."

The makeshift band was plucking out a familiar country love song, but there was something tight and anxious crouched there inside Abby's chest.

"You're marrying me because I'm practical, remember?" She searched that dark green gaze of his, though she couldn't have said what she was looking for. "This is me. Being practical."

She couldn't read the expression on his face. As if he was considering her in a new light, and that didn't make the crouching thing in her chest ease any.

For a while, all they did was dance.

When the band started a second song, other people joined them out on the dance floor that was nothing more than a cleared space between blankets, and Abby didn't

know why some part of her felt like crying. It was the ache
that never seemed to go away, that she was starting to think
was a part of her. Or a part of her when she was around
Gray, and she'd married him now, hadn't she? Maybe this
was how it was going to be from here on out.

When the second song ended, she could admit she was
grateful he stopped dancing. They could go back to talking with the people who'd showed up for them, instead of
not talking to each other.

It had never occurred to her that maybe, just maybe, it
was easier to love a man from afar.

Abby chatted with more of these people she'd known
all her life and ordered herself not to look for pity on their
faces when they offered her congratulations. Because
maybe Gray was right. Maybe they were just looking.
Maybe she was the one adding *intention* to it. She took a
few moments with Becca, as much to make sure she
stopped acting as if she was the hostess when she should
have been enjoying herself as to make sure she was okay.

"Of course I'm okay," Becca replied. She'd frowned.
"Why? Are you not okay? Can I do something?"

"You can have fun," Abby suggested.

But she didn't push it when her brand new stepdaughter stared back at her as if she'd suggested she turn herself
into a dragon and breathe fire on the nearest pastor.

Then, finally, she went and sat with Grandma in the
corner of the room where they could look out and see
everyone.

"This is a very nice party," Abby said as she settled in
the chair next to her grandmother. "I didn't think I wanted
one. But then it turns out I wanted exactly this."

Not only because she was enjoying the fancy picnic
thing, she admitted to herself. But because she hadn't realized she'd needed this small break between marrying

Gray and tossing herself headlong into her life with him, whatever that looked like. A reception meant some breathing room. She could sit with what her friends had told her about sex. She could observe the way her new brothers-in-law behaved to Gray and to the town and to her, comparing Brady's sharp charm to Ty's lazy ease.

It meant she could be only Abby for a little while longer.

Next to her, Grandma smiled and reached over to pat her on the thigh. "I expect you're like me in more than just looks, Abigail."

"I hope so. I'm not sure I like the alternative."

Neither one of them looked over to where Abby knew Lily was, holding court in a corner with a few people from town that Abby had always had to challenge herself to find the goodness in. But at least that was better than Lily standing there at Abby's side, whispering her poison directly into Abby's ear.

Punching yourself in the face would also be better than that, she told herself sharply.

"I married your grandfather when I was sixteen," Grandma said, her steady gaze trained on the crowd before them. "I knew he was the only one for me. And that I wouldn't be marrying again, no matter what happened."

"I'm surprised you could know something like that at sixteen."

Her grandmother turned, her eyes bright. "Seems to me you knew who you were going to marry at sixteen too. It just took you a minute or two to get to the altar."

Abby let out a shaky sigh and pressed a hand to that fluttery place below her chest. "Someday he's going to find out that I've had a crush on him for all these years, Grandma. And I'm afraid he's really not going to like it."

"Maybe so. But that day isn't today. And until that day

comes, there's no point worrying about what he might or might not say about something he might or might not already know. You work on the marriage, not what made it happen."

It was the same great advice everyone had been giving her today that didn't help at all, because the people dispensing it knew exactly what they were talking about, and Abby had no idea what language they were using. Sex, marriage, men. Garrulous old Lucinda Early had even started talking about babies.

"How am I supposed to know—"

"Every marriage is different," Grandma said with that calm certainty that had always soothed Abby. Today was no different. "And then again, every marriage is the same."

"You said the secret to staying married was not getting divorced."

"That's rule number one. Rule number two is that you don't have to be right even if you are. And rule number three? You're never alone in a marriage, maybe especially when you think you are."

Abby sighed. "I don't know what that means."

Grandma only patted her on the thigh again, the way she might a fractious animal or a finicky pie crust. "You will."

When Gray came to find her this time, he nodded to Grandma with that old world courtesy that made Abby's stomach swoop around inside of her, then pulled her up to her feet.

Abby leaned down and kissed Grandma on her forehead, inhaling her familiar scent of lavender and sugar, and tried not to let the tears well up as Gray pulled her away.

It wasn't goodbye. It was a change. Just a tiny change of address, that was all.

"Grandma—" she began.

"Go on now," Grandma replied, all serenity and a wisdom that made Abby shake. "I'll see you soon, Abby. Very soon."

Abby held onto Gray's hand and let him tug her out of the flow of traffic, so he could look down at her. There were too many things sloshing around in her head, so all she could think about was how strange her left hand felt clasped in someone else's with that brand new ring biting into her finger. Well, that and the fact that Gray remained the most handsome man she'd ever beheld. She wondered if she'd always lose her breath when she looked at him.

And something she didn't want to acknowledge, deep inside her, wondered if he'd ever lose his breath when he looked at her.

She shoved that away as if it were on fire. Because she was terrified it would turn her into ash, right there in her wedding dress.

"I think we've hit every note there is to hit," he said in that drawl that felt like heat all over her. "Vows were exchanged, and we had a little party to make everybody feel better about it."

"Do people feel badly?" Abby tried to focus on someone or something other than Gray and failed. "I figured they would think it was unexpected, sure, but not necessarily *bad*."

"I don't know what they think. I don't care what they think. I don't know why you do," Gray replied evenly. "But you do, so here we are."

Abby knew exactly why she cared what people thought, and it was mostly because she didn't like the things she was sure they were thinking. About her. But she didn't want to say what those things were out loud. Not to Gray. Not when she'd much prefer to pretend he wasn't thinking all those same things himself. She'd come close enough to putting it all out there on Thanksgiving.

And besides, the man was looking right at her. He knew who she was and what she looked like. If there was anyone to blame for the tide of gossip she was sure might sweep them both away any moment, Abby knew it was her. She was the one shameless enough to marry a man who could do so much better because he'd asked her a few days after burying his father. She would have to live with the small town judgment on that.

When she didn't say anything, Gray's mouth crooked. "I think we're done here."

"Done?"

"My daughter, who it turns out is a whole lot more devious than I ever gave her credit for, tells me that she and your grandmother and those friends of yours arranged everything."

"The party, you mean."

"The party, yes. But they also got us a room. Here."

"A room?" Abby was suddenly so aware of her own heartbeat it was shocking that she could hear anything else. "But . . . we agreed we would go straight back to the ranch because you'll have things to do in the morning."

"There will always be things to do." Gray's hand seemed tighter around hers when she knew—when she could see—that what he actually did was loosen his grip and look down at the ring he'd put on her finger. "But there's a reason I have a foreman. He can handle things one morning."

"Oh. Well." She was flustered and her *heart*, and she'd never wanted to take that long, long ride out into the Everett fields so much before in her life, to win more time. When it had been all these years and surely that was more than enough time for anyone. "I've always wanted to spend the night at this hotel. Haven't you?"

"You're not getting my point," Gray drawled, laughter dancing in those dark eyes of his and making her pulse speed up, which really shouldn't have been possible. "We're standing here in this party when we could be upstairs. Right now. In a room with a bed, which I guarantee you is nicer than a freezing cold yard on Thanksgiving afternoon with nothing around but dirt."

Sex.

He was talking about sex.

With her.

With. Her. At last.

Abby was afraid that maybe she'd died. Died and came back, only to die again, because she couldn't quite take it all in.

But maybe that was the point. She could stand here and continue to *think* about sex, and specifically sex with Gray Everett, the way she had for years. The way some part of her clearly wanted to continue doing forever.

Or she could claim her rights as a married woman, and *do* it.

That trembling thing inside her was still there and going strong. But she didn't mind. Holding onto Gray's hand, looking up into that direct, dark gaze, was a lot like finding Hope and Rae at the bottom of the farmhouse stairs this morning.

Pure joy. Sheer relief.

And the promise of something better.

She ignored her wild pulse and the voice in her head that urged her to break away and do another round of polite conversations she'd already forgotten. "You're talking about consummation."

His smile was still so unexpected. Especially when it flashed over his face the way it did then, as pure and fierce as the Colorado sun. "I believe I am."

"In some places a marriage isn't really legal until it takes place."

Gray's smile widened. "So I've heard."

"I don't know if Colorado is one of those places," Abby said primly. She drew herself up straight, holding that gaze of his as if her life depended on it. "But I suppose we'd better go ahead and make sure that we're as legal as possible."

12

Gray couldn't bring himself to drop Abby's hand.

They said their goodbyes and left Martha and the rest of the town to their celebrating. Gray was well aware that the real reason he was prepared to leave the ranch in hands other than his own for the first time in about a decade— not to mention, his daughter with her uncles—had a lot more to do with the bed he knew waited for them upstairs than any particular recognition of his newly married state.

He was a man, after all.

Though it occurred to him when he and Abby stepped into the gold-plated old elevator in the lobby and left the crowd behind them that he'd had some doubts on that score over the years. He hadn't meant to become a monk, but he had. He hadn't meant to bury himself on his land before it was his time, but he'd done that too.

He'd married Abby because he wanted a wife. A good wife, a mother for his daughter, and a decent marriage that they could roll on into the future. A marriage for the right reasons that would let future Everetts become stewards of the land, not prisoners of it.

But tonight wasn't about that, he admitted to himself as the elevator slowly rose.

Tonight was about Abby.

It was about the way she looked at him with all that wonder and heat in her gleaming eyes that made him so hard he felt like a fifteen-year-old all over again.

The elevator chugged its way from one floor to the next as if it was taking the time to tour through its own long history as it went. Gray felt the weight of what they'd done in the courthouse, and what they were about to do, thank God, sitting on them both a little too heavily. Abby stopped looking at him once the elevator cleared the second floor. She was staring down at the floor as if she'd never seen her feet before and was unduly fascinated by them.

"I had the hands pick up your boxes," he told her.

She jolted as if she hadn't been expecting the sound of his voice. He could admit that had come out on the abrupt side, but it was better than the thick silence that pressed at him.

When she looked at him again, her cheeks were rosy. "Thank you."

"I want to make moving in as seamless as possible."

She nodded, though he noticed she wasn't quite meeting his gaze. She was looking slightly to one side. "I appreciate that."

If he'd been calmer, he might not have been able to feel his pulse in his sex the way he did then. Insistent. Demanding.

He was half afraid she could hear it too.

The other half wanted her to.

"Your mother didn't cause any trouble today," he heard himself say, because apparently this woman was the only thing on earth that could turn him chatty. "I was waiting for her to—"

"Can we not talk about my mother?" Abby asked softly. "Please?"

Gray studied her for a moment. There was color on her

cheeks, yes. But there was also something hectic in her gaze that seemed wired directly into him. As if she could feel that pulse in him. As if they were both locked into that same insistent, demanding rhythm.

He nodded.

They traveled the next two floors in silence.

When they arrived on the top floor of the hotel, the elevator doors slid open and Abby stepped out. She hesitated in the hall until Gray caught up to her, his hand dropping to the small of her back naturally. As if they'd walked like this a thousand times before.

He kept having the nagging sensation they had. Or they should have.

It made even more sense that he'd married her, he told himself, shaking off the odd sensation. He liked that they fit, that was all. He didn't have to stoop, and it surprised him *how* good that felt.

Especially when he knew what they were heading off to do in all the Grand Hotel's hushed luxury.

This was why he would never have done well picking up women in bars. There was something about walking down a quiet hallway with a woman when both of them knew exactly what they were going off to do. He expected the anticipation and *greed* of it would shift as time went on. It would hopefully become a part of the fabric of the life they built together. But tonight, here, he and Abby didn't know each other that well.

And still, they were on their way to a hotel suite for sex.

Gray really didn't understand how or why people did this casually.

Their suite was at the end of the hall. Gray unlocked the door with hands that looked steady yet felt shaky, but when Abby went to step in ahead of him, he stopped her.

She frowned up at him. "What's wrong?"

He didn't think about what he was doing. He just did it.

Gray bent, then swept her into his arms, lifting her high against his chest.

All the air went out of her in a *whoosh*. With a little laugh on the end. A whole lot like no one had ever picked her up before.

"You'll give yourself a hernia," she said, but she was breathless.

"I doubt that very much," Gray murmured, because he wasn't breathless.

Just needy. Hungry.

And more of each with every second.

He carried her over the threshold of the hotel room, but he didn't put her down on the other side. He kept hold of her, taking in the suite's old world furnishings without stopping to admire them.

He didn't stop until he found the bedroom and could set her down near the foot of the big king bed.

She was trembling, and his heart tipped over inside him.

"You okay?" He didn't sound like himself. He sounded gruff and soft and something else entirely.

Abby's eyes looked too big, suddenly. She swallowed, visibly, then pressed her lips together as if she was trying to figure out what to say.

And for a moment Gray let himself enjoy her.

He hadn't known what to expect when he was waiting for her this morning. But the moment he'd seen her get out of her friend's truck, he'd felt a rush of something too powerful to be simple relief that she'd actually showed up to their unorthodox wedding.

It wasn't that he was relieved, though maybe he was. It was more that she was so . . . *right*, there with the Colorado sunshine painting her bright and gleaming. Or maybe that was just Abby.

Her dress was a deceptively pretty thing that suited her perfectly. It was an ivory column with no adornment, which was perfect because she didn't need any. The dress didn't call attention to itself. It brought attention to her instead.

Those bright eyes of hers, shining like gold. That mouth he wanted to taste a lot more deeply tonight. And the hair she'd done up in pretty curls, hanging down to her shoulders and reminding him that she was more than a convenience. She was a woman.

Gray was a lucky man.

He lifted his hand to marinate in his luck, but she stiffened.

"I have something to tell you," she blurted out.

"That sounds alarming."

Though he wasn't alarmed. Not really. This was Abby.

"It's not alarming." She considered, while her eyes darted around like she was panicked. Or trying not be panicked. "It's mostly embarrassing."

"Are you drawing out the suspense on purpose?"

She let out a sigh. He watched her chest rise as she took what was clearly meant to be a deep, steadying breath.

"I've never done this before."

She tensed as if anticipating some kind of response.

"Well, Abby, I did actually know that."

"You did?" She looked horrified. "Does it . . . You mean, by *looking*?"

He frowned at her. "Not that it would have been a deal breaker if you'd been married before, but I know you haven't been."

"Oh." The deep red color on her face deepened. "*Married*. I am . . . I'm not talking about marriage, Gray."

"Then I'm still in the dark."

He knew, somehow, that she wasn't about to confess to

an opioid addiction. Or a selection of secret boyfriends she refused to give up. Or a bunch of kids she hadn't mentioned before. It probably wasn't gambling debts or ruinous credit card balances, because he didn't see Abby holding on to those kinds of secrets when she lived at home with her grandmother and spent her days so visible in that coffee shop. Someone would have whispered something. That was how it went. He would have had an inkling.

Even if she were harboring all of those secrets at once, he doubted she would be confessing like this, standing there in front of what he had every intention of making their marital bed.

Not that it mattered. Gray would deal with it, whatever it was.

"This," she said, with more urgency and a fresh wash of red all over her face and down her chest. She nodded toward the bed in question, then looked back at him. Nervously. "I've never done *this* before."

Gray stared at her. Then blinked.

"I'm sure you think there's something wrong with me now," Abby said hurriedly, and now she was gripping her fingers too tightly in front of her. "There's not. I mean, I wouldn't know, necessarily. But I never felt there was something *wrong* with me. I didn't . . . It never seemed . . ."

She was sounding more frantic with every word, and Gray reached over and tugged one of her hands away from the knot she was making of the pair of them and held it.

"I don't think anything's wrong with you."

But he was afraid there was something wrong with him. He was very possibly having a heart attack. That was what it felt like, primitive and dark and *insane*. It was like something in him *roared* from the inside out. He'd never felt anything like it before.

Possessive.

Bordering on savage.

Because he could hardly believe his ears, and he really, really wanted to. She was all his.

No one had ever touched her, or would ever touch her, but him.

It was a gift he hadn't seen coming, and wasn't sure he knew what to do with. Well, except all the obvious things repeatedly—if on a less intense rotation than he'd initially imagined.

"Well, maybe I think there's something wrong with me. I didn't want to, you know, jump in and try to fake my way through. And maybe it's an obvious thing anyway, and you'd see it, and then you'd know—"

"Abby." He rubbed his thumb back and forth over the back of her hand and waited until she breathed steadier, her gaze glued to his. "I have this."

He could feel fine tremors winding through her, one after the next. He pulled her closer and moved with her, backing her toward the bed until she could sit. Until she had to sit.

He stood there a moment, not quite between her legs, looking down at her as if he'd never seen her before.

Maybe he hadn't.

She had to tilt up her head farther than usual, and Gray fit his hands to her cheeks, reveling in the softness. The heat.

"I don't want you to be disappointed," Abby whispered, and he felt that pressure against his ribs again. Harder.

"How could you disappoint me?"

She gave a jerky sort of shrug, but didn't say anything. She didn't have to. He could see all that emotion and apprehension in her face. Her gaze. The way she was trying to keep her lips from trembling.

"Maybe you haven't noticed, but I'm a traditional kind

of guy. I don't think it's weird you waited for marriage. I like it." He brushed his thumb over one cheekbone, then the other, and told her something no one else knew. "So did I."

Abby looked at him in disbelief. "You mean . . . You can't mean . . . ?"

"That's exactly what I mean. Both times."

Her lips parted as if she couldn't take that in.

Gray didn't know how the practical exercise he'd been expecting had tipped over into something that felt a whole lot more sacred. But he didn't question it.

He leaned down until he could get his mouth close to hers.

"You really don't mind that I'm the oldest living virgin west of the Mississippi?" she whispered, there against his lips, as if she were asking him if he believed in Santa Claus.

He wanted to laugh, but there were too many intense things in him then, fighting for supremacy. All the ways he wanted to taste her. All the ways he wanted to touch her. Learn her. Know her.

All the ways he wanted to celebrate this woman and all the gifts she was giving him, but this one particularly.

This one he couldn't believe he got to unwrap, right here and right now.

"I don't mind it at all," he told her, so gruff he didn't sound like himself and far past caring.

Then he proved it with a kiss.

13

Abby hardly knew what to do with herself.

Rae and Hope's sex talk had kicked her anxiety about her virginity into high gear. Every step she'd taken down this hallway toward the hotel's honeymoon suite had felt as if she was walking straight into her own humiliation.

She kept playing it over and over in her head. What might happen. How terribly wrong it could go. What he might do or say or how he might *look* at her. It was all a kind of blurry mosaic in her head, cobbled together from books and movies and television shows, and all the things she'd overheard over time. All the ways pretending she'd had sex before could humiliate her and ruin her marriage before it started.

Not to mention, it was a lie. A lie of omission, but still a lie.

A practical, dependable, *appliance* sort of woman would never dream of doing nothing but hoping it all worked out the way it was supposed to. Kissing had been one thing. She'd figured that out all right on the fly, but it wasn't the same. Even she knew that.

Abby could handle anything, including every horror story she'd heard about *deflowering* as if virgins were recalcitrant garden projects, except Gray's disappointment.

Gray being disappointed in her might kill her.

Then he'd picked her up, which had sent her head spinning. Because it was so unexpected. Because it was *romantic*. No one had ever picked her up, not since she'd been a baby. She was too tall. Too solid. Too . . . something. She'd spent all of high school watching the petite girls get picked up and carted around by their boyfriends, twirled in the hallways, even bench pressed in one memorable history class. She'd always wondered what that would be like. Would she squeal and carry on? Would she pretend to beat her fists and kick? Or would she go supple and boneless and smug-eyed?

She'd imagined every variation from the secure position of her feet firmly on the ground because no one was likely to fling a girl like Abby aloft and tote her about like a trophy. That was for pretty girls. She'd accepted that long, long ago.

So she hadn't been prepared to be lifted up at all. And she certainly hadn't been ready for how little she felt like squealing or carrying on or offering a token show of half-hearted resistance.

Because there was nothing funny about being lifted up in Gray's arms so easily.

It felt like a kind of homecoming. It felt like the kind of marriage they weren't supposed to be having.

And worse than that, it had made her feel even more terrible about the glaring secret she was hoarding inside of her. That was the question she should have asked her friends downstairs. Was it worse to tell a man up front that he'd married the last true spinster of the American West? Or was it worse to brazen it out and hope he wouldn't notice?

Men were notoriously unobservant. Or so Abby had

been repeatedly informed by every form of popular
entertainment available and most of the women she
knew.

Still, she'd made her choice. And instantly regretted it.

Except now . . . Gray was kissing her.

Kissing her again and again as he stood there between
her legs. Kissing her until the slide of his tongue against
hers was another vow. Slow and luxurious, as if that was
all he planned to do. Ever. As if the fact they were alone
in this hotel suite was neither here nor there. He angled
his head one way, slowly, then the other, trying out the
best fit.

She mimicked him. Then, as she grew confident, she
matched him.

She was vaguely aware when he shrugged out of his
jacket, but she didn't hear it hit the floor. And she didn't
care. He straightened, taking his mouth away from her and
grinning when she made a small sound of protest.

"Patience," he said gruffly.

I've been patient my whole life, Abby thought.

Then realized she'd said it out loud when that curve in
the corner of his hard, delicious mouth kicked up.

"Be more patient."

He kicked off his boots, then he crawled onto the bed,
hooking her beneath her arms and carrying her with him
as he went. Once again displaying so much easy, thought-
less strength that Abby was tempted to imagine she was
someone else. Someone darling and tiny and effortlessly
charming. Someone pretty and light and airy.

Someone worthy of a man like this.

But then they were stretched out in the middle of the
bed, and there was no time to think about pretty or worthy or anything but the man there above her, blocking out

the light. Gray was holding himself up on one elbow, so he was angled over her. Not pressing her into the bed, or not entirely.

It was better than the very wildest of her dreams.

"Here's what we're going to do." His tone of easy command made the trembling thing deep inside her settle. "You don't have to worry about anything. You can touch me as much or as little as you want, and I'll do the same. All you have to think about is whether or not you like something. If you don't, say so. Does that work?"

She frowned at him. "Aren't we supposed to have a serious conversation about birth control?"

His eyes crinkled in the corners, and she felt it, everywhere. Like lightning, bolt after bolt until she was electric.

"Sure," he said, and he was close enough—he was *touching* her—and she could feel the rumble of his voice as well as hear it. It felt like magic. "But you told me that you were a virgin, so I'm guessing that means you're clean. And I told you I haven't had sex in ten years, which means I'm pretty clean too. So that's covered."

He started to trace a pattern along her jaw with the tip of one finger. It was distracting. It was a lick of flame and a roll of thunder, tumbling through her and pooling in the most wonderful places. Her breasts felt heavy. Between her legs, she melted.

Gray didn't stop at her jaw. He kept going, just the faintest touch of his finger, making his way down her neck and then along her collarbone. Then lower still. "And I already told you I want more kids. The question is if you do, the way you said you did."

They had talked about children on the phone, in even more detail than that first day in the farmhouse when Abby hadn't believed this would ever really happen. In a sort of *someday I'd like some* way.

But maybe this was someday. They'd just gotten married. Abby was already thirty. When she'd imagined what her life would look like, she'd expected to have kids by now. More than one. More than two, even. She could wait longer, of course. But why?

She already felt as if she'd been waiting forever.

Because she had been.

"I do," she whispered. "I do want kids."

Your kids, she thought, and that time she didn't accidentally say it out loud.

She told herself it was practical. That people entered into marriages like this one all the time, for exactly these reasons. Companionship. Shared goals. Babies. A life.

But when Gray's dark green eyes gleamed with approval, and something infinitely hotter, she knew there was absolutely nothing *practical* about the way she wanted to carry this man's child.

Or anything else.

The fire in her was too hot. Her need for him was too great.

And still his hand moved in that lazy trail, winding its way down her body as if he didn't know he was touching her.

As if he had no idea the storm he was stirring up within her when his fingers skirted her breasts and found a pattern to follow across her belly. Her dress felt insubstantial one moment and like a prison the next.

She found herself shifting from side to side. Lifting her hips, as if she could catch his hand.

There was a desperation building inside of her, thick and insistent.

Gray watched her as if he'd never seen anything so fascinating, a glint in his dark green eyes that made everything in her pull tight.

Then he set his mouth to hers once again.

And Abby . . . lost herself.

There was the way he kissed her, each slide of his mouth against hers more drugging than the last. There was the taste of him, rich and heady, that made her feel drunk.

He was so big, and he was pressed against her. And the more they kissed, and the more she shifted, the more he moved until he was on top of her.

God help her, he was *on top* of her.

She might have died from the sheer, unmanageable beauty of it when he held himself there, his lower body pressed to hers, and the thick, unmistakable ridge of his arousal jutting into her. Maybe she did.

She felt shivery and silvery at once. She felt fragile and vulnerable, vast and unstoppable.

Abby hardly knew who she was.

He used his hard, callused palms against her, holding them over her breasts until her nipples stood at attention. Then he moved them in slow, heated circles until she was arching her back to meet him.

All the while he kissed her. He played with her. She moved her hips against him, and he rode her until she was whimpering there beneath him, and desperate. Wild. Outside her head and yet entirely in her body and the things he was making her feel.

She hardly knew what she was doing when she reached for the waistband of his jeans, then tugged at his shirt.

But she sighed in satisfaction when she pulled it out, then slid her hands onto the bare skin of his abdomen at last.

It was better than she'd imagined, and she'd imagined it often and intensely. He was hot, smooth in some places and dusted with hair in others. Abby found herself breathing hard, as if she was running when she was definitely not running.

She fumbled with his buttons, pulling them apart, and baring the wonder of Gray's naked chest to her hungry eyes at last.

He was perfect.

He was even more perfect than that one time she and her friends had tracked him down on a bright May afternoon out there in the fields, shirtless in the sunshine.

He outdid any dream she'd ever had of him, and that hardly seemed possible, given the dreams she'd had about him. But she could move her head and lick her way across him. She could taste him, she could feel him pressed so heavily against her, and she wanted to slow down every sensation so she could drown herself in it. While at the same time, she wanted more. She wanted faster. She wanted everything.

He muttered something she didn't catch, but she didn't care. There was that breathtaking hardness between her legs, and it was a wonder. She rocked herself against him and moaned when he pulled the top of her dress down so he could find her breasts again. But this time, with his mouth.

Nothing in her life had prepared her for Gray's mouth opening over her nipple. Then sucking, with enough pressure to make her head rock back against the pillows.

And everything in her tightened.

Everything.

"Keep going," he said, and she didn't understand.

But then she did. The more she rocked herself against him, the more wonderful everything felt. She thought, *this is how it happens.*

This was how it was going to happen. Her first orgasm with another person.

Maybe it was thinking about it that threw her toward that edge. Maybe it was the way he hummed as he tasted one breast, then moved to the other.

But when it hit her, it hit hard.

She didn't know if she was crying or laughing. She shook and she shook, she wanted to go on forever, and she worried it might tear her apart.

When she was done, he was still there over her, that handsome face of his almost severe, though his dark green eyes glittered bright and hot.

"Do you want more?" he asked, and his voice was nothing but a delicious scrape that seemed to track its way down her body.

She couldn't speak. She only nodded, amazed that she was even capable of that.

And astounded that there could be *more* when that had been . . . everything.

Gray's hard mouth curved, and it was like getting walloped with heat all over again.

He was connected to her somehow, as if the curve of his mouth cut deep between her legs, and she loved it.

He shifted, stroking his hands down to where her legs were splayed wide open, and then tugging.

She wanted to help him, she did. She prided herself on being helpful and hadn't she married him to be useful? But she couldn't seem to move, and she knew he understood that when he laughed.

He kept tugging, until she realized he was pulling the skirt of her dress up to pool around her hips.

She couldn't think about what was happening then. That she was exposed. Open to his gaze, with only the panties she wore between them.

But then he was tugging them off too. She was limp as he moved her where he wanted her, pulling the panties down one leg and then the other, and then tossing them aside.

He left her for a moment and Abby felt she ought to

protest that, but when he came back again, everything was better and she didn't feel like protesting anyway. Because Gray was naked. And then, better yet, he pulled her up so she was sitting, and yanked her dress up and over her head. Then reached around, his fingers lighting fires wherever they touched her skin, to unhook her bra.

He made a low, very male noise that she knew was approval, even though she'd never heard it before.

And that, too, washed over her, a shower of flame and need.

Gray stretched out beside her again, and this time when his hand tracked its way down the length of her body, he didn't stop where the top band of her panties had been.

He went lower, and Abby wondered if she ought to be embarrassed by how wet she was. How open and needy. That couldn't be right, surely.

"Don't close your legs," he told her.

She was burning up; she was blushing so hard and deep. It was all over her body, so intense she was sure she must have turned the color of strawberries.

But if she had, he didn't comment on it.

He was too busy drawing shapes through all the wetness he'd found. He stroked his way through her folds, as if he wanted nothing more than to play with her all day. She hardly knew which sensation was the most intense. All she knew was that soon enough, she was lifting her hips to him again. She was rocking herself against his hands.

She shuddered all over when he used his finger to find his way inside her.

He tested her, then he stroked her. He seemed to do that for a long, long time, while she rocked against him and made herself go crazy with the feel of it. He tested that part of her where no one had ever gone. One finger, then two.

And when she was moaning because everything felt

great, he looked up at her, grinned with a deep kind of satisfaction that made everything burn at the edges, and did something impossible with a twist of his hand.

Just like that, she was shaking and shuddering all over again, bucking up against him with her head thrown back.

As she shook, Gray moved on top of her and settled himself between her legs again, this time with no clothes between them.

Then he was stroking his way through all that melting with something broader and heavier than his fingers.

She knew what it was. Of course she knew.

Abby was so busy picturing it that the only thing she could do was buck against him, shattering all the more.

He reached down between them and wrapped his hand around himself.

Then she felt the pressure, pressing where his fingers had been.

Gray pushed inside her, but he did it slowly. So slowly, she felt stretched wide open. There was a kind of heaviness, but right when it should have tipped over into pain, it dissipated. And he knew that too, because that was when he pushed again. Slow, steady, as if he was prepared for it to take all night.

But Abby wasn't the only one shaking when he was finally settled deep inside of her.

Inside of her.

Gray Everett was *inside* of her.

"Oh my God," she whispered.

"I'll take that as a compliment," he said, low and lazy, his voice another caress over her heated skin.

He pulled out then, even as he settled himself more firmly against her. Her breasts were pressed against his chest and his elbows were on either side of her head. He tipped her face back with his hands, letting his thumbs move on her jaw as he set his mouth to hers.

Then he was inside her in two ways, and Abby could hardly handle it. It was too much. *He* was too much. Gray kissed her deeply, ravenously. His tongue stroked hers while below, he pulled himself out of her, then thrust himself back in.

It was all impossible. Too greedy, too hot.

Too real.

Flesh against flesh. He tasted of salt and something she knew was all man. All him. She could hear the sounds their bodies made. She could feel how hard his heart beat in his chest.

And most of all, she could feel him deep inside of her.

She lost herself in the rhythm. For a long while, the rhythm was the world.

Until there came a point where she could no longer kiss him because she had to tip her head back to gasp for air. She had to wrap her arms around him and dig her fingers into the smooth, rippling muscles of his back.

He dropped his head down into the crook of her neck, and she could feel his breath there in the hot crease where her shoulder met her neck.

She didn't know how she could handle it. How she could survive it.

He thrust inside her, deeper and then deeper still. He moved faster, and she did too, finding a way to meet him. Finding a way to rock her hips against him to feel even more. To go deeper. Harder. Further into that liquid, impossible thing they were making between them.

When it happened again, she knew what it was. She gripped him, and she arched herself against him. She felt herself fly apart as if there had never been anything holding her together in the first place.

But this time, he groaned out her name, and then she felt him jerk inside of her. The same kind of shuddering moved over him, as if they had always been made to match each other this way.

As if this was all meant to be. As if they were.

And as he came down over her, a delicious weight pressing her into the bed like glory and joy, Abby shut her eyes. She tucked her head against his chest, breathed him in, and just for a second—just for tonight—let herself believe it.

14

The days grew even colder, harsh and raw. Snow hit hard, covering the mountains and blanketing the fields. The dark seemed to take over the world, leaving only the sparkling Christmas lights in town to stand proud against the night.

It was December in Cold River, and Abby was married.

To Gray Everett.

The simple truth of that threw more light everywhere, inside and out, than she knew what to do with. She was married. She loved him the way she always had, and maybe more now. Because now she got to live with him, share his bed, be a part of his life . . . all things she wished she could go back in time and tell her distraught teenage self would happen one day if she was prepared to wait.

No wonder Abby felt like her own set of Christmas lights, wrapped tight around the heart inside her chest, blazing out all that love and heat she'd only ever wanted to give the man who'd become her husband.

Her *husband*.

"Do you think we can decorate the house?" Becca asked, snapping Abby out of her daydreaming and back into the car she was driving home from town that chilly evening.

Becca sat in Abby's passenger seat, her gaze out on the

twisting road that danced in the gleam of the car's head-lights. Where Abby's attention should have been.

"I don't see why not," she said, with more intensity than necessary to make up for letting her mind wander when surely she should have been focusing on something suit-ably *stepmothery* instead.

"I've always wanted to do real decorations," Becca con-tinued, a dreamy sort of note in her voice. "On the front of the house and maybe the barn too. Wouldn't that be pretty?"

"Do you not normally decorate for Christmas?"

Abby and her grandmother had always spent Thanks-giving weekend putting up the tree, placing garlands every-where, and getting the stockings tidy and ready over the fireplace. Some years they wrapped the posts on the front porch in lights, and there'd been a few years when they'd put lit-up reindeer in the yard.

This year, she'd stopped by a few days later and done it with Grandma one afternoon.

She felt the same pang she always did when she remem-bered all the things she took for granted about her life were different now. Abby figured it was up to her to de-cide these changes were all good, no matter the odd grow-ing pains that went along with them.

"Well, no," Becca said, and her voice was less dreamy. More . . . reserved. "My grandfather didn't like Christmas decorations. He called them 'blackmail.' And I don't know that my dad ever cared either way because I don't think he likes Christmas."

Abby felt Christmas spirit surge within her like a glit-tery, tinsel-festooned tidal wave. "That's going to have to change. I like my Christmas decorations. And I *love* Christmas."

She didn't know what pleased her more, the prospect

of decorating a new house and bringing the magic of Christmas to her brand new family, or the pleased smile on Becca's face.

Her *stepdaughter*, Becca. Abby allowed herself a pleased moment of pride in the fact that so far, at least, she was handling the whole *step* thing well. Or not wickedly, anyway. If the prospect of a few Christmas lights could make a teenager smile like that, she was determined to make the Everett ranch house a winter wonderland. Tonight, if at all possible.

She made it down the icy mountain into the sprawl of snowy fields without letting her mind wander again, and it was funny to drive down the county road she knew so well but not turn down toward the Douglas farmhouse the way she had for so many years. It didn't feel *wrong* necessarily. Just different.

Abby still wasn't used to it. The other night she'd paid no attention to what she was doing, driving home from her shift at the coffeehouse on autopilot while she relived a few of her favorite scenes from that night in the Grand Hotel. Becca had been catching a later ride from a friend, so she hadn't had any stepmothering to attend to. She'd found herself halfway down the farmhouse's drive before she realized it. At which point she'd stopped the car, surprised herself with a rush of emotion, and had continued on to say hello to Grandma as if she'd meant to stop by all the while.

Tonight, however, she continued on toward Cold River Ranch. Five miles farther along that county road, then a mile into the fields, down another old dirt road that had been there about as long as there'd been dirt.

She saw Gray's truck in the yard as she pulled up and felt the same familiar catch in her chest. And lower, these days. Her head spun at how quickly the world could change, but it turned out she could settle into a routine no matter how strange and new everything was.

Abby loved a routine.

Gray had come back in from the fields and the winter pastures already. That was why the lights were blazing in the house. He came in and turned them on before he headed back to the barn to do his evening rounds, and Abby liked to consider that a token of his affection, whether he meant it that way or not.

Abby and Becca got out of the car and went inside, and Abby didn't even look around to see if she could catch a glance of Gray. Progress, as far as she was concerned. Because she was a rancher's wife now, and there was a routine, and her part definitely did not involve mooning after the man when he was working.

Not in front of his daughter, anyway.

Becca slung her school bag onto the dining room table, stamped her feet into a pair of old boots she kept in the mudroom, and then headed out to her own nightly chores that Gray insisted were part and parcel of life on a ranch.

While Abby got to play house the way she'd always wanted to, deep in her heart. It wasn't any different from what she had done at the farmhouse when she'd come home in the evening, and yet it still felt charged. There was something about making food for her husband, for the man who would eat what she made and then crawl into the same bed with her at night. It gave her a deep sort of satisfaction that made her feel . . . settled. Warm, inside and out. She was conscious of it as she moved around the kitchen, pulling things together. It added a kind of extra layer of meaning to the familiar ritual of making a meal. By the time Gray and Becca came inside, knocking the snow and mud from their feet and then heading off to wash up, Abby was putting dinner out on the table.

She'd always enjoyed cooking, but there was something about preparing a hot meal for a man who spent the day outside that pleased her. Deeply.

Or maybe she wasn't the happy homemaker she imagined herself. Maybe, she thought as Gray walked into the kitchen, fresh from the quick shower he took at the end of his work day, it was just Gray.

Her husband.

She still couldn't get over that

Though if she was honest, she was adapting to the married part. It was the sex that kept making her feel . . . giddy.

Even now.

Because it was nighttime again, and nighttime meant that soon—never soon enough—Gray would head up to bed ahead of his early morning, Abby would go with him, and he would proceed to turn her inside out.

His dark green gaze touched hers as he took his seat at the kitchen table, and Abby turned red the way she always did. Instantly and completely.

Her reward was that curve in the corner of his mouth.

"No Ty tonight?" Abby asked as she sat down.

Ty was like a ghost. Abby sometimes caught a glimpse of him out of the corner of her eye, but he flickered there and then disappeared, leaving nothing but that lazy smile of his and leftover plates in her sink to indicate he'd been digging around in the refrigerator in the middle of the night.

He'd showed up for dinner exactly once since Abby had moved in and had kept them all entertained with bull-riding war stories throughout the meal, so it hadn't been until afterward that Abby realized he hadn't actually said a single thing that could be considered personal.

"You can depend on my brothers for one thing," Gray said now, without any particular inflection, though his eyes

were glittering harder than usual. "And that's to be unde-
pendable. I wouldn't count on either one of them to do anything else."

That sounded harsh, but what did Abby know? She'd
grown up an only child with only adults around. Both
Hope and Rae had spent the bulk of their lives complain-
ing endlessly about their siblings one minute and then
dropping everything to support them the next. Gray viewed
both of his brothers with flat-out suspicion, but Abby
couldn't say they didn't deserve it. If there was one thing
she knew all about, it was navigating life with a family
member who could turn on the charm to outsiders whenever she felt like it while acting like a monster in private.

She knew too much about it, in fact. Lily had left after
the wedding—with threats to return for Christmas, according to Grandma—but her insults lived on, burrowing
beneath Abby's skin and setting up camp the way they always did.

Abby was hungry. She wanted to pile her plate high
with the dinner she'd made, but Lily's arch comment about
"stick-to-your-ribs farm dinners" echoed around inside her
head, and she restricted herself to salad.

"Abby says we can decorate the house," Becca announced, filling her plate with mashed potatoes and the
chicken Abby had left simmering in the slow cooker all
day, because she wasn't *plodding*.

"Decorate the house?" Gray asked, as if he'd never
heard of such a thing. Or maybe Becca was speaking in
tongues. "What house?"

"This house," Becca said, with something much sharper
than usual in her voice. "For Christmas."

Abby's ever-present swirl of body issues faded away at
that because everything was suddenly very tense around
the bright red, barn-door table. The sixth sense that always

told her when her mother was going to strike shook itself into sudden awareness, and she didn't know what to do with it. Not here, in Gray's house, when Lily wasn't even present.

"You know we don't really do Christmas," Gray said in that stern way of his. Shot through with warning and finality all at once.

But Becca didn't appear to hear that warning. "Abby said we could."

Abby froze where she sat as both Gray and Becca turned to stare at her.

Becca's gaze was imploring. Gray's, on the other hand, was unreadable. And Abby's throat was entirely too dry.

"We don't do a big thing for Christmas," Gray said.

As if the subject was closed.

"What does that mean?" Abby asked, very carefully, because her stomach was twisting into some kind of pretzel.

Gray's gaze was steady on Abby's. "We like it simple."

Across the table, Becca made a scoffing sound. "You might like it simple, but I don't. I never have. Because 'simple' to you means ignoring the fact it's even Christmas!"

"Enough, Becca."

Gray returned his attention to his plate as if that was all the conversation the topic required.

Abby and Becca stared at each other across the table. Becca widened her eyes, silently encouraging Abby to say something. Abby didn't understand why there appeared to be a hand around her throat, preventing her from speaking. She felt speechless and furious, the way she did whenever Lily started in with her snide commentary.

You understand, a voice inside argued. *You understand perfectly.*

It nagged at her while she did the dishes after dinner, having waved off Becca's halfhearted offer of help and having assured Gray that she was happy to do the dishes while he tended to the ranch paperwork he could never seem to get on top of. "Happy" might have been a strong word, but she didn't mind washing dishes. She found a kind of peace in the running water, the scrubbing, the careful loading of the dishwasher. In a clean kitchen with the surfaces wiped clean, the coffee ready to brew at four thirty the next morning, and the following day's meals plotted out in her head. In a job well done and well-executed, as her grandmother had taught her.

Or she usually found peace in it.

They'd been married such a short while. Slightly over one week. And it was nice to have a routine and a relief to feel things falling into place—but that didn't mean this felt like home. None of this was hers. She'd taken over what duties and chores she could, to prove how committed she was and what a great choice he'd made, but she still felt as if she were auditioning. He touched her body at night, up in that big bed of his where she wasn't sure she'd yet had a good night sleep, no matter how he made her shake and cry into her pillow, so riled up was she at the notion that she was sharing a bed with *Gray Everett*. And that she would be doing so for the rest of their lives.

Maybe if she lost herself in routines and schedules and all the domestic things that fell under the banner of *rancher's wife* that she'd signed up for, then she'd start to feel like Gray's wife. Instead of an imposter on a trial run who could be dismissed at any moment.

Becca wasn't her daughter. She had no right to interfere with the way Gray parented her. Or to complain about the way he ran this house, for that matter. He had been nothing but kind to her, but he'd never promised her an equal partnership. He'd promised her a very specific role, and she'd chosen to dive into it because, quite apart from imagining she could make herself useful, she loved him. She'd always loved him. And because she loved him, she'd been sure she could push the boundaries of that role into something that more closely resembled her grandparents' relationship. The kind of relationship she read about in her books.

Gray hadn't volunteered for any of that. She couldn't fool herself into thinking otherwise, no matter how his hands moved over her and in her in that wide bed upstairs.

But on the other hand, she certainly hadn't agreed to whatever "a simple Christmas" was.

When she found herself wiping down the kitchen counters for the third time, because she was obviously stalling, Abby pulled herself together.

Fretting is the same as standing still, Grandma always said. *And worry never did solve a single problem.*

Maybe this was the benefit of the kind of marriage Abby had chosen. She didn't have to worry if something she did might ruin Gray's love for her, or make him think less of her, or any of the things she imagined people in more romantic relationships might feel.

All she had promised him was practicality.

She rubbed absently at her chest as she started down the small hallway that led to the ground floor bedroom that had been Amos's and was now the guest room where Brady like to make himself at home on the weekends. And farther still, the room Gray used as his office.

Her heart beat faster as she padded silently to the open door and stood there a moment.

She kept telling herself this wasn't a romance, that there was nothing romantic about the life they'd both agreed to live together and that was fine, but there was no stopping that seesaw of longing and hope and need that rattled around inside of her when she looked at him.

Every time she looked at him.

Gray was bent over his desk, frowning at a stack of papers and raking one hand through his dark hair, and Abby could have lost herself forever in the sheer perfection of his profile.

She wondered how long it would take before she stopped marveling at the fact that she'd tasted him now. That she'd kissed him. Repeatedly. She'd given him her virginity, and he'd given her a whole lot more in return.

He'd showed her a whole lot of other things in that hotel room, leaving them both gritty-eyed and smiling the next morning. Abby should have felt self-conscious about wearing her wedding dress that following morning, especially when she'd gone in to the coffeehouse as a customer, but she hadn't. Not with Gray there beside her, quiet and solid, the foundation holding up everything her life had been missing all this time.

She'd sat in his truck with her hands cupped hard around her favorite coffee drink, taking careful sips as he steered them home.

Home, she'd marveled.

The home they would make together.

The fields had looked different as they'd made their way down the other side of the mountain. And not only because the snow was falling, sweet little flurries that promised not to stick.

When they'd arrived at the ranch, she'd wondered if he would repeat what he'd done at the hotel and carry her over the threshold—

Abby had wanted to kick herself for the stab of disappointment she'd felt when he didn't.

Gray had immediately turned all business. He'd showed

her the way to their room—*their* room, which she still couldn't get her head around—and had nodded at the boxes that were stacked there beneath the window, and out into the hall.

"Feel free to settle in however you like," he'd said. "I'll call when I'm headed in for the night."

And that had been that. She'd been a newlywed, newly *deflowered* as well as newly a bride, and she felt so many things she didn't know how to name a single one of them as she stood there in a bedroom that hadn't felt the least bit like hers.

But she hadn't cried. Because she had nothing to cry about.

He had never promised her anything emotional.

Abby's great-grandmother hadn't had the benefit of knowing her husband-to-be when she'd ventured out west. Abby was *lucky*, or so she lectured herself that first day as she set herself to her boxes, unpacking things and putting them away as best she could while not wanting to take up too much of his space. She was lucky that she'd known Gray all these years. She was lucky that he'd showed her all the deliriously exciting things he'd showed her the night before. She didn't need romance when she had sex and certainty, surely.

Abby hadn't shed a single tear. Not even when she stood in his shower, then sunk down into the bath for longer than she'd usually allow herself, because her body felt like someone else's. Tender and fragile when she had never felt anything but strong and sure.

But maybe that was a gift for a girl who'd always considered herself *plodding*, like a Clydesdale surrounded by show ponies.

She'd lectured herself extensively on how she needed to behave and what she needed to do to hold up her part of the bargain. When dark began to creep in, it made sense to start dinner because that's what she would have done at home.

Your former home, she'd snapped at herself in the ranch house's kitchen, scowling at the big, red table with all its marks and scars that made it look better, not worse. Like a monument to all the Everetts that had come before her and had sat around it, weaving the bonds of land and family tight together.

She'd traced what looked like words carved into the table's surface and told herself she needed to make this her home. She needed to make herself a good wife.

The only example Abby had of a good wife was Grandma, who had never let Grandpa walk into the house at the end of a day without a hot meal waiting. Cooking for her new husband didn't only make Abby feel like a wife, it made her feel connected to her grandmother. And less homesick for that quiet, easy life she'd given up for this still-alien one that felt so strange all around her.

When Gray finally came in, he'd stopped in the back door with an arrested look on his face, not even finished with stamping off his boots in the mudroom.

"Is that dinner I smell?"

"I made a roast," she told him, nerves leaping around inside her. "I hope you don't mind that I helped myself to the meat in the freezer. If it was being saved—"

But the smile that cracked over Gray's face told her everything she needed to know. And better yet, made her feel that warm, settled thing inside her again. As if this was all meant to be. As if it was *right.*

He'd helped her with the dishes afterward in an easy, matter-of-fact way that told her it was a task he was well used to doing. Then he'd disappeared into his office for a few hours, which Abby had gathered meant she was left to her own devices for the evening.

You knew what you were getting into, she reminded herself as she sat on Gray's big, leather couch with her book. She found herself tracing cabbages against the leather, as if she could make them appear that way. *You know how little Grandpa was around when there were things to be done in the orchards.*

She ought to have been happy. Ecstatic, even. She got to live her life exactly as she'd been living it, only she got to spend time with Gray too. It was her dearest fantasy come true, and she should have been *joyful* as she sat out on that couch.

She hadn't meant to fall asleep in the living room that night, but she'd stirred awake when she'd felt herself lifted, then turned against his shoulder.

"Are you waiting for me?" Gray had asked in that deep, low rumble while he carried her, his arms and chest so warm it was better than a fire.

Abby hadn't meant to wait for him. But once he'd asked the question it was clear to them both that, of course, that's what she'd been doing. Because she didn't have it in her to slip into a bed she was expected to share with him. Not without any guidance.

She scolded herself not to get used to being carried around in his arms. It felt too good. It made her too . . . dreamy.

Upstairs in the bedroom, *their* bedroom, she'd been flushed and overly aware of every move she made as the two of them had navigated their way around the room together, in and out of the bathroom they now shared. Getting ready to *sleep together.*

"I didn't want to take any space that you were keeping

for you," she said nervously when he paused at the closet door, and she knew—she just *knew*—he was eyeing the clothes she'd hung in there. "I can move everything around again if this doesn't work. I wanted to get the boxes—"

"It's fine." He turned and studied her expression a moment. "It's good, Abby. Whatever you want."

She'd wanted more of the things he'd taught her the night before, stretched out in that hotel bed, all sensation and greed. But she certainly didn't know how to ask for it.

Abby had pulled on the usual long T-shirt she wore to sleep in and did her best to ignore it when Gray stripped down to his boxers. Meaning, she'd nearly fainted, but hadn't *actually* toppled over.

And when he'd headed toward the bed, she'd done the same, afraid that her heart was thumping loud enough for him to hear it. Or possibly kill her. They both crawled under the covers, as if that was normal. As if they did that every single night and always had. Abby was wired and wide-awake, but still, when Gray turned off his light, she turned off hers too.

Then she'd lain there in the dark, her eyes wide and her heartbeat wild, having no idea what was supposed to happen. Or if anything was supposed to happen. She didn't know how any of this was meant to work.

Her head was spinning so fast she was surprised it wasn't rocking the bed when Gray turned over and wrapped his arm around her middle, and everything in her . . . stilled.

"Hello, wife," he'd murmured, there in the dark, his mouth to her neck.

And then he'd taught her how to melt.

Tonight, standing in the door of his study, Abby was used to their routine now. Gray didn't touch her much during the day. He saved it all for those nights when the lights went out and it was only the two of them in a hushed dark of their bedroom.

Abby told herself that would have to be enough. It was so much more than she'd ever imagined.

"You going to say something?" Gray didn't look up as he spoke. "Or are you just going to stand there?"

Abby moved into the room and took a seat on the other side of his desk. "Do you have to do this much work every night?"

"I swear the paperwork grows and grows," he said darkly. "If something happens and I skip a few days, I'm backlogged for months. And then sooner or later, all hell breaks loose. I took over most of it for my dad a few years ago, but there were still a few things he was supposed to be doing. He wasn't."

He threw down the pen he was using and sat back in his chair, looking tired. And rumpled. And delicious.

"Can I help?" Abby asked.

"Help?" he echoed, as if he couldn't comprehend the word.

"I like office work. I'm good at it. There's no reason I can't do some of it, is there?"

"Not at all. I guess it never occurred to me that you would want to."

"Isn't this supposed to be a team effort? You shutting yourself away in here every night to do a few angry hours of work doesn't seem right. Not when I'm sitting around doing nothing."

A look of surprise moved over his face. He followed it with his hand. "I can't say I've ever been on a team. I got used to doing things by myself a long time ago."

Abby wanted to rub that part of her chest that ached again as she pictured solitary Gray, always alone no matter how many people lived in this house with him. She didn't.

She smiled instead. "You? A lone wolf of a rancher? Never."

He blinked at that, and then a different sort of heat lit those dark green eyes of his.

"Did you come in here to poke at me?"

His drawl was different then. Thicker. And thrilling.

It kicked around inside of her, so many brushfires they might consume her whole.

"No," she replied. "I didn't even come in to help you, though now I feel badly that I didn't offer that sooner."

Those crinkles in the corners of his eyes made her feel giddy. Again. "We've been married for eight days. There's not a lot of *sooner* to worry about."

"I came in about Christmas."

The mood in the room shifted, abruptly. Gray's gaze went cool and those laugh lines disappeared. Having convinced herself she'd misunderstood the tension at the dinner table, Abby wasn't prepared. It was alarming, so Abby sat a bit straighter and swallowed, hard. She couldn't say she liked the way Gray was studying her.

Too much steel. Not enough heat. "I told you I like to keep things simple at Christmas."

That look he was giving her made her even more nervous than she already felt. She tried to ignore it. "Becca talked to me about it on the drive home today. I don't know if you remember what we do over at the farmhouse—"

"I don't like Christmas, Abby. I don't know how to be more plain."

It was like a wall had come down between them. Abby wanted to shove at it with her hands, but she couldn't move.

"I don't know what that means. No tree? No lights? No decorations of any kind?" A more horrible possibility occurred to her. "You don't mean no presents?"

"Becca took you for a little ride," Gray said after a moment. "She already knew what the answer would be. She wanted it to be directed at someone else, for a change." He stared at her for another moment or two, and then a faint crease appeared between his brows. "You're staring at me as if I'm not making sense."

"Because you're not. Are you telling me that you don't celebrate Christmas?"

"That's what I'm telling you."

". . . at all?"

He shifted in his chair, impatiently.

As if she was annoying him.

Treating her like an annoyance was a surefire way to make her curl up inside herself and crawl away, but Abby forced herself to stay where she was. Gray's frown deepened.

"I don't appreciate being spoken to like something's wrong with me," he said, low and clipped. "You don't have to understand it. Everetts haven't celebrated Christmas in years. Not my brothers, not me. Definitely not Amos. That's just how it is."

"You're all grown men who can do as you like. What about your daughter?"

What about me? she didn't quite dare ask.

Because she doubted she'd like his reply.

"Becca goes and sees her grandparents at some point over her Christmas break every year, and from what I hear, they do it up. That's more than enough Christmas."

"Gray. You sound very sincere and very certain, but you really should have brought this up before. Because I would have told you that 'no Christmas' is not a concept I understand."

"You'll figure it out."

There was a note of finality his voice. But on the off chance she'd missed it, he redirected his attention to his paperwork, effectively dismissing her where she sat.

Abby had loved this man forever. She was already discovering the image she'd had in her head was very different than the reality, but until now, all those differences had been kind of wonderful.

There was a huge part of her that was urging her to walk out of the room. There was no point drawing lines in the sand if she had no intention of doing anything about them. She wasn't going to leave him after a week, no matter what holidays he celebrated. She didn't want to leave him at all.

But there was small voice inside of her whispering that if she backed down on something that mattered to her now, she always would.

She'd married this man because she loved him. He might not love her back. Maybe he never would. But if there was any chance at all that he might, however small, Abby knew with every fiber of her being that she had to be *her*. No matter if that disrupted these routines she'd already come to like so much.

It didn't matter that a huge part of her wanted to slink away and do what he asked, for fear he'd take all the marvelous things he'd given her away. His body. That smile. This marriage she'd never dreamed could ever happen.

"I don't know how to tell you this," Abby said quietly. "But that's not going to work for me."

15

Gray had never seen that expression on Abby's face before.

Stubborn, yes—but not in that adolescent way that Becca got stubborn. Abby didn't look emotional at all. Her gaze was cool and direct. There wasn't any trace of red on her cheeks.

There was no reason that should make Gray uncomfortable.

He refused to use the word "nervous."

"What do you mean it's not going to work for you?" he demanded.

He expected her to crumple and blush. She didn't.

"I love Christmas," Abby said simply. "I decorate the farmhouse with Grandma every year, and I do the coffee-house too. And it's still not enough. I love the lights. I love stockings over the fire. I love baking Christmas cookies, delivering them around town, and then baking some more. I like the house to smell like mulled cider and sugar at all times. And that's not even getting into the Christmas tree."

"We're not doing any of that."

His teeth were gritted and his hands were balled into fists, and he hated that she was making him feel out of control. He'd already done *out of control*. He'd married Abby for peace.

"I love going through the boxes of ornaments that Grandma and I have collected over the years," Abby continued as if she hadn't heard him. Or worse, didn't care. "Every ornament is a story. A memory. They're precious and beautiful, and if I could wear them on my heart, I would."

"No." Gray was astonished they were still discussing this.

He preferred the Abby who gazed at him as if he were a dream she'd had, come true there in front of her. He'd overlooked the fact that she'd managed that coffeehouse for years, which suggested she had more backbone than he'd ever seen in action before. Given that managers had to deal with hiring and firing and other kinds of decisive action. And it wasn't that he had anything against a backbone in general. He wanted her to have one, out here in these fields that could take far more than they gave, but he didn't want it used as a weapon against *him*.

"I think you're misunderstanding me." Abby smiled at him, but it wasn't that sweet smile he'd been getting used to this past week, up there in that bed of his that he'd never spent so much time obsessing about before. "I'm not asking your permission."

An old, familiar darkness roused itself inside of him, shook itself off, and sat up tall. And as much as Gray hated the things that made him like Amos, he did nothing to tamp it down.

He should have known better. He should have laid down the law from the start. The problem was, he hadn't expected all that damned chemistry. It had knocked him back, that first kiss. And then the sex had been way too good. Not only the night they'd gotten married, which Gray supposed he could chalk up to having waited all those years, but every night thereafter. If anything, it kept getting better. Abby was built for his hands, his mouth. He wasn't sure he could ever get enough of her— but it had made him lose sight of his actual goals here, which had nothing to do with what happened between them in bed. That was a bonus.

Gray needed to put more distance between them. Maybe he should have been glad she was apparently throwing down about Christmas, of all stupid things.

"I get it," he said, his voice hard. "You thought you'd come in here, butter me up with an offer of something you know would help me, and then demand something in return. Guess what? This isn't a transaction. That's not how this is going to work."

"This?" Abby repeated the word, and she looked paler than usual, but other than that, she was still. And no less focused than before. "Do you mean this marriage?"

"This marriage. This life. This."

He jutted his chin to indicate the space between them. Him, her. *This.*

Abby tipped her head to one side, her gaze darker than he'd ever seen it outside of a bed. "Do you get to decide what our marriage is? I could have sworn that was a team activity."

"I'm starting to remember why I don't do teams. If you think you can come in here and manipulate me, whether it's offers to do paperwork or access to your body or whatever else you have up your sleeve, you have another think coming. And I'd suggest you go on out there and get working on that second thought."

She stared at him for much too long. "Access to my body?"

Gray shouldn't have said that. He was folding the past into the present, and he knew better.

But this was classic Cristina. It was like a terrible flashback. Her endless bait and switch, giving him something he wanted so she could take something he didn't want to give, and he could still feel that cold shock fall through him when he'd realized what she was doing.

It made him furious that Abby was no different.

But it wasn't a simple fury. It was threaded through with betrayal, and that was the part that gnawed at Gray, making him angrier than he ought to have been.

"I didn't trick you into this, Abby," he gritted out. "You knew exactly what you were getting into."

"Really? Because I don't recall you mentioning that you were the Grinch in the middle of our wedding ceremony."

"This isn't a debate. You already got your answer. I'm not going to waste my time arguing about the fact you don't like it."

Finally, color flooded her pretty face. But it didn't make him feel any better.

"So this is it? You get to lay down the law, and that's the end of the discussion? Because I didn't sign up for that either."

"I never made any secret about who I am or what I expect. Maybe you need to ask yourself why you imagined that would change once you moved in."

"Gray—"

"I married you because I needed help, Abby. Not because I wanted grief. I get enough of that from my brothers. My kid. I don't need it from you too."

He was letting that darkness in him get the better of him, he knew. But he couldn't stop it. Just as he couldn't control the rawness that had taken over his voice. God knew what expression he might have on his face.

And the worst part was he had no idea what his new wife might do next.

For a moment, she did nothing. She sat across from him, her cheeks hot and her eyes burning, and merely stared back at him. And it hit Gray how little he really knew her. He didn't know what that steady gaze meant. He didn't know how she handled her temper. His own mother had gotten quieter and more thin-lipped. His short-lived stepmother had preferred stomping around the house in a fury, sharing her feelings with slammed doors, the heavy tread of her feet, and the odd glass or plate against a wall. Amos's other girlfriends had run the gamut between operatic tears, threats, and in one particular case, actual attempts at bodily harm.

Cristina, meanwhile, had preferred a war of attrition. Burned dinners. Sleeping in the guest room or once, notably, on the bathroom floor. Refusing to do any housework for weeks at a time. And then, when she was really mad at him, she'd sweetly agreed with every word he said and had gone out and cheated on him behind his back.

He told himself it was curiosity, nothing more, rolling around inside of him as he waited to see which way Abby would go. There was no reason for him to feel tense, or scalded by a familiar and acrid disappointment.

After an eternity, Abby shifted slightly. Then rose to her feet in that unconsciously graceful manner of hers that drove Gray crazy. Not least because she was totally unaware of the effect it had on him.

"My offer to help with the paperwork stands," she said, and there was something about the even tone she used that set his teeth on edge. "I don't offer my help with strings attached."

"Meaning I do?"

Abby shrugged. "I can't possibly answer that. As you've made very clear, I don't know you at all."

Gray didn't want to yell. He didn't want to start down

that road. He wasn't sure why he felt halfway down it already. "You know everything you need to know."

"I know a whole lot more tonight."

"Don't make a holiday into a war, Abby."

"Because, of course, there's nothing between obedience and war. Certainly not anything that looks like compromise. Got it."

"I get that you want to fight about this." But it was Gray whose fists were clenched. "I still have a couple hours of work left, and this isn't making it go any faster."

Abby looked down at him and she didn't *do* anything, particularly. And still, he felt small. Like a tightly-packed ball of all that ugliness he'd never wanted in his life. All that darkness he did his best to pretend wasn't there inside of him, even when it sloshed around the way it did now.

He wanted to blame her. But he had the lowering notion that there was no one to blame but him.

"My apologies," Abby said stiffly.

And it made him feel even worse when all she did was walk out of the room. No stomping feet. No slammed doors. The house was quiet until he heard the dryer go on in the laundry room off the kitchen, suggesting that no matter how pissed she was, Abby wasn't planning to shrug off the domestic labor they'd agreed to split up between them.

Gray felt like a jackass.

He tried to concentrate on the stacks of papers before him, but he kept going over and over the night in his head. The fact that Becca had set them up. The fact that Abby hadn't backed down. What was he supposed to make of that?

He shoved the papers away and sat back in his chair. This was exactly what he didn't want. This was what marrying Abby had been meant to circumvent. He couldn't count the number of hours he'd sat in this very chair, try-ing to figure out what the hell he was going to do about Cristina. He didn't like the flashback. But it was more than a flashback, because he was . . . antsier. And this was a lot sooner in the marriage. Cristina had fooled him for a good long while.

Abby is not Cristina, he growled at himself.

He didn't believe in ghosts. And he had no intention of retreading old ground.

But here he was. Sitting up in the office, letting his wife interfere with his work. Exactly what he wanted to avoid.

Sounds like the common denominator is you, whis-pered a rough voice deep inside him that sounded a hell of a lot like Amos.

But Gray wanted to think about his father even less that he wanted to think about his late wife.

He didn't like Christmas. He didn't get why that needed to be a federal case. He had no warm, fuzzy Christmas memories rattling around inside of him. The holidays had always been an opportunity for the adults in this house to act even worse than they normally did. He remembered his mother's attempts to pull off a decent Christmas and the way they'd failed, time and again. They'd either been filled with nearly unbearable tension as everyone tiptoed around Amos and counted his drinks, or Amos had started the whole thing off drunk, ruining it before it started. What-ever happened, it was always awful.

The best part about Amos's last ten years or so was that they'd all stopped pretending.

Gray rubbed his hands over his face. Once, then again. But that didn't help. He was still raw. There was that dark thing inside him, but then there was the look on Abby's face. He didn't want to feel like this. He didn't want to *feel*.

The whole point of this marriage was to get around the

weight of the relationships Gray had witnessed, disliked, and lived through himself. It wasn't supposed to be weighty at all. It wasn't supposed to divert his attention.

Much less make him feel like his own, rotten father.

He reached out and jabbed his finger on the flashing message light on his phone. Two robocalls, one political and one claiming he'd won some kind of cruise. Gray rolled his eyes and deleted each one.

"Jonathan Townes here," came the final message. "I'm calling from Townes Realty down here in Denver. We represent high-end, once-in-a-lifetime properties, and I've had a nice chat with your brother Brady about the family ranch."

Gray didn't hear the rest of the message. He was too busy noting that it was actually, physically possible to see red. He had the vague impression of a request for a return call, an invitation to view a website, but all he really heard was his brother's name.

He pushed back from his desk and stopped pretending he was going to get any more work done that night.

Temper stormed through him, mixing with something less sharp and more painful, deep inside him. He left his office, not sure if he was happy or further irritated that Abby was nowhere to be seen. Wasn't that how this went? He'd done this before. It started with a few sharp words. Then, like tonight, Abby had already gone upstairs rather than reading on the couch until he was finished.

He knew where it ended. He knew it all too well.

Instead of heading up to his bedroom, he blew out a breath and went into the kitchen.

He expected to find it empty, so he had to take a minute when he saw the figure bent over the open refrigerator door.

"You don't have to forage, Ty," he said, aware that he was letting his pent-up temper get the best of him. "You're welcome at dinner anytime. Of course, that would mean you'd have to put down the bottle long enough to sit at the table with the rest of us."

It seemed to take Ty a long time to straighten. And even longer to shut the refrigerator door and turn around.

But he was wearing that damn smile of his when he did.

"Spoiling for a fight, big brother?" he asked, his drawl more pronounced than usual to Gray's ears.

"Just pointing out that you've been here for a month already and, as far as I can tell, you drink all day, sneak into my kitchen at night, and then do it all over again."

Ty's smile got broader. But it didn't reach his eyes.

"That sounds like vacation to me. I didn't realize I needed to report in for duty."

"Of course not." Gray regretted this conversation already. He could have let Ty eat in peace. His brother's choice to drink his life away had nothing to do with him. But here he was, standing in his own kitchen with his arms folded over his chest, doing his best to be his brother's keeper. And he couldn't stop talking. "Why would you bother to help out? Brady's down in Denver selling our land out from under our feet. You're up here drinking like you want to fill the hole Dad left behind. I guess we're not really the Everetts if one of us isn't falling down drunk all the time."

Ty ran his tongue over his teeth. There was a spark of something in his brother's gaze—temper, feeling, *something*—but Ty never dropped that affable expression of his.

"I don't believe I'm falling over," he said, mildly enough. "Just like I don't believe it's your business how much I drink."

"There are no answers at the bottom of a bottle, Ty. You know that as well as I do."

"Who says I'm looking for answers? Maybe I like the journey."

"Great. You're on a journey. You might want to stop and ask yourself what's going to happen when this land is all condos and you don't have a rent-free place to enjoy your downward spiral."

"What's rent-free?" And this time, that smile of his had an edge. "This conversation feels a whole lot like rent."

"What the hell happened to you?" Gray demanded.

"About two thousand pounds of pissed-off bull."

"I know that's the excuse. But you were just as drunk a year ago when you came home for Christmas. Or do you not remember?"

Ty's eyes glittered, and for the first time in as long as Gray could remember, he didn't even pretend to smile. "Maybe you should worry less about me and more about your own crap."

"My crap? You mean, like the ranch that's up and running entirely because of me? That crap, Ty?"

"Climb on down from your cross, Gray. No one asked you to take on responsibility for everything in the whole damn world."

"You're right. I should have run away from this place like you. Dad could have run it straight into the ground, and the bank could have foreclosed years ago. Why didn't I think of that?"

He heard his own voice. Too loud. Too rough. Too much like he was the one reenacting the life and times of Amos Everett, not Ty.

And that burned in his gut like a whole new shame.

"I may be a drunk," Ty said quietly. "I'm not going to deny I like my whiskey. But one thing I don't do, big brother, is stand around having fights with drunk people who aren't in the room. You should think about doing the same."

He offered Gray a sardonic salute, then turned to walk back out of the kitchen into the night.

Leaving Gray in this mess he'd made.

He didn't know how long he stood there, Ty's unwelcome words echoing around inside his head. He knew his brother was right. Gray was spoiling for a fight—but not with Ty. He wasn't sure he was even all that mad at Abby. Or, for that matter, Cristina, who'd paid a pretty high price for her inability to deal with the toxic atmosphere in this house.

But Amos was another story.

Take Christmas. Gray felt like an alien that he couldn't even fake his enjoyment of something that seemed to bring every other person he knew so much happiness. What kind of messed-up, bitter creature was he that he couldn't put up a stocking? Throw some plastic lights on a tree?

But he knew why the very idea made his stomach turn.

There was the Christmas that Amos had gotten wasted and thrown all the presents under the tree into the fire. There was the Christmas Amos ran their mother off, throwing her clothes out into the snowy yard while *A Christmas Story* played on an endless, mocking loop on the television in the living room. The Christmases where pretending Santa existed couldn't make up for the sense of dread that choked all of them as they waited to see when, not if, a table would get flipped. Or when, not if, Amos would use his fists. Or any combination of those holiday treats.

He'd tried with Cristina when Becca had been young. Amos had been too old to be an actual threat, but that hadn't kept the old man from shooting off his mouth.

It'd been a relief to stop.

Abby standing there in front of him talking about cookies and sugar and Christmas trees made his chest hurt. He wasn't the one who'd ruined Christmas. He was a survivor of too many terrible holidays to count.

But he didn't want to be this guy. The one standing in his kitchen, alone, fuming at things that could never be fixed or changed.

Gray forced himself to slap the lights off, then head upstairs. And if he had a moment when he considered bunking down on the couch, well, it wouldn't be the first time.

But he refused to accept that his shiny, new, deliberately practical marriage had already ended up there. No matter Abby's feelings about his position on Christmas.

He expected the lights to be off, so it was a surprise to see light under the door when he made it to the second floor. He set his jaw as he walked toward it, bracing himself. He should have known that Abby's quiet, dignified retreat wasn't the end of it.

When he opened the door and walked in, she was sitting up in bed with one of her books. Gray busied himself with his usual bedtime ritual, telling himself that just because she was quiet didn't mean there was a problem. She was reading. Maybe he should take that at face value.

When he walked over to crawl into the bed, she set the book down and fixed her gaze on his.

"Did you wait up so we can keep fighting about this?" he asked.

Her eyes narrowed at his tone, but she didn't say anything when he threw himself down. Or when he tucked his hands beneath his head. Gray stared at the ceiling, much too aware of her beside him. The silence stretched out.

Abby reached over and extinguished her light, but Gray knew she was as wide awake as he was.

Wide awake. Tense. Ready for the next shoe to drop.

Welcome to your marital bed, jackass, he gritted out at himself.

"I don't know how this works," she said into the dark of the room, approximately twelve years later.

"Which *this* is it now? Because I don't care how mad you are me, Abby, I can't stay up all night fighting about nothing." He sounded angrier than he was. Much angrier than he wanted to sound. "Even if I wanted to."

At first he couldn't comprehend what happened. She moved fast, and it took him too long to understand that she'd actually rolled over and swatted him.

With her book.

"Did you just . . . *hit* me?"

"Your arm can take it. You have enough muscles."

"I didn't say it hurt. I'm wondering if this is really the road you want to go down. You might want to think it through."

She shifted in her place beside him, and he stopped pretending he was fascinated by his own ceiling.

"That's the thing, Gray. I don't know how these fights work. I don't usually fight with anyone besides my mother, and she tends to win. Do we just lie here? Does it take a few hours to feel better? Or do you never feel better?"

"That's up to you."

"But—"

"Freeze me out as long as you want, Abby," he said, and he didn't know if she could hear how bitter he sounded. But he could. "Feel free."

When he heard her move again, he braced himself. And again, he didn't understand. Because this time, she wasn't trying to beat him with the paperback. Instead, she'd rolled herself toward him, so he could feel that lush, long body of hers flush against his side.

Or, he thought on another rush of bitterness, so she could torture him more by withholding herself.

It was all well and good to claim this marriage wasn't transactional. But he couldn't actually make her quit bartering with whatever she imagined he'd want if that was how she played it. The very idea made him feel sick.

"You're not getting my point," Abby said, and his eyes had adjusted to the dark then. She was frowning at him, but her hand was smoothing its way across his bare chest. "I don't want to freeze you out."

"You don't?"

"I like what happens here, in this bed, when the lights go out." Her voice was fierce. And he was a dimwit because it only just dawned on him that she was naked. "I don't see why you being an authoritative ass should mean I have to miss out."

Gray's heart kicked at him. In his chest and, far harder, in his sex.

"I believe it's called hate sex," his untouched, virginal wife informed him, even as her hand move down his abdomen to grip him.

Just the way he'd taught her.

"That's not what it's called," he told her, but he was already moving. "Not exactly."

He rolled her on top of him, lifting her so he could move the heat of her against him. He found her wet. Ready. *His.*

"But we can practice if you want," he growled, gripping her hips and bringing her down on him. Hard.

Abby rode him as if she'd been born to move over him like this in the dark, temper and passion fusing into a white-hot, blistering kind of need that Gray wasn't sure they'd both survive.

He wouldn't call it "hate." It was too rich. Too furious. *Too good,* he thought, as they hit that edge and shot over into the flames he was sure would burn them both alive.

But at least they'd turn to ash together.

16

It was almost two weeks later when Abby closed down the coffee shop at six p.m. as usual, which in the deep, inky dark of December felt more like eleven p.m. She did the last check and clean of all the machines and the kitchen, then bustled around between the tables to make sure they were wiped down and ready for the morning rush. She called goodbyes to her baristas as they made their way out into the night, the frigid blast of air from outside making her shiver, and locked up the front doors behind them.

Everything was the same as it always had been. She might have changed addresses, but the core of who she was and what she did was the same.

She chanted that to herself as she wound her way into the back room to collect Becca, who was doing her homework at Abby's desk the way she did on the evenings Abby closed. She reminded herself that her life was *great*.

Yes, she asserted inside her own head. *Absolutely* great *in every way.*

She had her marriage now. A ranch house that was hers to change or keep as she liked, as long as it wasn't Christmas-themed. She had a teenage stepdaughter who she genuinely liked and who seemed to like her in return. And she had a husband who, sure, was a touch uncompromising, but almost made up for that flaw every night in their bed. What more could anyone want?

That was a question Hope had asked her directly earlier this afternoon when Abby had wondered, out loud, when she would stop blushing every time she heard Gray's name.

"You're still in the newlywed stage," Hope had said, rolling her coffee cup between her palms after Abby had pulled her drink. She hadn't done much to hide her big grin at the bright red shade of Abby's face. "I'm pretty sure that will wear off. The pheromones go, and then it's all arguing over the television remote and lives of quiet despair, right?"

Abby had rolled her eyes. "You know that from your great wealth of experience with marriages, I take it?"

Hope had laughed, but a moment later had sobered. "Maybe it's different for you. You're married to the love of your life. What more could anyone want?"

What indeed, Abby thought now. Maybe with unnecessary darkness.

Because maybe she'd been a bit too cavalier about the idea she could love enough for the both of them. And maybe she should have listened to Rae when she'd suggested that some of Gray was actually not better than none at all.

But she'd made her own bed, hadn't she? And she decided to focus on what they did in it every night, no matter if they'd agreed with each other much ahead of time. Abby had heard people say that sex didn't solve anything, but she figured they'd never had sex with Gray.

He was the same in bed as he was out. Stern. Uncompromising. And very, very sure of himself.

She shivered again, but this time, it had nothing to do with the cold.

Last night, he'd taught her the fine art of taking the length of him into her mouth, and had then returned the favor, until Abby had not only been wrung out and beside herself—she'd been tempted to imagine she was as pretty as he made her feel.

She shut that down hurriedly, and not only because it was inappropriate to think about such things while staring at Gray's daughter.

Abby cleared her throat. "Are you ready to go?" she asked Becca when the girl looked up. "I have to stop—" She almost said "home," but caught herself at the last second. "I need to swing by my grandmother's house on the way."

"And upset my dad's beloved routine?" Becca asked, something a touch sharper in her tone than in her smile. "How will he survive?"

"I like a routine myself." Abby wasn't sure if she was defending Gray or herself. Or both of them. Or why she felt that little prick inside her that urged her to do it in the first place. "My grandmother always says, 'A place for everything and everything in its place.' That goes for people, places, and things, in my opinion."

Becca flashed that smile that Abby wasn't sure she still considered quite so self-possessed. It was too studied. Too deliberate. "That's why you and my dad are so great together."

Abby didn't quite believe that cheerful tone either. But what could she do? Demand that Becca tell her father's brand new wife all her true thoughts and feelings? Abby was pretty sure that was a quick way to establish herself as the evil stepmother no one wanted.

Still. She'd married Gray, and Becca was a part of the new family they were supposed to be building. She braced herself as they headed out the back of the coffeehouse together. She wasn't Becca's mother. They weren't even friends, necessarily. But Abby spent the bulk of her days with people far younger than herself, including a handful of baristas who were still in high school. Surely she could handle one conversation with a fifteen-year-old.

"You know," she said, as carefully as possible once they'd climbed into the car and were letting the engine warm up. "It's okay if everything *isn't* great all the time. I know you're disappointed about the Christmas situation. I'm disappointed about it myself. We can talk about that too. I mean, if you want."

"But everything *is* great," Becca replied quickly, and when Abby glanced at her, she was frowning. "Isn't it? Would you tell me if it wasn't? I never should have brought up Christmas. I knew what my dad was going to say."

"Everything is fine," Abby said with as much conviction as she could muster. Because it was. Her *feelings* weren't supposed to be involved, so what did it matter if they'd gotten bruised? "I didn't know your dad's position on Christmas, so I'm glad it came up. I guess I'm trying to say that your dad and me being together is an adjustment. A big change. You might feel one way about it one day and another the next, and that's fine."

She didn't want to admit that she'd spent hours in Capricorn Books leafing through self-help volumes with names like *The Complicated Family: How to Connect with Your Stepchildren*. That had to be cheating. Surely everyone else was a natural. Or felt less like a fraud.

Of course, Abby assumed that most people reading about their complicated families and stepchildren hadn't actually gotten together for all those purely practical reasons she listed in her head. Like a prayer. Because it helped her remember the thing she kept forgetting—that she was the only one in love in her marriage.

And that was okay. That was what she'd signed up for. It was her own fault if she found it hard to bear.

That was the thing she hadn't told Hope this morning. That was what she hadn't told anyone. She carried it around instead, an anvil where her heart should have been, and it only seemed to shift when Gray was moving deep inside of her.

You have no one to blame for your feelings but you, she reminded herself as she headed down Main Street, very deliberately not looking at all the bright and shining Christmas lights as she went.

"I meant what I said before the wedding," Becca said. With great fervor. "I'm happy my dad got married, and I'm even happier that it's you."

"Well, I'm happy too," Abby said, aware that she wasn't really scratching beneath Becca's deliberately cheerful surface with her attempt at this conversation. And might even be making things worse if Becca was now concerned about her father's brand new marriage.

She held her breath, but Becca only waited a moment, then bent her head to send out as many series of texts as she could before they lost service up on the mountain. And Abby couldn't help wondering if she was as obviously *not great* to her friends as Becca was to her.

It was clear to her the girl was not only wound too tight, she was deeply committed to staying that way. And there was nothing wrong with that. Abby didn't really believe there was anything *wrong* with Becca, but she did wonder what was beneath all the forced cheer.

And more, why Becca felt the need to act that way in the first place.

Then again, Abby knew a whole lot about motherless girls and all the ways they had to parent themselves and find a way to explain the gaping hole right there in the center of their lives.

Abby had certainly had her own struggles. Lily had been like a black cloud hanging over her no matter what. No matter if Lily came around or stayed away. But Abby couldn't remember beating herself up worrying about being perfect and happy and *fine with everything* . . .

But maybe she hadn't called it that. She'd been so worried about acting out the way Lily had. The way she knew folks expected her to do, because like mother, like child. She'd heard all the stories. More than she'd wanted to know. What Lily had got up to in high school with all the boys who'd followed her around—and were now the fathers of people Abby had gone to school with, pastors and shopkeepers and *gross*. The implication had always been clear.

Your mother liked the boys, Lucinda Early had told Abby years ago in church, and had made a great show of saying nothing more. As if saying anything to Lily's abandoned fourteen-year-old daughter was her tactfully restraining herself.

Abby had understood too much, even then. The way Lily talked about her "friends." The lengths she was willing to go for them—like driving clear across the state to Grand Junction on Christmas Eve after a phone call—when she'd made it clear she wouldn't cross a street to see her own kid.

Abby couldn't remember beating herself up about that and other unpleasant truths about her mother, but she'd had a remarkably conflict-free adolescence with her grandparents, hadn't she? She'd even been smug about it. She'd chalked up her easy relationship with Grandma and Grandpa to simply being that much *better* as a *person* than her mother.

Lily might have been beautiful. Everyone said so. But Abby was *good*.

She'd gotten a lot of mileage out of that distinction. It had filled her with light, some dark seasons. It had made her feel *right*, no matter what horrible things Lily might have said to her.

But as she sat next to Gray's daughter, heading back to Gray's house, where he would eat her food with appreciation, show her more of his paperwork so she could actually help him, and tear her up in his bed later but never, ever love her, something else occurred to her.

Her stomach sank.

Was it possible she'd been putting on an act all those years the way she was fairly certain Becca was now? She would never admit it to Hope or Rae, but she certainly could have gone to that dance with Tate Bishop way back when. She'd known he liked her. Or could. But Abby had been far too dedicated to her endless, impossible, unrequited crush on an older man who'd never given her the time of day.

It had never crossed her mind that she might have chosen to love Gray *because* he was unattainable. That the high school boy who might have liked her was real and scary, but the dream of Gray was safe. That all this time, she hadn't been following her own path as much as she'd been doing whatever she could to make sure she was different from her mother. In every possible way.

Lily liked the boys, so Abby was a vestal virgin who loved only the man she couldn't have.

Lily fought with everyone, so Abby went out of her way to find the good even in those neighbors she didn't much like. Like Amos Everett.

Lily caused her parents nothing but sorrow, so Abby

had dedicated herself to being a source of joy for her grandparents.

Lily moved from place to place like a ping-pong ball, so Abby had stayed put.

She'd prided herself on being nothing like her mother—but she'd never stopped to think that doing the opposite was nothing but a twisted way of proclaiming a person's importance.

That unpleasant notion sat in her belly like a hunk of the mountain itself as they climbed up the steep side of the hill. Becca messed around with the music, and Abby was fiercely glad when she turned it up too loud for conversation.

Because she didn't quite know how to sit with that. She preferred the image she carried around of herself. A good citizen, a conscientious granddaughter. A dependable worker. A great friend. And so selflessly devoted to Gray, all these years. Delighted to take any scrap of his attention. *Honored* to marry him when he'd made it clear love and affection weren't anywhere on the menu.

She hadn't complained. It hadn't occurred to her to ask for more.

Because she'd spent her whole life making sure she was the anti-Lily. The one who made no waves. The one who was rational and easy about anything and everything. A thirty-year-old virgin. A practical *appliance*. The perfect wife for a man who didn't want any emotional attachments.

Not even to Christmas.

Congratulations, Abby, she told herself with a surprising slap of bitterness as she made it over the mountain and coasted down into the dark, cold fields. *You've done everything perfectly.*

Maybe she shouldn't have been surprised when she pulled in to the farmhouse drive and saw that newly familiar sedan parked next to Grandma's red truck. Had she known? Had it been there in Grandma's voice when Abby had called earlier to say she'd be swinging by? Was that why she'd spent this whole drive turning herself inside out and exposing things she'd never, ever wanted to look at straight on?

She was reeling from too many revelations that she really hadn't wanted, so it made sense that Lily would be here. Of course, she was here.

"What's the matter?" Becca asked worriedly when Abby parked the car but didn't get out.

"Nothing at all," Abby said, trying to sound upbeat. And realizing the instant she did that she sounded a lot like Becca always did. She assumed that made her about as convincing. "It looks like my grandmother has a visitor, that's all."

"A visitor?" Becca echoed, but Abby didn't answer her.

She was too busy lecturing herself instead as she climbed out of the car. She would not react. She would not sink to Lily's level. She would not let her mother get to her, no matter what she said or did. She would not engage. She would not play this same old sad game that she'd imagined she'd outgrown years ago—until she'd had to walk out of another Thanksgiving dinner.

Abby let herself in the side door that led into the kitchen, Becca at her heels. Maybe too close on her heels, but Abby wasn't about to complain about having backup, even if it was in the form of a fifteen-year-old. It was always possible *something* might shame Lily into holding her tongue.

Possible, but not likely.

This time, Lily was sitting in Abby's usual seat at the kitchen table, cutting up vegetables the way Abby would have been doing herself a few weeks ago. And all the things Abby had been telling herself disappeared.

Because it felt sharp and hot and nearly crippling. It felt like a betrayal.

It was as if Grandma had used that sharp paring knife of hers. As if she'd picked it up, hurled it across the kitchen, and hit Abby square in her gut.

Abby knew she wasn't being fair. Lily had lived in this house long before Abby ever had. Lily had her own relationship with her own mother, no matter how Abby felt about it. She knew all that.

But knowing it didn't take away from the thick, painful kick in her stomach or the sudden prickle of tears she refused to let fall.

"I came to borrow those baking sheets," Abby said instead, and she could hear her own stiffness in her voice. Her much-too-loud voice. She knew she was probably standing there the same way, formal and awkward, here in this kitchen that still felt like her real home.

A home that Lily was invading. Again.

And the fact Abby had a different home now didn't seem to help.

"Help yourself to as many baking sheets as you like," Grandma said in her mildest possible voice.

Normally, when faced with an unexpected repeat of a visit from Lily—especially when it came so soon on the heels of the unpleasant one before—Abby would have marched in, done what she needed to do, and then cleared out as quickly as possible without acknowledging that Lily was back.

But today she wasn't alone. Becca was standing there at her side, and Abby was sure she could feel the girl vibrating with tension. Which meant Abby had to decide, then and there, if she was going to do the same damn thing she always had, which had never resulted in anything but more of Lily's same behavior. Or if she was going to be the person she wanted to be regardless of what her mother did.

Abby didn't want to give Lily the satisfaction of ignoring her. That only gave her power. And Abby had learned a few things about power these last weeks in Gray's bed. What it felt like to make a hard man shudder. What it meant to surrender to someone she knew without a doubt would hurt himself to keep her safe. How different the world felt around her when he ran his hands and mouth all over her body as if she were spun sugar and pretty straight through.

She didn't owe Lily a thing. Especially not her emotions.

"You're back so soon," she said. She even managed a smile and didn't have to look in a mirror to confirm it looked a whole lot like the one Becca was always using on her. "I wasn't sure we'd see you again this year."

Polite. Easy. The way she would talk to anyone who came into the coffeehouse.

"It seems I can't stay away," Lily murmured, in that overly suggestive way she said everything, with a hundred pointed knives bound up in every syllable. It made Abby want to scream. But she didn't. "I wanted to try out a homespun, country Christmas for a change."

Abby would usually snap back at that, even if she'd been trying to pretend Lily wasn't there. She'd pick a statement like that apart for all the disparagement she knew was bound up in it. She'd do her best to hurt Lily in return, even though, as long as she'd been alive, she couldn't remember a single time she'd managed to get beneath her mother's skin at all.

Maybe it was time to stop slamming her head against walls that were never going to break. Or even bend.

That resonated inside her like she'd gone and turned the music up way too high.

"You must be happy about that," she said to Grandma, and she tried her best to mean it. Not for Lily's sake, but because she knew her grandmother loved her daughter. Of course she did. "I hated imagining you alone on Christmas."

Grandma's steady gaze met hers and held, and Abby felt it like the hug she was pretending she didn't need.

"Your mother thinks she might stay a while," Grandma said in that same mild, serene way that told Abby she was conflicted. But possibly also hopeful, as little as Abby wanted to admit that. "Give Cold River another chance."

Abby felt all the usual emotions boiling up in her. She wanted to scream that Lily had given up her right to live here. She wanted to demand that once, *just once*, her grandmother stand up for herself and tell Lily exactly how her behavior had hurt her over the years.

Or if Grandma couldn't stand up for herself, stand up for Abby. And tell Lily she wasn't welcome here. Just this one time.

But Abby didn't live here anymore. She had no right to that hollow, scraped-raw feeling inside of her.

"That sounds great," she made herself say. She moved then, walking stiff-legged over to the cupboard beside the stove where Grandma kept her baking things. She pulled out her favorite cookie sheets and hugged them to her chest.

"It's nice to see you, Becca," Grandma said in that way of hers that had always made Abby feel better. Yet didn't tonight. "We appreciated you sharing your Thanksgiving with us."

"Of course." Becca's voice was strained. "Any time, Mrs. Douglas."

"You should watch our Abby carefully," Lily chimed in then, that usual malice spiking her voice. "Learn how to cook and clean and run around pretending that's all you want from life. Doesn't that sound fun?"

"Grandma, I'll talk to you later," Abby said instead of replying to her mother, still keeping her voice even. "Come on, Becca, we need to get—"

"I'd rather be like Abby than like you," Becca threw out into the kitchen, not moving an inch. She was frowning at Lily, but Abby was much more concerned with the way she was shaking. "Any day of the week."

"Would you?" Lily asked huskily. Abby knew that tone. And its danger. "That doesn't exactly shock me. You're the kind of pretty that disappears completely by the time you're twenty. You better lock down that high school boyfriend while you still can, little girl."

"Leave her alone." Abby didn't recognize her own voice. Or the way she was holding the baking sheets before her like a shield.

"This is the place to do it," Lily continued, almost merrily. But Abby could see her face. "Teenage marriage is a crime some places, but not here. There's nothing more to a happy life in Cold River than imprisoning yourself, barefoot and pregnant, in some cowboy's kitchen." Her cold gaze moved from Becca to Abby. "Isn't that right?"

"Is the alternative abandoning your family to chase after a parade of men who never want to keep you once they get to know you?" Abby retorted, because she could have ignored it if it was directed at her. But not when Lily aimed it at Becca. "I'll pass on that, thanks."

"I'll remind you that I was a teenage bride, Lillian," Grandma said, in that sedate way of hers that nevertheless sounded shot through with steel. "And I never spent my time barefoot in this kitchen when there was work to be done in the fields. It seems to me that the point of progress is so all women can make their own choices. None of the rest of us have to like them."

Lily laughed. And Abby knew that laugh. She knew it boded nothing but ill, but she couldn't seem to move. She felt frozen solid.

"We're not talking about you and Dad, Mom," Lily said dismissively. Deliberately. She tapped her knife against the cutting board on the table in front of her as if she couldn't contain herself, and worse, she smirked at Abby. "We're talking about Gray Everett, a man whose first wife hated him so much she slept with everything that moved and drove herself off a mountain road to get away from him. And let's not kid ourselves. He married Abby because whether she loses it or not, it's not like *she's* going to find anyone to cheat with." Her voice turned sharp and mocking. "Cowboy, take me away."

There wasn't a sound in the kitchen. Abby heard a kind of roaring and understood only distantly that it was in her head. Next to her, Becca made a small, hurt sound that pierced Abby straight through. She didn't wait for a response; she turned and slammed out of the kitchen.

Abby didn't watch her go because her eyes were on her mother.

"Lillian—" Grandma began.

"That was her father you were trashing," Abby bit out, interrupting her grandmother and unable to feel sorry about it. "Her *father.* What is *wrong* with you?"

Lily's dark eyes glittered, and she opened her mouth— but Abby wasn't done.

"I'm used to you. I'm used to you rolling into town and wrecking everything you can get your hands on. You're no different from any other storm. We weather you, we survive you, and we forget about you the minute you're gone.

But you leave that poor girl out of it. She deserves better in life than you."

"The angry lion mama thing looks great on you, Abby. Really. It's been, what? A couple of weeks? Very convincing."

"Mock me all you want," Abby said, her voice quiet and shaking with an emotion so violent she was afraid it would knock her over. "I stopped worrying about your approval when I was still in diapers. I've been waiting thirty years for you to stop embarrassing me, but I guess that's not going to happen. And it doesn't matter." She leaned forward, her fingers clenched hard on the metal edge of the baking sheets she was still gripping to her chest. "I understand that you're miserable. You're an empty, angry, jealous woman who wants attention any way she can get it. And since you've burned every bridge you've ever been near, the only way you can get it around here is by spewing out your ugliness on every possible surface. I get it. But if you ever talk to Becca like that again, it's not your own ugliness you're going to have to worry about. It's mine. And I should warn you, I have thirty years of it all saved up and ready to go."

She didn't wait for Lily's response. She turned on her heel and headed for the door.

"Marriage is clearly doing wonders for you, Abby," Lily said from behind her, a harsh edge in her voice. "Now you're threatening your own mother."

"Hush, Lillian," Grandma said, sounding tired and old. "You reap what you sow."

Abby didn't pause to revel in that unexpected show of support, though she tucked it away inside. She pushed her way out the door and all but ran to the car, wrenching the door open and shoving the baking sheets into the back as she climbed in. She expected to be greeted with tears, at the very least.

But Becca wasn't crying. She wasn't even breathing heavily. She was sitting with her hands folded, her spine rigid, staring straight ahead. Out into the dark, frozen fields that were only partly lit by the light from the farmhouse.

"I am so, so—" Abby began.

"Don't apologize. It's all true."

Abby sucked in a breath. "Nothing she says is true. It's always some twisted, horrible shadow version of the truth that has nothing to do with anything. Don't let her work her way inside you. She's poison."

Becca turned slowly, her face pale even in the dark. "I know who my mother was. I know what she did. You don't have to pretend."

Abby had never imagined she'd ever find herself called to defend Cristina Everett, but here she was, faced with Cristina's daughter and that terrible look on her face. She swallowed.

"Marriage is complicated, Becca. People don't always do the things they should. They hurt each other without meaning to. What happened between your parents was between them. You must know that your mother loved *you*, no matter what. She would never have left you on purpose."

Becca's mouth twisted into something much worse than a sob.

"You're wrong." Her voice sounded thick, as if she *were* the sob. "My mother left me *all the time*. That night wasn't anything special. She liked her boyfriends a whole lot more than she ever liked me."

"You were very young. You don't—"

"My grandfather." Becca shook her head, her mouth

still in that sad, vulnerable shape. "It was his favorite subject. He liked to flip the kitchen table and count all my mother's boyfriends, right there in my father's face. Why do you think the table is a door? It's the only thing he couldn't break."

Maybe every family had their own version of Lily. Abby didn't know why that possibility hadn't occurred to her before now.

"You shouldn't have had to hear any of that," Abby said softly. "I'm so sorry."

"Don't feel sorry for me," Becca fired back at her. "I'm fine. It's my dad you should feel for. First, my mother did what she did. Then, he spent years listening to my grandfather throw it in his face. And people in this town still think he *drove her to it* when maybe, just maybe, she was nothing more than a terrible person."

Abby's heart was beating so hard inside her chest, she was shocked it didn't pound open her car door. She tried to shake it off.

"She was confused, that's all. She wasn't a terrible person."

"She was disgusting." Becca's voice rose, and her eyes tipped over into tears that she jabbed at angrily when they hit her cheeks. "She was *disgusting*. I hate that I look like her. I hate that every time my dad looks at me, he sees *her*."

"When he looks at you, he sees *you*."

"In a couple of weeks I'm going to have to go to my grandparents' house. They have pictures of her everywhere, and they want me to sit with them and pray for her, and I *hate* her. Every year they tell me I need to forgive her. Everyone tells me I need to forgive her, but she's like your mother. She doesn't deserve forgiveness. She doesn't deserve *anything*."

Abby didn't know what the books would suggest she do

at a time like this. She didn't care. The pain in Becca's voice ate at her, and not only because it was so raw. But because she recognized it.

She reached over and grabbed her stepdaughter in a hug, holding Becca tight as she finally broke down and sobbed. And sobbed. Abby rocked her. She smoothed her hand over Becca's hair.

And when the storm subsided, a long while later, Abby wiped at the moisture in her own eyes.

"I'm never going to sit here and tell you that you need to forgive someone just because," she said, low and fierce in the chilly dark of the car. "I've never figured out how to do it myself."

If this was a preview of what mothering felt like, this unbearable ache for someone else's pain and the knowledge she'd dig it out with her own hands and carry it inside her if she could, if it would make Becca feel better, Abby felt something like seasick. Except far more humbled.

"But, Becca," she whispered. "Sweetheart. You're going to have to find a way to forgive *yourself*, because nothing that happened was ever or could ever be your fault."

"I don't know how." Her voice was a ragged, muffled wail into Abby's shoulder. "I don't know *how*."

"Me neither," Abby confessed, holding her tighter. If she had to, she would hold her forever. Two motherless daughters bound together now into something better. Something much, much brighter. "We'll figure it out together, Becca. You and me. I promise."

They sat there like that for a long, long time. Until they were both shivering from the cold. And when Abby finally started the car, they were both red-eyed and blotchy-faced. They sniffled at each other, and even laughed too, as if to wash themselves clean.

Then Abby drove them home.

17

When he heard the back door in the kitchen slap open, Gray assumed it was Abby and Becca back from town.

At last.

He'd expected them much earlier, but not, he'd assured himself every time he'd looked at the clock, because he *needed* them. He wasn't helpless. He'd been cooking for himself and others for years, and he was used to sitting in his office and eating there while Becca did her homework on the rug. That had kept them both away from Amos's drunken rampages or, worse, those nights when Amos seemed almost normal and cheerful. Until he lured you close so he could *really* stick the knife in.

Gray had discovered tonight that he much preferred the new life he was living in this house. It made the old house itself feel new.

His childhood had been marked by the turmoil here, all of his father's making. Divorces and all the messiness that went along with relationships imploding when the adults in question didn't much care about collateral damage. Then, he'd done his part and brought his own bad marriage home, adding to the chaos. Gray knew that was on him. But he'd had ten years since Cristina's accident to get used to setting himself apart from the drama that his father could kick up in an empty room.

It was funny looking back on it from the perspective of these weeks with Abby. Because he hadn't considered his life bad at any point. It had been his life with a few complications he couldn't do much about. There'd been no changing it that he could see, so he hadn't tried. He'd let Amos do what he liked even if that meant the old man did his worst—because it had been Amos's house and Amos's land, like it or not—and he'd done what he could to minimize the damage to Becca.

He'd focused on the land and his daughter, because they were the only things that were his, or would be eventually, once Amos finally kicked off.

Gray couldn't say he'd paid much attention to the house itself. His ancestors had built various structures here to take advantage of the well water. His great-great-grandfather had built the oldest part of the house that still stood and was now the living room Gray was sitting in tonight. And every successive generation of Everetts had built onto the ranch house, making it a sprawling, rambling place that had seemed to go on forever and yet had never been big enough to avoid Amos entirely.

But now even the house felt different, as if Abby had moved in and changed it from its foundation on up.

When he came in from the cold these days, even if Abby wasn't there, it was as if the rooms were altered now that she lived here.

Maybe it was Gray who was altered.

Abby was the most extraordinary woman. She hummed when she cooked, though Gray didn't think she knew it. He found himself lingering there in the door to the kitchen more often than he wanted to admit when she thought he was still in the shower, listening to her as she moved around getting dinner ready.

She hadn't changed much around here, so it didn't make sense that it felt as if she'd overhauled the whole ranch the way women sometimes did. He remembered one of Amos's short-lived live-in girlfriends who'd moved in, thrown out furniture and started repainting rooms—only to move back out long before the painting was done, leaving paint cans and oil cloths everywhere. The only visible change Abby had made was that she'd set up her own craft projects on the far end of the dining room table Becca used as her desk. And last weekend, she and Becca had sat there together, working on what Abby had called "neighbor gifts."

Gray didn't know what that meant. He didn't like gifts because he didn't want the obligation or all the intensity that came with the giving and the receiving, much less having to remember all the occasions people thought were important enough to merit gifts in the first place. And meanwhile, Abby clearly believed not only that there were different levels of gifts for different people, but that it was worth spending her free time *making things* to give them.

It baffled him. He thought maybe that should have annoyed him more than it did. Instead, Gray found it cute.

She was cute. More than that, she was determined. Ever since that talk about Christmas, which still left a bad taste in his mouth when Gray wasn't the kind of man who suffered from indecision over judgments he'd already made, Abby had come into the office every night after dinner to learn about the ranch and help him with the paperwork.

He hadn't had to cajole her. Or even remind her.

It made him feel like an ass for suggesting she was anything like Cristina, because she wasn't. On any level. In case he'd been harboring any doubts on that score, she hadn't been lying about her affinity for office work either. She obviously enjoyed it. She was good with numbers. And she had a flair for organization that made Gray's head spin, because who *liked* filing?

"I do," Abby had said when he'd asked that very question a few nights back. She'd looked up from where she'd been sitting cross-legged on the rug, papers spread all around her as she sorted years of ranch life into appropriate piles. And she'd grinned at him, making it impossible not to grin right back. "How can you ever really relax if you know things aren't in order?"

Gray maybe hadn't relaxed much. In years. And he wasn't a man given to unruly optimism, but with every day that passed, it was clear that having Abby in his life really might take a huge burden off his shoulders.

Another burden, that was, besides the office stuff.

She hadn't wanted to give up her job at the coffeehouse, and Gray hadn't seen any reason why she should.

"I guess that's something we should talk about," she had said. Very seriously, that first morning they'd woken up together here at the ranch. *Together.* Meaning, she hadn't stayed in bed half the morning and then staggered around acting as if it was early when Gray had been up and done half a day's work by the time she rolled out from under the covers. She gotten up with him before dawn, watched the way he fixed his coffee, and had then made sure it was programmed and waiting for him every morning thereafter.

"You mean like birth control?" he'd asked her, so he could see her flush bright red, there in the kitchen with nothing but the surly dark outside.

Her cheeks had heated up, and he'd liked that as much as he'd imagined he would.

"It's what married couples do, isn't it? Discuss how they want to order their lives together? Communicate, even?"

"Are you asking me my permission to keep your job, Abby?" he'd asked. "Or do you want me to throw out my opinion so you can react to it?"

Maybe he'd sounded too cranky. And he couldn't have said if that was because it was early and he wasn't used to company at that hour, or if he had already been defensive about a marriage he wasn't in any longer. Thank God.

But Abby hadn't gotten mad. She'd actually considered the question, her hands wrapped around her own coffee cup as she leaned there against the counter in the thick, flannel pajama pants she'd pulled on, a thick wool sweater wrapped around her like he'd been the night before, and her hair up in that messy ponytail that made him want to get his mouth on her neck again.

"I wouldn't like it very much if you made sweeping announcements about what I should do or not," she had said after a moment. Almost shyly, which had lodged inside him. Like a splinter he couldn't work out. "But I want your input, of course. We're supposed to be in this together, aren't we?"

The memory felt more pointed, now. She'd wanted a conversation about Christmas, and he'd come down on her like he was . . . Amos.

But the ways he was like that bitter, angry old man haunted him enough as it was. He'd told her he didn't see any reason why they should talk about her job until and unless there was childcare to consider, and that had been that.

Then it had made more sense, she had pointed out, for her to drive Becca because she was already going back and forth to town, freeing up a few more hours of Gray's day. He almost didn't know what to do with himself.

It was a weird thing when a man actually got what he wanted.

"Is it okay with you if Abby takes you to school and picks you up after?" he had asked Becca out in the barn one evening while they were tending to the horses.

"I would love that!" Becca had cried, as if she'd never wanted anything more than a woman in her life to drive her around.

As if the fate of the world depended on her enthusiasm.

Gray had blinked at that. "You don't have to prove anything. I expect you to treat Abby politely and with respect, the way you'd treat anyone, but you don't have to pretend you're best friends." He'd frowned into the stall where Becca was leaning against her favorite horse. "I know this is new. And fast."

"You worry too much, Dad," Becca had said dismissively. And then had been all smiles when she'd realized he was frowning at her. "Abby and I are going to get along *great.*"

And they had.

That was what Abby had already done for his life. She fit into it so easily and so fully, it was hard for Gray to remember what it had been like before. He already couldn't imagine this house or this life without her.

Which was why he scowled when the person who walked through his back door, across the kitchen, and into the doorway that led into his living room was Brady.

"To what do I owe this honor?" Gray drawled, and he didn't work real hard at keeping that dark edge out of his voice. He was kicked back on his couch, waiting for his wife and kid to come home, which was as relaxed as Gray ever got. Brady, however, was not relaxing. "It's the middle of the week, little brother. Don't you have important things to be doing down in Denver?"

"Nice to see you too."

"I see you all the time. More in the last month than in the previous year."

"Not that you're counting."

Brady stayed where he was in the doorway, and Gray watched as he shifted the duffel bag—a fancy leather duffel bag, naturally, because that was Brady—from his shoulder to drop it on the floor. With a *thunk* that struck Gray as ominous.

"You look like you're staying a while." Gray's tone was not welcoming. In the least. "Am I missing something?"

"It's Christmas, Gray. People come home for Christmas. Even me."

The last thing Gray wanted to hear about from anyone, but especially his little brother, was the looming horror of another Christmas. Especially after what had happened with Abby.

"Christmas isn't for weeks."

"Just about ten days, actually. You do know the date, right? And how Christmas is on the same day every year, rain or shine or seven feet of snow?"

"You usually rush in Christmas Eve and head out as soon as possible Christmas Day, weather permitting. Why the change?"

A kind of shadow moved over Brady's face, and if Gray didn't know better, he might have been tempted to imagine he'd hurt Brady's feelings. He didn't like the dark, oily thing that kicked around inside him then. It was much too close to outright shame, and it just made him mad.

"The reason I used to avoid coming home is dead now." Brady was stiff. "Though you're shaping up to be the same kind of reason."

Gray had no memory of getting to his feet. One minute he was sitting on his couch, a sports channel playing on the TV, pretending he was still enjoying his quiet evening alone. And the next he was standing there like he was getting ready to throw down with his brother the way they had as kids.

It was Christmas. Christmas, again. He was so damned tired of hearing about Christmas. Brady should have known better.

But then, Brady should have known better about a whole lot of things.

"I know you didn't just compare me to Dad."

"If the lonely ranch house fits, brother," Brady retorted, offering Gray the kind of slick smile that was as good as two raised middle fingers.

Gray didn't have it in him to hold back. Not anymore. Not when things were finally okay—so okay, in fact, that he'd actually allowed himself a measure of cautious optimism that they might stay that way.

"You have realtors calling me on the phone when I told you I didn't want to sell," he gritted out. "You roll in here every weekend to live off the ranch you don't do anything to support. Maybe you're counting your money in advance. But you think I'm like Dad? Me?" He let out a bitter laugh. "Take a look in the mirror, Brady. You give nothing. You complain and you take and you complain some more. You act like you're owed something, but you don't do a single thing to earn it."

Brady rubbed a hand over his hair, and Gray recognized it as a thing he did himself when he was trying not to lose his cool. He didn't like the comparison.

"I'm more than a little tired of you talking to me like I'm still in diapers."

"Then don't act like it." Gray was aware that they were squared off with only a few feet between them. His hands were in fists, and he could see Brady's were as well. And he didn't want to be that dark thing he could feel inside of him, pulsing and thick. He didn't want to give into it. But the urge to punctuate this conversation with the fist to the face Brady so richly deserved was almost overwhelming. "You keep telling me you're a grown man. Prove it. The world doesn't revolve around you, Brady. Let me know when you figure that out."

Brady took a step toward him, that same shadowed look on his face, even with that temper crackling his gaze. "You might want to put your persecution complex aside for five minutes, Gray. Everyone's not out to get you. *I'm* certainly not out to get you."

"You're real supportive. I can tell. That's why you had some slick scumbag from Denver call and talk at me about 'parcels' and 'build lots' and 'planned communities.'"

"That wasn't supposed to happen. But it doesn't hurt us to have all the information, does it? It's not an attack on you that I want to know exactly how much we're worth after all those years of Dad claiming the bank was three seconds away from taking everything." He blew out a breath. "Doesn't it make sense to figure out exactly what it is you're fighting so hard to protect?"

"Because you're just that altruistic."

"You could try trusting me," Brady threw at him.

"Oh, son," came Ty's lazy drawl from the kitchen. "Don't you know by now? Saint Gray doesn't trust anyone but his own self."

Saint Gray. Gray didn't care for the way that echoed around in him, settling too hard in his gut. He also didn't like the fact that Ty had walked into the house while Gray had been too busy trying not to kill Brady to notice.

"Great. A pile on. It's like the two of you are still the same little brats who used to follow me around."

"I've been called many things," Ty said, that grin of his

taking on a hard edge. "Terrible things, as a matter of fact, and most of them true. But I haven't been a little brat following you around for a lifetime or two, Gray. You might want to let that go."

"He can't lord it over everyone if he lets a single thing go, ever. Not one single thing." Brady made a show of rolling his eyes. "The world would fall apart."

"Why are either one of you here?" Gray asked, more loudly than he'd planned. He glared at one, then the other. "You're happy to move right into an outbuilding and pretend you're not on a bender, Ty, but the truth is, you could do that anywhere. And there's a lot of real estate in these mountains, Brady. You're so rich and fancy these days, go buy some. There's no reason for either one of you to subject yourselves to being in my house, under my roof, eating food that's in that refrigerator because of the work *I* do with my own two hands. I didn't invite you. I certainly don't need you—"

"You made that part clear," Ty drawled, daring to sound bored.

"Repeatedly," Brady agreed.

"Is this where you tell me off for fighting with drunk people who aren't in the room again, Ty?" Gray demanded. "Because guess what? I'm actually fighting with you. The drunk person who won't get the hell out of the room I'm in."

"Once again, I don't recall asking for your commentary on what I drink, how much I drink, or anything else," Ty murmured, with a dangerous glint in his dark eyes. The way a man had when he was about one second away from taking a swing.

They were all facing off now, in a weird trinity right there between the living room and the kitchen. Gray wanted to knock their heads together as if they were in an old movie. His hands twitched as if they planned to do it on their own.

He wasn't sure he had it in him to stop them.

"Dad isn't here anymore," Brady said, his quiet tone cutting through the tension in the house like an axe falling.

Ty blinked at that and looked away.

Gray frowned. "What are you talking about? You were at his funeral. We all were. You know he's not here."

"Dad's not here," Brady said again, more urgently. "But he might as well be sitting at that table, scribbling out that stupid will again and again. The man's been in the earth for over a month, and he's still pulling strings around here. We're still at each other's throats. We're still fighting. Everything is exactly the way he left it. He'd be thrilled."

"Don't be so dramatic," Gray gritted at him.

"Gray's the martyr. Ty's the drunk." Brady listed both things off much too easily, glaring at each of them as he said them. "And I'm the kid. Congratulations, jackholes. We're the living legacy of Amos Everett, exactly as he made us."

Gray didn't know what to say to that. Because it wasn't true, he assured himself, even as his gut twisted. It wasn't *completely* true, anyway—

But that was when Abby and Becca finally came home. First the headlights swept along the front windows. Then Gray could hear Abby's car pull up out in the yard. And he guessed he wasn't the only one who didn't know what to do with the tense atmosphere in the ranch house. His brothers stared at the floor, the walls. Gray found himself with his hands on his hips.

"What's the matter now?" Becca asked the second she came inside, sounding weird as she shrugged out of her jacket and looked from her uncles to Gray and back again.

Gray took in his daughter's appearance with a single glance. Red eyes. Too pale. And her voice was dull, which wasn't like her—especially not these days when she seemed to be auditioning to be the world's most constant cheerleader. He cut a glance to Abby as she came in behind Becca, who met his gaze and made a quick face that told him, without a word, that whatever it was, she'd handled it.

It took Gray a minute to understand why that felt so warm inside of him. And when he did, he didn't know where to put it. He wasn't used to having another parent around. He wasn't used to sharing the load.

Or any load at all, a small voice deep inside him chimed in.

"Your uncles and I were just having a family meeting," Gray told Becca. "Everything's fine."

He ignored the scoffing sound that Brady made at that, the same way he was ignoring the way Ty lounged against the nearest wall as if he was entirely too lazy—or too drunk—to stand up straight. And maybe it was the steady way he held Becca's gaze that let her blow out a breath, then nod.

"I assume you've all already eaten," Abby said briskly, heaving a bunch of metal cookie sheets onto the nearest counter and then going back to hang up her coat. Cookie sheets that Gray knew, without having to ask, had something to do with Christmas. Hadn't she said something about cookies? But he couldn't get into that right now. "I was going to throw something together for Becca and me. Unless anyone else needs some food? Ty? Brady?"

"I made chili," Gray said gruffly. Reluctantly. And he wasn't sure he liked the way everyone swiveled to look at him like he'd suddenly grown horns. "What? I can cook. Who do you think fed everyone around here the last ten years?"

"Dad's actually a great cook," Becca said staunchly, because she was his girl. She straightened her shoulders like she was heading into battle. "And you're lucky, because his chili is actually *amazing*."

Which was how Gray found himself sitting at the kitchen table with his entire family, all of them eating his chili and talking about random, impersonal things like traffic on the I-70 at this time of year and the icy, treacherous conditions on the Vail Pass that claimed unprepared tourists and the unwary every season because they braved it without the proper chains, snow tires, or four-wheel drive.

But Gray had already eaten, so he didn't have as much to distract him from what Brady had said.

Or the fact the little brother he wanted so badly to dismiss had been right.

Amos wasn't here, but he might as well have been, slumped at his end of the table with that mean glitter in his narrowed eyes as he looked for his next target. Amos had loved nothing more than keeping everyone at each other's throats. And Gray hadn't noticed before tonight that it had only benefited Amos when they'd obliged him.

Did he not trust his brothers because they weren't trustworthy? Or because Amos had convinced him that he shouldn't?

Was he afraid of the darkness in him because he was like his father? Or had his father convinced him that all it would take was the slightest slip on Gray's part and he'd be exactly the same as Amos—because he liked watching Gray fight himself?

Gray didn't know how to answer those questions. But he was all too able to identify the feeling that squatted on his chest then, heavy and misshapen.

Grief.

The grief he hadn't felt at the funeral. The grief he hadn't felt since, every single day on the ranch that passed without him missing his father at all.

He felt it now.

For the father he'd never had, sure. But more, for the family he'd missed out on, all these years with these brothers he hardly knew. The lies he'd swallowed down, one after the next, never bothering to ask himself if they were true. Or if Amos had always had a really good reason to make certain that everyone in the house hated each other and did nothing at all but react to him.

He didn't know how he was supposed to handle that revelation.

It reminded him of the night he'd realized exactly what Cristina was doing. What she must have been doing for some time. The cell phone she never put down, always texting "friends" when she'd often complained she didn't know anyone local, and taking care never to leave it out where he could see anything. Her sudden interest in nighttime "meetings" in town when he should have known that other mothers weren't gathering together that late on school nights.

He'd watched her get ready to go out one night. She'd been sitting at that prissy little princess table she'd loved, with all its mirrors, that he'd long since turned into kindling. Gray had pulled a muscle out in the fields that day and had been giving himself an extra long soak after the baby went down. And he'd been toweling himself off, standing there in the bedroom while she'd pouted at her reflection and made her eyes smoky.

Just like that, he'd known.

Everything had slipped out of place, all at once. The

world. Him. As if the bottom gave out, everything was suddenly in a different language, and worst of all, it wasn't only that Gray had lost the life he thought he was living. But the entire future he'd had planned too.

It was knowing himself one moment and discovering he was a stranger to himself the next, trapped in a life he didn't recognize.

Because he remembered when Cristina had dressed up like that for him. And how long it had been since she'd bothered.

Tonight that grief had a different flavor, but it was shot through with the same regrets that he hadn't seen what was right in front of him. That he hadn't noticed the signs. That he'd gone along with it until it was much too late to turn back.

Maybe it was always too late to turn back.

Becca left the dinner table first, murmuring something about homework and having to wash her hair. Gray let her go without comment, knowing enough about his daughter to understand that pushing her to share something with him before she was ready wouldn't end well. She was too much like him for that. Ty headed out not long after, not meeting Gray's gaze as he went. And Gray got the impression that Brady was deliberately biding his time at the table to prove that *he* wasn't bothered by the conversation they'd had. Or the fight they'd almost let themselves have. But even Brady eventually excused himself, swiping up his duffle bag and heading down the hall off the living room toward the guest room he'd taken over.

Then it was Gray and Abby in the kitchen, quietly doing the dishes together, making him feel a kind of peace he didn't feel anywhere else. Not in this house, anyway, no matter how she'd changed it since she'd moved in. Not unless he was far out on his land somewhere, surrounded by nothing on all sides but silence and mountains.

But that was how it felt to do this domestic dance with the woman he'd expected would help him, but not like this. Not quite like this. He ached to touch her. He missed her when she wasn't home. He wanted her more by the day and the truth he was trying so hard not to admit to himself was that he liked it.

He more than liked it.

"What was that when we came in?" Abby asked quietly as she wiped down the counters. Gray finished loading the dishwasher and leaned back against it when it was closed. "You looked like you were about to rip each other's throats out."

Gray's instinct was to tell her that nothing had happened. That it wasn't her business if something had. That he was on top of it, anyway.

But she was bustling around his kitchen like she'd lived here forever. She liked to organize things, and she did it without a second thought, from the cupboards to the pantry to the overstuffed fridge. She made everything better, and Gray didn't know what he was supposed to do with something so sneaky and impossible to ward off. Not when her gaze was so kind and gleamed like gold, and he wanted to be inside her so much it hurt. It actually hurt.

Maybe that was why he opened his mouth and said the kind of things he never, ever said out loud. Because he had no one to say it to. He never had. And because he'd never wanted to make it real by admitting it.

"I don't want to be like my father." He sounded like a stranger, strained and rough. Abby froze, her eyes wide on his, and Gray supposed he looked like a stranger too. "I don't want anything of him in me. Not one drop. I told myself it didn't matter what he did because I was different. And yet somehow he died a month ago, but he might as well be alive and well because he's living it up right here." His fist hit his own chest. Hard. "He turned me into him year by year, and I didn't even notice. I let him do it, Abby. *I let him.*"

18

Abby had been right.

Gray's mask of unbothered perfection was just that—a mask.

But the fact she'd suspected it didn't make the anguish on his face or in his voice any easier to bear.

She'd always loved this man from afar. But she knew, without a shred of doubt, that she was *in* love with him tonight. Because she wanted to reach inside him and tear out the things that made him hurt. She wanted to do this with her own two hands and she would have done a whole lot more to ease that terrible look on his face, and that awful sound she'd never heard before in his voice.

"What did you let him do?" she asked. She wanted to touch him, but she suspected that he'd be even more skittish than his daughter.

And she knew that if she ever said the word *skittish* to him—about him—he would hate it.

"All I want to do is take this dark *thing* inside of me and let it out. I want to punch through walls. I want to beat down both of my brothers for being the same jackasses they were when we were all teenagers. I want to flip tables like my father did. Why not? He might not have gotten what he wanted, but he always got a rise out of anyone unlucky enough to be around him."

Abby let him talk. She stayed where she was, leaning back against the counter in this kitchen that didn't feel like home, exactly, but still felt like hers. The same way Gray did.

And she kept her hands to herself. No matter how hard it was.

"Sometimes I think I'm nothing like the old man," Gray said bitterly. "But then nights like tonight, it turns out I'm a mirror of him. He would have loved knowing that. He always told me I was made like him, head to toe."

Abby had known Amos Everett all her life, and except for a vague height comparison, she didn't think Gray was made like him at all. She'd always assumed that all the Everett brothers had gotten their looks from their mother.

But she knew Gray wasn't talking about superficial likenesses.

"Tonight, when I stopped by my grandmother's place, I saw my mother's car," Abby said after a moment, when it was clear Gray wasn't going to continue letting that bitterness pour out of him. Likely because he was keeping it inside instead, where it would do nothing but poison him. She knew all about that. "I knew it was hers. And all I wanted to do in that moment was accelerate. Ram that car straight out of my grandmother's yard. Then hit it a few more times, for fun."

"But you didn't."

"I didn't. The car is in one piece. So is Lily, which is probably more miraculous."

When he started to shake his head, Abby reached over and slid her hand into his. She braced herself for him to pull away. And his gaze was too dark as it touched hers, but he didn't shake her off.

Speaking of miracles.

"It doesn't matter what you *think*, Gray. We all think terrible things, all the time. We all have dark parts inside of us that whisper things we worry and sometimes hope we might listen to one day. But what matters is what you *do*."

"Sometimes," Gray said with quiet conviction, "I worry I'm holding on by a thread. Just the thinnest little thread. And the next time Brady shows his face . . ."

He shook his head, his fingers tightening around hers as he stiffened.

"Brady is a thirty-four-year-old grown man. How many times have you beaten him up in all that time?"

Gray gave her a look as if she was deliberately misunderstanding him. But he didn't let go of her hand. "We were all a lot rowdier when we were younger."

"Roughhousing as a boy is normal. It doesn't make you your father. You're *not* your father."

"You don't know that."

"I do know it."

Abby shifted then, so she could take his other hand in hers too. Then she was standing there in front of him, her chin tilted so she could look him full in the face. Eye to eye. As if they were made to see each other clear, just like this.

"Your father couldn't hide who he was. I didn't live in this house, but I knew. Everyone in the valley knew. And maybe what you should ask yourself isn't why you didn't fight him off yourself, but why no one intervened."

"You can't tell a man how to raise his own children. I'm not sure anyone tried, especially once I was old enough to act like the adult in the house."

"But when was that?"

She could feel the emotion in her gaze. She made no

attempt to hide it. And Gray's fingers tightened around hers, matching the almost convulsive way he swallowed, his gaze locked to hers.

Which was answer enough.

"I don't think you're talking about turning eighteen, Gray. If I had to guess, I'd imagine it was a long time before that. Were you eight? Twelve? How much responsibility did you give Becca at that age?"

His hard mouth tightened. "You don't understand."

"You're not the only one who spent their whole life trying so hard to be perfect it crippled them, because the alternative was being like the parent you hate most in the world."

"I don't hate my father." The brackets around his mouth stood out. "And I wouldn't call myself crippled. Or you."

"Hate. Love." Abby shrugged. "All I ever wanted growing up was to be able to count on my mother. Just once. But I wanted that so desperately, with every single part of me, that sometimes I was afraid it might suffocate me. What word would you use to describe that?"

"I felt sorry for him." Gray's voice was rough. As if the words were leaving marks as he spoke, and he wasn't sure he could handle it. "I thought living here was some kind of steadying influence. I was taking care of Becca and keeping the old man from killing himself. Two birds, one stone. It never occurred to me that he was spending all that time getting in my head."

"All the voices in my head are my mother," Abby whispered, and it hadn't dawned on her before that moment how true that was.

Ponderous. Plain. *A big girl.* A not-very-bright country simpleton. Sneaky and two-faced one moment, plodding and dull the next.

Not worthy of love—or even a telephone call, some years.

Abby was the first to call herself forgettable. Except maybe she wasn't the first. Maybe these days she said things like that—even if only to herself—to make sure it was clear that she knew what she was. That being exactly what her mother had always told her she was. With words, often. And with her neglect, always.

It was one thing to fight Lily off when she was right there in front of Abby with that smirk at the ready and her running snide commentary. And it was something else entirely when Lily hadn't been seen for years, and yet Abby still took care to dress herself so that her "hefty farmer's shoulders" were minimized.

But this wasn't the time to think about her mother. Not when Gray was finally opening up to her, one hard crack at a time.

"You should know that when my mother said nasty things to my face tonight, Becca didn't hesitate to jump right in and defend me. It's possible that even if your father is in your head, he's not in hers."

"She's a good kid. Maybe wound too tight, but I know where she gets that from." Gray shook his head, his mouth tightening again. "I never thought too much about where I get things from. Maybe I should have. It took Brady, of all people, to point out that the old man is the only one who ever benefited from the three of us at each other's throats."

"Maybe. But also, you do know that brothers are kind of famous for fighting with each other, right? Cain. Abel. Ring any bells?"

Gray did nothing but look at her for a moment. A long moment. So deep and so long that it felt as intimate as a kiss. He squeezed her fingers in his, then let go.

Abby figured he wouldn't appreciate it much if she complained about that. So she bit her tongue the way she always did. And she headed upstairs, her husband behind her as he turned off the lights and made sure all the doors and windows were shut against the cold.

It was still hard to believe that she got to live with this man. That she got to call him *her husband*. She got to move around the same bedroom as Gray every night, when the dark pressed in and the wind rattled the windows. She got to watch him strip down, toss his clothes in the hamper, and stand there in the bathroom with all his hard, muscled perfection on display. Better still, she got to crawl into the same bed with him.

She kept waiting for it to get old. For the excitement she felt every time she slipped into her side of the bed to fade out.

Tonight, Gray lay there beside her the way he often did, his hands stacked behind his head as he gazed up at the ceiling. And as much as Abby liked to keep this time sacred—or whatever the opposite of sacred was that included a whole lot of wholesome, married sex—she knew there was still more to talk about tonight.

As little as she wanted to discuss Cristina here in this bed.

"Becca didn't just defend me from Lily," she said, forcing herself to launch into it before she talked herself out of it. "She got very upset."

Beside her, Gray tensed. "What did Lily say to her?"

Abby had almost forgotten that part. "She said something cutting about Becca's prospects. The way she does." When Gray only waited, she pushed on. "That Becca is the kind of pretty that disappears fast, so she'd better grab onto a high school boyfriend and settle down while she can. The usual Lily foolishness, though she usually directs things like that at me."

To Abby's memory, her mother had never told her she was any kind of pretty.

She wondered what was wrong with her that she was even thinking something like that. As if she wanted to compete with Becca to get her feelings hurt by Lily. It shouldn't matter what Lily thought or said. About anything.

Gray took his time before he answered, his tone even. Steady. It made Abby feel steadier too. "Seems to me Lily spends a lot of time talking about other people's looks and not a whole lot thinking about all that ugliness she carries around inside of her."

"Well. Yes. That's her whole thing."

Gray shifted so he met Abby's gaze. "Then why do you believe her?"

That hit her. Much too hard, especially after what she'd been thinking down in the kitchen. "I don't."

But her voice was weak. And she felt the way she had the first time she'd been thrown off a horse. Winded and . . . betrayed, almost.

"I know she's your mother," Gray said, something glittering in his eyes that Abby could tell had to do with how stiffly he was holding himself. As if he was keeping himself from jumping up and *doing something* to protect his daughter by sheer force of will. "And I respect that. But I don't like her dumping her poison on Becca. She's had enough to deal with. Is that why she was crying?"

"She was crying because my mother reminds her too much of her mother," Abby said. Carefully. "Who she hates. Or wants very badly to hate."

"She doesn't hate Cristina."

"She feels responsible." When Gray frowned as if that was impossible, Abby forced herself to keep going. "Of course she feels responsible. She said her grandfather took every opportunity to tell her how her mother never wanted to stay home with her. As if that was the reason she . . ."

Abby didn't finish that sentence. And she knew the reason she didn't wasn't to protect Gray, though she wanted that too. But because she couldn't imagine what would make her crawl out of Gray's bed and into someone else's. She couldn't conjure up the kind of loneliness she assumed Cristina must have felt to do something like that. Repeatedly.

But you didn't marry him expecting him to love you, another voice whispered, deep inside, neatly cutting her in two.

"Great." Gray sounded distant. *Wrecked.* "All this time I believed I was keeping her safe, and I wasn't. Perfect."

Abby could still feel the way Becca had shook against her. She could still hear the younger girl's sobs—and she felt the same wave of fury and grief and pain she'd felt in that car.

But really, Gray was just another motherless child. Except instead of growing up with wonderful grandparents to balance out his mother's desertion, like Abby, or even with a great dad like Becca, he'd had nothing but Amos.

"You need to forgive yourself," she told him, with far more conviction than she felt when she was trying to find her own way to the same place.

"I don't need forgiveness. I'm fine. But apparently my kid isn't, and that's on me. The same way the situation with Ty and Brady is on me. I'm the oldest. I should have known better."

"Becca blames herself for her mother leaving," Abby said quietly. "Because that's what kids do, Gray. I did it. I still do it, when if you asked me, I'd be the first to tell you that I don't even want Lily around."

He scowled at her. "I told you I'm fine."

"Becca does it. I do it. Maybe you do it too."

"Of course my mother left. The only reason to live in this house with Amos is the land, but that means you need to love it, and she hated it here. She hated the winter. The mountains made her feel claustrophobic." He rubbed his hands over his face like he was trying to rub the memory away. "She's much better off in California."

"That sounds very adult. Kind of like when I say my mother is actually tremendously sad because she doesn't have the slightest idea how to have relationships with other humans. But it doesn't change the fact that she gets under my skin. Still. And easily."

"What are you trying to say, Abby? Because, like I said, I don't have issues with my mother. My father was nothing *but* issues. Neither one of them is here."

"Haven't you noticed how determined Becca is that you be happy with me? Don't you think it's a bit over the top? There are a lot of teenage girls who wouldn't be that excited about a new stepmother. Who'd have some growing pains with another woman in the house after all these years on their own."

"Do you *want* her to have a problem with you?"

Abby sighed. "I want her to be happy for us because she's truly happy for us, Gray. Not because she secretly believes that she's the reason your first marriage broke up."

"She doesn't think that."

"Are you sure? I can tell you that I spent a lot of years making sure I was as perfect as possible because I hoped that might bring my mother back. Becca know she can't bring *her* mother back, but what she can do—"

"Is act like a cheerleader who never gets the day off."

Abby didn't realize how tense she'd been until then. "Yes."

"It's like I'm turning into him whether I want to or not," Gray said after a moment, and there was so much raw despair in his voice.

As if he'd already given up and given himself over to his fate.

Abby wanted to crawl on top of him. She wanted to show him how little he was like Amos. She wanted to prove it to him with her mouth, her hands. With all the love she had bottled up inside of her and didn't dare say out loud.

"That's up to you," she said instead, her voice wasn't harsh, exactly. She sounded like her grandmother. Matter-of-fact and unafraid of what the response might be. "If you don't want to be like your father, don't be like him. You get to choose that every day. Amos's life didn't *happen* to him. He made it. Day by day, year by year, until even his own sons didn't tear up at his funeral. You can do the opposite. If you want."

She had never taken that tone with him before. Or anything close to that tone.

Abby wished that she'd laid down too, so she could have been staring at the ceiling and pretending she didn't notice the sudden, dangerous stillness that hunkered between them.

But instead, she was looking directly at Gray. She watched his expression shift from something like *arrested* into something . . . molten.

When she'd gotten into the bed, she'd sat up against the headboard, curling her body toward Gray while they talked. Now she felt frozen there as he shifted again, his wide, work-sculpted shoulders lifting from the mattress. His hands found her face, then cupped her cheeks.

"You giving me a little tough love?"

"Just a little."

She didn't know which one of them sounded grittier. Too much emotion. Too much truth. *Too much.*

He looked stern now, but she could see the heat in his gaze. The combination made her shudder, deep inside until her bones felt like rubber. And between her legs, she was nothing but needy.

Greedy. Again.

Always, a voice inside her whispered, and this one had nothing to do with her mother.

"Good," Gray said gruffly.

Then his hard mouth was on hers, and Abby couldn't tell the difference between tough love and this love and that same, giddy love she'd been carrying around inside her all these years.

It didn't matter. She melted against him, and she poured herself into him.

He could cancel Christmas. He could turn out to be different in so many ways from the character of *Gray Everett* she'd carried around in her head all this time.

But there was still this.

The way he kissed her, deep and sure. His callused fingertips against her skin, stirring up heat wherever they brushed her.

And there was nothing she wouldn't find a way to live with if it meant she could have this. Him. Naked and hot and hers.

Because this was worth putting up with anything.

His strong, muscled arms wrapped around her, and then he was pulling her down against that steel wall of his chest. And she knew him now. She knew how to settle herself astride him, so she could push herself up on her hands and gaze down at him, breathless with wonder and need.

"You're still wearing underwear." His voice was dark like honey, and it pooled in her like all that sweetness was lit on fire. His thumbs moved lazily at her hips. "Didn't we agree that was pointless?"

A month ago Abby wouldn't have believed it if someone had told her she could smile the way she did then, beaming down at him while laughter bubbled out of her of its own accord. Surely sex was no laughing matter, she would have said. It was serious. Mysterious, despite the internet.

But tonight she laughed. And laughed some more.

"Martha Douglas's only granddaughter can't go to bed *naked*," she told him, shaking her head in mock-seriousness, as if she was scandalized. "The world would end."

She knew him now, so she reached down to the hem of the oversized T-shirt she wore and pulled it up, then tugged it over her head, glorying in the way his expression went tight. Fierce. He moved his hands from her hips to find her breasts, and she found herself arching into his palms.

The fire burned hotter. Or maybe it was Abby who was on fire. She couldn't tell the difference. She didn't care.

She could feel the thick, hard ridge of his need jutting against her, and she moved against it until they were both breathless and lost somewhere between laughter and a curse.

They got lost there so much, it was starting to feel like home.

"I told you what would happen," Gray warned her.

But Abby didn't care. She felt the tug at her hip, then he was tearing the panties off of her, and she couldn't seem to do anything but feel the thrill of it.

Inside. Outside. Everywhere.

Then her own hands felt clumsy between them as she

reached down and wrapped her fingers around the hard length of him, sitting up so she could work the thick head inside her, where it belonged.

Then everything was better.

Perfect, even.

Because Gray was inside her at last, again. And she settled herself back to take more of him, shivering with pure delight as he slid deep, burying himself to the hilt.

And suddenly, neither one of them was laughing.

He reached up and tugged her hair out of its ponytail so it tumbled down over her shoulders and teased the tops of her breasts. Abby braced her hands against the taut ridges of his abdomen as if they'd been put there for her fingers, then rocked herself against him.

Again and again.

He was so hard, everywhere. Inside and out, and she loved that too.

She loved everything about this man. She loved more and more by the day.

Gray let her control their pace, but she knew as well as he did that he could shift that in a moment. And probably would.

She took her time. She moved up, then down, as if she was trying to feel every last inch of him. She experimented with pace and depth. She . . . enjoyed him.

The glory that was this thing they did. The slick, impossible beauty of it.

Meanwhile, she couldn't seem to look away from the dark passion that made his cheekbones stand out against his beautiful face. She couldn't seem to jerk her gaze away from all that hard, possessive green.

Abby thought about walls. All the time she'd slammed her head against them to no avail. She couldn't seem to break or bend a thing, but it occurred to her as she lowered herself on Gray and then lifted herself up again that she was looking at things the wrong way.

A man like Gray couldn't break. It would kill him. But Abby didn't mind bending. And God, but she loved the way they bent together.

Over and over and over again.

And after all the things they'd lived through out in these fields, in these houses that looked so pleasant from a distance with their windows lit up bright to hide the heartache inside—so much heartache over so many years—she couldn't see how a lie by omission was any different from a full-on, flat-out lie.

Abby wasn't her mother. She certainly wasn't Cristina. She was Martha Douglas's only grandchild, and she wasn't a liar.

So when things began to get crazy, when Gray tugged her down and rolled her over so he could brace himself on his elbows and thrust that much deeper inside of her, Abby stopped biting her tongue.

"I love you," she told him, with her head tipped back, too much pleasure to bear stampeding through her body.

Gray went still for a single second, so brief Abby almost missed it, and when he started again, he was wilder. Darker.

But he didn't stop.

"I've always loved you," she said as he moved her closer and closer to that edge, because the confession felt like part of this thing they were doing. The way their bodies danced together and made better sense that way. "My whole life."

He dropped his head close to hers, pounding into her with a beautiful fury that she felt flood through her.

"I love you, Gray," she cried out as everything exploded.

Inside her. Around her.

But it was only when she'd fragmented into a trillion sparkling pieces, glittering and perfect, that she realized that he'd followed her over but hadn't said a word.

19

She didn't say it again.

After they were done, Abby went boneless. Gray couldn't move with those words echoing in the air, eating up all the oxygen in the room and pounding at his temples like a hangover, but Abby seemed to have no trouble slipping off into sleep. He shifted himself off of her, flipping over to his back, and he expected her to curl up on her side of the bed the way she often did.

But she curled up on him instead. And when he went to right the situation, she made a tiny sound of protest, like she was a sleepy cat, and burrowed her face into his shoulder.

He didn't have it in him to do anything about that.

Gray lay there, wide awake and much too agitated. He stared at the ceiling until he was surprised he didn't rip off his own roof and send it spinning off into the fields.

But nothing changed. She'd said what she'd said, and there was no taking that back.

Gray didn't want love. He didn't believe in it. He didn't want to be anywhere near it, and he sure didn't want it in his bed.

He didn't know how long he lay there anyway, staring into the dark of their bedroom, feeling a lot like Abby had strangled him.

When his relentless alarm went off the next morning, he was cranky from lack of sleep. Abby murmured something before burying her head in her pillows, and all Gray could do was sit there on the edge of their bed like it was a cliff. And he'd already lost his footing. He took a shower to try to wake himself up, pulled on his clothes, and was working his way toward full-on surly by the time he made it downstairs.

Where his predawn coffee was made already, waiting for him in the sparkling clean kitchen that no longer felt precarious. Because Amos wouldn't be swaggering in, ready and willing to throw down at the slightest opportunity, and if he had, he wouldn't have recognized the place. It was organized, well-stocked, and . . . comfortable.

Gray had lived in this house his whole life, but he'd never considered it *comfortable* before.

He slammed his mug down on the counters Abby kept clean enough to eat off of, and watched as the hot coffee—from beans she ground herself at Cold River Coffee and brought home to him, a major upgrade from whatever supermarket coffee he'd been drinking all these years—sloshed over the side. And he didn't rush to clean it up as it formed a pool.

Because it was Gray who was spoiling for a fight these days, he realized when he'd stood there scowling at the dark puddle in front of him for much too long. A lot like he was waiting for someone to come into the kitchen and give him a reason to get mad.

The way his father had done every day of his miserable life.

It doesn't matter what you think, Abby had told him. *It matters what you do.*

But Gray was pretty sure that his thoughts were like kindling, just waiting for a match.

He kept up the bad mood all day. Normally some time out on the land sorted his head out, no matter what had happened. The sweeping views. The grandeur of the mountains. The big sky that stretched out over everything like a prayer. Somehow it all usually worked together and lightened whatever load he was carrying.

But not today. He was grumpy with his foreman. He was short with his hands.

He was a jackass, in other words.

For a man who had always vowed he'd never be anything like his father, Gray was sure doing a dead-on Amos impression.

When he got back to the house that afternoon, he saw Abby's car in the yard. He'd forgotten that this was her early day, and that Becca would come home later with one of the kids in her class who lived out this way.

Or maybe he hadn't forgotten, he thought grimly as he pushed the back door open and stepped into his kitchen. Maybe he'd taken the dirt roads too fast on his way home because he was still spoiling for the fight he hadn't gotten this morning.

Because he needed her to take those words back before they burned him alive.

Except when he pushed his way through the back door, it didn't smell like his kitchen. He was momentarily disoriented, like he'd accidentally walked into someone else's house.

It smelled like sugar and cinnamon. Chocolate and a sharp vanilla. It smelled like . . .

"Are you baking cookies?"

His voice rang out, a gruff accusation that didn't make the burning in his gut any better. But Abby didn't jump. And when she looked over her shoulder at him, she didn't look guilty. Or worried, for that matter, the way she ought to have been after what happened last night.

After what she'd done.

Those words seared through another layer inside him, like a brand.

"I am." It took Gray a minute to process that she was actually smiling. *Smiling. At him.* Like it was perfectly normal and even okay that she'd turned his ranch house into a bakery, which it wasn't, and that wasn't even touching on the whole love thing. "Six dozen for the Winthrops' annual cookie exchange and another few dozen just for fun."

"Fun?" He didn't exactly spit the word out, but he made it sound like some kind of disease either way. He could have been talking about mad cow.

"Yes, Gray. Fun. Baking cookies makes some people happy. And by some people, I mean me. And then when you're done baking, as a bonus, you have delicious cookies to eat."

He knew there was a straight line from her *I love you* last night to this. A straight, dangerous line with that burning thing in his gut and Christmas a mess right there in the middle. There was that same hollow feeling scraping at him, the one that had kept him up half the night—while she'd slept there beside him, warm and cute and cuddled up against him like she belonged there.

The worst part was that he'd been starting to think she did. He'd let his guard down.

It was the betrayal that was getting to him today. The fact that she'd taken it upon herself to fundamentally alter the terms of their marriage—and she didn't seem to be the slightest bit concerned about what she had done.

"We already agreed about Christmas."

If she heard the darkness and warning in his voice, she didn't heed it.

Instead, she laughed. First the smiling. Now the *laughing*. When nothing was funny.

Gray couldn't remember ever feeling less like laughing.

"We did not agree about Christmas. You made a great many proclamations about Christmas, and I stopped arguing with you about them."

She said all that as if she was telling a charming story about something hilarious, which was not how Gray remembered that conversation. Then she wrinkled up her nose, and he saw there was flour on her cheek. His fingers itched to brush it away. To touch her, whatever the reason. It was too much.

"And then we had sex," Abby continued brightly. "It's hard to stay mad after sex. Don't you think?"

Gray did not think. He'd been mad all day.

"That's sidestepping the point by a mile or two." He sounded as grave and grim as he ever had. And it didn't seem to matter because it still felt like everything was out of control. Like *he* was out of control. "I'm pretty sure I made myself clear."

"Have I decorated the house against your wishes?" she asked, whisking something in a big bowl with quick, sure strokes. She eyed him as she did it, and he saw too much of her grandmother in her. All that quiet steel. "Is there a giant, decorated tree by the fireplace? Do you hear Christmas carols playing?"

Gray wanted to say something about the spirit versus the letter of the law, but caught himself. Because he wasn't actually pissed about *cookies*, surely. Or issuing actual proclamations about anything. There weren't laws, only his preferences, and he wasn't that much of a monster.

Not yet, anyway.

He waited because Abby was still studying him in that disconcerting way. And he figured she would surely bring up what happened last night. Any second now. He stared back at her, ready for her to ask him why he hadn't responded. Or point out his obvious bad mood that he wasn't exactly hiding. Or do something—anything—so he could tell her what he thought about her declarations.

But Abby only held his gaze, hers mild and steady, while the whisk made that scraping sound against the bottom of her bowl.

"I'll be in the barn," Gray muttered.

And he didn't really appreciate Abby's sunny "goodbye" as he headed out the door.

He stayed out in the barn for a long time, until even the horses were sick of the black cloud he was carrying around today.

So long, in fact, that when Becca's friend dropped her off and she headed out to the barn to do her share of the evening chores, Gray had already done them.

"Why?" Becca asked worriedly, her gaze darting around as if she expected a judge and jury to be waiting for her in the stalls. "Was I doing something wrong?"

"You do your chores just fine. And even if you didn't, you wouldn't have to panic about it." He considered her for a moment. "There's nothing to panic about. You know that, right?"

Becca blinked at him. She shoved her hands into the pockets of her coat, rocked back on her heels, and tucked her chin into her collar. Pulling herself together, he knew, and Gray felt something clutch in his chest. She wasn't a little girl anymore, but he could still see the little girl she'd been whenever he looked at her. Her sweet face and too-smart eyes. He could still remember the first time he'd ever held her right there in the Longhorn Valley hospital, tiny and hot, red-faced and squirming, with that same clever gaze when she'd been minutes old.

He knew better than to mention it. Because she wasn't his baby these days. She was fifteen and . . . complicated. She was pretty like her mother had been, but she didn't have Cristina's too-delicate fragility, like the next wind might break her in half. Everything about her made Gray proud.

He wished he could find a way to tell her that.

"I guess Abby told you what happened," Becca said after a moment, her voice cautious. "I asked her not to."

"Did she tell you she wouldn't?"

"She told me she wouldn't keep secrets from you, but that if I wanted, we could tell you together."

That was another sucker punch. Gray didn't know where to put it or how to breathe through it. He didn't know what to do with relentlessly cheerful Abby, who flung love words and smiles around like tinsel, baked dozens upon dozens of cookies in a kitchen where no one had done anything so sweetly domestic in decades, and knew without his having to tell her that secrets were something he couldn't abide.

And more than that, she'd assured his daughter—the only one who'd suffered more from the secrets that had polluted his first marriage than Gray himself—that secrets and the lies that went with them weren't going to be a factor any longer.

It made him kind of lightheaded and much too aware of those damned words still on fire in his gut, so he shoved it aside.

"I'm not sorry," Becca declared, and even squared her shoulders. "I know I'm supposed to be respectful to my elders, but you didn't hear how Abby's mother was talking to her. It was worse than Thanksgiving."

"Becca. I'm never going to have a problem with you defending family." That word poked at him. "Family." It had come out on its own. And now he couldn't think about anything else but what that word meant. What it had always seemed to mean to other people not trapped in Amos Everett's family, that was. "I'm more interested in what happened after."

"Oh." Her shoulders drooped. "You mean about Mom."

"I do."

She seemed to get smaller while he watched, but to her credit, Becca didn't look away. "I don't think I'm going to apologize for that either."

"No one's asking you to apologize for anything."

Gray felt gruffer than usual. Awkward, even. But then, while he'd always cared a whole lot about his daughter's feelings, they didn't usually spend a lot of time talking about them. Her emotions struck like storms, they both weathered them as best they could, and then they moved on. Until Abby, he'd thought that was the right thing to do. Now all he could think about was the way Abby had said "motherless girls." More words to careen around inside of him, burning wherever they touched.

"I didn't know how you felt about it," he said, feeling like he was picking his way over ice on a pond when he had no idea if it would hold his weight.

Becca shifted from one foot to the other, reminding him of one of their fall colts, all legs and emotion.

"Really, Dad? How did you think I would feel about it?" He recognized that slap of pure teenager that took over her voice then, and it was amazing how much a dose of attitude could ease a man's mind. But before he could answer her, she kept going, the words spilling out. "She made you so unhappy. You've been unhappy for as long as I can remember."

He wanted to deny it. He would have, a few months ago. Gray hadn't considered himself unhappy.

But everything had changed since Amos had died. Since he'd looked up after the funeral and seen Abby Douglas standing in his back door like she belonged there. And whatever he was now—or had been until last night— was so markedly, inarguably different from what he'd been before that he was forced to consider the possibility.

That he'd been unhappy all that time. And more amazing by far, that he was happy now.

Him. *Happy.*

It felt like another sucker punch. As did the fact he didn't know how to think about himself or his life if he wasn't fighting something.

But this wasn't the time to dig through his own mess.

He focused on his daughter. "That's not your fault, Becca. You shouldn't have to worry about something like that."

"I shouldn't worry about whether or not you're happy? You're my *father*." And Gray watched helplessly as her face crumpled. "And I know the worst part is that I look like her."

The hits kept coming. Gray didn't know what to do first. Punch a hole in the side of the barn. Go outside and shout at the stars until this made sense. Yell at Cristina herself, the way he'd done too often after the accident, out there where there was no difference between the sky and the land, and no one to hear the things he said to her that he would never have said to her face. Out there where the wind stole his guilt and shame and fury away like it had never been.

Whether any of those things could actually make him feel any better was debatable, but it certainly wouldn't help Becca.

He reached out, wrapped an arm around her and cradled her head in his hand as he took her in a hard hug.

"What is this?" he asked softly. Very softly, so he wouldn't yell. "How could it ever be a bad thing that you look like your own mother?"

"She was evil. *Evil.* You must look at me and see nothing but—"

"She was beautiful," Gray said, as if he was laying down the law. Because he was. There was no ambiguity here. "You got your laugh from her, and that smile that could light up this entire valley in the dark. There's no shame in that."

"She was a whore."

Becca words slammed into his chest, bitter little bullets. And he knew without asking that someone had said that to her. Someone had put that in her head.

It only took a breath more for him to understand that it had been Amos.

Of course, it had been Amos, night after drunken night while Gray had been busy trying to hold on to the ranch and keep his dysfunctional family together, one way or the other.

"I don't ever want you to use that word about your mother again," he gritted out now, because he couldn't go back in time and keep this from happening. He couldn't retroactively deal with his father the way he should have before all this damage had been done. "What happened between her and me is nobody else's business. Nobody gets to judge her. It seems to me she paid a pretty high price for the choices she made. The truth of the matter is that we weren't any good for each other."

He'd never said that out loud before. He wasn't sure he'd known those words were in him.

Becca shuddered in his arms, and he pushed on. "And

I was too stubborn to let her go when I knew that was what she wanted. So she found a way to leave anyway."

Because you couldn't force someone to be anything but who they were. God knows Gray had tried. Wasn't that why he'd married Abby? He'd known who she was. He'd known what he was getting. He'd been so sure he'd figured out a way to make certain there was no leaving this time. They'd both committed to riding this thing out, no matter what, no emotions to cloud the vows.

I love you. I've always loved you.

But it turned out Abby had lied to him too.

Becca made a snuffling sound against him that reminded him of her toddler years, but when she pulled her head back, she looked much older and sadder than her fifteen years.

"Yeah," she said hollowly. "She was good at leaving. With anyone and everyone she could find."

Gray rubbed his hands over his face, wondering why no one had ever bothered to tell him that being a father would be like this. The terrible need to fix her tears, whatever had brought them on. The urge to wrap her up in armor to keep her from getting hurt. And worse than both, the unpleasant realization that he had to find a way to be okay with Cristina and what she'd done to the both of them because Becca needed that from him.

His fury would only warp her the way Amos's bitterness had bruised all of them. What Becca needed from Gray was forgiveness.

Not because he wanted to forgive Cristina, particularly. But because the only thing the two of them had done well was Becca. And if he wanted to protect her, well, hell, he needed to give her the tools.

He had to make it all right for her to forgive her mother for abandoning them.

"That sounds like your grandfather talking." Gray shook his head. "You can feel whatever you need to feel, Becca, but don't take your cues from a bitter, lonely, old drunk whose only joy in life was making other people miserable."

"But he said—"

"It doesn't matter what he said. He was wrong. I don't even have to hear what it was to know that." Gray would do anything for his daughter, anything at all. So he proved it. "I forgave your mother a long time ago. She deserves better than the way this town talks about her. And so do you."

Becca didn't say anything, but she swayed on her feet, like Gray wasn't the only one taking body blows.

"What I want to know is why this stuff about your mom is bubbling up now. Is it Abby? Are you having a harder time with her than you want to admit? I'm not going to get mad at you if you are. You can tell me."

"I love Abby."

"You don't have to say that because you think I need to hear it." Gray shook his head, trying to wish away the constriction in his throat. "It's my job to worry about your feelings, not the other way around."

"I love her," Becca said again, her voice thick. "I love her with you. And it will be even better in a few years, probably. You'll have kids, and I won't be here, and things will be the way they should be."

He tipped his head to one side. Scratched his chin. "Where are you going?"

She frowned. "I don't know. I'll be eighteen."

"Is somebody throwing you out of the house at eighteen? Because I know I'm not. You might have noticed your uncles are still wandering around the place. Why would I kick you out and keep them?"

"Dad. Come on. Everyone knows it will be easier for

you and your new family if your old family isn't hanging around like a bad memory."

It wasn't the first time he had stared at this child he'd helped create and marveled that they could be related at all. It wasn't even the first time she'd made his head whirl around like he'd had far too much to drink.

But it was the first time he would have cracked her open with one hand, right here in his barn, and dug all this ugliness out with the other if he could have.

"You need to get your head on straight, Becca," he said, very seriously. In the tone that always made her stand taller, eyes a bit wider. "You are my daughter. You will always be my daughter. There is nothing on this earth that you could do that would make me love you any less or wish you were gone. There's nothing your mother did years ago that could change that. And there's no way anything that happens between me and Abby that could change it. Are you hearing me? Nothing can change that. Nothing ever will."

He let that sink in for a moment. He watched the way Becca's chest rose and fell rapidly, telling him everything he needed to know about the mess inside of her that he should have seen sooner.

I also don't know any fifteen-year-old motherless girl who's fine, Abby had said.

Gray was going to have to carry that too.

"If there comes a time that you want to go somewhere because *you* want to go somewhere," he continued in the same grave and steady way, "then you'll go. But you will always have a home here. You will always have a home with me. Do you understand me?"

"I only wanted . . ." she whispered, but her words trailed off.

"Listen to me. It doesn't matter what happens between Abby and me. It doesn't matter if we have babies or don't.

That will never change the fact that you're my first. There's only one you, Becca. And I can't do without you. Ever."

He watched her face crumple again, but she fought it off this time.

"Okay?" he asked her. He needed to hear her say it.

"Okay," she whispered. "Okay, Dad."

Gray slung an arm over her shoulders, steering her around so he could walk her out of the barn and back toward the house. For a few moments all they did was walk together, side-by-side. He could hear her sniffing back tears. He could feel the unconscious way she swayed into him and then away, with that sturdy body he'd once held in his hands. The lights from the house beamed into the night, bright and cheery like the woman inside who'd made the place smell like cookies.

He was glad they were still outside for a moment, so he could get a hold of his own expression and keep himself from showing exactly how much he hated the idea that his little girl had imagined for a moment he might wish she was somewhere—anywhere—but here.

But he was a grown man. He couldn't howl out his feelings at the December sky. Not where anyone could hear him. No matter that he could taste the howling on his tongue.

When they got to the door, Becca turned and threw herself against him in a hard hug. Gray hugged her back, aware the way he was sometimes of how fragile this was. This family thing he hardly understood himself and clearly wasn't doing all that well.

But God help him, he wanted better for his kid. He wanted her to feel all those things he'd stopped believing in too long ago to count. He wanted to give her the big Colorado sky that arched over them, dark and lit up bright with stars, prayer and love and *home*.

He wanted things for her he couldn't fit into words.

"I love you, Daddy," Becca whispered. She pulled back and grinned up at him. "And I really am so glad you fell in love with Abby. It's made everything so much better."

She whirled around on that, dancing into the house and leaving Gray frozen there at the bottom of the steps.

Frozen solid—except for all the places that terrible, treacherous word burned through him, brighter and more painful with every breath.

Love.

Gray couldn't be around love. He couldn't be *in* love.

It was impossible. He didn't believe in it.

No matter how it glowed too hot and seared its way around inside him, like it was cauterizing him where he stood.

20

"I told Gray I loved him."

Abby could probably have timed that announcement better.

She and Rae and Hope were gathered around one of the self-consciously rustic tables at the Sensitive Spoon, having their traditional December twenty-third Almost Christmas Party. Every year they dressed in festive attire, brought each other silly presents, and basked in each other's company. With wine. And cake. They'd been doing it for so many years now that it wouldn't feel like Christmas if they missed it.

Not that she planned to test that theory, given all the things that didn't feel like Christmas this year.

She told herself the clutching, hollow, scraping sensation in the pit of her belly was an excess of massaged kale and vegan cheese, not emotion.

"Oh *no*," Hope breathed, as if Abby had announced the onset of the stomach flu. But she leaned in closer, clearly not fearing contagion.

"Did you really?" Rae whispered in much the same tone, looking stricken.

Abby actually laughed. "You guys could have at least *tried* to sound less dire."

Hope shrugged. "It's not as if you came dancing in here singing love songs at the top of your lungs. I feel like we know where this is going."

"For all you know I'm singing love songs internally, Hope. Nothing but happiness and married bliss cartwheeling around and around in my soul like a Disney montage scene."

Hope reached over and patted Abby's hand where it lay on the reclaimed wood table. She didn't actually say "there, there." That part was implied.

"What did he say?" Rae asked, her tone neutral.

Very carefully neutral.

Abby smiled at her friends, sitting back in her chair in the clingy velvet dress she never would have worn a year ago. Or even a few months ago. Because that was the other thing regular sex had done for her, she had realized while getting dressed at home this evening. She hadn't transformed into any kind of goddess overnight, but there was a different kind of confidence in her lately.

Because how could it matter what she looked like if Gray enjoyed her body so much?

"Well, that's the thing," she admitted, holding onto her smile. "He didn't actually say anything."

Rae's expression was as carefully neutral as her tone. "Nothing at all?"

Hope frowned. "You mean when you said it. In that particular moment he didn't say anything."

"No, I mean he didn't say anything then, and he hasn't said anything since." It was getting harder to keep smiling. Abby tried to force it and was pretty sure the concerned expressions on her friends' faces were a clue to how badly she was pulling it off. She let it go. "It's kind of like it never happened at all. Except he's a lot more grumpy than he was before."

"*More* grumpy?" Rae sniffed. "That's hard to imagine."

"What would that even look like?" Hope chimed in. "Did he finally turn into an actual stone, like a hunk of forbidding granite?"

"But, Abby, seriously." Rae's gaze was direct. Then something worse than direct. "Did you really expect him to say something?"

Her tone wasn't exactly pitying, so Abby knew she shouldn't have taken it that way. Still, she felt the scrape of it down into the center of her. Because it turned out that one thing regular sex with the man of her dreams couldn't do was make her feel any better about being the object of people's pity. No matter how well meant it was.

"I expected him to say something, yes," Abby said, hoping she didn't sound like a petulant kid because that was pretty much exactly how she felt inside.

"But you didn't expect him to say he loved you back." Rae shook her head. "You can't have expected that, right?"

"And why not?" Hope demanded, frowning at Rae. "Why shouldn't the man be head over heels in love with Abby?"

"Of course he *should* be," Rae threw right back. "*Of course*, he's an idiot. I'm just saying it's not the biggest surprise ever that *Gray Everett* wasn't suddenly spouting love poetry."

Rae was right. It wasn't a surprise at all. Abby had been almost 100 percent certain that there was no possibility Gray would return her feelings or respond to them positively. Or respond at all, for that matter.

But it was that *almost* that had sunk its teeth into her. It was that *almost* that had made her imagine a world of *maybe* . . . Just *maybe* . . .

Instead, this brand new marriage of hers had gone quiet. On the surface, everything was the same. They both seemed to like their routines and how easy it was to sink deeper into them. They both seemed to enjoy their division of labor. Becca had seemed lighter in the aftermath of her run-in with Lily, walking in from the barn one night with a spring in her step and a silliness about her that hadn't been there before. Abby assumed that was because Gray had actually talked to her about her mother.

Which meant Abby had done her job.

More than that, it meant that Gray did in fact remember that night. Just in case Abby was tempted to tell herself that he didn't.

Everything was great, really. On the surface. And yet below it, everything had changed.

Where there had been an ease in her interactions with Gray, now there was tension. He had opened up to her that night—in the way she had always imagined he might—but he didn't do it again.

At night he stayed late in his office, gruffly telling Abby to go on up to bed before him. Which she did, because what else was there to do? Fight with him about bedtime like a child? Every night she would get into bed, read until her eyes were heavy and she sometimes dropped her book on her own face, until she was forced to give up and turn out the lights.

She never heard him come to bed. But at some point or other in those long, dark, late December nights, they would turn to each other. And it was like they . . . combusted.

Gray was like a fury, dark and intense as he moved over her, under her.

There was no laughter in those dark, wild moments, lost somewhere between dreams and waking. There was only the way he pounded inside her and the way she came apart in his hands. No words, no unwanted *I love you*s, nothing at all but need and passion until they were both limp.

On the long, frigid drive into town in the mornings, Abby would blink out at the snow and tell herself that what happened in the middle of the night *was* Gray's response. It was the way a man who didn't or couldn't talk communicated.

In the dark, deep inside her with his mouth against her skin, he was eloquent.

Abby didn't know how exactly to share that with her friends.

She didn't know how to explain what it felt like to love someone so much that she was tempted to tell herself— and them—that it didn't matter that he clearly didn't feel the same. That she almost wanted to pretend she didn't like Christmas herself so he wouldn't feel so alone and angry.

There was a part of her, threaded through the hurt feelings she was trying so hard not to nurse, that didn't mind if he didn't love her as long as he let her love him in peace.

How could she say that to either one of her friends? They would hate that for her. They would see it as a loss. A terrible surrender. They would lecture her about reciprocity and losing herself in a man, and they would mean well. If she wanted them to, they would leap up from this odd, yet surprisingly tasty experimental hipster dinner, and charge out into the nearest vehicle. They would mount their own small army in her defense and get directly into Gray's face if that was what Abby wanted.

But she didn't want it.

Because love wasn't as simple as Abby had always imagined it. It wasn't as simple as a sweet kiss in a fairy tale that charged the air with magic and changed everything, complete with singing mice and animated household articles.

It was what happened after the kiss. It was what happened in the dark as well as the sharp winter light. It was protecting as much as it was possessing, and she understood both.

Just as she understood that if she tried to stumble through an explanation of this, both of her friends would argue that Gray ought to have been the one protecting her.

But Abby was the one who had spent her whole life sifting through her confusing responses to the things her mother had done to her. Abby was the one who had known that no matter what happened with Lily, or what gross feelings she might carry around about it, she had her grandparents. Her friends.

What had Gray ever had? He and his brothers didn't get along, all of them too angry at each other and their father to realize they were more alike than not. Then he'd had Cristina, who had taught him to trust even less than he might have already.

Abby knew he had friends, though the ranch kept him too busy to see much of them. She knew he enjoyed his foreman, his hands. But she also knew he didn't depend on them the way she depended on Hope and Rae.

Does he depend on anyone? she asked herself. *Does he know how?*

Abby didn't know if Gray would ever love her. But she found she couldn't blame him for that. She wasn't entirely sure the man knew what love was.

It was lucky she was around. She could show him. Over time, she told herself, she would show him. She would love by example.

Something she knew her friends would think was a cop-out.

Or worse, deeply sad.

"Are you okay?" Hope asked, bringing Abby back to the Sensitive Spoon with a jolt.

Abby knew that if she wanted, she could turn this whole

night into a forensic examination of every word that Gray had ever said to her. And every response she'd ever had to him in return.

The three of them would leave no stone unturned. They would parse and dig, extracting meaning from every lift of an eyebrow or moment of silence. They would build out stories and tell them back to each other, and they would make sense of Gray that way. They would make Gray and Abby *work*, one way or another.

This was what the three of them had always been for each other. The kind of safe, supportive space Abby had always imagined family ought to have been. Because in every way that mattered, Rae and Hope *were* her family. Her sisters.

But as much as they were in her life and integral to it, they weren't in her marriage. And Gray wasn't the older boy she'd talked about in high school, all daydreams and *what ifs* and *maybe when I'm older*. Not anymore. That boy had been a construction the three of them had put together around tables a lot like this one, telling each other stories about the character of Gray they'd made up who was solid and gorgeous and perfect for Abby.

The real Gray was a living and breathing man. He was complicated and often grumpy and a stern, brick wall when he wanted. He was also delightfully wicked, could stop the world with that rare smile of his, and a good deal funnier than she'd ever imagined.

The real Gray was just that. *Real*. And if Abby truly wanted to be married to him, if she wanted it to work, she somehow knew that chewing over every detail of their life together was exactly the wrong way to go about it.

At a certain point she had to talk about her marriage with the person she was in a marriage with. Or it wasn't real. It would never be real.

And if she had any kind of Christmas wish at all, it was that somehow, someday, this thing with Gray might feel real all the way through.

So this time, when she smiled, she made it a good one.

"I'm more than okay," she said, and she looked at each of her friends in turn to make sure they were hearing her. "Really."

"You don't have to prove anything," Rae shot back, a kick of emotion in her voice that surprised Abby. And Hope too, whose eyebrows rose. "It's okay to admit if you made a mistake. No one's going to think any less of you."

It was a clue—not that Abby had needed another one—that Rae wasn't as over her doomed marriage to Riley, the most dangerous of the Kittredge boys, as she liked to pretend.

"I knew what I was signing up for," Abby said quietly. "That doesn't make it a mistake."

"I'm not saying you made a mistake," Rae replied fiercely. "But if you did feel that way, at any point, there's no shame in admitting it. People talk about marriage like it's a prison sentence. That you're locked in it forever with no key or way to escape."

"Or, you know, you made vows," Abby murmured, curling her fingers so she could press her thumb against the gold band Gray had put on her left hand.

"All of those things are important, I'm not saying they're not." Rae shook her head. "But that's part of the reason it's so hard for people to admit that they were terribly, horribly wrong about someone. And it shouldn't be that hard to admit. You should be able to acknowledge if you made a mistake, and move on."

"Abby doesn't think she's made a mistake, Rae," Hope said, a warning in her tone. "Just because things aren't all love songs on a loop doesn't mean they're wrong."

"I knew what I signed up for," Abby said again, when all eyes swung her way. "I'm good."

"You deserve to be happy," Ray said with quiet intensity. "We all deserve to be happy. If there's another point to life, I don't know what it is."

"I am happy," Abby replied simply. "I know you don't think that's possible, but I am."

"You told your husband that you love him, and he said nothing in return," Rae retorted, that directness of hers like a punch. "How can anyone be *happy* with that?"

Once again, Abby felt that wall between them that she didn't think her friends even knew was there. Because she could answer that question. She could talk about what love was for a man like Gray, how much of it he'd experienced, and what she thought he needed . . .

But her husband was a man who kept his own counsel. Always. And there was no way he would view her discussing his deepest, darkest feelings with anyone as anything but a betrayal.

A terrible, unforgivable betrayal.

Abby had no intention of joining the list of people who'd betrayed Gray.

"I'm sorry if my happiness doesn't look the way you think it should, Rae," Abby said as evenly as possible. "But when I tell you I'm good, I am. I promise."

"But—" Rae began.

"I have to change the subject," Hope said, leaning forward. "We can come back around to arguing about Abby's marriage in a minute, but I need both of you to stealthily turn—*stealthily,* Rae—and check out who just walked in the door. Looking hale and hearty, healthy as a horse, and notably, not on fire."

"Are we in seventh grade again?" Abby asked with a laugh. She didn't swivel around in her seat like Rae. She kept her gaze trained on Hope. "Are we checking out boys in the rearview mirror?"

"It's better than seventh grade." Hope looked satisfied. Smug, even. "Because seventh grade was apparently the beginning of a long-term downward spiral. But since you refuse to look for yourself, I'll share with you that it turns out a downward spiral isn't the end of the story."

Abby sighed. "Somehow I'm certain I don't actually want to know what you're talking about."

"Oh," Rae murmured, still turned around in her chair, "but you do. It's like a phoenix rising, and right before Christmas."

"A Christmas phoenix? Is that a thing?"

Hope leaned closer to Abby, dropping her voice dramatically. "It's Tate Bishop, back from the dead or prison for arson or wherever he was." Her dark eyes met Abby's then, something knowing in them. Something kind. It felt a lot like a hug. "See that? It's proof that anything can happen at Christmas. Anything at all."

Abby considered the Tate Bishop situation the next morning while she packed up her car with her cookie deliveries, then spent her morning driving all over the Longhorn Valley, dropping off her version of Christmas cheer the way she did every year on Christmas Eve. Assuming the roads were passable.

The Tate who had come in to the Sensitive Spoon, with two people who had Aspen-by-way-of-California written all over them, was certainly not the Tate Bishop that Abby remembered. He'd looked more than simply healthy, she'd confirmed when she'd finally snuck a look. He'd looked pulled together and prosperous. Hot, even.

Abby was happy for him in the abstract. What stuck with her was what Hope had said. *Anything can happen.*

Like love, maybe, Abby thought when she'd dropped off the last of the cookies and was finally headed back toward the ranch. Not from town this time, but from way out in the outer valley, where all the Kittredges lived. This particular drive was one of Abby's favorites, especially at this time of year. The county road wound out through the fields, on and on forever, as if it might go straight on up into Wyoming if she wanted to risk the mountain passes at this time of year.

As she took the road back toward the ranch, driving slowly because the road was packed with snow and icy just beneath the surface, she could see the whole valley spread out before her. Snow on the fields and clinging to the trees. Frozen creeks and rivers. And the dark blue, snowcapped mountain heights that her Douglas ancestors had stared at as they'd carved their lives out of the land more than a hundred years ago. They'd settled this valley next to Everetts and Kittredges, all those years ago, and here they all still were.

Delivering cookies to each other on Christmas Eve. Marrying and farming and breeding cattle out here, shouldering the enduring weight of these Colorado skies as they did it.

History was a funny thing.

It meant Abby could feel rooted here, as much a part of this land as the dirt and the trees. The crystal blue rivers that ran with snowmelt in the summer. The fields and pastures that had been the center of Abby's world for as long as she could remember.

But history could also be like last night, when everyone in that restaurant had turned to stare, most of them immediately leaning in to whisper stories about Tate Bishop and that arson rumor, back in the day.

It was no different for Abby.

Rae wasn't the only one who felt the need to perform a happiness check on Abby. Every person she'd seen today had done the same thing, some more skillfully than others. Old family friends she knew from church. Folks she'd worked with at the coffeehouse. People she'd gone to high school with and was still friendly with. Each and every one of them seemed to look much too closely when they asked her how she was *doing*.

As if she was a janky old car with its engine light on for everyone to see, no matter how many times Abby kept insisting the motor was *fine*.

She laughed a bit at that, her own throat feeling rusty, as she passed the turn for the ranch and continued along the county road toward the farmhouse.

There were worse things than being a beater with all its warning lights on.

Her mother, for example.

Abby ordered herself not to worry about that when she pulled up into the yard and parked next to Lily's car.

She had saved the best of the cookies for Grandma, of course. Abby gathered up the baking sheets she'd used, holding the cloth bag of cookies in her other hand. She slammed her car door closed with her hip, then started toward the back door.

She was working on the calm, unbothered, *serene* face she planned to show her mother when her grandmother appeared at the back door and pushed it open.

"Merry Christmas Eve, Grandma," Abby said, smiling up at Martha from the foot of the steps. "I brought you your favorite cookies."

"You always were my favorite grandchild, Abigail."

For a moment, everything felt easy. Good. The way it should on a crisp Christmas Eve with no storms in the forecast. Just the dusk falling headlong into the perfect silent night.

Grandma took the cookies while Abby carried the baking sheets into the kitchen. Then busied herself putting them away, taking her usual odd pleasure in the loud noise kitchen items made. She supposed it was as close as she got to clanging pots together, the way she had as a little kid.

"I wasn't sure you'd come back," Grandma said. Mildly enough. "Even if it is Christmas Eve."

When Abby looked over, her grandmother had gone back to take her place at the kitchen table. Where her hands were never idle, ever, and today were occupied with clipping her coupons.

"I'm not going to hide away," Abby said, matching her grandmother's mild tone as best she could. "I'm not going to pretend I don't know the way home because she's here."

"Good." Grandma stopped what she was doing and set her scissors down on the table. "I'm glad to hear that."

"I'm not going to pretend I don't know the way home, and I'm not going to pretend I don't know you," Abby said, more fiercely. "You can depend on that. I love you, Grandma. No matter what."

They both stayed where they were for a moment. Abby could hear the television in the other room because Lily liked to watch her television shows a whole lot more than she liked to, say, pitch in around the house. The way Abby would have been doing if she still lived here.

There was a part of Abby that would always be furious about that. Part of her that wanted nothing more than to charge into the other room and demand that Lily do something useful for change, knowing full well that it was a futile gesture. That all Lily really wanted was the fight.

Maybe she doesn't know any better, she told herself, because it was Christmas Eve and Tate Bishop was a surprising local phoenix, so why not Lily too? *Maybe she really can't help herself.*

But she knew her mother was fully aware she was here. Lily was deliberately staying out of the room because these were the games she played. The games *they* played.

It stung, but Abby had to accept that historically, she had a part in this. Because she kept playing.

Today, she refused. Because it was Christmas Eve, and she wasn't having her usual Christmas. And because it turned out she was pretty much done with playing games. All across the board.

"This is the thing about love," Grandma said into the cozy quiet of the kitchen that still felt as if it belonged to the two of them alone. "It never, ever looks the way you think it will in your head. Those are fantasies. Real life has wrinkles and a bad back. An ugly tongue when it gets riled, and no good reason for half the things it does. Real life is angry and ungrateful, sometimes ugly and spiteful, but you love it all the same."

Abby tried to smile, but knew she'd missed it by a mile. "Even if it hurts?"

Grandma didn't smile. But her eyes were steady and kind, with steel there too.

"Especially when it hurts. Whoever told you love wasn't supposed to hurt?"

"Everyone. Valentine's Day. Corinthians."

Grandma smiled then, the way she did when she knew better. Which Abby had learned was pretty much all of the time.

"Love isn't supposed to *hurt you,*" Grandma said. "But that's not to say it won't *hurt.* It's the difference between an assault and an ache."

Abby wanted to deny that she ached. That anything hurt at all. But her throat was too tight, and there was a hard knot in her stomach.

"It's like any muscle in your body, Abby. If you use it, it's going to hurt at some point or another. That doesn't mean it's bad for you. It means you need to practice more, like anything." Grandma's smile turned sad. "Some people never learn this."

Neither one of them looked out toward the front room, where the television was blaring and Lily was practicing nothing. Because the only thing she'd ever practiced consistently was leaving.

"Some people never learn," Abby agreed, but the words seemed to tangle themselves around her as she spoke. And she suddenly didn't know who she was talking about—her mother? Or herself?

"If I could tell you one thing, it would be this," Grandma said quietly. "Don't be afraid of what hurts. That's how you know it's worth it. How you know it's—"

"Real?" Abby supplied, barely more than a whisper.

Her grandmother nodded. "Real things matter, Abby. Because they stick. Because they take work and time and care. And yes, sometimes, because they hurt. They're supposed to." This time when she smiled, Abby felt it everywhere, like a burst of hard winter light. Or the shattering beauty of a cold and dark Christmas Eve out here in these mountains, blooming deep inside her like a song. "Or what would be the point?"

21

Gray managed to make it all the way to dark before anyone forced him to recognize the fact it was Christmas Eve.

He would have congratulated himself on that being some kind of record, except it was his kid who was staring right back at him, daring him to pretend he didn't know.

"I heard you, Becca," he said gruffly when she continued to stand there in the door to his office, staring at him as if the sight of him behind his desk was an outrage. Which was how he felt about the sparkly little dress she was wearing, God help him. "I know what day it is."

"Do you? Because you're sitting there working like it's any other night."

"Because it is any other night. To me."

He took the way his once too-perfect-to-live daughter rolled her eyes then as a compliment. It meant she really was comfortable at last.

So comfortable, in fact, that she could revert to being a regular teenager.

Careful what you wish for, he told himself, just keeping himself from grinning. He knew she'd take it badly if he did.

"Well, I have *several* Christmas parties to attend," she

told him grandly, after staring at him long enough for Gray to wonder if she *wanted* him to comment on her outfit—a risky proposition at best, he knew from experience. As long as she was covered, he tried to let her do her own thing. "Don't worry, I already have a ride home."

"I wasn't worried." He leveled his sternest look at her. "I trust you."

To make good choices. To call if she had a problem. To be back by her curfew. To be the good kid he'd raised. Not the always-worried kid who'd raised herself.

"Merry Christmas Eve, Dad," Becca said, a certain defiant glint in her gaze that he blamed directly on Abby.

But all Gray did was smile back at her. Without taking the bait.

Long after he heard the back door slam shut, he stayed where he was.

The reality was, he didn't have any work to do. Nothing pressing, anyway. With Abby's help in the office over the last weeks, he was in better shape than he'd been in as long as he could remember.

He didn't know why admitting that felt like surrendering.

Or why, when he finally left his office and walked into the main part of the house to find Abby sitting at the dining room table wrapping Christmas presents, he didn't feel as pissed as he should have.

If anything, he felt like Scrooge and the Grinch wrapped into one.

Except a whole lot uglier.

"Don't worry," Abby said in that cheerful way of hers. Gray couldn't even tell anymore if it was forced or real. "I won't assault you with a present. These are for other people."

"I never said you couldn't give people presents."

"I think you'll find, Gray, that when you cancel a holiday, you generally cancel all the things that go along with it. So I understand if you feel like me wrapping something for your brothers is breaking the rules."

Something pricked at him that he didn't want to define. He scowled at her instead. "It's fine."

"That's good. Because I also wasn't going to stop."

She smoothed a piece of tape into place with one finger, and he didn't know what to do with the way she smiled at him. Sweet and defiant all at once. It shouldn't have been possible.

And it certainly shouldn't have been . . . *cute*.

He didn't know what to do with her. That had been the trouble all along, hadn't it?

"You don't have to pretend," he heard himself growl at her, because maybe the real truth was that he didn't know what to do with *himself*. "Pretending only makes it worse."

Her smile dimmed a bit, but didn't disappear. "What am I pretending?"

It had been about ten days since she'd said she loved him. Every one of which had felt, to Gray, like a stone-cold eternity.

"You said something to me. You made it clear. Impossible to miss."

"You're right. I did do that."

"You said some things, and I gave you the chance to take them back, but you didn't."

"I have no intention of taking them back." She was sitting too straight in the chair at the end of the table, that hazel gaze of hers locked to his and her chin tilted up. "I love you. I'm sorry if that's upsetting."

"That's not what this was about." He sounded rough. Scratchy. "That's not what this was ever supposed to be about."

"I know it's not what you want to hear," Abby said, her voice steadier than that look she was aiming at him. "But I've been in love with you forever. Maybe this wasn't about that for *you*. It's what this has always been about for me. Do you really think I would have up and married a random neighbor? Just like that?"

"This is supposed to be a practical arrangement. This *is* a practical arrangement."

This time her smile was sharp. "I happen to think it's eminently practical to marry a person you already love. Some people might consider it essential, in fact."

"You shouldn't have said that out loud, Abby. You know better."

She considered him for so long that he started to feel strange in his own skin.

"Why not?" she asked, and he wondered how much it cost her to keep her voice so light. So *easy*. Because it had to be costing her something. He couldn't be the only one paying. "At a certain point, things begin to feel like lies of omission."

"No one says they love you without wanting something in return," Gray gritted out. "And I can't. You know that."

"I know that you think you can't," she agreed quietly, and that easiness was gone from her voice. Replaced by something that made Gray tense. "That doesn't mean I agree with you."

"And this is where it starts." All the agitation of the past weeks rolled through him then. That dark fury he was always afraid was about to erupt. The hollow, metallic space in him that he refused to call loneliness. The good thing she'd ruined by opening her mouth like that. Right when he'd been starting to think too highly of the whole situation. She'd sandbagged them both, for no reason at all. "These are the kind of demands that ruin marriages."

"What demands did I make?"

"I can't love you," he belted out, aware that he was too loud. Too unhinged. Too unlike himself, but he didn't know how to get himself back under control.

He didn't know how to hide from her, and that galled him.

Abby stared at him for a long time. Too long.

Gray watched as the color drained from her face. And there was a futility in those eyes that were usually bright and gold.

You did that, he snarled at himself. *Good job.*

"I never asked you to love me," she said, her voice very precise, as if she was fighting to keep each syllable even.

That notion scraped at him.

"Of course you did," he said, because he couldn't seem to stop himself. "It's not a statement. It's the kind of thing that demands a reply. And you know it."

"I didn't ask you to say anything. I didn't ask you to reply." There was an odd, sick note in her voice to match that awful look on her face. "And I certainly didn't have the temerity to ask you to love me. Don't worry, Gray. I would never be so stupid." Her gaze burned into him. "I know my place."

He could tell they'd stumbled onto uneven ground—or he'd pushed them there—by that note in her voice. By the look on her face, as if he'd punched her in the stomach. And then by the way she pushed back from the table and rose to her feet gingerly.

Gray was all too aware that he'd done that too.

"You and I made a very specific agreement," he said, trying to put it back on track. "We made vows, Abby. We agreed on what they meant."

She stood there, her fingertips on the edge of the dining

room table, as if it was helping her balance. As if she needed help balancing in the first place.

As if he'd taken her knees out.

"I spent most of the day today delivering cookies all over the valley," Abby said softly, almost like she was talking to herself. Though she was looking straight at him. "Then I took Grandma to church because she likes a Christmas service, but she also likes her Christmas mornings."

"Did I say you couldn't do those things?"

Abby sighed. "I spent all day out there, talking to people. Exchanging Christmas greetings. Chatting about life at the end of another year. That's the *point*. You make a little something, and you celebrate the people you know by giving it to them. It's neighborly. It's nice. It's a tradition, is what I'm saying, and it's always been one of my favorites."

Gray didn't know why he wanted to argue with that. She was telling a story, not mounting an argument. He didn't know why his hands were in fists at his side.

Or why there was that dark thing curled up in his gut that felt a lot like shame. Guilt. Self-disgust. None of them new to him. But Gray had imagined he'd buried them with his father.

"Some of the people I give my cookies to are friends. People I love and who love me." She wrinkled up her nose as if she was trying not to laugh. Or cry. "But some are just people I know. People who are part of the map of this valley and the map of my life, which are always overlapping whether I like it or not. Usually I like it. But on a day like today, it was hard to love it the way I usually do. Do you want to know why?"

Gray was certain he didn't. But he nodded anyway. He couldn't help himself.

"Because there's always someone—or in this case, a lot of someones—who have been pitying me all their lives. And now there's even more reason."

Gray frowned. "Why would anybody pity you?"

"Because they know what I am," Abby said with a horrible matter-of-factness. "And even if I had somehow forgotten what I am, today would have reminded me."

"What are you? What are you talking about?"

"I'm a plain, overlooked girl who was a virgin at thirty not because I was virtuously holding out for marriage. But because no one ever looked at me twice. I'm too tall. Too boring. I fade into the background when other girls shine. I'm not sexy, exciting, or any of the things girls need to be to catch the attention of boys. That was clear when I was Becca's age, and it only got more apparent as time went by."

Gray shook his head, but what she was saying didn't make any more sense.

"I know who I am and so do you," Abby said, and her voice was more ragged and more fierce. "I never pretended to be something I wasn't. You decided to take pity on your plain, awkward neighbor who no one else wanted. And I decided that I wouldn't care about all the pity. The whispers. The gossip that would either say I took advantage of a grieving man or worse, that you married the most dull and dependably unattractive woman you could find because there's no chance *I'll* cheat on you."

"Abby—"

But she was on a roll. There was an awful light in her eyes, and she was holding herself so stiffly Gray was surprised she didn't break.

"And they're right, of course. I won't cheat on you. I would never cheat on you. Because I loved you when you were nothing but a daydream in my head, older than me and completely unaware that I existed. I loved you when I heard what was going on in your marriage, and I loved you after the accident, when you had to raise Becca on your own and keep your head up despite the fact everyone knew why and how Christina had left you." Her voice was hoarse with too much emotion. Gray could see it on her face. Worse, he could *feel* it. "I've always loved you. I loved you when you were perfect in my head, and I love you more now that I know who you really are. Now that I get to live with you. Work with you. Sleep with you."

"Abby." He tried again, his own voice suspiciously thick. "Abby, don't do this."

"I never asked you to love me because I don't need it. I've never needed it. I'm perfectly happy to go on as we always have. You're the one who can't seem to handle it." She let out a hollow laugh that slammed through Gray like a punch. "Because I guess a pity marriage is okay with you, but not if you know that there's emotion behind it. Not if you suspect for even one second that I might have real feelings for you. You can marry the ugly girl, work on building a family, but the idea that I might love you revolts you."

His jaw hurt, he was clenching his teeth so hard. "It doesn't revolt me."

"I guess this is the grown-up, marital version of cooties. I guess I still have them. Nothing ever changes, does it? Merry Christmas to me."

"Don't stand here putting words in my mouth."

"It was fine when there were no words in your mouth, Gray," Abby threw at him, and whatever hold she'd had on herself was gone. He could see that. He could hear it. "I can think of a thousand reasons why a man who grew up like you did doesn't know how to love anybody. You didn't have to say anything. I would have been happy to leave it where it was because I'm used to loving you from afar. Why should this be any different?"

"This is the problem with emotion," Gray bit out. "You don't even know why you're angry. You let an emotion rule you, and it takes over. It's the same every time, and you might not know where it ends, Abby, but I do."

"Great call. The only thing that could make this conversation better is for you to once again confuse me for your former wife."

Gray swore beneath his breath. He dragged his fingers through his hair. "Listen to me."

"I always listen to you," Abby replied, her voice hard. "I listened to every single thing you've ever said to me. But I'm not sure you can say the same."

"I heard you," he threw that out there, hard and cold. And maybe even more unhinged than before, though he couldn't seem to care about that any longer. "I don't want you to love me, Abby. I don't want *love*."

"I understand. No love. No Christmas. Just angry, silent sex and shared chores."

"That's what a marriage is." It was only when the sound bounced back from the walls that Gray realized he was shouting. "That's all a marriage is."

"That's all our marriage is, yes," Abby threw at him. "Don't worry. I won't make this mistake again."

Gray had no idea why he had the urge to run after her when she pushed back from the table and left the room.

Just like he had no idea why he was standing there, his chest moving up and down as if he were running from something, when he'd said nothing but the unvarnished truth.

Staring at her pile of Christmas presents made something in his gut pull tight and uneasy, so he wheeled around and moved into the kitchen. Where he found himself staring at that barn door of a kitchen table, with all the scratches and scars that had been left there over the years.

So many of them left by Amos. And that damned red pen.

Adding things, then taking them away. Keeping a running list of transactions and debts, grudges and obligations. Revenge, pettiness, fury, all carved into the wood.

That was the true will and testament of Amos Everett. Discord. Unhappiness. As long as they all should live.

You'll die of loneliness, bitter and mean and crazy, just like the rest of them, Brady had said after the funeral. Like a prophecy.

Gray shouldn't have been surprised that he was no more and no less than the sum total of his own cursed blood. His father's son. Doomed to exactly this.

He could hear Abby upstairs, the old floorboards creaking as she moved around their bedroom. He wanted to go to her with a longing inside him so deep and so intense he was half afraid it would double him over where he stood.

But only half.

He couldn't do what she wanted. He couldn't be *who* she wanted. He wanted no part of her teenage crushes and her grown-up love, wrapped up in cinnamon sugar and vanilla extract, tied in bows and made pretty.

That had never been what he'd wanted.

Because, deep down, if Gray had learned anything at all from his father, it was that he didn't deserve it.

Something broke in him then. Gray didn't think, he just headed for the door, shrugging into his jacket and stamping into his boots before he pushed his way out into the night.

Outside, the stars were bright, the night was clear, and the cold was sharp and deep.

It almost hurt to take a breath.

Gray didn't question where his feet led him. He trudged through the snow, skirting the horse pens on his way toward the hill. His boots crunched in the hard snow underfoot, and his breath was smoke against the night. He kept his gaze on the moonlight bouncing back off all the gleaming white around him, so the fact he hadn't brought any kind of flashlight didn't matter much.

Not that it mattered anyway. It was like he had a homing device inside him, leading him back to the place he'd always known he'd end up one day.

The family plot was buried under a few feet of snow, with only the tips of the gravestones sticking through, but Gray knew who they were. He could name his grandparents. A handful of uncles and distant cousins. Family on both sides, stretching back to the pioneer days, all of their lives leading to this quiet place. Near a river, in sight of the mountains, and free beneath the stars.

He stood there, the cold air an ache in his lungs and that hollow thing where his heart should have been, and tried his best to feel the land.

The land he had given himself to all his life. The land that would take his life back into itself in time.

There had always been a comfort in this. Standing here, looking at his future. It was the circle of life, and he was a man who lived by the seasons. Hopeful spring into the sorrow of fall. Bright summer into cold winter. It was the simple truth of who he was and who he would remain, no matter what happened.

But tonight, he didn't see his fields. His cows. Everett beef and Everett land, acre upon acre, like it was the blood in his veins.

Tonight, all he could see was Abby.

She loved him.

And Gray didn't know how to love. He didn't know how to love another person who might love him back the same way.

Becca was his daughter. His love for her made sense to him because it was so much like the way he loved this land. Enduring. Permanent. So vast and so deep it might have scared him if it wasn't just a simple fact of his existence. A fundamental truth of who he was.

But then there was Abby.

She loved him, whether he wanted her to or not.

As Gray stood alone in the dark of a crystal, cold Christmas Eve he'd done his best to ignore, he finally understood the darkness in him wasn't his father's violence.

Because Abby was right about that too. If he'd been likely to give into it, he would have already. And he hadn't. The dark thing in him was far more insidious than the urge to pop his brother one.

The darkness in Gray assured him he was meant to suffer. It whispered that marriages in this ranch house never stayed together long, and hadn't his first attempt proved that?

The darkness in him wasn't his father's rage. It was Amos's bitterness.

What lived in him was that bitter, cynical old man writing up that will, only to tear it up as soon as he was done or another temper hit him. Over and over and over again, so he could be sure to cause the most harm.

Gray understood, out here in the snowy cemetery where he would lie himself one day, that he had always assumed this was the cost.

He could have the land. He could steward it, exult in it. He could carry the Everett name forward and do his duty to his ancestors and descendants in turn.

But deep down, he truly believed the price of that stewardship was suffering.

His own suffering.

He didn't believe in love. Because he'd never had the opportunity to try, not really. He'd had Amos. The mother who'd left too fast and had barely looked back. The woman who'd given him a baby and then betrayed him again and again.

He didn't know what it was that cracked open in him then, but he knew it felt a whole lot like Abby's hands on him. In him. Tearing him open and exposing his heart whether he wanted it or not.

Gray didn't know what love was. But he knew Abby. As far as he could tell, that amounted to about the same thing.

"This is goodbye, Dad," he said to the old man's gravestone. To the night that surrounded him. To the stars so far above. To the future that waited for him here—but that didn't mean he had to live the way his father did, one bitter foot in the frigid ground already. Simply *being alive* wasn't enough. Gray didn't want to *exist*. He wanted to *live* his life. Every minute of it. "I don't want what you had. I can do better. I will."

It felt like a burden was lifted off him once he said it. As if he'd been carrying around more than Amos's poison all this time. As if he'd been carrying the old man himself, tied to his back like one of the watching, waiting mountains.

Gray didn't want it anymore. He didn't want stone and cold, poison and regret.

He wanted Abby.

He wanted that smile of hers and the way she laughed, particularly when he was inside her. He wanted cookies and even the bright madness of Christmas, if it meant that much to her. He wanted the joy she never tried to hide, and that he could see now was the reason why she'd slid so seamlessly into his life.

Because all the while, she'd loved him.

Gray didn't know what he needed to do to deserve that. But he intended to find out, if it took every remaining day of the life he planned to live in full before he returned to this place for good.

He blew out a breath, rubbed his hands together because they were cold even with his work gloves on, and only then turned and started back toward the house.

Toward his life, not his grave.

He trudged his way back over the snow. And as he climbed the gentle hill, it seemed, for a moment, that his eyes were deceiving him. He blinked. But the two figures waiting for him at the top of the hill didn't go anywhere the closer he got.

"Well, what to my wandering eyes does appear but my very own big brother," Ty drawled. "Visiting cemeteries on Christmas Eve, like you do."

"I think that makes him the ghost of Christmas past, Ty," Brady said from beside him.

"What are you two idiots doing out here?" Gray asked gruffly.

"What are you doing here?" Brady fired back. "Stomping around in the dark with a death wish, or is the grave-yard a coincidence?"

Gray made it to the top of the hill, and then they were all standing there, the three remaining Everett men with the moon cascading all over them and nothing but Everett land for miles.

Everett land around them and between them, as it always had been. But Gray reminded himself that was his father talking.

"It turned out I had something to say," Gray muttered, feeling exposed. Silly. But he guessed that as long as he was feeling something, that was what mattered. "To Dad."

Neither of his brothers said anything to that. But all the same, it felt as if something eased between them.

Or maybe, Gray thought acidly, *it just eased in you, and that makes all the difference.*

"I heard you and Abby fighting," Brady said with studied indifference, when it seemed another December or two had come and gone with them out here in the cold, like the born and bred Coloradoans they were.

"And you figured you could fix a marital fight?" Gray shoved his hands deep in his pockets. "You obviously learned nothing while growing up in Dad's house. I admire your optimism."

"Then you came out here," Brady continued. "I couldn't tell if maybe you decided that instead of acting like Dad you'd come on out here, stretch yourself out on his grave, and *be* him. Melodrama and all."

Gray didn't know what had changed in him, but something had. Because he knew that before tonight, a comment like that would have had that violent thing inside him clenched in a fist, battering at his rib cage, demanding he teach Brady a lesson.

But tonight, he laughed. A real laugh that surprised him as much as he could see it surprised his brothers when they exchanged a quick look.

"It's kind of cold for that." He could feel the wind chill biting at his face as he said it. "But you go ahead, Denver. I can see you got that extra fancy, microdown, whatever the hell parka on."

"It's a special jacket," Ty interjected, all drawl and more of that same laughter. "A very special ski jacket, hand-crafted for life in subzero weather by people who want to look like they could stay outside all day without having to actually do it."

Brady snorted, but there was no temper in it. "Don't blame me that you were so jealous you went and looked it up. If you ask nicely, Santa might just give you one for Christmas, Ty."

"Everybody wants a special jacket, of course," Ty said blandly. "We have to walk around in expensive uniforms that tell everyone how fancy we are or people might forget to be envious."

Gray felt himself smile as Brady gave Ty the finger. He waited until they were both looking at him.

"I don't want to sell," he said, but he wasn't growling it out this time, all dark and furious. He just said it. And he met Brady's gaze. "But I know that's not my call to make. I have a proposition for the both of you."

"That sounds racy," Ty drawled. "But I'm betting it's not."

"I want you both to give me a year," Gray said. "And I mean a full year. Not just living here, tying one on in the outbuildings." He waited until Ty's expression changed, then looked at Brady. "I'm not talking about weekends up from Denver when you feel like it. I mean a full year, working on this ranch, acting like the full partners you are without Dad around to cause trouble."

"Full partners," Brady said, his tone surprisingly even, "except you're the boss."

"I'm the boss because this has been my job since I was eighteen," Gray said, and he was uncompromising on that point. "But it's *our* ranch. We're it. We're the same Everetts who've been here since the eighteen hundreds. If you two are willing to really, truly dedicate yourself to this family's legacy, and this land, for a year, then at the end of it, I'll give the same amount of respect to the idea of selling. I can't say that I'll be for it. But I promise I'll listen to what you have to say. And we'll figure it out together."

That word seemed to sit hard and heavy there between the three of them.

Together.

"A year is a long time," Brady said. But he didn't say it hotly or angrily.

Gray shrugged. "It doesn't seem like a lot of time to me. Not next to all the years this ranch has been in our family."

"Seems fair," Ty said, in that amiable way of his. As if he'd just been waiting on an invitation to help out.

It occurred to Gray that it was entirely possible Ty really had been. Something Gray never would have noticed because Brady had been right the other night. They were all programmed to think of each other the way Amos had always thought of them.

They'd been taught to distrust each other. But that had only ever served one member of this family, and he was dead.

"I don't want to be a martyr," Gray told his brothers. "And I'm sure as hell not a saint. I don't know the first thing about working *with* anyone, but it seems to me that we're brothers. We have that going for us already. We might as well figure out who we are when we're not playing roles the old man assigned us."

"Who knows?" Ty said, a grin in his voice. "We might actually like each other. We might turn out to be friends."

Brady made a scoffing sound. "Let's not get carried away."

They all laughed at that. Even Gray.

Maybe especially Gray.

Then, out there in the dark, December chill of a frigid, silent night, with the moon shining down and their ancestors listening in, the last three Everett brothers shook hands.

Which was only the first of the Christmas miracles Gray intended to work before morning.

22

Abby woke alone in the big bed upstairs, and that was the first kick of disappointment.

Then she sat up, and what had happened last night poured through her. The things Gray had said. And more humiliating, all the things *she* had said.

She took a long time staring at the clear evidence of the unmarked pillow beside her that told her he hadn't come to bed at all. For the first time since their wedding night, they hadn't shared a bed.

It was ridiculous, really, to feel the slap of that.

Abby had been okay with all of this when they'd both said a lot less, even if the silence was sometimes painful, and then came together in this bed at night.

She hardly knew what to do with this new version of her supposedly practical marriage, which was filled with painful things and no sex in the middle of the night to smooth it over.

Whoever told you love wasn't supposed to hurt? Grandma had asked.

Abby rubbed her hands against her chest, pressing hard against that aching, hollow spot.

Maybe she should have asked her grandmother *how*

much it was supposed to hurt. And whether or not that ever went away.

She rolled out of bed, only realizing as her feet hit the floor that there was a different scent in the air.

Bacon, something in her whispered in sheer delight. And something else that smelled a lot like coffee cake.

Smells that Abby would have loved to attribute to Christmas morning, but this was the Everett ranch house. There was no Christmas here.

Maybe not, she told herself briskly, because she wasn't one for too much self-pity. It made her feel thick and sullen, and she didn't like it. *But you get bacon and coffee cake of some kind or another, and that's a nice morning either way.*

She fixed her hair, pulling it back into her usual pony-tail, which always made her feel better. More in control. She pulled on her favorite cozy leggings, her scrunchy boot slippers with the fleece linings, and the thick, comfortable wrap sweater she used as a robe. Or a blanket, depending on her mood.

Becca, she told herself as she hit the stairs. It would be Becca doing some kind of Christmas morning break-fast, though maybe she'd call it something else to spare her father's feelings.

Not that Abby really wanted to think about Becca's father at the moment. Because if she did, she would cry. And there was no point crying over the spilt milk that was her marriage.

Abby had known exactly what she was signing up for, as she kept reminding herself and anyone else who would listen. She'd been the one doing the signing. It was her own fault, and no one else's, if it turned out she was feeling ever so slightly dairy intolerant these days.

That was what she'd told herself last night, curled up in

that empty bed in a miserable little ball. That was what she'd told herself, again and again, because that was what she had to believe.

The truth was, it was perfectly possible to live without hope.

It just wasn't pleasant.

But no one had promised her *pleasant.* Or a rose garden. Or happiness, or love, or any of the other things it turned out she wanted.

Her broken heart was her own damn fault.

She was so lost in her own head, so busy trying to box up all her hurt feelings and shove them somewhere else, that when she got to the bottom of the stairs, it took her a moment to notice that everything was . . . different.

Abby looked up. Then she looked around the living room.

Then she did it again, more slowly, her jaw dropping open of its own accord.

"Merry Christmas, Abby," Gray said, gravelly and grave from one of the leather sofas.

Abby had to reach out and grab the banister before her legs gave out from under her.

Her heart, which she would have said was smashed to smithereens and entirely useless, was whole enough to pound at her. Hard. Then again. And again.

Because when she'd gone up to bed last night, the living room had looked the way it always did. Cozy, masculine, a lot like a fantasy Western ranch house, but in no way Christmasy.

So what she was looking at now didn't make sense.

There were lights everywhere. White lights over the mantel and down the sides of the fireplace. Colored lights hanging from all corners of the room. There were evergreen boughs on seemingly every surface. There were even stockings hung over the fire, wrapped in more lights.

And there, in the corner between the fireplace and the window, there was a tree.

A tall, bright green Christmas tree, covered in lights. And thick with ornaments—that when she looked closer, Abby could see weren't real ornaments.

In fact, it looked like someone had emptied all the cabinets in the kitchen, found as many small utensils as possible, and then attached them somehow to the branches. She saw ribbons from the spools of ribbon she'd had in the dining room. And what looked like balled up wrapping paper, as if someone had been trying to make traditional Christmas ball ornaments.

It was the most beautiful thing Abby had ever seen.

"We all helped," Gray told her from the middle of the transformed room. Where Abby could hear Christmas carols playing from the tiny speaker on the mantel. "Ty, Brady, Becca. Me."

Abby's heart beat a little harder. A little faster.

"I don't understand what's happening . . ." she whispered, still holding onto the banister for dear life.

She looked at him, but looking at Gray was even more overwhelming than looking at the tree. The stockings. Actual presents nestled beneath the tree.

Gray was kicked back on one of those leather couches, looking every inch the same stern, uncompromising cowboy she'd been in love with all her life.

Even the glow of Christmas lights couldn't take away the hurt she still felt. But Abby told herself it was okay. No one was guaranteed to get everything in life. She had this. She had a good home, and a decent marriage, even if it wasn't the fantasy one in her head.

She vowed to herself that she would find a way to be okay with that too.

Because it was more than okay to call what she had enough. It was greedy to think she deserved *everything*. Especially when he'd done all of this for her.

"This is Christmas," Gray told her, snapping her attention back to him. He held her gaze as he slowly rose to his feet. "The first of many, I'm imagining, so it might be a little rusty this time. We'll get it right as we go along."

"As we go along . . . ?"

Abby felt frozen solid as he started toward her, even though every part of her seemed to be trembling at the same time. Her knees. Her belly. Even her mouth.

To say nothing of that soft place between her legs that was his. Ever and only his.

When he reached her, Gray only took her hand in his. She should have argued. Done something.

But instead, his hand was warm and hard around hers, and she let him pull her with him toward the fire. She stood there with the flames crackling merrily on one side, a decorated Christmas tree on the other, and Gray there before her.

Like everything she'd ever dreamed.

And then, to her complete surprise, he dropped down to his knees.

"What is this?" she asked nervously.

Gray took her hands in his again. More securely, if possible.

"I want you to listen to me," Gray said, very solemnly.

He was her husband, and it was Christmas morning, and her heart was already so full she wasn't sure how it could continue to function.

Abby nodded, not sure she was able to speak.

"I love you, Abby," Gray said, in that stern, certain way

of his that was better than heat as it washed through her. "I love you so much I'll even try Christmas on for size if that makes you happy."

"Gray. . . ."

She hadn't meant his name to come out the way it sounded, with that hurt note so obvious in the middle of it.

Gray's gaze searched hers, deep green and serious.

"We have a few things to cover here," he told her, in the same way he'd laid out his reasons for why she should marry him in the first place. "First and foremost, I didn't marry you out of pity. Let's make that perfectly clear."

Abby tried to pull her hands back, but he wouldn't let her.

"We don't need to talk about this." She could feel her cheeks, hot and shameful, and she didn't want to remember the things she'd thrown at him. She could feel them, humiliating and revealing, deep inside. "I don't want to talk about this."

"I haven't done a single thing out of pity in my life." Gray kept his gaze steady on hers until she couldn't do anything but sigh, as if he'd gentled her from the inside. "I don't know why you think I'd start with a marriage."

"You don't have to do this," she managed to get out. "You don't have to create this fake thing when we both know—"

"Abby. Baby. Look at me."

She did, again, but only because there was a riot inside of her. And she didn't know what to do except lose herself in him, because it still felt a whole lot like finding herself.

"We both know who got in your head a long time ago and told you that you were something less than pretty." He made a rough, low sound. "She's flat wrong. She's always been wrong. You'd go to war for Becca without a second thought, but when it comes to you, you accept everything Lily ever told you as if it were the absolute truth."

"You married me because I'm practical," she whispered, horrified that she sounded so unsteady. So utterly impractical it should have hurt. "Rational. Well, I am. And I know what I look like."

"I don't think you do." Gray's gaze was so hot it hurt. It all hurt. She couldn't understand why all of this *hurt* this much. "And I want to be very clear that this is objective. It's not an opinion. You're a beautiful woman. You're tall and built with a mouth that gives a man ideas. The only person on this earth who thinks you're plain is you."

"And my own mother."

"Your mother doesn't think you're ugly," Gray said with that matter-of-fact certainty that made her feel . . . protected. Free. Both at once. "If she did, she wouldn't comment on it." When Abby started to protest, he shook his head. "Look at all the things you have. You're the true love of your grandmother's life. You have a home with her, always. Now you have a new one with me. You have roots and a future here. You're happy with a life she doesn't want to live, but keeps coming back to anyway. You're all the things she couldn't be, and she resents it. Lily doesn't know how to have any of the things she left behind. But you do it effortlessly. If you believe nothing else I ever tell you, believe this. She's jealous."

Abby only realized she was breathing too heavily when Gray's mouth curved in the corner.

"I don't . . ."

But Abby couldn't seem to finish the sentence. Maybe it was the wetness she could feel on her cheeks. Maybe it was the way her hands shook, despite the fact they were wrapped in Gray's strong, callused ones.

"I didn't marry you out of pity," Gray said again, his

expression even more severe. But his eyes burned. "I told you and myself a whole lot of things about why you were the only possible choice for me. And all of those things were true. I knew we'd make a good match. I wanted a practical, down-to-earth, salt-of-the-earth woman, and yes, that's a compliment. You're not an appliance to me. You're not a condiment. I . . . trust you."

He said that as if it hurt. As if she wasn't the only one hurting here. As if they got to share this ache the way they shared everything else.

Something about that made her heart flip over inside her.

"I stood out back the day of my father's funeral, looked up, and you were there," Gray told her, his gaze softening, though his voice remained stern. Just the way she liked it. "And I told myself it made sense. I told myself it was practical. Reasonable. Rational as hell and good for my daughter. But the truth is, I just wanted you."

"You have to stop," she whispered to him. "Please, you can't say these things."

"I don't really know how to love," Gray told her solemnly, the same way he'd said his vows in city hall. As if he was carving them into stone with his voice alone. "I know how to give myself to the land. I know how to be a father, more or less. But I never believed I was capable of anything else. I never believed I deserved it."

She moved then, pulling her hands from his so she could hold them against his jaw. "That's your father talking."

"I thought I was him," Gray said simply.

"No," Abby said with her own quiet certainty. Like another vow. "You're nothing like him at all."

"Baby, listen to me."

He smiled up at her, and it dawned on her that it wasn't the first time he'd called her "baby." It wasn't the first time

the endearment had tumbled through her, wild and bub-
bly and *right*. Another tear made its way down her cheek,
but she didn't wipe it away.

She was too busy holding on to Gray for dear life.

"I want to love you for the rest of your life," he told her,
smiling this time. "I want to take care of you. I want to
live with you. I want to fight with you and sleep with you
and wake up in the morning to do it all over again. With
you, Abby. Only with you."

"I already said yes, Gray. I already married you."

"You married me for all kinds of reasons," Gray agreed.
"You're already my wife. But, Abby, I want you to be my
everything. My love. My light. If you want words, I can
give you words. If you want actions, I can do that too. I
just want you. Because this is love, and I want more of it.
I want all of it."

"Of course, this is love," Abby whispered, through tears
and laughter that felt like the same thing. "I told you. I've
always loved you."

"And I made you feel like you were alone in that," Gray
said gruffly. "That's not going to happen again."

Abby sank down on her knees, pressed herself against
him, and wrapped her arms around his neck.

"Yes," she said. "Yes to love. To words and actions, light
and happiness and everything else. Especially the everything else. I want it all."

"We'll make a new deal," Gray said, low and urgent.
"I'll believe that I'm capable of love, if you'll believe you're
beautiful. Because you are. More and more, every time I
look at you."

She had never believed that. She'd have assured anyone
who asked that she knew better. But Gray was looking at
her as if she was his very own Christmas. And she could
almost see the woman he saw.

"I believe in you," she whispered.

"And I love you," Gray told her, like he knew she could never get enough of those words. "I love you, Abby.

"I love you too," Abby whispered against his mouth, so much happiness inside her she might burst. "Merry Christmas, cowboy."

Then she kissed him in the glow of all those unexpected Christmas lights.

She kissed him because it was Christmas morning, and of all the things he'd given her this morning, the sweetest by far was hope.

Hope. Love. *Him.*

Abby kissed him and she kissed him, until they were both laughing, because his brothers were in the doorway and Becca was clapping her hands together with tears wetting her cheeks.

Hope, Abby thought. *Love. Family.*

And the perfect Christmas she'd always wanted, after all.

A week later, Gray and Abby planned to stay up and watch the New Year's ball drop from the comfort of the couch, leaving the parties to Gray's brothers and the all-night sleepovers to Becca.

By nine o'clock they were upstairs in bed, which suited Gray fine.

It was coming on eleven when he'd finally sated himself, for the moment. The sheets were tangled around them, and Abby's beautiful, naked body was stretched out next to his in the cool air while they both fought for breath.

"I have something for you," Gray said.

He twisted to reach for his bedside table, and when he turned back, Abby had curled on her side, propped up on one elbow and smiling that sleepy, lazy, sexy smile of hers that Gray knew he'd love looking at for the rest of his life.

He wasn't a man of too much ceremony, so he took her hand in his and slid the ring into place.

For a moment she said nothing.

"You got me a ring," she breathed.

"I gave you the gold ring for all the practical things we wanted out of this marriage," he told her, playing with the wedding band. Then he moved to the new, much more sparkly ring. "But this one is for the rest of it."

"Love," she whispered. "A Colorado aquamarine, in case I need reminding what the sky looks like."

"Yes." He lifted his gaze to hers. "Together, they're forever."

"That's what we are, Gray," she said, and she kissed him again.

Sweeter. Deeper. Until he could feel the heat roar in him anew.

He pulled her into his arms, but paused when she took her mouth from his.

"I have something for you too," she said.

"I don't think a pretty ring will look that great on me."

Abby smiled. Then she took one of his hands in hers and slid it down to cover her belly.

Gray froze. It couldn't—

His hand tightened against her. He searched her face until she nodded, her smile wide and happy.

"It's better than a ring," she said. "It's the future. Our future."

Gray leaned over so he could press his mouth against the place where his next child grew.

Once, twice, until Abby's eyes were damp, and they were both laughing again.

Just the way his future should feel, Gray thought. Because there was a lot of road to travel between this bed and that grave by the river, and he intended to acquaint himself with every colorful, beautiful, glorious inch of it.

With his practical, wonderful, perfect wife by his side. One kiss at a time.

Dear Reader,

Thank you so much for joining Gray and Abby for Christmas at Cold River Ranch!

I hope you loved your trip to the Colorado mountains. And I really hope you loved a little glimpse into the complicated Everett family.

The story doesn't end here! Look for *Cold Heart, Warm Cowboy* next summer (2019). We'll head back to Cold River and out to the Everett ranch to see bull-riding rodeo star Ty and the life—and love—he can't quite remember . . .

Until then—

Happy Reading!